MASON'S KEEPER

Cynthia J Stone

TREATY OAK PUBLISHERS

PUBLISHER'S NOTE

This is a work of fiction. Other than a few historical figures, none of the characters or events is based on actual people, living or dead, or their lives or circumstances. When I have used actual last names from historical records, the characters, their actions, and the events described are a product of my imagination, Eisenhower being the exception. If you think you recognize anyone and want to make something of it, you're dreaming and should try-ing writing your own book. Seriously, it's just a coincidence and purely un-intentional.

Printed and published in the United States of America

TREATY OAK PUBLISHERS

ISBN-13: 978-1-938749-24-7

ISBN-10: 1938749243

DEDICATION

For my parents, aunts and uncles, and grandparents
who endured more than I'll ever know...

To the ones who survived and thrived:
thank you for your faith and determination.

Also by

CYNTHIA J STONE

Mason's Daughter

This riveting mystery unlocks the secrets of a husband and father's supposed suicide.

Stone's debut novel takes readers down South, where a broken family tries to makes peace with their recent loss. Sally Mason and her 13-year-old son, Colton, have been reeling since Sally's husband, Jack, died. ... As Sally unearths tales of staggering debts, familial betrayal and lies, she discovers what the cost of truth and how deeply her mother's love runs. With candor, sensitivity and suspense, this novel weaves together elements of mystery and emotion. Sally's quest and determination to help her son serve as the catalysts for a host of exciting events. Her dynamic character and the many people she encounters while piecing together her husband's death—and life—prove to be memorable and well-sketched.

An exciting read that shines light on the secret layers that can exist between two people who think they know each other.

KIRKUS REVIEWS

MASON'S
KEEPER

CHAPTER ONE

By the time Nate Wallace returned to the cabin, the late afternoon sun stuck to the top of the corn stalks like a giant pat of butter melting in the heat. Coins jingled in his pocket as he climbed the front stoop. He tucked the leftover pie tins under his arm and and stooped as he pulled open the rickety screen door.

Standing at the cast iron stove, his mother didn't turn around even when he let the door slam shut behind him. "How many orders?" Evie stirred the steaming pot, banged the wooden spoon on the edge, and wiped the sweat from her face with the hem of her green calico apron.

"Eleven." Nate recited the orders for homemade berry pies while he set the pie tins on the rough plank table and emptied his pocket of coins, as if tithing on Sunday morning. "What's for supper?"

"Same as last night. Mustard greens and butter beans."

Nate bent forward to sit at the table but stood upright when his mother turned toward him. She handed him the glass pitcher with the chipped spout. "Go fill this from the well bucket. And bring in another load of short wood."

After he took the pitcher from her and set it on the table, he put his hands on her shoulders, turning her toward the light from the fireplace. The fresh bruise on her left cheek had swelled with red streaks. Frowning, Nate clenched his jaw. "I'm going to kill him. Where is he?"

"Now don't go setting yourself in a temper." Evie bent her

neck sideways, craning her face away from Nate. "Your pa left here a while ago."

"Tell me where he went."

"Getting all riled up won't fix anything. One hothead in the family is more'n plenty."

"What did you fight about?"

"The usual. He took the money I saved and went into town. You know what's he's like when he's drinking. It wasn't so bad this time."

"How much?"

"Oh, about five dollars, I guess." She touched her cheek with her fingertips. "I should learn to hide it better."

Nate took his mother's roughened hands in his and stared down into her pale blue eyes. "He won't never lay a finger on you again. Not Mary nor Lillie neither."

"A boy, even one mostly growed up like you, can't teach his own father nothing." She shook her hands loose and began picking up the coins from the table. "Look, here's one of them new buffalo head nickels. I heard they started striking them right before the war." She turned it over and held it up to the light. "Mary's cough is worse and she needs some elixir, now she's come down with the fever, too. I have to go see Dr. Broomfield." Evie sighed. "You stay here with your sisters and bring Mary some water if she wakes up."

Nate held out his palm. "Let me take care of it."

She dropped the nickel and other coins into his hand and folded his fingers around them. "If it's not enough, tell him I'll pay the rest next week. He's a good man." She squeezed his hand and let it fall. Arching her back, Evie rubbed her palm over her bloated belly as if polishing it and tried to smile. "Won't be long now."

"You got to get some rest." He pulled out a wooden straight-back chair, the one with the deerskin seat cover he had repaired last spring, and eased her down until she could lift her swollen feet off the floor. "Want anything?"

Evie shook her head and dabbed her mouth with the corner of her apron. For a moment, she toyed with the torn pocket. "I'll mend this while you're gone."

He slid the coins back in his pocket, picked up the pitcher, and started for the door. A tiny cough from the open loft made him turn around. He glanced up, then looked at his mother with raised eyebrows.

She fluttered her hands at him, shooing him out the door like a pesky puppy. "Remember, President Wilson and the country already done fought the Great War. Don't be out looking for trouble, you hear? I'm counting on you to come right back."

Within minutes of depositing the full pitcher and the load of wood in the kitchen, Nate trudged down the path toward the turn-off to Clark's Common. The dirt road took him past cotton fields and rice paddies, and as he quickened his pace, he inhaled the salty air from the Gulf. He passed the Baptist church next to the cemetery where two younger sisters and a baby brother were buried. He missed the one closest to his age, figuring she'd be about fourteen by now, but the babies had seemed like toys to him. Fever took all three of them the same winter, as if it had come to collect an overdue debt.

His father Roy had pulled boards from the back fence to build the coffins, but he got too drunk to help with the burials. His mother couldn't afford to pay anyone, so Nate had dug the graves himself. He wondered if he would have to shovel another one soon, realizing it would be easier now than when the ground turned frozen. Roy wouldn't be any help this time either.

By the time Nate crossed the railroad tracks and rounded the corner by the Methodist church at the edge of town, he decided to ignore his mother's warning. Roy would have to learn he couldn't let loose his bad temper on her, and Nate had grown big enough to teach him the lesson. Finding his father wouldn't be difficult. Just go where they serve rotgut whiskey and deal crooked cards.

HALFWAY DOWN MAIN STREET, he stopped at a yellow clapboard house surrounded by a white picket fence.

Ma deserves a house like this. She works hard enough to earn one.

He unlatched the gate and scampered up the frontwalk. Dr. Broomfield met him at the front door and led him to a room at the back of the house where he examined patients.

"Ma says Mary's cough ain't getting any better. She needs some elixir."

"Have a seat, young man. It'll take a few minutes."

"No, thank you sir, I'll stand."

The doctor turned to the medicine cabinet and chose several small vials, plus a medium-sized bottle which appeared to be empty. He pulled out the cork stoppers and began to pour one of the liquids, but set it down immediately. He reached back into the cabinet and replaced the empty bottle with a smaller one.

"We have money." Scowling, Nate shifted his weight from foot to foot. "We can pay for the medicine."

Dr. Broomfield smiled at him over wire-rimmed spectacles. "Mary's only five. She doesn't need a big bottle." He began measuring and mixing.

Nate stared at the doctor's white collar and black pinstriped vest and suit and wondered what it felt like to dress up like a gentleman. His own Sunday clothes were always clean, but never starched or ironed. He glanced around the room until a large document, framed and hanging above the medicine cabinet, caught his eye. The fancy script twined like ivy, and he couldn't decipher the block letters either. Nate wished his mother had taught him to read better.

After a vigorous shaking, the doctor corked the bottle with the dosage, and handed it to Nate. "One dollar and six bits, please."

Nate counted out five quarters, three dimes, and two nickels, including the buffalo head. His face felt burned and he couldn't look the doctor in the eye. "I need another dime."

"Forget it. Tell your mother to bring me one of her scuppernong berry pies, when she feels up to it. That baby's going to come early, I expect."

"We don't take no charity." Nate turned toward the door. "I'll be back in a little while with the rest of the money." With deliberate motion, he closed the door behind him.

AT THE FAR END OF MAIN STREET, he lingered on the sidewalk in front of the Seven Roses Saloon. Nate had gone inside several times before, ever since he grew strong enough to carry his father home after he passed out. Roy was the smaller of the two, and Nate rarely struggled with the burden of his weight.

With two urgent goals, he had to plot his strategy before he entered the saloon. Retrieve the money first, then give Roy a lesson he'd never forget.

The air inside hung thick with smoke that swirled around him as Nate pushed open the swinging door. He strode up to the bar and handed the bartender the medicine bottle. "Keep this safe for me, will you?"

"For how long?"

"Not more than a few minutes." Nate turned around and surveyed the room, table by table. He didn't let the chatter or laughter distract him while he waited for his eyes to grow accustomed to the candlelight from tin chandeliers. After a few moments, he spied Roy seated at a round table against the wall, five playing cards held up covering most of his face.

Nate wove his way through the crowd, ignoring greetings from men who labored in the cotton fields with his father, until he came to stand at the edge of the round table, opposite Roy. He waited until Roy lowered the cards.

Roy's steely blue eyes blazed at him. "What do you want?" He filled his shot glass from the half-empty whiskey bottle near his elbow.

"Give us back the money you took."

"Why should I? Law says it's mine."

"Ma worked for that five dollars, not you. We got to have it to pay the doctor for Mary's medicine."

The gambler seated in front of Nate half-twisted in his chair to look over his shoulder. "How much you need, son?"

Nate's dark gaze flashed his answer. *Not a single thing from you.* The man backed his chair away from the table.

"Go on back home to your momma. I ain't giving you nothing." Roy flung a nickel into the pile of coins in the center of the table, then laid two cards face down. He gestured toward the dealer.

Nate put his hand on the dealer's shoulder, lightly clasping it. "It ain't for me. It's for our family, for my sister."

"Sister, hah!" Roy spat his words out as if they were tobacco juice. "More like half-sister."

Scowling, Nate released his grip and bent over the table, fists down. "What do you mean?"

Two other men scooted their chairs away from the table. The one seated next to Roy stood up and leaned against the wall near the window.

From one side of his mouth, Roy grinned at Nate. "You ain't

got no family, boy."

"She's my family. Same as Ma and Lillie." Nate sneered. "And you. Now give me the money."

Players at the tables around them grew silent, as they turned to observe the argument. Even the steady clink of whiskey glasses subsided. The bartender came out from behind the bar and watched.

Roy tapped his index finger twice on the table and pointed across the pile of coins, but the dealer held the deck without moving. Tilting back in his chair, Roy glared up at Nate. "She might be your sister, if I was your father."

"What are you getting at?"

"Before I married your ma, you was already on the way, courtesy of some other guy. Hell, it could have been ten other guys."

With his fists clenched, Nate jerked upright and started around the edge of the table toward Roy. Two gamblers sprang forward, grabbed him by his arms, and held him back. "Don't pay him no mind," one whispered from the side of his mouth. "Roy gets mean when he's stinking drunk."

Nate shook them off and, taking a step backward, smiled at Roy. "You ain't my pa? That's fine. Then I won't feel too sorry after I teach you a lesson. You rough up Ma again and I'll kill you."

The dealer gasped. From the corner of his eye, Nate spotted the bartender moving closer. Roy squinted and shook his head. "Like hell you will."

After a moment frozen in time, Roy shoved the table. Nate caught the edge and flipped it back against Roy, scattering coins, cards, and shot glasses. Roy's chair tipped over backwards with a loud crash. Nate charged at the pile of furniture. Flinging the table to one side, he grabbed a dazed Roy by the front of his shirt. Blood steamed from Roy's temple.

Nate yanked him to his feet. Roy was too drunk or dizzy to do more than lurch toward him, and Nate planted a solid fist on his jaw. As Roy staggered backward, Nate slammed him against the wall, then hurled him toward the window behind the table. The glass shattered like an explosion, and Roy landed in the alley with a loud thump, his head shoved sideways against a hitching post.

The man leaning against the wall peered through the window and gave a low whistle. "Somebody better call the doctor. Roy's not moving."

Fists clenched, Nate whirled around. The gamblers and the bartender had formed a semicircle. Never taking his eyes from their faces, Nate crouched down and scooped up a few coins in his left hand. Before he stood up, he grabbed a broken whiskey bottle by the neck and brandished it like a pitchfork.

"Get Sheriff Kelley," said the bartender to no one in particular.

Nate took a step toward them. They backed up and parted in the center, clearing a path. The instant he sensed enough opportunity, he darted through the crowd and out the front door.

In the gathering darkness, he ran all the way down Main Street, not slowing down as he turned the corner by the Methodist church. He had almost reached the cemetery before he realized he had left Mary's medicine bottle behind the bar at the Seven Roses.

CHAPTER TWO

Nate arrived at the cabin, breathless and jumpy. The last quarter mile he spent looking over his shoulder, expecting Sheriff Kelley to shout his name and wave handcuffs in the air. The country noises of day folding into night couldn't calm him. Every bird's rustle or cricket's chirp sounded like someone coming to get him.

He found his mother, eyes closed, her slat-backed rocking chair by the fireplace, holding a crockery bowl of black-eyed peas, ready to shuck. Not much room left in her lap for preparing tomorrow night's supper. In careful silence he picked up the heavy bowl and set it on the table. He'd shuck the peas later, after his mother went to bed.

Evie stirred and opened her eyes. "Oh, I about fell asleep." She yawned and arched her back, raising her arms over her head.

"Don't get up."

"Well, maybe not for another minute yet." She settled in again and gave a little push with her foot to start the rocking motion.

"Ma, I have to tell you something." Nate pulled a chair close to her, sat down, and stared at his feet. "Something awful."

"Did you see your pa after I told you not to?" She stopped the rocker and stretched out her hand to raise his chin. After a moment, his gaze met hers. "Did you have words?"

"More'n words."

She scooted back in the rocking chair and turned her head to face the fire. "I warned you. Now what are we going to do when your pa gets home? He'll be drunk for sure and in a temper again."

"No, he won't."

She tsked a few times and shook her head. "You don't know him like I do. When your pa staggers through that door—"

Nate stood up. "He's not my pa."

"What do you mean?" Evie put her hand to her throat. "Where did you hear that?"

"He told me while we were arguing." Nate coughed and half-whimpered. "Right before I hit him. I don't know, maybe he's dead."

"Dead?" The rocking chair creaked as Evie sat up straight. A stray pea fell from a crease in her apron and landed on the floor near her shoe.

"He wasn't moving after I threw him out the window." Nate picked up the pea and dropped it in the bowl. "That's what somebody said."

"Maybe you better start at the beginning."

Evie rocked back and forth in rhythm to match Nate's monotone. She kept her eyes on him without expressing opinion, doubt, or judgment, and showed no surprise when he said he wasn't sorry.

She bit her lip. "Are you sure he isn't just knocked out cold?"

"Well, somebody went for the doctor." Nate lowered his head and pounded his fist into his palm. "I forgot Mary's medicine. I asked the bartender to keep it for me, in case Pa got rough."

"Guess you'll have to run back yonder and get it now. We'll go into town tomorrow and see about everything else."

"I can't go back. Somebody called Sheriff Kelley. If Pa's really dead, am I in trouble?" Nate paced in front of the mantel. "Lots of people stood around watching, guys who heard me threaten him. Everybody saw us fight."

They both jumped when footsteps pounded up the front stoop. Someone knocked on the door as if they were hammering a nail into it. Mother and son locked eyes without moving.

After a long moment, Evie pulled herself to her feet. "Stay put. I'll see what they want." She waddled to the door and called out, "Who is it?"

"Sam. Sam Warner."

Evie opened the door just a crack and peered through it. "Roy's not home. He's gone to town."

"I know. That's why I'm here, Miss Evie. The doc says you should come right away."

"What's the matter?"

"Uh, Roy, well, he… he's not feeling too good. Didn't Nate tell you?"

"Nate's not here neither. I don't know where he went. Maybe out coon hunting. They been getting at the chickens lately."

"I brought the wagon, so's you can ride back to town with me. But Doc says come now."

"Hang on a minute while I get my things." She closed the door and turned to Nate, finger to her lips. "Sam can get the medicine from the bartender while I'm at Doc's. You stay here," she whispered. "Wait for the wagon to leave and then bolt the door after me. I won't likely be back 'til the wee hours."

Nate did as he was told and then sat in his mother's rocking chair, staring into the fire. He didn't move until the wagon approached the house again.

NATE STOOD AT THE front window and waited. The breeze fluttered the curtains and he pulled back, fearing Sam would spot him.

The three-quarter moon rode high in the sky, casting enough light to see the pale sandy road and the fence lines on either side.

Sam pulled up on the reins, tethered them, and jumped down to help Evie from the buckboard.

"Too bad about Roy," Sam said. "Thought he'd pull through, right enough."

"Bound to happen sooner or later. He was an ornery old cuss." Evie let her shawl fall off one shoulder and drag the ground. "Always in a temper and fighting."

"Well, I sure am sorry Nate got mixed up in it. I expect Sheriff Kelley will drop by in the morning. Doc didn't see much point in waking him up in the middle of the night." He shoved his hands in his pockets. "You take care now. Maybe put another wet rag on that eye. It looks a mite swoll up."

Evie said nothing, panting as she climbed the front steps. In the watery light, Sam waited in the yard. She turned to thank him.

His face had turned red.

"Don't worry, we'll be fine."

"Uh, Miss Evie, there's a spot of blood on the back of your skirt." Sam spun around and scampered back to the wagon.

After he disappeared around the bend in the road, she tapped softly on the front door. "Nate, it's me."

The bolt slid with a clunk, and Nate opened the door. She reached for his arm, and he led her to the rocking chair. "I can't sit down right now. You go get your things. All your clothes and that old brown satchel from under the bed." She set the medicine bottle next to the kitchen basin.

Nate did as he was told, and, after scooting the pie tins aside, laid out everything on the kitchen table.

"Pack it up. We don't have much time." She rolled up his two extra pairs of denim pants and wool socks, then folded his shirts in half, and half again. She laid them on top and smoothed them with her palm. "Here, put all these in there. You're going to need them."

Evie waddled to the kitchen, cut two thick slices from a loaf of bread, and wrapped them in a fabric strip from a flour sack. She returned to the table and tucked the bundle inside the canvas satchel.

"What about Pa? Is he—"

"Roy passed about an hour ago." She pressed her hand on her lower belly and winced, sucking in her breath.

Nate grabbed her arm. "You should go lie down."

"Just your little sister telling me it's too cramped in there." She gave him a weak smile and leaned against the edge of the table. "Or little brother."

"Half-brother." He stared at her belly, then looked her in the face. "Is it true, what he said? About him not being my pa?"

Evie blinked and looked away. "Your real father died just about the same time you was born. I should've told you before now."

Nate dropped into the chair and put his head in his hands. "You had a baby and lost your husband at the same time?"

"Oh, no... well, he was away at college up north. I worked for his family in South Carolina, over on the East Coast."

"How did he die?"

"He drowned. Boating accident on the Charles River, somewhere near Boston in the state of Massachusetts."

"What was his name?"

Evie gazed into the distance, as if she could see through the wall. "Ransom Beauchamp Rutledge, the third."

"What was he like?"

"Beau was wild and fun-loving. And so handsome, he melted this poor girl's heart. I never in my life met anyone as charming and good-looking. You're the spittin' image of him, you know?"

"So why'd you marry Pa instead?"

"The Rutledges didn't see fit for their son to bring a servant into the family, baby or not. They offered Roy some money, and he agreed to take care of me and the child on the way. That was you." Evie shook her head. "Besides, he worked hard when he wasn't drinking. In the beginning, Roy was steady, not always running off somewheres else."

The low sound of a distant train whistle brought her back to the present moment. "Train's coming. Grab the satchel." She jerked her thumb toward the door. "Let's go."

"But there's no station in Clark's Common. And we got no money for a ticket."

"You got to travel without one." She turned toward the door. "Come on."

He followed his mother down the path to the dirt road, all the way past the Baptist church. Nate paused at the cemetery. "If I'm gone for a while, how are you going to get a grave dug here?"

"The Baptists won't allow Roy, since he wasn't baptized in their church. We'll go down the road to the Methodists instead."

"Was Pa, I mean, Roy, was he baptized there?"

"No, but the Methodists will take him anyway." She kept walking and stopped at the side of the road about ten feet from the tracks. "Stay low behind the bushes."

"Ma, I don't want to leave. Our family should stay together. Now Pa is gone, I'm the man of the house. I can look after you and the girls. And even the new baby."

"And take your chances with Sheriff Kelley? No son of mine is going to jail. Especially not for what happened to Roy." She looked up into the moonlit sky. "Durn, I wish them clouds hadn't scattered."

"But how will you manage? How will you get along without me?"

"It won't be easy, but you can't stay. Even if you didn't mean to kill Roy, we can't afford no lawyer." She placed a hand on his arm and squeezed. "Look, I know you was defending me. The sheriff probably won't see it that way. I'd rather send you away than have them haul you off."

Evie stopped to catch her breath. "You're my first born, the only one I ever set much store by. I can't let this be your future."

"I don't know what kind of future I'd have anyway. Seems like we never get a break."

"A body can't give up. Best not to let others see you suffer neither. Keep your burdens to yourself." She wiped her nose with the back of her wrist. "Nothing else has ever cut my heart this much."

Evie snorted. "There I go, not taking my own advice."

"Ma, I'm truly sorry."

"I know you are." She took a few more steps. "Now, when the train passes, watch for the empty cars with the sliding doors left open. Sling your bag inside and grab on."

"But you'll have to explain to the sheriff what happened to me."

"By the time he gets to our house come morning, you'll be long gone and I'll be having the baby. Too distracted to answer questions. He won't bother me none."

Nate glanced down the track in the direction of the faint clatter. "This is the train that goes to New Orleans. I'll be back next week." He dropped the satchel in the dirt.

"No, you won't. I done some thinking while I was at the doctor's waiting for Roy to pass. I'm going to write to the Rutledges. The stingy old folks has surely given up the ghost by now, but his sister, Miss Vivian, was always nice to me. Said to let her know if I ever needed anything. After the baby comes, I can take the girls to Charleston and go back to work for her."

"Someday you'll have a house of your own. I'm going to

work harder than ever so I can buy you one, and we'll all live there together. And Lillie and Mary can go to school, and—"

"Hush now." She wiped her face with her apron and turned toward the sound of the second whistle. "You're the only one I ever got attached to... wasn't much point with the others, with 'em dying and all." Her lip quivered as she gazed into the distance.

As Nate bent down to pick up his satchel, the coins in his pocket jingled. "Here, I almost forgot." He pulled out a handful of coins and gave them to her. "I scooped these up off the barroom floor. Some of it's bound to be the money Roy took."

Evie spread them out in her palm. "There's a twenty dollar gold piece here." She smiled. "We can get to South Carolina all right, as long as I don't have to pay for tickets for the girls." She selected a few others. "Slip these back in your pocket. You'll need them when you get to New Orleans."

The third whistle blew and the train rounded the bend.

After glancing over his shoulder, Nate took a step backward. "How soon can I meet you in South Carolina?"

"I don't know. Depends on the baby and if Mary..." She shook her head and swallowed hard. "Wait here in the shadows 'til the engine passes, then run for it. Jump with all your might."

She reached out her hand to touch his shoulder, but Nate had already backed away to pause in the opening between the pine trees. Their eyes met for a moment before he turned and ran toward the tracks.

THE RUMBLING OF THE WHEELS matched the pounding of his heart. The engine thundered past, huffing smoke. Nate ran alongside.

As an open freight car rolled nearer, he tossed his satchel

inside and grabbed the metal rail, now forced to pick up speed. He lifted himself by the door handle and slung his leg through the doorway. When he landed inside, the forward motion spooled him backwards, but he was on his feet in an instant, swaying from side to side to catch his balance.

Nate leaned out the doorway to wave at his mother, but she had already headed back to the cabin. He wondered how long it would be until he saw her again. Would she leave for South Carolina soon? She'd wait for the new baby to get big and strong enough to travel. Mary would have to get well from her cough or … Nate shut the other solution out of his mind.

He reached in his pocket for the coins and sat down. The moonlight disappeared as the train headed through the trees. After a few moments, the soft glow returned and Nate picked out a single coin.

He held it up to the light. A buffalo head nickel.

CHAPTER THREE

A few moments passed before Nate realized he wasn't alone. He jammed the nickel in his pocket and sat up straight, staring at two smudged faces on the other side of the railroad car. When the larger of them grinned back at him, Nate clutched the satchel tighter.

"Ain't seen you before on this run," the man said. Without taking his eyes off Nate, he nudged the younger one in the ribs. "Where you headed?"

Nate hesitated. "East."

Once his eyes adjusted to the dim light, Nate could pick out the shoes with holes and no socks, denim britches worn thin at the knees, buttons missing. And nothing, not faces, fingernails, or clothes, was clean.

Not so different from me.

"We're getting off, come Houston. Should be there right before dawn."

"What time will it be?" Nate wondered if Sheriff Kelley would be knocking on his mother's door by then.

"I can't rightly tell you. I left my gold pocket watch back at the hotel." He jabbed his companion in the ribs again while they each snickered.

"Yeah, Spike, y-you left it at the Ritz," the younger one wheezed. A fit of giggles consumed both of them once more.

Nate shifted his satchel behind him and scooted down to rest his head on it. He wished he'd packed his old threadbare quilt, the only thing his mother had ever given him. He could describe every piece by heart, and it would have been some small comfort against the night air and the wooden floor under him.

Yawning, Spike said, "I guess it's time for bed. We best get some shut-eye, too."

In his mind's eye, Nate started with the square in the corner, a red gingham triangle paired with a blue one, repeated to make a pinwheel. Green and yellow cotton slivers stitched with white thread at random in the middle. Every scrap was left over from clothes his mother had sewn for the family. Turning on his side, he counted around the edge in rhythm to the gentle rocking of the train along the tracks.

The next thing he realized, someone was shaking his shoulder. Nate bolted upright and swung his arm in a semi-circle above his head.

"Whoa there, partner," said Spike as he ducked Nate's fist. "Did you wake up on the wrong side of the feather bed?"

"Where are we?" Nate scrambled to his feet as he glanced toward the door and squinted into the dark gray sky.

"J-just outside Houston," said the younger man.

Spike turned and pulled his friend forward. "Marty, don't you have something for this gentleman?"

Marty grinned. "Sure do." He stretched out his arm with a closed hand, palm down. "This fell outta your p-pocket and rolled across the floor." He jiggled his fist until Nate cupped his hand under it. "I saved it for... for you." He opened his fingers and the buffalo head nickel fell into Nate's palm. In a flash, his grin faded into a frown. "Bet-better jump off 'fore we get in... into the rail yard."

Nate pocketed the coin. "Why? Can't we just keep riding until we get there?"

"We got to dodge them bulls." Spike shook his head. "Those guys'd just as soon kill you as look at you."

"Who are the bulls?" Nate picked up his satchel.

"The railroad hires them to keep folks like us from riding the empty freight cars for free. They all carry blackjacks and most of them are armed, too. Mean as hell. Marty got caught by one and he ain't never been the same in the head ever since."

"I dunno, Spike," said Marty as he knotted a large bandanna around his neck. "This fella here... tall 'nough to hold his own."

Spike looked up at Nate. "You can walk far beyond to sneak back on the next train. The railyard'll be busy, guys loading cotton bales, rice, and other crops. Go 'round through the woods to the far side, and keep out of sight."

"How will I know which train to catch?"

"Heading east, ain't ya? Just jump on one pointed toward the sunrise. There'll be plenty going that direction."

Nate reached out his hand. "Thanks, you've been a big help."

"Good luck to you, mister, wherever you end up." Spike shook Nate's hand and then turned to check on Marty. "Ready?"

Marty waved the ends of the bandanna at him. "We d-done ate all our vittles yesterday. My stomach's so em... so empty now, bounce... when I hit the dirt."

"One more thing," Spike spoke over his shoulder as he gathered his scant belongings. "A big strong guy like you should have no trouble getting work at the loading dock. Either at the rail yard or at the port."

"The port? You mean, on the ocean?"

"Well, it'd be the Gulf of Mexico unless you're going all the way to the Atlantic. You might think about staying in Houston."

Nate pretended to study his shoes. "Ma said I have to get out of Texas ..."

"I left the farm because there were too many mouths to feed," Spike half-whispered. "We all got our reasons." As he limped toward the doorway, Spike glanced over his shoulder.

"C'mon, Marty, let's get moving."

Marty stepped forward. Nate watched both men take deep breaths and fling themselves into the dark air. Holding tight, he craned his neck out the doorway a moment later. About twenty-five yards behind, Spike was still rolling through the weeds and undergrowth, but Marty had sprung to his feet and waved at Nate to jump, too.

In the doorway, Nate clutched his satchel as he repeated the motions of inhaling and then launching. The train seemed to pick up speed while he hung in midair. He landed on his feet, knees bent, and let himself drop and tumble along the ground. By the time he stood up to return the wave, Spike and Marty had disappeared into the woods.

Easy as that, come and gone. He didn't even learn where their homes were. Just as well they didn't ask him either. The fewer people who heard about what happened in Clark's Common, the better.

Chapter Four

Before long, Nate found the path through the woods leading to the far side of the rail yard. Along the way, he dodged scattered remains of campfires and remnants of old newspapers, and a few people huddled in the morning mist. They gave him short nods, as if they already knew why he sneaked through the forest. He passed them without speaking.

The cool air carried odors of salt and pine, but Nate's pace drew sweat across his brow. He eyed the approaching sunrise, his feet snapping fallen twigs as he hurried among the trees.

Beyond the woods, he reached a clearing with curved tracks in the distance carrying a train toward the east. With only fading darkness to hide him, he took off running across the field, planning to catch an open car in the middle of the train where Spike had told him neither the engineer in front nor the brakeman in the caboose could see him. All he had to worry about were the bulls Marty mentioned.

With the same precision as yesterday, he tossed his satchel into an open car and grabbed the handle to follow it. This time, he rolled only once before he was on his feet. In moments, Nate collected his satchel and glanced around the empty space. From the far corner, three young boys stared back at him, the biggest one looking no more than twelve years old.

"Who are you, mister?" one said. "You ain't a bull, are ya? We was warned 'bout bulls."

Nate shook his head and sat down against the wall.

"He's giant enough to be a bull, ain't he?" said another one.

"Shut up," said the eldest one.

The littlest one began to cry. "I'm hungry."

"I told you to shut up."

"When are we gonna eat?" said the middle one.

"Not now. Not today. Quit your damn whining."

"You promised Poppa you wouldn't cuss no more."

"What's he gonna do about it?" His voice quavered. "He ain't here. He ain't nowheres."

Nate sat up straight and opened his satchel. He felt around inside for the cotton bundle. Pulling it out, he said, "Here, you can all share one of these."

The boys didn't move. Nate dangled one slice of bread toward them, and the youngest one licked his lips. In seconds, all three pounced on his hand as if they'd been sprung from a trap. Before Nate could determine how they divided it, the bread disappeared.

"Much obliged, mister," said the middle one. The two others thanked him as well.

Nate ate his remaining slice, first in small bites, but as he realized the boys had fixed their gazes on him, he shoved the rest in his mouth and chewed as fast as he could. After he swallowed the last of it, he said, "A glass of buttermilk'd be nice about now, wouldn't it?"

The youngest one pointed to his satchel. "You got milk in there, too?"

The eldest one swatted his arm. "No, stupid. That's a travel case, not an ice box."

"Let's get some rest." Nate settled against the wall with his satchel behind him. The boys returned to their corner and sat down. As Nate's eyelids grew heavy, he watched the youngest one climb into the lap of his eldest brother and lean against his chest. The middle brother twined his leg over the eldest's and rested his head against his shoulder. Just before Nate fell asleep, the eldest brother put his arms around his little brother and pulled him closer, tucking his head under his chin.

In his dreams, Nate wrestled his younger sister for his fair share of the quilt.

AS THE TRAIN SLOWED DOWN, Nate resisted admitting it might be close to morning. He pulled his jacket closer around him and slid back into sleep in the dark corner.

A sliding door's loud slam and screaming voices woke Nate up. As he opened his eyes, a man, his back to Nate, leaned over the terrified boys and struck them with his blackjack. The bull snatched up the youngest brother and held him over his head like a bloody trophy, but before he could turn toward the door and pitch him out, the eldest boy began hitting the man in the stomach.

At first, Nate thought he must still be dreaming. He rubbed his eyes.

The man flung the child to one side, where he landed with a cracking thud. He grabbed the eldest boy by the shoulder and swung his fist, clubbing him across the jaw. As the boy staggered and collapsed backwards, the man lunged toward the middle brother, who stood against the wall, wide-eyed and stiff as a statue.

Nate sprang to his feet.

When the bull cocked his arm backward to land a harder blow, Nate grabbed him by the wrist and spun him around. He ducked the surprised man's left-handed swing and punched him in the stomach. Dropping his blackjack, the man bent forward. Nate raised his knee into the man's face. With a loud moan, he went sprawling, landing near the two brothers who lay still on the floor.

Nate glanced at the middle brother, paralyzed in fear against the wall. "Quick! Get behind me." He didn't wait to find out if the boy obeyed. Nate seized the blackjack and struck the bull, not stopping until the man's eyes grew bloated and his mouth and nose oozed blood. He leaned back and wiped his hands on his trousers.

A small hand on his shoulder startled him. "Did you kill him?"

Nate caught his breath and realized he'd been sweating. He put his finger on the side of the man's neck and waited for movement of his chest, the way he'd seen his mother do when someone in the family took deathly sick. "He might live." He took him by the ankles and dragged him to the doorway.

When he rolled the bull to the edge, metal clunked against the floor. Nate reached down and pulled a pistol from the man's coat pocket. "You won't be using this on anyone from now on." He searched the man's other pockets and found bullets, along with a roll of dollar bills. After dropping the bullets in his pants pocket, he tossed the money toward his satchel against the wall.

Nate rested his foot on the man's chest and pressed down. The man groaned. With a little ache in his throat, Nate exhaled. *At least I didn't kill anyone else.* Eyes closed, he slid his heel to the man's shoulder and shoved his body out the door.

Nate turned toward the middle brother and followed his stare to the others, pale and motionless on the floor. He walked over to where they lay and squatted beside them. Without touching them he knew. He'd seen death often enough to recognize when it claimed someone, especially the young.

The one remaining brother swallowed hard, his eyes pleading with Nate's. "Will they wake up soon?"

In one fluid motion, Nate swept the boy up into his arms and carried him to the far side of the car, cradling his head against his shoulder. "Not… not yet." He spun around to face the two bodies so the boy wouldn't have to. "They're—"

"Dead, ain't they?" The boy clutched Nate tighter around his neck. "Say it ain't true."

"Maybe not, I don't know." Nate sat on an empty wooden crate and leaned against the wall.

All the air seemed to escape from the boy until his body sagged. Without warning, he stiffened and pushed back to sit up straight and looked Nate full in the face. "Are you sure you didn't kill that man what done this to 'em?"

"He was still breathing when I shoved him out the door."

"Too bad. He needed killin'. That's what Poppa would'a said."

"I know." Nate stared into the distance, forcing the memory of Roy's body from his mind. When the boy snuggled up against his chest again, Nate stroked his hair, the way he would have done with Mary or Lillie. "What's your name?"

"Walter. But Poppa calls me Walt."

"What does your mama call you?"

"Nothing. Leastways, I was too little to remember. She died when Jimbo over there was born."

"So his name's Jimbo. What's the other one called?"

"Albert. But he never answers to that. Just Bertie, to ever'one."

"Where is your papa now?"

"Killed in the war." The boy sat up again. "You ever heard of France? He's buried somewheres in France."

"I guess so. It's a long ways off." Nate studied the boy's face. "If both your parents was gone, who'd you live with?"

"Our granny. She'd get in a temper and beat us some, but Bertie, he always set against her and took ours for us. But then she up and passed, too. That's how come Bertie said we had to leave." He rested his face against Nate's shoulder. "It's why we took off on this train."

"You got other family somewhere?"

The boy was silent for a few moments. "They ain't nobody."

As Walter gave way to sobs, Nate felt tears soak through his shirt.

"Bertie said no how was we gonna live in an orphanage or get split up to diff'rent folks. They'd likely be strangers. He said we'd never see each other again. So we just got on the train and left. All three of us, together. He said that's the way it gots to be." Shuddering, his voice dissolved into gasps and moans.

For several hours, they rode the train into the rising sun, stuck together, breathing in tandem as if they had become one person. When the light changed, Nate realized the water at the coastline reflected it. He arose and set Walter down on the box, peeling his arms from around his neck.

He stood at the doorway and gazed out at the water, green and murky below its surface but shiny, bright as crystal, toward the horizon. As the train's whistle blew, he looked down at the edge of ruffled tide, which seemed to reach under the tracks from far below and lap the bottom of the train.

We're way up over the water.

When Nate turned around, Walter had walked over to the bodies of Jimbo and Bertie and sat down. He rested a hand on each one's shoulder, but looked at Nate. "What you gonna to do with 'em?"

"We'll stop somewhere soon. I'll get off the train and bury them." Nate rubbed the back of his neck. "I can try to find some wood for a coffin, if you like."

"No, don't leave me on the train by myself." Walter stood up and peered out the door. "Are we really over the ocean?"

"I'm not for sure it's the ocean. But I heard they have lakes and swamps, so maybe…" Nate nodded. "We must be in Louisiana by now."

"Bertie always wanted to jump into the ocean. He saw a

picture of it once, in a book the preacher had. Showed a man asleep in the back of a boat while ever'body else fretted about the storm, big waves and all. After that, Bertie said the creek wasn't no fun without no waves." Walter took Nate's hand. "He can't swim, none of us learnt, but I think you ought'a put Bertie in the ocean. Jimbo, too. They'd both like it. Easier that way anyhow."

The boy was right. Nate tried, but he couldn't think of a better solution, or even a different one. He asked Walter if he wanted anything, meaning clothes or shoes, as the boys owned nothing else, but Walter shook his head.

"Do you want to say a prayer or anything, before I..."

"You say one for us."

With Walter following at his side, Nate carried the bodies and laid them in the doorway, first Bertie, then Jimbo.

"They can go together," Walter said.

Kneeling, Nate prodded them forward, as if they were still alive and needed waking. When he realized they wouldn't clear the tracks unless he tossed them, he clenched his jaw. It wouldn't be too different than the time he lifted his little brother's body into a coffin, he told himself. He picked up Bertie by the shoulders, but didn't look into his colorless face. One by one, he flung them out the doorway until they disappeared over the edge. The train's wheels masked the sound of the splashes, one after the other.

Nate stood up to face Walter, but before he could take his hand, the boy jumped through the doorway to follow his brothers.

"No! No!" Nate yelled as he stretched out his hand, but Walter had already fallen beyond his reach. Squeezing his eyes shut, Nate spun backward until he slammed into the wall next to the door frame. "Oh, God, no," he panted.

After a moment, Nate's knees buckled and he sank to the floor, unable to support his own weight. He waited until his breathing slowed down before he opened his eyes. He shuddered, trying to block out the memory of Walter's squeaky voice and the warmth of his body when he cuddled in Nate's lap. How could he and his brothers be gone forever so fast?

Near him lay the roll of dollar bills he had taken from the bull's pocket. Nate picked it up and held it high until it caught the sun's rays. "When I get enough, I'm coming for you, Ma. I promise."

The whistle blew again. New Orleans.

Nate picked up his satchel, stroked the pistol in his coat pocket, and made ready to jump as soon as the train crossed into dry land and slowed down at the edge of the city.

Chapter Five

Nate didn't expect to find the ground so damp or the city so noisy. He walked several miles until he reached pavement. Within a span of several blocks crowded with pedestrians, Nate passed musicians playing wild tunes he had never heard on brass instruments he had never seen. On one street corner, a newsboy held his papers overhead and alerted residents to another murder by the mysterious ax man.

"Keep your back doors locked at night," he yelled, as he held out a newspaper to Nate. "Little Italy, beware!" The front page displayed a photo of an elderly Italian man.

Nate shook his head and kept walking until he reached the corner, asked for information, and was told to turn east toward the French Market. He figured there must be something to load or unload where supplies of farm produce met big city buyers. Remembering the wad of money in his pocket, he stopped at a food vendor's cart.

"Po' boy?" The vendor raised a square of yellow newsprint holding a long sliced roll while he stirred a kettle with a spoon in his other hand.

Sighing, Nate wished he had bought a newspaper to shield his face from the sun. He gaped at the large expanse of water beyond. "Is that the Gulf of Mexico?"

The man gave him a quizzical look. "Naw, it's the Miz-sippi."

In the distance the river snaked through the neighborhood of buildings crowded together, rolling past like it had an important meeting in the Gulf. Nate turned his gaze to the vendor. "I'm pretty far from home now."

"Oysters or shrimp?"

Nate hesitated. He'd heard of people getting sick after eating things cracked out of shells from the ocean.

"Mebbe mud bugs 'nstead?" The man set the paper down on the makeshift wooden counter. "Or I got muffs, too. Sturdy gentl'man like yo'self must have a fulsome appetite."

"I don't eat bugs. What are muffs?"

"Aw, you be new heah." The man grinned. "Muffulettas. Eye-talian salami and ham on a round loaf, stuffed with olives. You like spicy or plain?"

"Never had either. Ham sounds good for a change." Nate patted the wad of bills in his pocket. "How much?"

"Nickel, tha's all. Cain't find a bettah sandwich anywheres than Ol' Hootie's." He pointed to the hand-painted sign hung on poles above his cart. "My woman bakes the bread, fresh ever' day. You want some red beans and rice, too?"

"If they're like butter beans or black-eyed peas, I don't want any." Nate pulled a nickel from his pocket and imagined he smelled his mother's scuppernong pies hot from the oven. He checked to be sure the coin wasn't the buffalo head before he handed it to the man. "I'll take the spicy."

While Hootie piled the ingredients between two round slices of bread, he whistled as if he flirted with the notes. "Say, you be needin' sumpin' to wash it down. How 'bout a col' beer? Local brew, just bottled this mornin'."

"REPENT, SINNERS!" called a voice from the opposite corner.

Nate whirled around. Balancing on his tiptoes on a crate, a man in black clothing and white collar bawled out penitence to passers-by. "Join the Anti-Saloon League in fighting drunkenness and debauchery. Take the pledge today and avoid the fires of hell."

Three women, also clad head-to-toe in black, stood in a semi-circle behind him, wearing wooden placards like aprons. Nate could make out a few letters, but couldn't read all the words. "What's that about?"

Hootie pulled a dark brown bottle from a lower cabinet of the cart and twisted out the cork. "Another nickel, if you please." He wiped his forehead. "They's just the Woman's Christian Temp'rance Union. They show up ever' day, tryin' to shut us hard workin' folks outta business. Not much luck so far."

"Why are they still here?" Nate took a bite of his sandwich and chewed slowly. He removed a wad from his mouth and examined it. "Are these green things olives?"

The man nodded. "The Looziana legislature done ratified the Eighteenth Amendment las' year, but N'Awlins ain't gonna pay much 'tention to the Volstead Act."

"How do you know all this?"

Hootie waved a stack of papers. "I reads the newspaper 'fore I wrap food in it. No sir, prohibition don't stan' no chance here. Peoples wants their beer and their Sazerac."

"You mean whiskey? They passed a law against whiskey?"

"Won't do no good. Rumrunners is too fast for 'em, they gonna bring it in anyways, if'n not unloadin' barrels down by the pier, why then, in coffins or some such." Hootie snorted. "The city only got 'bout five thousand saloons. How many customers you figure that comes to?"

"At least twenty thousand."

Hootie's eyebrows shot up. "Lordy, you is quick. No matter, sellin' booze is a heap o' trade, what make N'Awlins a great place." He wiped the countertop with a dirty towel and then licked his fingertips. "And the food, o' course, is sumpin else. Well, I 'spect I oughta not leave off the jazz neither."

Nate took a swig of his beer. "Tell me about rumrunners."

"You come back t'morrow and try my gumbo, ya heah? I be in this spot right early." Hootie laughed as he shuffled through a dance step and whirled around in time for another hungry patron, snapping his fingers all the while.

By the time Nate finished his meal, Hootie had given him as much information as he needed, including which saloons might be hiring. Nate waved as he started down Decatur Street toward Canal Street.

AFTER THREE INTERVIEWS with various managers, Nate was hired at the Napoleon House Bar and Café on Chartres Street. Starting that night, his job was to toss unruly drunks out into the street. Before midnight, he broke up two fights and whistled for twelve cabs to take patrons back to their hotels. In tips, he earned a dollar seventy-five, enough for Mary's medicine, he recalled with a pang.

By the time the restaurant closed at two a.m., he took a different spot at the back of the building to stand guard by the rear exit to the saloon. "Keep an eye out for Izzy," his boss told him. "He puts on disguises, but try not to miss him. He's five-and-a-half feet in both directions."

Nate glanced up and down the sidewalk. "Who is Izzy?"

"Izzy Einstein. Not exactly a Fed or a cop, but he patrols the bars anyway, all across the country. Every time he comes to any city, he registers how long it takes him to get a drink. New Orleans holds the record at thirty-seven seconds."

"He won't get past me."

"Be damn sure he doesn't. But watch out for him and his tricky squad. Sometimes they dress up real nice and drive fancy cars. I heard Izzy wore a fake mustache in El Paso." The boss shook his finger in Nate's face. "We get caught selling booze, he can shut us down. Then you're out of work."

Nate clenched his jaw. "I'll take care of it." For over an hour, Nate held the door open for exiting customers, both men and women, many of whom giggled as they linked arms and staggered down the side street toward the corner.

At least the drunks aren't slapping their wives.

He suppressed memories of Roy and wished he could recall his mother's face other than bruised.

Nate jerked to attention as a long, shiny-looking car pulled up and stopped to block the side street. Two men dressed in suits climbed out of the front seat and headed in his direction. Neither guy was very big, and Nate figured he could take both of them. He patted the gun in his pocket and waited.

The first one pulled his hat low as he approached Nate. "Bar still open?"

"What bar?" Nate's eyes flickered to the second man behind his partner.

"Napoleon's, you idiot."

"Why don't you go around and use the front door?"

The man nodded toward the waiting car. "Because, as a highly respected local citizen, His Honor doesn't want to be seen entering."

The car door opened again, and a short, fat man emerged. As he strolled toward Nate in the dark, the ember tip of his cigar glowed.

Nate sucked in his breath and held it for a moment. "So he's playing a rich guy this time?"

The second suit stepped forward and sneered up at Nate. "Listen, pal, I don't know what cockamamie idea you have, but you're going to open the door and let us through."

"Not tonight." Nate shifted sideways, blocking the doorway.

"What's going on here?" The short, fat man blew a puff of cigar smoke toward the sky as he stopped about two feet in front of Nate. "Trouble?"

The first suit spoke. "No trouble, sir. We just need to get this bumpkin out of the way."

Nate's muscles tensed as both suits flanked him. He clenched his fists, trying to decide if he should strike first.

Before anyone could move, the heavy wooden door burst open, banging Nate in the back. As if a bucket had spilled, drunks gushed out the back door. Nate stumbled forward, knocking the fat man to the ground, and landed on top of him. He tried to roll off, but the two suits grabbed both his arms and yanked him upright.

The drunks swarmed and shouted to each other. Nate swung his arms together, smashing the two suits against each other. As they tripped backward stunned, Nate snatched the short, fat man by the lapels and wrested him to his feet. He spun him around and grabbed his collar and the seat of his pants. One of the suits groped his way upright and leaped on Nate's back.

Nate jabbed him in the gut and the man fell backward. Lifting the fat man off the ground, Nate took one stride, thrusting him down the alley toward the car.

The other suit pulled on Nate's arm, but one of the drunks hit the man over the head with a whiskey bottle. The first suit scrambled to his feet and punched the unsteady drunk in the face. A high-pitched scream pierced the cool air.

Whistles blew and two uniformed officers charged down the side street. The next thing Nate knew, something blunt jabbed him in the ribs, while the cops tried to knock him to the ground. Without letting go, Nate shoved the fat man sideways, sending one officer toward the brick wall.

"Hey, you! Put the judge down!" yelled the other cop. "We got you now!" Handcuffs clattered to the pavement when he couldn't catch either of Nate's wrists.

Nate rammed the fat man toward the only cop left standing, turned, and raced down the alley toward the street. Oh, God. Someone told the police he had killed Roy. How did they know where to find him?

As he passed the corner, he glanced over his shoulder, but collided with three more policemen. Too late to dodge or run the other way.

Amid shouting and scuffling, one of them batted Nate on the head and he collapsed to his knees. A dark silhouette loomed overhead, his mother smiled at him, and then the sidewalk rose up as everything faded to black.

Chapter Six

Nate awoke to the sound behind him of someone urinating against a wall. When a few sprinkles struck his face, he bolted upright. The man finished, buttoned up, and turned around, nodding at Nate as he slid his back down the wall until he flopped on the wood floor.

"You're sitting in your own piss." Nate glared at him, as he wiped his cheek with his sleeve.

"Huh?" The man grinned.

"Where are we?" Nate tried not to inhale the sour air through his nose as he studied the space. Dark walls, no window, other men lying scattered on the floor. But no sound except snoring. He looked to the right. Iron bars from floor to ceiling, wall to wall.

"Slammer." The man scratched the whiskers on his creviced cheeks.

Nate sprang to his feet, and a dizzy flash behind his eyes reminded him of the beating he had received in the alley. Last night or this morning? "I got to get out of here right now."

"Priest'll be here soon." The drunk tipped over sideways and sprawled on the floor.

"Who is the priest?"

Another man near him stirred and rubbed his eyes. "Father Antoine comes by the drunk tank every morning to get me and a few others."

"Can he tell them to let me go?"

"I dunno. Always takes us back to the mission for breakfast.

Sometimes beignets. Other times just beans and rice, but it's better'n nothing."

"How soon will he be here?" Nate paced several steps away from the two men until another sleeping body blocked his path. He spun around.

No answer. The man's head tilted sideways, leaving his mouth to dangle open as he passed out again. His breathing came in bursts of sputters and honks, but his eyelids didn't flutter. A vision of Roy lying unconscious on the cabin floor passed before Nate's eyes, and he gave up expecting the man to reawaken.

Nate had no wish to sit on the plank floor, and he stepped into the corner where the dark was thickest. The walls felt damp and sticky, and he stood without leaning against them. With no idea of the time, it seemed to him several hours passed and it must be early morning.

When I get out of here, I'm heading to the train. New Orleans is no place for me.

After a moment, Nate realized he couldn't go back to Texas. Not where the sheriff would find him. Maybe never again.

Down the hallway, a door opened and the sound of clanking keys provoked a few of the sleeping men to stir. A uniformed guard flipped on the lights and stopped in front of the door to the cell, a few feet away from Nate. Standing behind the guard, a silver-haired man in a long black robe held a large wicker basket. From a chain around his neck hung a heavy gold cross decorated with fancy vines, and he stooped forward, as if the weight of both might topple him.

The guard unlocked the door, opened it, and stepped back. "Here ya go, Father." As the priest entered the cell, the guard crossed himself.

In center of the cell, the priest set down his basket and

opened the lid. One man approached him and stretched out his hands. The priest pulled a long white towel from the basket and began to wipe the man's hands and wrists. "Are you hungry, my son?"

The man nodded and turned to wait by the open door, as if he knew a familiar tradition. Other men followed him, first the cleansing from the priest, then the standing in line.

Hoping no one would object or even notice, Nate joined the ritual.

The priest peered up into his face. "You're new here, aren't you?"

Nate nodded. "I'm hungry, too."

"He stays." The guard cleared his throat. "I got my orders."

Nate sucked in the musty air. Did someone see Evie take him to the train? His mother would never give him away. She'd die before ever telling. The sheriff back in Clarks Common must have sent the news of Roy's death to the police in New Orleans.

One by one, the priest wrapped Nate's hands in the towel and rubbed his palms. He took extra care with his knuckles where the skin was broken. When he pushed the sleeves up Nate's arms, he gasped at the bruises. "Mon Dieu! What happened?" he whispered.

Nate winced. "It's nothing."

"Turn around, please."

Nate eyed the guard while behind him the priest lifted his shirt to give his back the once-over. He muttered what sounded like curses in a strange language.

The guard dusted off the shoulders of his jacket. "He was like that when they tossed him in here early this morning, Father." When he realized the priest was frowning at him, he stood up straight and crossed himself again. "I swear I didn't do it."

At the end of the hallway, the door swung open again and

the guard pulled down on the front of his jacket, trying to cover his flabby stomach. The men in line tensed their stance against the wall and seemed to hold their breaths. The priest continued his duties, ignoring everyone, even the heavy footsteps coming down the hallway.

Nate couldn't stifle his surprise when one of the suits from the fight in the alley stopped at the door to the cell. He spoke in a low tone to the guard, who glanced at Nate and nodded.

Despite his clean and freshly pressed clothes, the suit's swollen eyebrow gave Nate a pinch of satisfaction, and he smirked.

"Are you acquainted with that man?" the priest whispered.

"Not really. We had a run-in last night."

The suit entered the cell and stood next to the priest. "Excuse me, Pastor," he said. "I've got some business with this guy."

The priest slung the towel across his shoulder, brushed the lapel of Nate's jacket, and mouthed, "Beware," before he turned to the next cell mate.

When Nate clenched his fists, the warmth from the swabbing faded. His skin had tightened around his raw knuckles, and fresh pain swept across the backs of his hands.

Through narrow slits, the suit glared up at Nate. "Relax, buster. Someone wants to see you."

Nate's gut tightened. "It wasn't my fault. I didn't mean to kill anyone."

The priest whirled toward Nate, a question on his face.

The suit turned to leave. "You didn't," he said over his shoulder. "Not yet." He paused at the doorway and tucked a small white envelope inside the guard's breast pocket.

With a sigh of relief, Nate hung back. Maybe the guy hadn't heard about Roy's death.

The suit sneered at him. "You coming or not?"

"Why should I?"

"Because it's the only way you're getting out of this stinking place." He spat on the floor. "As of last night, you're out of a job. But you're in luck. A friend has something special in mind for you."

"Doing what?"

"You'll find out."

"I don't work for free."

"Don't worry. You follow orders, use that humongous brawn, and you can earn more loot than a dumb hick like you ever dreamed of." He winked at the guard before he sauntered down the hallway toward the steel door at the end.

The priest laid his hand on Nate's arm. "Remain here instead. I'll bring you a warm breakfast from St. Louis Cathedral. Then later I can attempt to talk to —"

Nate tried to catch his mother's voice telling him to work hard, but all he could remember was the doctor saying he didn't have enough cash. He closed his eyes and Roy's pile of coins on the poker table flared up like flames. Lack of money caused his family such misery by breaking them apart, and he vowed never to be without it again.

He lifted the priest's hand from his arm. "Thank you, sir. Maybe I'll see you later."

Without any more hesitation, he stepped through the doorway and followed the suit down the hall.

Chapter Seven

As Nate emerged from the holding cell and plodded down the hallway, the suit waited for him at the doorway of a small room. He motioned for Nate to sit across the table from him in one of the metal chairs.

"You're pretty good in a fight," the man said, his face muscles twitching. "You think fast."

Nate shrugged.

"The judge wants to know if you'd be interested in some work."

"Doing what?"

"For now, let's call it delivery. You have to move quick and keep an eye out."

"What for?"

"People who'd rather you didn't deliver the product."

Nate studied the man's brown pin-striped suit and polka-dot tie. His white shirt was pressed stiff, as if he couldn't bend forward without cracking the front. Trimmed and even, the man's fingernails showed no sign of grime or grease. His haircut gave proof of a barber's touch, smoothed back and parted toward the center.

The man must have taken Nate's indecision for refusal. "Or you can go back to the cell and wait for your punishment."

"You mean I'm blamed for a crime?"

They found out about Roy after all? Nate held his breath.

"You can't beat up a federal judge without consequences."

"Oh, you mean, the judge." Nate exhaled.

"But His Honor is willing to, shall we say, look the other direction, in exchange for the use of your special talents. You should be grateful."

Nate looked down at his filthy clothes, unchanged since he left Clarks Common three days ago. When he raised his gaze to the man's face, Nate clenched his jaw. "I can start right now."

"Relax. The product gets delivered at night. You don't get paid 'til afterwards." The man stood up and handed Nate a business card. "Be at the judge's office by two o'clock. If you're late, don't even bother knocking."

Nate took the card, glancing at it. He didn't want the man to suspect he couldn't read.

"You can pick up your personal stuff on your way out. Bring the pistol. And get yourself cleaned up."

Nodding, Nate stood up and slipped the card into his pocket.

The man opened the door and turned back toward Nate. "One more thing. Can you swim? I mean, you ain't afraid of the water, are you?"

"Sure." Dog-paddling must count for something. "Why?"

"Just a precaution. Not that I care." He departed without a sound except for his heavy shoes clunking against the wood floor.

Within five minutes, Nate had collected his belongings and emerged from the building onto the front sidewalk. Squinting, he held up his hand to shade his eyes.

Somewhere in the distance, a church bell chimed nine to match the rumbling in Nate's stomach. Warm breakfast, the priest had said. Nate stopped the first passerby to ask for directions to St. Louis Cathedral.

Food first, then questions. Nate needed to learn why the priest had warned him.

ALL THE PARK BENCHES were occupied when Nate strolled through the town square. He stopped in front of a statue of an army officer on horseback and leaned on the black wrought-iron fence that surrounded it.

A woman and two young children stood on the other side, as she read aloud from a bronze tablet embedded in the grass. Nate strained to listen to a brief history of General Jackson. The general's bronze rearing horse loomed dark against the bright blue sky and seemed poised to trample Nate into the cinders in the pathway where he stood.

Beyond the statue stood a large white building spread wide in three sections, each with an arched front door. At first Nate thought it could be a courthouse or a government building, similar to the ones he had seen in Houston, until he looked up at the black pointed roofs with their crosses on top.

He couldn't remember what day it was. Surely not Sunday yet. He glanced over his shoulder before he skirted the small fountain. After a moment's pause, he pushed the massive center door open and stepped inside. Two stone statues of angels holding large seashells greeted him. The long aisle leading to the front of the church was laid in a black-and-white checkerboard pattern.

Nate looked up and caught his breath. Flags lined the balconies on either side, and the arched ceiling stretched toward heaven.

Why would people spend so much money? What good is a fancy church?

The wooden pews were all empty, no pastor behind the pulpit, no choir in the loft. Weariness settled on him like an unwelcome visitor, and he dragged himself to the last row of pews and wedged in as he dropped to a seat. Maybe he should pray.

Sighing, he crossed his forearms on the back of the pew in front of him and leaned forward to rest his head. God would have to wait. He concentrated on the sound of his own breathing until he lost all sense of time and space.

"Have you come for our breakfast handout?"

Nate bolted upright and turned toward the sharp voice behind him. A dark-browed woman wearing a long black dress and a strange hat that hid all her hair waited in the center of the aisle. Her clothes looked familiar. "Are you from the Women's Christian Temperance Union?"

The woman half-smiled and shook her head. "I am Sister Ida-Emily. May I help you?"

"Uh, I'm looking for Father Antoine. Is he back from the jail yet?"

She pointed toward a small wooden closet beyond the opposite end of the pews. "He'll return in about an hour. He can hear your confession then."

"Well, meanwhile, I'd like to earn my breakfast. I don't take no charity."

With a stern look in her eye, she motioned for Nate to follow her up the aisle. "You must be only just arrived in town. What's your name, young man?"

"Nate. Rutledge." His new name rolled off his tongue easier now. He picked up his satchel. "You got some wood needs chopping?"

"How are you at gardening?"

"My ma has a garden."

"Flowers or vegetables?"

"Just vegetables. And one rose bush. She digs it up and takes it with her every time we move." He figured his mother would have to give up the rose bush when she left Texas.

"Is that recently?"

"Er, no, not since …"

"Where is your family now?" She bowed before the large hanging cross at the front of the church and turned right, padding silently next to the railing.

Nate swallowed hard. He could not tell anyone, not even someone who worked in a church, where he came from. "They've been in South Carolina for quite a spell. We have other family there."

"Charleston? Or maybe closer to Savannah? I'm familiar with Savannah."

His stomach heaved. "Charleston."

Please, Lord, don't let her ask me anything about the city.

"I'm on my way back, soon as I get enough money."

AFTER HE SPENT AN HOUR raking and clipping dead branches off palm trees, Sister Ida-Emily showed Nate where to clean himself up. He splashed water on his face and upper body, dried off with his dirty shirt, then changed clothes. A shave would have to wait. He wondered what the judge would think of the dark whiskers on his chin, more than stubble now.

The nun led Nate to the dining hall, where a plate of food awaited him. He sat at the long wooden table and stared at the rectangles of fried batter dusted with sugar.

"I never had any pancakes 'cept flat, round ones." He glanced at the light brown liquid in the mug. "Or nothing but plain black coffee." He closed his eyes and inhaled. "Smells great."

"Beignets and café au lait. You are in New Orleans now, Mr. Rutledge."

"Thank you, but I ain't staying long. I got plans elsewhere."

She refilled his coffee. "Tell God your plans. He'll be amused."

Halfway through the meal, Father Antoine arrived with the crew from jail. They joined Nate at the long wooden table, none looking surprised he had arrived before they did. The sister busied herself filling blue tin plates and mugs.

When everyone had finished eating, the group wandered out of the dining hall, leaving Nate and the priest together. Sunlight through the arched windows warmed Nate's back and shoulders.

After Sister Ida-Emily cleared the last of the dishes and left the room, Nate waited for the priest to speak, but he worked at wiping a smudge from the table instead.

"Back there in the jail, you warned me. How come?"

"You perhaps have discerned that New Orleans can be a treacherous place. Full of crime and violence."

Not that different from Clarks Common, just larger. Or the train.

"Seems a little rough."

"With the new law in effect, the roughness will escalate. The man who spoke to you in the jail, where is he employed?"

Nate fumbled in his pocket for the judge's business card.

Father Antoine pulled a pair of thick glasses from a pocket in his robe and wrapped the wire stems around his ears. He took the card from Nate and studied it. "Ah, Judge Carolla. Rumor has it, he's deeply connected to the New Orleans Mafia. Any employment he offers you could be dangerous, if not illegal."

"Who are the Mafias?"

From the old priest, Nate learned some of the Sicilian immigrants who settled in New Orleans had their own style of doing business. The Matranga family had always operated saloons and brothels, but about thirty years ago they also wanted to gain control of the commercial shipping, especially fruits and vegetables from South America.

"They extorted payments from the Italian dockworkers and eradicated their competition, the Provenzano family. The Matranga Black Hand engaged them in violent gang wars until they were forced out. Seems like we held funeral services twice a week back then."

Nate stared at the priest and wished he could take in all the big words. "We've had some trouble with our neighbors, too."

But it had been all Roy's fault.

Nate stood up and tucked his chair under the table's edge. "So I need to watch out for anyone named Matranga?"

"Not just them, but I hear Judge Carolla has a nephew or a cousin who has risen in the ranks of their family. Be on your guard for a man named Sam Carolla." Father Antoine shook his head. "He seems destined for great misconduct."

"I just need to find a job." Nate shouldered his satchel. "Thanks for the breakfast. What time it is, please?"

"Not quite eleven. You are welcome to remain here, if you wish."

"Can you please tell me how to get to that address?" He pointed at the card. "I need to be there before two."

"So you're determined to go see the judge? I wish you'd stay here instead."

"I can't live on charity. If he's got work for me, I don't have a choice."

The old priest sighed. "Piazza d' Italia. Not far. Head south-west for several blocks on Chartres Street and turn at the —"

"Just give me all the names of the streets I'll pass, in order, if you please."

The priest raised his eyebrows. "Would you prefer I draw you a map instead?"

"I can remember them." He stood up and held out his hand for the card. "I'll count them out."

And maybe recognize a few letters on the street signs.

"Would you do something else for me?"

"If I can."

Nate held out his satchel. "Hold on to this 'til I come back for it."

"Of course. It'll be here awaiting your return. Soon, I pray."

Nate thanked Father Antoine again for his kindness and promised to return for more visits or if he needed other help. "By the way, why is your church called a cathedral?"

"St. Louis Cathedral, named for King Louis IX, the sainted king of France, has a bishop appointed by the Archbishop and approved by the Pope." The priest waved his arm through the air, as if addressing a large crowd. "We have a rich history as the oldest cathedral in America."

"Holy smokes, my pa would pitch a conniption." The instant the words left his mouth, Nate wished he could shove them back in. "Sorry, I don't mean to be ungrateful." Besides, Roy wouldn't have any conniption, not ever again. And Nate's real father lay buried in South Carolina, not Texas.

The priest chuckled as he recited the street names for Nate. "Just listen for the chime on the Century Clock Tower, so you'll know when it's two o'clock." Then he walked him out through the sanctuary and waved as Nate headed southwest on Chartres Street. "Take care of yourself."

As Nate counted out the streets, he brooded on what his job with Judge Carolla might be. It couldn't be doing anything worse than what he had already done. His mother would just have to understand that he had no choice, if he wanted to make it all the way to South Carolina.

CHAPTER EIGHT

As he hurried away from the church, Nate counted out the streets exactly as Father Antoine had recited them, matching his memory to the first letter on each street sign. When he paused near the intersection at Toulouse Street, he glanced around for Hootie and his cart. Up or down the long street, no sign of his acquaintance from yesterday.

Nate slowed his pace to a stroll until he stopped altogether. What could be illegal about unloading and delivering product? It's not likely the judge would expect him to steal or murder someone. Surely Nate's size and strength had impressed the judge, and the suit made it sound like the product needed protecting. Could be as simple as the beer Hootie sold from the bottom of his cart.

I can't tell Ma about this job. She'd have plenty of objection. It's not like I'll be delivering her fresh pies.

Nate crossed the street. After several blocks, he turned south onto Camp Street and the buildings appeared more like businesses than homes. He came to Poydras Street, a wide avenue the priest had mentioned, and continued to Lafayette Square. This time, the statue of the hero wasn't on horseback, just a man standing in old-fashioned clothing.

Nate lingered to listen to a brass band play marching tunes, probably from the Great War. Some he recognized went back to the Civil War. He marked time with one he remembered his mother humming.

Shouldn't the musicians be parading up and down like soldiers instead of seated in the gazebo?

After several thumping pieces, the music changed to an irregular rhythm, as three black performers stood and blew notes from different instruments, one short horn that stuck out in front of his face, one curled down the chest and stomach of the player, and a long one with an extra bar that slid back and forth.

Several passers-by stopped to enjoy the music and clapped with enthusiasm when the piece was finished. Nate decided the musicians had earned the clapping, so he joined the other fans.

A well-dressed middle-aged couple turned to nod and smile at him. As they continued applauding, a small boy skipped in front of them singing and chattering while another boy behind them, almost identical to the other, sneaked his hand into the gentleman's pocket unnoticed.

Before he could make his getaway, Nate snatched the boy by the collar and lifted him off the ground. "Give the man his money back."

The boy whimpered and tried to kick Nate in the crotch. "Let me go, damn you!"

The couple wheeled around and the wife fussed at Nate not to hurt him. The second little boy began to cry and make a loud commotion, as several people gathered in a circle around Nate.

"Here, here!" said the man. "Put the little urchin down. He's not bothering anyone."

"That's because he's a good thief." Nate shook the boy like a crumpled rag. "Empty your pockets or I will."

Glaring at Nate, the boy reached inside his pants. Two fat wallets, a roll of bills, and a gold watch tumbled about four feet to the ground from the bottom of his pant leg. The crowd grew silent, while the other boy slipped away.

"Hey, that's my watch!" said one bystander.

"And my wallet," said the gentleman in front of Nate.

His wife apologized and thanked Nate as people collected their belongings. "You should call the police," she said to her husband, then to Nate, "You deserve a reward."

Nate set the boy on the pavement and held up his palms. "Oh, no, I don't want no police or reward." As the boy scurried off, Nate backed away from the crowd, but the wife followed him.

She gestured to her husband. "Angelo, give him something."

"Of course." He pulled a crisp five-dollar bill from his wallet. "Here you go, young man. We appreciate your quick eye and strong arm of justice." He grinned, revealing four gold front teeth.

"I don't take no charity, thank you anyhow."

The man urged the money at him. "You deserve it. Besides, it's a lot less than I would have lost if you hadn't spotted those little pirates."

That much money would have paid for Mary's medicine almost three times over. Or bought twenty of his mother's pies. Nate wasn't sure he earned it, but he accepted the bill and thanked the couple.

As he blended into the crowd, he wondered if the two little boys had a third brother somewhere, too small to join their band of thieves yet. Maybe home with their mother, if they even had one.

Was that what became of youngsters without family? Forced to choose between stealing or dying of hunger?

He pushed from his mind a vision of Walter leaping after his brothers out the door of the train.

IN THE DISTANCE, the Century Clock Tower chimed. Nate stopped to number off the gongs and bells and figured it was one-thirty. He turned east onto Lafayette Street, took the next three blocks in long strides until he reached Piazza d' Italia. The building stood at the corner of Lafayette and Commerce Streets, a red brick structure with arched windows. Nate climbed the stairs to the judge's office on the fifth floor, where the woman at the reception desk asked him his business.

"The judge said to come see him today at two o'clock. I'm early."

"By twenty minutes." She sniffed and wrinkled her nose. "Have a seat over there."

Nate assumed from her pout she didn't like being watched as she sorted papers and opened mail. From the corner of his eye, he observed as she snapped the drawer to the filing cabinet open and closed and then signed for a package from a delivery boy.

"Is there an invoice in the crate?"

"No, ma'am," the delivery boy said. "No paper. Boss say get cash today."

"You'll have to sign a receipt anyway. How much?" The receptionist pulled keys from her pocket and unlocked a bottom drawer.

"They's sixteen of 'em, boss say, at three dollars and seventy-five cents each for his discount. That's … uh, hmmm."

"Well, how much is it?"

The delivery boy scratched his head and whirled around to shrug at Nate with a sheepish grin.

"Sixty dollars," Nate said. "Total. Unless you add a tip."

The receptionist glared at him as she stacked the bills and counted them again before handing them to the delivery boy. Nate returned her frown until she added a quarter. On his way out the door, the young man winked and tipped his hat to Nate. The receptionist locked the drawer and stepped toward the east window to haul up the shade.

As the light poured in, Nate raised his gaze. "Gosh, is that the ocean?"

She frowned instead of looking where he pointed. "The Mississippi." Her tone came out flat, as if she had told people a thousand times what lay beyond.

"Too bad you don't realize how lucky you are, all this glory lost on you," Nate said under his breath. He stood up and walked to the window, leaning his forearm on the glass.

"Hey, you're blocking the light."

"Oh, sorry." He stepped back. "When will the judge be available?"

"Whenever he shows up."

"He's not here?" Nate lowered his voice. "Sorry, I didn't mean to holler. But you didn't tell me that."

"You'll have to wait until he returns." She shooed him away from her desk. "Take your seat over there."

An hour passed before the judge came through the door. Nate stood up, but the judge ignored him. He sauntered past the receptionist's desk into his inner office and closed the door.

The receptionist didn't look at Nate. He took a step forward. "Sit down."

Nate blinked and stared at the floor. After a few moments, he returned to his chair.

Five minutes later, the judge came out to drop some papers on her desk and whisper something in the receptionist's ear before returning to his office. This time, he didn't close the door.

The receptionist announced, "You can go in now. He'll give you three minutes."

When Nate entered the office, the judge was already seated behind his desk, elbows resting on top, fingertips touching to form a steeple under his chin. The man might as well have been sitting on a throne. He never took his eyes off Nate. "Think you're ready to go to work?"

"Doing what?"

"Special deliveries."

"Like that boy who was just here?"

"Similar product, much bigger shipments, a few impediments to overcome. Can you handle it?"

"How much will you pay me?"

"I'm not the employer, but you'll receive twenty dollars a week, plus a room. You can begin with that crate in the front office."

"Where do I take it?" Nate figured he could fool the receptionist into deciphering the address for him.

"Downstairs, to the back loading dock. Someone will meet you there with a truck. Get in and do what he says. Create any trouble and you'll land back in jail, where you'll likely rot." The judge opened a wooden box on his desk and took out a cigar. After clipping one end of it, he struck a match. "Questions?"

Nate shook his head.

"One more thing. You help yourself to any product without permission, there'll be other unpleasant consequences." He puffed on the cigar and blew a stream of smoke toward Nate. "Understood?"

"Sure." Right then, Nate set his heart on learning big words. People with proper speech got what they wanted, even if they were crooked.

Nate stepped up to the edge of the desk and stared down at the man, not to threaten him, but to make sure he grasped the value of Nate's size and strength. "I got here before two, just like you asked. Why did you keep me waiting all this time?"

One of the judge's cheeks was redder than the other, a souvenir from last night's fight. Didn't he realize Nate could toss him out the window behind him?

"I was testing you. You passed."

If he didn't know before who held the power, Nate became aware at that moment. He scowled down at the judge.

"You wouldn't have a chance to treat me that way if I was the one with the money. Even if you own the law, you don't own me."

Instead of looking alarmed, the judge flashed half a smile, which faded to a sneering indifference. "Now get out of here."

Nate turned to leave, but stopped when the judge spoke. "By the way, if you didn't bring a pistol, the driver will provide you one."

As Nate fingered the bull's gun in his jacket pocket, the priest's words echoed in his ears. He strained to catch the judge's expression through the cigar smoke. "How dangerous is this work?"

"The swamp around New Orleans is full of 'gators and cot-tonmouths." The judge raised one eyebrow. "You have to be pre-pared so you don't get bitten or swallowed whole."

His mother had once told him that lies and half-truths can be just as hard to recognize as death because you don't always see them coming. What hadn't the judge told him? For twenty dollars a week, Nate would put up with lies. But he'd keep a sharp eye out for them and an even keener one in case death showed up again.

Nate returned to the front office, hoisted the crate from the floor, and tucked it under one arm. The receptionist gaped at him. After a moment, she held the door open for him, and he nodded as he passed by her into the hallway, wondering what kind of trouble lay ahead.

CHAPTER NINE

The alley opened to the street at one end, with the loading dock at the other. Just as the judge described, the truck was already parked with its rear backed up to the edge.

The driver, a handsome man of about thirty with dark hair slicked back, leaned against the side of the truck, smoking a cigarette. He glanced up as Nate approached and dropped the butt to the pavement, not bothering to grind the burning tip.

He jerked his thumb over his shoulder. "Why didn't you come out the back door?"

"Didn't know it was there."

"Anyone see you with that crate?"

"Just the woman who works in the judge's office."

"Ah, sweet Matilda." He opened the truck's rear door. "What's your name, kid?"

"Nate Rutledge." The momenet the words left his mouth, Nate winced. Maybe he should have used a different last name.

"I'm Franco de Angelis. Slide that in here and then get in the front."

Nate did as he was told, noting the painted M on the sign on the side of the truck. The drawing with the fancy gold letters told him the product was fruits and vegetables, but wooden crates, sealed shut and stacked on top of each other, crowded the back of the truck. If the goods also belonged to the Matranga family the priest had mentioned, the crates were packed with something else.

He climbed in and wished his mother could see him. Wouldn't she be impressed that he finally got to ride in a truck, and not just watch them pull away after unloading at the general store in Clarks Common? She would have something else to say, however, about working for a crook.

Franco drove down the alley and turned left. "The judge says you need a place to stay?"

"He told me it comes with the job."

"You got anything besides what's on your back?" He sniffed. "You need some new clothes."

"I'll get 'em later."

"Don't wait too long."

They rode for a while without talking, and Nate sucked in the open, fresh air. If he leaned back far enough, he could watch the view from the oval window in the side panel.

Driving didn't look too hard. Mash something on the floor with both feet, every now and then move the stick in the middle, and turn the wheel in a circle at the corner. And watch for bumps and holes in the road.

After several blocks, the neighborhood changed from businesses to homes, big fancy ones that could be palaces, with large gardens. Franco slowed to turn into a driveway, and Nate's eyes grew wide as they passed through a snazzy wrought-iron gate. Toward the front door, the garden overflowed with roses that covered the branches of small round trees. His mother's rose bush had never bloomed that thick.

But instead of stopping the truck in front of the house, Franco pulled around the back toward the garage. He motioned for Nate to get out and meet him behind the truck.

The same man who had visited the jail and arranged for Nate's release waited on the back porch. Nate could feel him watching as he unloaded the crate from the judge's office.

Franco signaled toward the house. "Fetch this up on the veranda and leave it for the bartender."

Nate headed up the brick sidewalk and climbed the stairs to the columned porch. He nodded at the man waiting, who ignored him. As he set down the crate on a table, the man called out, "Hey, Frankie, what's new?" The two men met halfway on the lawn for private conversation.

The back door opened and an elderly black man in a dark suit and white shirt with a black bow tie stepped out on the porch. He pointed at the box. "That be the hooch?"

"I guess so. Are you the bartender?"

The man pulled a small metal spoon from his suit pocket and pried the lid off the box. Nate peeked at the contents, sixteen bottles, the same number the delivery boy had recited to Matilda. Nodding, the black man counted twice. "This'll have to do. His Honor 'spects only 'bout forty guests."

"Judge Corolla lives here?" Nate gazed up at the high ceilings with brass light fixtures and gave a low whistle.

"Quit your gawking and let's go," Franco yelled.

Nate leaped off the porch, clearing a flowerbed by about two feet, and hurried across the lawn to the truck. Franco started backing up before Nate closed the door.

"Where to now?"

"Deliveries, then back to the warehouse. Then more deliveries 'til we're done."

Nate learned the routine that afternoon and into the evening. Franco drove the truck into alleys behind restaurants and bars, and while Nate unloaded the crates, Franco collected the payments and flirted with the waitresses.

Sometimes they parked in front and interrupted the flow of pedestrians. Despite the manager's warning at Napoleon's, Nate wondered why nobody cared enough to call the police.

At the warehouse, they worked together as one of several teams, and Nate figured there must be enough shipments to serve a drink to everyone in New Orleans.

After the last delivery, Franco showed Nate to a musty store-room behind the warehouse. "Foreman says you sleep here. I'll be back late tomorrow afternoon."

"What do I do during the day?"

"Here's a five-spot. Go treat your girlfriend to a fancy lunch at the Court of the Two Sisters."

Nate stared at the printed face of President Lincoln and shook his head.

Franco tucked the money into Nate's shirt pocket. "I don't care what you do. Just stay outta trouble. And rest up."

"It's the wee hours already. I won't get much sleep."

"The wee hours?" Franco laughed. "Who talks like that?"

Nate clenched his fists. "That's what my ma called any time after midnight."

"Hey, relax, hit the hay now. The real hard work starts late tomorrow night." Heaving a big yawn, he left.

The bed consisted of a straw-filled tick mattress with no sheets or blankets. Nate rolled up his jacket to use as a pillow. Then he opened the window to let the cool night breeze freshen the air inside. When the drizzle started, he closed it again.

He lay on his back and stared up into the dark. If he were at home, he would smell beans with onions boiling on the stove and pies in the oven. Mary would be coughing, Lillie would be trying to sleep, and his mother would be sitting in the rocking chair, shucking peas or mending someone's clothes. His pa, or Roy, the name Nate would use from now on, would be... gone.

When would he see them all again? Nate closed his eyes and calculated how many weeks he would need to work until he could afford to bring his family back together. It didn't matter where. South Carolina was just as good as Texas.

So far the job had turned out to be easy enough. He hadn't needed to use his pistol or swim through deep water filled with gators and snakes.

Maybe he would tomorrow or the next day. He prayed the time would never come, but if it did, he'd be ready.

CHAPTER TEN

Franco hadn't told Nate what the actual hard work was. Instead of loading the truck at the warehouse, he drove it empty to the far end of the port, away from the night lights of the city, and parked under a cypress tree with drooping branches. Soon at least a dozen other trucks lined up next to them. A few yards away, waves lapped the shore like a playful puppy.

"We wait here for the signal." Franco rolled another cigarette and offered one to Nate.

Nate shook his head. "What's the signal?" He rubbed his forearm against the windshield, which had turned foggy from the humid air.

"Someone will show up."

"Then what?"

"We move fast. Got to get them crates off the skiffs and into the back of the truck."

"Where do the skiffs come from?" Nate wished he knew what skiffs were.

"You mean the big boat? I dunno. Haiti. Cuba. One of those islands in the Caribbean where they grow sugar cane."

After several minutes of dark and silence, other trucks pulled up beside them. Franco lit another cigarette. "Looks like a big haul tonight."

The sound of a door slamming came from the truck parked next to them. Nate sat up straight and followed Franco's gaze as he strained his eyes toward the water. Black as far as he could see, as if the ocean had swallowed the horizon.

"There they are." Franco got out of the truck. "Come on. Take off your shoes and roll up your pants legs. Watch out for the big rocks."

By the time Nate stood barefooted in the surf, twelve small rowboats headed toward him and the others.

Gliding low in the water, the rowers looked like they might sink at any moment. They rode in the last ten feet on the tide to where the ocean was only about two feet deep. Franco handed one of them something, palm to palm.

Before Nate had finished unloading and stashing all the truck could hold, Franco started the engine. "We skated by lucky this time. No Feds."

Nate got in the truck and dried his feet with his socks. "I counted 147 crates in the back." He wondered if he should mention the man in the shadows watching every transfer they made.

Franco took off ahead of the other trucks. "Counting them is my job, kid." He made so many turns, Nate couldn't tell which direction would take them to the warehouse making one stop on the way.

After turning down a darkened street, Franco pulled over to the sidewalk and stopped near an alley. "Stay in the truck. I'll handle this."

Nate waited in the front seat while Franco unloaded seven crates from the back of the truck. The alley was too dark to see the other man, but Nate caught a hint of an unfamiliar accent.

Franco climbed into the driver's seat and fixed his eyes straight ahead. "You saw nothing, you say nothing, got that?" He held out a five-dollar bill.

Nate stared at him. Despite Franco's extra dealings, Nate hadn't done anything wrong, and if no one asked him any questions, he wouldn't have to lie. Or tell the truth either.

"Sure." Nate took the money and stashed it in his shirt

pocket. "But you gotta teach me to drive this truck."

Franco laughed as he opened the driver's door and slid out. "I'm gonna show you how to change the tires and service the engine, too. You can be the one who gets greasy from now on." He turned to face Nate. "Be smart and you can do all right for yourself."

After leaving the door open, Franco scampered around the back of the truck to find Nate still in the passenger's seat. "Slide over, will ya?"

Following Franco's instructions all the way to the warehouse, Nate stared straight ahead. By the time he turned off the engine, Nate hadn't decided if Franco was a cottonmouth or a 'gator.

EACH DAY WAS JUST like the one before. Between the warehouse and deliveries, only trips to the waterfront interrupted Nate's routine, but he never knew when to expect the change in schedule.

About every other shipment, Franco slipped something to a rower, not always the same one. Only the warehouse foreman kept track of supplies and orders. Nate wondered how often he checked the delivery math and if he would find Franco coming up short.

After three weeks, Nate got used to sleeping until ten o'clock. That gave him freedom to stroll around the business district and find Hootie and his cart in time for lunch and the local news. He returned to St. Louis Cathedral to thank Father Antoine and reclaim his satchel. Nate was tired of washing his one set of clothing in the basin at the back of the warehouse. With the New Orleans weather so humid, most days his clothes weren't completely dry when he put them on.

Over café au lait with Father Antoine, Nate relaxed for the

first time since he arrived in New Orleans. But within a few minutes, he fidgeted with the metal spoon.

"You seem preoccupied," said the priest.

"What if you know someone's doing something they shouldn't?" Nate tapped the spoon against the tabletop. "Would you turn them in? I mean, this guy I work with, he's not hurting anyone."

Father Antoine gave him a sad smile. "Do you mean to imply that certain sins are only a little bit wicked?"

"Well, I can't figure how it matters to the big bosses. They got so much stuff in the warehouse to begin with." Nate shrugged. "But the guy told me to keep my mouth shut. That's how I know."

"That he's defrauding his employer?"

Squirming, Nate frowned. "I never said ... uh, what do you mean?"

"Cheating," the priest said. "He's wagering high stakes against the devil on earth."

"I guess so. But I don't want to get into any trouble."

"So you ignore his malfeasance?"

"His mal... yeah, I just turn the other way. Nobody can prove much without seeing the extra stuff and..." His voice soft, Nate paused, until louder he said, "I didn't know they would match it to delivery tickets. But if Franco gets caught, his mess could land on me. I have to watch out for myself."

"In your line of endeavor I suspect there are no true comrades."

"Franco has been good to me, so he won't expect me to rat on him to the boss. Maybe I can just ask to partner with someone else."

"Won't that prompt some suspicion?"

"Either way, I'm too close to the fire and I don't want to get burned. What should I do?"

"Short of finding another job?"

Nate shook his head.

"Well, then, my son, you are on the horns of a dilemma."

"Gosh, I wish I could talk like you. Big words and all. You must have gone to school."

"Yes, to university."

"Could you teach me?"

"I could lend you some books to read in your spare time. We could discuss them later."

"That won't do me no good."

"How much education did your parents provide you?"

"Not much. My ma, she tried to teach me to read when I got big enough, but then the babies started coming every spring or summer, and what with most everyone sick and some dying, we never got too far. Then I had to go to work after my pa, that is, Roy, took off for awhile to work elsewheres. Pretty regular, he'd come back when the crops farther north gave out."

"You've had some difficult years for such a young man."

"Ma had it worse, but I'm going to change that. I'll get enough money to bring her and my sisters back to ... back to ..." Nate's eyes filled with tears and he blinked to keep them from running down his cheeks. "I don't rightly know where."

The priest patted his arm. "Come back this time tomorrow. We'll find a remedy for your lack of education." He stood up. "Meanwhile, you have to decide how you'll fix your other problem. Remember, the Matranga family, and now the Carollas, won't look benignly on someone who ignores the rules. They are quite territorial."

"That's plain enough." Nate shook the priest's hand and left through the sanctuary. Now his familiar route, he passed the two angels holding the bowls shaped like seashells, rubbing one on the head for luck.

On the way to the warehouse, Nate practiced what he could

say to the foreman about Franco's extra activities. He wouldn't say Franco had skimmed the product more than once. Maybe his partner would get assigned some other duties. He hoped the foreman believed he had no part of it.

On the other hand, Franco had been a pal to Nate, treating him to late night meals at musician's dives, teaching him to drive, tipping him when the loads were extra heavy. He wouldn't take it kindly if Nate sold him down the river.

How do I not get blamed?

Either way, he determined not to take any more money from Franco.

After he dropped his satchel in his room, he reported to the loading dock, but Franco wasn't there. Nate waited and watched while the foreman supervised the other teams as they loaded their trucks and took off for their rounds of deliveries.

As soon as everyone else had left, the foreman approached Nate with a stack of papers. With every step, Nate's stomach tightened. He wished he'd taken the priest's advice and found a different job.

The foreman glared at Nate. "Can you drive that truck?"

"Sure." He craned his neck to get a look at the papers.

The foreman folded the papers and tossed Nate the keys. "Get going."

"What about the load?"

"Already in the truck." The foreman turned around and gestured to a thin, dark-haired man who leaned against the wall, the same man hidden in the shadows the first night on the beach. The man put on his cap and strolled toward them.

The foreman handed the man several sheets of paper. "Franco must've took sick today." He nodded at Nate and turned around. "Meet your substitute partner," he said over his shoulder as he walked back to the office.

Nate looked the new guy up and down, noting the bulge

under his jacket. Figured him to be about thirty and Italian. "Okay, what's your name?"

"You can call me Vincent." The man's face showed no emotion, not even friendliness.

'Gator or cottonmouth? Time would tell.

Nate climbed into the driver's seat. "Where to first?"

CHAPTER ELEVEN

T he rest of the week, Nate couldn't move without Vincent watching him. Nate thought some customers might ask about Franco, and he dreaded having to answer, or give them even a simple excuse of illness. But no one mentioned his name.

Aren't they even curious to know if something happened to him?

Nate received his pay on Saturday morning. He had never had his own money before, much less twenty dollars. After staring at the bills for several minutes and dreaming of seeing his family again, he realized he would have to find someplace safe to keep it. Not a bank.

He searched the storeroom for a box or a small chest. Nothing. He put the money in his pants pocket along with the five from Franco. Remembering the two little thieves, he stuffed all of it inside his shirt and tightened his belt. On the way to visit the priest, he patted his stomach several times and at last pulled the money out, clamping his fingers around it.

Father Antoine agreed to keep it for him in a green jar on the upper shelf in his office. "This once held incense."

Nate followed the priest to the library, a room with one window among walls of shelves brimming with books. "Have you read all these?" He drew one from the shelf and fanned its pages.

"Most of them." Father Antoine took the book from Nate and replaced it. "Let's start with English, not Greek."

After several false starts, Nate recited most of the alphabet, but not in order, and couldn't read a short sentence with small words. Father Antoine gave him pencil and paper and directed him to work on writing the letters, both capitals and lower case.

"Twenty-six letters, unless you count them double." Nate grinned. "Then you get fifty-two."

"How did you discern that so quickly?"

"I just see them and know."

"Like the day we met. You memorized the street names without looking at a map."

"Ma says I have a good memory."

"Practice writing them down. You'll make better progress if you can form the letters yourself."

Within an hour, Nate could not only keep the letters in order, but he could also match them to their sounds. Even vowels gave him no trouble. "Now we got thirty-one sounds."

"Numeric values seem to be the key to your mind, my boy." The priest patted his shoulder. "You'll be proficient in no time."

"I'll be able to read, too, and then get a better job."

Nate didn't tell the priest that learning to read might be his best protection.

THE CITY LIGHTS WERE too dim for Nate to see any street names, but he kept an eye out for signs hanging over doors of bars and restaurants where he and Vincent made deliveries. He found it easy to hide his lack of schooling from Vincent, but so far his job involved heaving crates in and out of the truck.

During the last delivery on Monday night, he turned to Vincent. "Maybe one day, I'll be the guy with the list and some other country cousin'll get the sweaty job."

"Forget it. You ain't smart enough." Vincent spoke loud enough for the customer checking the ticket to hear.

Nate hoped the darkness hid his red face. He slammed the

truck's back door and climbed into the driver's seat.

By the time he dropped Vincent off mid-town and returned to the warehouse in the wee hours before Tuesday's sun came up, Nate was bone-tired and in a temper. He had taken the insult without challenge, but he swore Vincent would one day be sorry for his cheap shot.

He plodded to the storeroom, but stopped when he found the door ajar.

Someone's been here. Are they gone?

He nudged the door open wider and fumbled for the light switch. A man propped up on Nate's mattress held up his hand, palm out, shielding his face against the shaft of light from the hallway.

"Who's there?" Nate's fingers glanced off the wall, searching for the button.

"It's me, Franco." His voice sounded husky, his breath coming in gasps.

"Where've you been? They told me you were sick."

"Shut the door."

Nate switched on a lamp and shut the door. When he turned around, he winced. "What happened?"

Franco held his stomach, blood seeping through his fingers. "Vincent found me." He laughed but no sound came out. "He thought he had me, but I fooled him."

"Are you shot?" Nate knelt beside the mattress and tried to pry Franco's hand up.

"I'll be okay." Franco grabbed the front of Nate's jacket. "You gotta do something for me."

"What is it?" Nate wished he'd had more deliveries to keep him out later. Or he could be sitting alone inside the cathedral, where he sometimes went when he couldn't sleep.

Franco pulled a small canvas bag from inside his shirt and held it out toward Nate. When Nate didn't take it, he dropped it on the floor. The back was smeared with blood. "Extra money I... earned."

"We both know how you got that money, and I don't want it. I don't want to get blamed for anything."

"You can't keep it, ya sap." Franco flopped on his back, exhausted from the effort of speaking. "Help me get out of here. I'll pay you."

Nate peeled away Franco's hand and lifted up his shirt. His mother knew more about gunshot wounds than he did, but it didn't take a genius to recognize that Franco wouldn't bounce back from this one.

He hoped Franco couldn't read any expression on his face. "Sure. I'll stash it somewhere. No one will find it."

"I'm taking it with me. Now help me up." Franco clutched at his arm, and Nate dragged him to his feet.

"How will you manage? Where will you go?"

"That's the favor I need. Take me to the waterfront. My Cuban friend, Paco, is coming for me."

"Now?"

"Get the truck and drive me there."

For a moment, Nate considered the possible outcomes. The worst one would be anyone finding a dead Franco in his room with the money he finagled. At this hour, no one was at the warehouse to notice a truck making an unscheduled delivery to the waterfront. He could be back in just over forty minutes.

Nate picked up the canvas bag. "Let's go." He tugged Franco's arm around his shoulder and together they lurched toward the door.

By the time Nate stopped under the tree with the low-hanging branches, Franco had stopped moaning. He slouched in his seat with his head tilted forward, his grasp of the bloody canvas bag gone slack.

Nate reached over and laid two fingers on the side of Franco's neck. After half a minute, Nate clenched his jaw. Father Antoine was right about the Mafia. Breaking the law when no one got hurt was one thing, but murder? A family who would kill its own wasn't family.

The moment the thought formed, he cringed.

Does that make me an outsider to my own kin?

But maybe his mother would say Roy was the one who didn't belong.

Leaning his head against the back window of the truck, Nate considered what to do. If he left the body in the tide, it might wash out to sea. Did Franco have kinfolks, or anyone who would miss him? Nate had never thought to ask.

In less than five minutes, Nate had dragged Franco's body over the rocks and into the water to a depth of about three feet, leaving it to roll back and forth with the waves. He climbed in the truck and drove back to the warehouse, grateful for the light mist that began to fall. It would wash any trace of sand from the truck.

After he parked under the shed roof, he pondered what to do with the money. He'd have to put it where nobody would think to look. Not his room. What if Vincent or somebody else followed Franco?

Should've thought of that before I left.

He stared at the bag until an idea came to him. He picked it up, the blood by now flaked and crusty, and shoved it under the passenger seat, wedging it tight.

As he lay in bed a few minutes later, it dawned on him that he hadn't counted the money. Maybe enough to bring his mother and the girls to New Orleans instead of South Carolina? What about the new baby? How much did Franco skim?

Except we can't stay here if the bosses think I was mixed up with Franco.

The straw in his mattress rustled as Nate turned over and

blinked at the ceiling. Dim light crept through the window, streaking the darkness with pale shadows. He needed sleep.

Tomorrow would be the hardest work he'd ever done. And, he hoped, the smartest.

Chapter Twelve

The next day after lunch, Nate returned to the warehouse to find all the trucks lined up in the center of the parking lot. Several of the crew held sponges and buckets as they scrubbed the sides and tops of each truck, one after the other.

Panic took hold of Nate, as he paced back and forth, trying to recognize which truck he had driven last night. All the writing on the side panels looked the same, and he never had found any numbers to identify. He'd have to try his key in the ignitions one at a time, but there were too many people around.

"Need any help?" he called out to one of the delivery men.

"Grab a broom and sweep out the back of each one. We're moving fruit today."

"How about the floors in front?" Nate pulled a broom from the storage closet.

"Go ahead, if you want to work that hard. The bosses'll like to see you sweat."

Nate started with the first truck on the left. The key didn't turn. He tried the next one, and the next after that. The key fit the ignition in the sixth one, and he heaved a sign of relief. Until he checked under the passenger's seat. No bloodstained canvas bag. He tried the key again.

The chance he'd be blamed for taking it or killing Franco made him gasp. He stepped backward from the truck and turned around, searching for anyone whose face hinted at even a little guilt. Had one of them taken the money?

Nate stopped pacing and looked at the pavement. Was Vincent any worse than he was? Father Antoine wouldn't split hairs over this question. Killing is killing, and it's wrong. The Sixth Commandment said so, in the Bible his mother used to read aloud.

Across the parking lot, Vincent strolled toward the office with a newspaper tucked under his arm. A few minutes after he disappeared inside, the foreman stood in the doorway and called Nate's name.

Trudging past the window that overlooked the parking lot, Nate squared his shoulders. Words of a heated argument stopped him at the door.

"This better not put me at risk," a man's harsh voice threatened.

Nate entered the office. The foreman was already seated behind his desk, pudgy stomach resting on the half-open middle drawer, the newspaper spread on top.

Next to the door, Vincent leaned with one shoulder resting against the wall. He scraped under his fingernails with the tip of a pocketknife and didn't look up.

On one edge of the desk sat a man dressed in an expensive-looking, dark blue suit, similar to the one the judge's bodyguard wore. From his posture and the way he let his leg dangle, as if he owned the desk, the office, and everything in it, Nate guessed the foreman reported to him. He kept his eyes down.

The foreman tapped his index finger on the photo on the front page, a dead body on the beach, covered with a tarp, surrounded by police. "Franco here washed up a few miles down river."

Printed below the picture of Franco was a second photo of a man standing in the center of a group of smiling police officers. Although a bit blurry and upside down, the man's smirking face seemed familiar.

Nate leaned forward and frowned, trying to keep the tone

of his voice even. "That's awful. What happened?"

"Evidently he got into a fight. Somebody shot him and dumped him in the delta. Police are looking for the guy."

Nate's eyes met the foreman's and held them for a few seconds before he stood up straight. "I hope they catch him real soon."

"Funeral's next week. At St. Louie's." The foreman folded the paper and set it aside. "Did Franco say anything to you on his last day at work?"

Nate's eyes flickered. "Sure, he always talked a lot. Don't recall anything particular."

"Maybe something about the deliveries? An angry customer? We were wondering if someone, an outsider, might have tried to bully Franco, perhaps take over his route."

Nate shrugged and hoped they couldn't hear the pounding of his heart. "I just loaded and unloaded what he told me." He glanced over his shoulder at Vincent. "Franco was the guy with the lists."

"Sooner or later, the police will be coming around, asking a few questions."

"I'll tell them the same thing I told you."

The truth, so far.

He swallowed but his mouth had gone dry. "I don't know nothing about any squabble, with a customer or nobody else. You know what Franco was like. Always in a good mood."

"Okay, Sam?" The foreman glanced up at the man in the suit. The man took his time nodding, but his steel-gray eyes never left Nate's face as he folded his arms.

The man in the newspaper photo! Sam Carolla, the judge's nephew.

The priest would snatch me out of here quick.

Sam Carolla stood up and buttoned his double-breasted jacket. "I'll be in my office if you find anything." He left through a doorway at the back of the room. A few moments later, the thud of his footsteps echoed as he climbed the stairs.

The foreman jerked his thumb toward Vincent. "Meanwhile, you'll keep the same partner."

Nate smiled and tried to keep his lunch from coming back up. "Fine with me." He rapped on his chest and burped. "Damn oysters."

"Go on. You've got deliveries." He spun his chair around and reached toward the group of keys dangling from rows of brass hooks screwed into a board hung on the wall. He lifted one off. "Here you go."

"Keep it. I came back too late to turn mine in last night."

The foreman and Vincent exchanged glances.

Nate turned around to find Vincent holding the door open. He gestured for Nate to go first, but Nate reached over his head and took hold of the door's edge. "After you."

THAT AFTERNOON, THEY DROVE from the docks to the open air market, the truck piled with fruits and vegetables to match the sign painted on its sides. The loads were lighter and Nate didn't work up the same sweat as with the crates of liquor and beer. Vincent didn't talk much, but Nate felt eyes on his back every time he picked up or set down a box.

By 11:30 p.m., they had made their final delivery. Nate sat in the truck without starting the engine. "Where do you want me to drop you tonight?" He rested his tired hands on the steering wheel and peeked at Vincent from the corner of his eye.

"I'm riding with you all the way back to the warehouse." Vincent shifted in his seat. "I have to stop by the office for something."

"The foreman won't be there this late."

"Shut up and drive."

Nate ground the gears and lurched forward, smiling when Vincent's head struck the back of the truck's cab. He aimed for every pothole, just for the jolt it gave him. Corners he tried to take on two wheels, as the tires screamed and the truck tilted. As he pulled into the shadowy parking lot at the warehouse, the only light came from the office window.

The foreman was working late after all.

Nate scanned the area for a parking place and screeched to a stop.

Vincent thrust his arms out to keep from pitching forward into the dashboard. "Watch out, ya maniac!"

"We're home." Nate got out of the truck and closed the door harder than he meant to. Without a backward glance, he reached the entrance to his room in a few long strides. The door stood partway open.

Not again. Who's in here this time?

He pushed the door all the way open and turned on the light. The mess before him sucked the air from his lungs. His satchel had been ripped apart and his few belongings torn and scattered. The mattress was shredded and its straw ticking thrown over every surface. The chair was set upside down with one leg broken off.

Nate bent over to pick up the wooden scrap and smacked his palm with it.

Thank God I left all my cash with Father Antoine.

He kicked at the straw, sending a few strands into the air. Maybe he could sleep in the truck.

"Here's the deal."

Nate whirled at the voice behind him. Vincent stood in the doorway, pointing a pistol at him. In his other hand he held the bloody canvas bag. With the barrel, he gestured at the chair leg until Nate dropped it at his feet.

"We know Franco was running extra product out of Cuba,

and you were helping him. See, the paperwork finally arrived, and the foreman caught a few discrepancies. So do yourself a favor and tell me who was Franco's contact from the boat."

"How would I know? I was always busy unloading. Just doing my job."

"Give me a name." Vincent waggled the pistol. "Or—"

"I only remember him mentioning some guy named Paco." Nate wished he hadn't left his pistol in the truck.

"Don't try this gag on me."

"What do you mean?"

"Paco is Franco in Spanish. Two guys with the same name? I oughta plug you right now."

"That's the only name I ever heard, I swear." Nate exhaled. "Looks like you've already got the money. Why shoot me?"

"Just protecting our turf. The foreman hasn't yet figured out how much moola your guy made off with. But Franco wasn't smart enough to make this work in the long run. Stupid bastard shoulda picked better associates."

"But you're smarter than Franco." Nate did some quick mental calculating. "You got friends in high positions." He nodded toward the bag of money. "You can keep his receipts and no one's any wiser." Slipping his hand in his pocket, he reached for the coins his mother had given him. He stroked the one his fingers recognized as the buffalo head nickel.

"Bring your hands out where I can see 'em." Vincent grinned, showing straight white teeth Nate had never seen. "You catch on quick. I can keep this money and keep my job, too." Vincent leveled the gun at Nate's chest. "Now let's get back in the truck. We're taking a little ride to the docks."

Clutching the coins, Nate freed his hand from the pocket. "Don't you want to take over Franco's sweet business deal, too? But you'd have to know which customers are in on it."

"All you did was unload crates. You never saw the lists."

Nate shifted his weight until the toe of his boot rested under the edge of the broken chair leg. "I didn't have to see the lists. I know who gets how much."

"I don't believe you."

In less than a minute, Nate rattled off the names of five customers on their route and calculated their weekly inventory and charges. Then he added the extra shipment Franco had provided and revised the total profit figure. "That's just the first week."

Vincent raised his eyebrows. "How'd you do that?"

Nate shrugged. "You think Franco pulled this off by himself? He needed a partner good with numbers. You'll have to give me what he paid me."

"I already got a partner." He jerked his head toward the office. "He's gonna be thrilled when I show him what I found. In your truck, by the way."

The foreman. Of course. Someone else had to be at the warehouse to tear up his room while Nate made deliveries with Vincent.

"Now let's get moving." Vincent took a step backward.

"You didn't find the rest of the money, did you? All that moola Franco paid me."

"Shut up. You're just stalling."

"You, or somebody, tore up my room and got nothing. If you was taller, you could have reached it, up in the rafters." Nate pointed at the ceiling.

In the second Vincent's gaze flew upward, Nate kicked the broken chair leg upward and threw the coins at him. Ducking, Vincent pulled the trigger as Nate twisted and lunged forward.

The bullet grazed Nate's upper arm, but he ignored it. He grabbed the gun by the barrel and curled Vincent's wrist sideways. The next shot fired into the wall.

Vincent squirmed and tried to wriggle free, but Nate tight-ened his grip, even when Vincent punched him in the gut. Nate shoved him against the edge of the door and wrenched the gun from his hand as Vincent staggered. Their eyes met in a hard stare. Bent backward and gasping, Vincent glared at him.

As soon as Vincent managed to take a breath, his white teeth flashed again while he pulled a knife from under his pant leg. No pocketknife this time, but a blade large enough to skin a deer. "You're just a kid. You don't have the guts to kill anyone."

Nate's eyes flickered to the bag of money Vincent had dropped on the floor during the scuffle. He straightened his shoulders and stood to his full height. "Are you willing to bet on—"

Vincent sprang forward, the knife thrust in front. Without thinking, Nate pulled the trigger, firing three bullets, the first into Vincent's neck, and two into his chest. Vincent fell toward Nate and the knife clattered to the floor. His hand clutched Nate's forearm, then his grip went slack. Nate let him slide until he lay sprawled face down.

He rolled Vincent over and watched the life drain from his face. Nate squeezed his eyes shut and tried to block the image from his mind. He concentrated on his mother, straining to remember her voice or her singing or reading aloud from the Bible. The last thing she said to him, before the sound of the train leaving Clark's Common drowned her words, was, "Now run for it."

Nate patted Vincent's leg near his ankle until he felt the knife's leather sheath and removed it. He searched the floor for the coins he had hurled and dropped them back in his pocket.

Two more dead guys in two days. I must be cursed.

The bloody canvas bag caught his eye. He picked up the bag, wrapped Vincent's leather coat tight around his dead body, and dragged him by his feet to the doorway. With some wads of straw, he wiped up the small streak of blood and turned off the light.

Once outside, he checked the moonlit parking lot to be sure no one lingered, and then he tramped across to the truck. No light came from the office now. Maybe no one heard the shots. Maybe the foreman already left for the docks to wait for them.

He opened the door on the driver's side, lifted Vincent's body to the truck, and propped it upright behind the steering wheel.

Right where ol' Sam Carolla and everybody else can find him.

Nate tucked the keys into the side pocket of Vincent's jacket. On the passenger side, he opened the bloody canvas bag and dumped the money in a pile on the seat. He hoped it would satisfy Sam and keep other killers from coming after him. The cash looked like enough to do anything a person could dream up.

After running his fingers over it for several moments, Nate slipped the cash back into the bag, tucked it under his arm, and headed to the foreman's office. The entry was bolted, but the butt of Vincent's pistol made short work of one of the small glass panes. He reached through and slid the metal bolt to open the door, then crossed the office in three long strides.

The door at the back of the room was unlocked. Nate turned on the light in the stairwell and climbed the stairs. On the second level, a row of desks and filing cabinets greeted him. He wound his way across the wooden floor, retracing Sam's footsteps that had made the ceiling creak that afternoon.

In the dim light, he made out the letters on the frosted glass door in the corner. Samuel Carolla's office. The door was locked, and Nate didn't want to break the big panel of glass. He looked around for a place to hide the money, where Sam would find it later. Maybe his secretary's trashcan or bottom drawer.

Nate's eyes fell on the newspaper the foreman had showed him earlier. He bent over the secretary's desk to look closer at the photo of Sam Carolla.

The police didn't care that a killer like Vincent worked for the Carollas. They would never trace his or the foreman's actions to Franco's death. Sam would use the money to pay someone else to murder the next guy or burn down the nearest restaurant whose owner didn't want to buy their booze.

Or...

Nate pulled the wads of cash from the bag and stuffed them inside his shirt. From the last bundle, he chose a fifty-dollar bill smeared with blood. After sliding it under Sam's door, he turned and dashed across the room, back down the stairs to the foreman's office.

The middle drawer of the desk was locked, but the bottom drawer slid open. Nate dropped Vincent's gun in and shut it.

Maybe he wasn't completely cursed.

Before he stuffed the bag in the trash, writing on the outside drew his attention. He held the bag above his head for better light and sounded out the letters. M-A-T-R-A-N-G-A.

The Matranga family. Tonight they were a couple members short. And a lot of cash.

Maybe Father Antoine would be glad to hear Nate had finally learned to read.

CHAPTER THIRTEEN

Nate crossed the parking lot, lit only by a sliver of the moon.

The money inside his shirt created too big a bulge to go unnoticed in daylight. He needed a new satchel, a bigger one to replace the one Vincent, or probably the foreman, had ripped into pieces.

He patted his waist. Now he could afford to buy another, even one made of leather this time. Meanwhile, he'd have to find a secure place to stash his spoils while he decided on his next move.

The only fix he could settle on was Father Antoine, but he couldn't go calling on him this time of night. Thank goodness the cathedral stayed open 'round the clock.

Nate tightened his jacket around him and lifted the latch on the outside gate of the warehouse. He looked both ways without a backward glance before he stepped into the street. Halfway to the corner he passed two men who chatted as they smoked.

Without warning, his knees felt like rubber and he leaned against the wall of a building. His stomach heaved and he vomited on the sidewalk. Words from the two men drifted back to him: "filthy drunk" … "can't hold his liquor."

After several minutes, Nate wiped his mouth on his sleeve and stood up. The two men had dodged around him to reach the corner. Nate crossed the street, turned left, and slowed his pace, hoping his recollection of the job, the crates, the docks, the dead faces of Franco and Vincent, all would fade like a bad dream.

He didn't know how long he walked the streets, glancing over his shoulder at regular spells, avoiding other pedestrians. Twice he refused a ride in a cab, then regretted it when the mist grew thicker. Before another half-hour passed, he found himself in front of St. Louis Cathedral. Its tall black spires were barely visible against the night sky.

Came here once before when I had almost nothing and nowhere to go.

Droplets of fresh rain sprinkled the top of his head and, with his mouth open, he lifted his face to the sky. When his skin felt cleaner, he entered through the heavy front door, found the sanctuary empty, and sank into a pew in the back row. The back of the church was unlit except for a few short candles on the right side. He watched the flames sink into the brass candlesticks until they all disappeared, save one.

After a few more moments, he leaned sideways until he could stretch out on the bench. Palms together, Nate tucked his hands under his head for a pillow and closed his eyes.

Maybe I can catch Father Antoine before he heads out to the jail and…

Nate let out a long breath, as weariness fell over him like a heavy blanket.

"NO, FATHER, HE DOESN'T seem to be praying," a woman's voice said.

Nate's eyes popped open and he jerked upright.

Sister Ida-Emily paused in the aisle as she peered down at him. Clutching a broom handle, the sister frowned and looked as if she might try to shoo Nate out the door like a stray pup.

Behind her, Father Antoine's eyes crinkled in kindliness as a warm smile played about his mouth. He erased it in a flash when Sister Ida-Emily turned to him and said, "Well, what should we do with him? Call the authorities?"

Gasping, Nate waited.

"Tsk, tsk," Father Antoine said, shaking his head. "Nate, what are you doing here this early? It's barely dawn."

"Can we go into your office?" Nate ran his fingers through his hair. "I have to… tell you something."

"The confessional is that way." Sister Ida-Emily pointed opposite the sanctuary and harrumphed as she continued her sweeping down the aisle.

"Come with me, son," the priest said.

Nate followed him to his office and waited until Father Antoine shut the door before he sat down in the tall leather chair. Rather than seat himself across the desk, the priest chose a matching chair next to Nate, swivelling it to face him.

Father Antoine folded his hands in his lap, but rose up in an instant and hovered over Nate. "There's blood on your jacket."

"It's all right. It isn't mine."

"Now, you'd best tell me what has happened." The old man settled back in his chair.

As Nate laid bare the events of the past few days, he watched the priest's face for signs of shock or disapproval. Other than nods and a few eyebrow twitches, the priest didn't react until Nate revealed he shot Vincent.

Father Antoine clutched his chest. "Lord have mercy, what have you done?"

"He attacked me with a skinning knife. I had no choice." Nate's voice grew softer. "He's dead. Are you going to tell the police?"

"You must ask God for forgiveness." The priest closed his eyes and was silent for several moments, as only his lips moved. Then he said aloud, "Are you certain he's dead?"

"Not a single…" Nate wondered which word would convince the priest. "…doubt."

The priest resumed praying. "Amen."

When he opened his eyes, he said, "Under different circumstances I would suggest you go straight there, but I wouldn't deem the New Orleans police department our finest public servants. You have more to worry about from the Matrangas, not to mention Sam Carolla."

Father Antoine sat up straight and leaned toward Nate. "My son, they will hunt you down."

"But it was self-defense. Besides, I wasn't the one who stole their money."

"I believe you." The old priest shook his head. "Although money is their deity, with them, it's also a point of honor. They will never give up until they find you and destroy you."

"I rigged it so maybe they'll think Vincent and the foreman fought over the money." Nate squirmed in his chair. "But just in case, I need to hide out here until I can leave town tonight."

"Where will you go?"

"Tonight I can take trains east until I reach South Carolina and wait for my ma and my sisters. Maybe they've already… arrived." With a smile, Nate stood up and pulled the front of his shirttail loose. "Meanwhile, I have to stash this money somewhere." The bundles of cash spilled onto Father's Antoine's desk.

The priest jumped to his feet and swung the chair in front of him. "But you said you didn't steal their money!"

"I didn't. This is Franco's stash. Vincent stole it after he shot him. I just ended up with it… you know, once Vincent—"

"You brought that blood money here? To this church?" His eyes widened. "What on earth has possessed you?"

"Did I do something wrong?"

"This is the house of God, not a den of thieves. I can't keep that tainted lucre here. Not for one more minute."

"All right, all right. I'll figure out something else."

"You must return the money."

"But I'd have to sneak back in to stash it in the foreman's office. I... I guess it's still early enough. No one should be there yet."

Nate picked up three bundles and stuffed them inside his shirt, but they fell to the floor. While bending over, he knocked others off the edge of the desk. As he tucked his shirttail in, the old priest came to stand beside him.

"A wise and virtuous choice. Let me at least find you something in which to transport it." He edged toward the door. "Wait here."

In a few minutes Father Antoine returned holding a burlap bag with a drawing of onions on the outside. "Here, use this. Sister Ida-Emily will never miss it."

"I've seen bags like this before." Nate held it to his nose and inhaled. "Ma used to—"

"Make haste. There could be parishioners stopping by at any moment."

"I'm sorry, but don't worry. No one followed me." Nate stuffed a wad of cash into the bag. "Aren't you bound for the jail this morning?"

"Not 'til later." Father Antoine sighed. "I'm full of regret it's come to this. Perhaps I should have taken a stronger hand with you, but I'm relieved you aren't murdered in your bed or returned to prison for who could predict how long."

"I have to leave New Orleans."

"Return the money before you depart, and you'll have naught to regret later."

Nate jerked his head sideways to look out the window. "You've been extra good to me. I won't forget it."

"I hate to see you leave," the priest sighed. "We were just getting started on your reading. Besides, you have to consider your future, which cannot possibly include involvement with gangsters. That is surely the path to eternal damnation."

"It's not like New Orleans was ever my home anyway. I was always headed elsewhere to meet up with my family."

"Family is most important," the priest said. "Remember the alphabet and attend to your reading comprehension. Don't allow anyone to tell you that you aren't capable. You're an exceptionally intelligent young man, Nate. Acquire a decent education and you'll go far."

Nate shouldered the burlap bag and shook hands with Father Antoine. The old priest looked as if he would throw his arms around him in a protective embrace, but Nate stiffened and backed up. Not even his mother hugged him.

As he passed through the sanctuary, he rubbed the heads of both angels.

I need all the luck I can muster.

The clock tower chimed 7:00 a.m. as Nate stepped onto the sidewalk. No one would show up for work at the warehouse this early. Except maybe Sam Carolla.

His growling stomach made him wonder if Hootie was up by now and stirring. He stood at an intersection and studied the street signs. After a minute, he said aloud, "Chartres and St. Ann." Smiling, he turned left. "Royal is one block up. I should be able to happen on Hootie somewhere along there."

Nate switched the burlap bag to his other shoulder and quickened his pace, as he headed toward meeting up with the only other person he could trust in the entire city of New Orleans.

NATE HADN'T GONE HALF a block when he realized he'd forgotten his earnings in the green jar on the shelf in Father Antoine's office. He turned around and headed back to the church, hoping to catch him before he left for the jail.

The clock tower rang out 7:15 a.m. when Nate entered the sanctuary a second time. Sister Ida-Emily had finished sweeping the aisle, and only three worshippers knelt in the pews and two at the altar. He tiptoed his way through the deserted hall and up the stairs to Father Antoine's office.

Nate knocked. No answer. He opened the door and peeked in. No priest. He entered, set the burlap bag on Father's Antoine's desk, and circled behind the desk. As he reached up to the top shelf for the green jar, the door banged against the wall.

"I knew you were up to no good the minute I first laid eyes on you!" Sister Ida-Emily's voice barked at him.

Nate fumbled the green jar, but caught it before it hit the floor. "What?"

The sister blocked the doorway, hands on her hips, a scowl on her face. "Stealing onions from the kitchen when my back is turned!" She stepped forward and snatched up the burlap bag in a chokehold. "All this time, I've been telling Father Antoine he was wrong to trust you." She turned to leave.

Nate set the jar on the desk and scampered around it toward her. "No, wait! That's, uh... those aren't onions. I didn't steal anything from your kitchen." He followed her to the door. "Father Antoine gave me the empty bag 'cuz my satchel got... ruined."

The way Sister Ida-Emily shook the bag reminded Nate of how his mother wrung a chicken's neck. She untied the strings at the top. "Well, if it's not onions, what—"

"My belongings. All I have left." He held out his palm. "I'm leaving town tonight. I won't bother you again."

She glared at him for what seemed like a full minute, then dropped the bag in the leather chair. "What did you come in here for anyway?"

Nate picked up the green jar and unscrewed the lid. He pulled out the few bills and showed them to her. "Father Antoine was keeping my earnings for me. I didn't have a safe place to put them."

"Money is the root of all evil," she snapped.

He put the bills back in the jar and replaced the lid. "Tell Father Antoine I want him to have it." Nate set the jar on the desk. "He can use the money to buy food for those poor drunks."

Sister Ida-Emily's frown softened a little.

Nate hoisted the burlap bag on his other shoulder out of her reach. She stood back, and as he passed her going down the stairs, he said, "It's love of money."

"I beg your pardon?"

He raised his voice in the stairwell. "First Timothy, chapter six, verse ten. You can look it up." Nate smiled when he realized how proud his mother would be that he could now read the Bible verse himself.

When Nate entered the sanctuary on his way out, several worshippers caught his eye. One group in the fourth row looked liked a family, with parents, four small children, and a grandma. The adults all kneeled and, with folded hands, mouthed words as they stared at Jesus' body fastened to the cross. Behind their backs, the children squirmed and poked each other.

Nate sighed and smiled at the children as he passed. One of the little girls waved at him.

Beyond the pews to the left and toward the rear of the sanctuary, two men in dark pin-striped suits lit candles and crossed themselves at the foot of a statue of a woman in a blue cloak. They turned around and watched him as Nate tiptoed down the aisle.

He fixed his eyes on them and walked faster, in case he should need to break out running. This time, Nate passed the two angels without rubbing their heads.

CHAPTER FOURTEEN

After fifteen minutes of searching, Nate found Hootie near the corner of St. Philip and Burgundy streets. With pride he read the street names aloud.

"Say it like this," Hootie chuckled. "Bur*gun*dy."

Nate repeated it.

"What you be up so soon this mornin' for?" Hootie unrolled the awning over his cart and fastened one loose end to the pole at the right side. "Not too early for sausage gumbo, is it?"

Waving a palm, Nate declined. "Nothing spicy right now." He set the burlap bag on the counter of the cart, but kept a firm grip around the neck. "I just came by to tell you I'm moving on."

Hootie let the tail of the awning drop. "You ain't been here that long. Leavin' N'Awlins right quick then, huh?"

Nate shrugged. "Things haven't worked out too good for me here."

"I s'pect you knows what's best. This can be a hard place, N'Awlins can." Hootie shifted to the other side of his cart and attached the rest of the awning. "Lordy, don't I know it!"

"You've been a good friend to me." Nate stuck out his hand. "Those are hard to come by."

"Awww, you all right yo'self." Hootie pumped Nate's arm. "Good fortune to you. Wherever you might land, it'll sho' be on your feet."

"I'll take one last crawfish pie for breakfast." Nate stood up straight and looked over Hootie's shoulder. "To go."

Across the street, a man in a dark suit leaned against the wall of the corner building, watching them. He took a drag from his cigarette and threw the butt into the street before he turned around and hustled down the sidewalk.

Nate fished in his burlap bag and pulled out a twenty-dollar bill. "Don't tell anyone I gave this to you. Just take it and spend it on your wife and your kids."

As he wrapped the pie in a piece of newspaper, Hootie's eyes grew large as hen's eggs. "Where you be gettin' that kind of bread?"

"I got paid yesterday, a double-bonus, plus a big tip." Nate scooped up the package of crawfish pie in one hand and his burlap bag in the other. "Take it. I'm spreading the loot. It's good for local business, like you explained to me, right? I learned a lot from you." Nate glanced behind him. "Gotta run. Take care."

Hootie slid the bill into his shirt pocket. "That's plum thoughty of you," he said.

Nate dashed down the block as the Century Clock Tower chimed eight. At the corner he bumped shoulders with the same man in the dark suit who had stood watching him a few minutes earlier. Nate clutched the bag tighter and jerked his knee up to reach for Vincent's knife, now strapped to his ankle. He wished he'd kept the pistol.

"Hey, be careful!" the man growled as he pushed Nate in the chest.

"Sorry," Nate stepped sideways and walked faster. He stopped at the next corner.

If he returned to the warehouse with the money, how would he explain how he came into possession of it, much less Vincent's body in the truck? If Sam Carolla had already confronted the foreman about the bloody fifty-dollar bill on his office floor, it wouldn't take much for him to shift the blame to Nate.

His word against mine.

Sam Carolla wouldn't care about the truth, only about getting his money back and punishing anyone who dared challenge him or cheat him. Franco was proof of that.

Very likely, the foreman would find another guy like Vincent and pay him to kill Nate. Or pull the trigger himself.

The sidewalks began to crowd with people jostling on their way to work. A few cars and trucks glided past at a slow pace.

Nate hadn't actually lied to the priest or promised to return the money, only to find another solution to stashing it at the church. Even if the foreman didn't kill him, Nate figured he'd end up in jail again. Left there to rot, the judge had threatened.

If his mother made it to South Carolina anytime soon, how could he be sure the Rutledge sister would hire her? What would become of his sisters? He couldn't leave them there unprotected.

With the burlap bag tucked under his arm, Nate turned and retraced his steps, figuring he could lose himself in the crowd if he weren't so tall. He headed in the direction of the rail yard, ducking in an alley every time he spied any man in a dark suit. He stopped under a bridge to eat his crawfish pie, not knowing where his next meal would come from.

AT THE RAILYARD, NATE kept to the edges where no one loaded or inspected shipments. He hoped to find someone desperate like him, but who knew which trains headed east. Any free riders stayed in hiding, and he couldn't find a single person to ask.

He didn't want to chance going to the ticket booth, but he puzzled over how else he would get the information. Creeping closer to the activity, where some of the trains had started rolling out or were arriving, Nate tried to gauge which way was east by the angle of the sun at mid-morning.

He crossed over two tracks, dodged a slow-moving engine,

and turned a corner. Two men ambled toward him, one with a stack of papers in his hand. The other carried a wooden club.

"You there!" the man with the club yelled. "What are you doing?"

As they hustled toward him, Nate reversed his course and caught up to the train he had just passed. He jogged along side it until he grabbed hold of a door handle and swung himself up into what he hoped was an empty car. Only one hand free made it more difficult, but the train wasn't moving fast enough for him to lose his balance and he scrambled to his feet a few seconds after landing.

What luck! I have the car to myself.

The wheels clattered under him as the train picked up speed. Clinging to his burlap bag, Nate kept to the shadows until any sign of city life was left behind. Once he could see nothing but open fields, he stood in the doorway and searched the sky. The sun wasn't directly overhead yet, but he couldn't tell which direction the train was headed.

Not until he spotted his shadow, straight behind him. North, not east.

I'm going the wrong way.

CHAPTER FIFTEEN

The train hadn't gone more than fifty yards when several other men scrambled into the freight car. They rolled along the floor and staggered to their feet at the back of the car.

Counting four of them, Nate sat on the dirty floor and leaned against the opposite wall, clutching his burlap bag. He made out bits of their conversation and wished he knew what a bindle was. Tightening his grip, he watched for any sign they might gang up on him.

Except they think I'm poor like them.

As they sat down, he nodded at them and then stared out the door.

"Headed to Bossier, are you?" One man jerked his thumb toward the front of the train. "We hear tell there's jobs in the cotton mills up that way."

"Just passing through."

The monotonous hum of the wheels and the flat landscape lulled Nate into a stupor, and he struggled to keep his eyes open. Spending a whole day and night with only a few hours' sleep on a church pew caught up to him, and his head dropped forward.

The next thing he knew, men were shouting and scuffling in the freight car. Someone kicked his foot while darting past. "Get out quick!" the man yelled.

The train slowed to a near-stop. Nate stood up and reached the doorway in three long strides. Without hesitating or checking the ground, he jumped and landed on his feet.

When he turned around, all the men riding in the car with him were scrambling to line up against the train, now at a standstill. A bull, a burly man of about fifty, pointed his pistol at them and then waved it at Nate to join the group.

"All right, you bums," he snarled. "Who's got money for a ticket?"

"We ain't bums," said a man toward the middle. "We're looking for work."

"That so?" The bull approached him and whacked the side of his face with the pistol. "Well, you can't ride the train for free." He walked to the far end of the line. "Come on, empty your pockets."

The first two men handed him a dollar bill and some coins. The man he had struck kept his palm against his cheek and shook his head. The bull moved on to the next man, who gave him another dollar. Nate slid his burlap sack behind him.

When he came to stand in front of Nate, the bull drew himself up to his full height, but he still had to look up into Nate's eyes. "What have we here? A road kid?" He sneered at the others. "You guys teaching this punk how to flip?" He sidestepped to face the man next to Nate.

"He was already there. Musta got on by hisself."

The bull turned to Nate again. "What you got in that bindle you been trying to hide?" He poked Nate in the stomach with the barrel of his pistol.

Nate stared straight ahead. "Just my stuff."

"You ain't added nothing to the kitty yet. Lemme see what's in that bindle."

"It's almost empty." Nate reached in his pants pocket and pulled out a few coins, hoping he hadn't scooped up the buffalo head nickel. "Here, take this."

While the man counted his profit, Nate calculated his options. The bull likely weighed at least forty pounds more than

Nate. Vincent's skinning knife was strapped to his calf, under his pants leg. The man's gun held six bullets. All five of them would be shot, maybe one of them twice.

The bull pocketed the money. "Now open it."

Nate wished he had put a shirt, or even a newspaper, on top of the wads of bills, but the foreman had left everything he owned in tatters. He untied the strings at the top of the bag.

The bull looked inside and gave a low whistle. "What'd you do? Rob a bank? There must be several thousand dollars in there."

From the corner of his eye, Nate glimpsed all four heads turn toward him. The bull hadn't punched him, but his empty stomach contracted anyway.

"I bet you killed someone for this much cash." While confiscating the sack, the bull aimed his pistol at Nate's chest. "I'm taking you in. The cops are gonna want to question you."

"No, wait—"

"Shut up. Get your hands in the air."

Before Nate could raise his arms, the man next to him fell forward in a heap. The other three hollered while they circled him. In the noise and confusion, the bull turned his back to Nate to threaten them.

In an instant, Nate took off running. A bullet zinged past him and bounced off the metal door of a train car, and he sped up. Two more shots were fired amid shouting, and the bull called out, "HEY! HEY, YOU!"

Nate glanced over his shoulder as he turned the corner by the caboose. One man lay on the ground, another bent over him, and the other two stood with their arms overhead. The bull held them at bay with enough bullets left in his pistol, one for each of them.

After he reached the woods, deep enough to hide, Nate slowed down to catch his breath. How could he go back and get his money? Was it worth getting shot or killing the other man, if he could even find him? The image of Vincent's pale face danced before his mind's eye.

With that much money, the guy could quit work forever. What about the police?

The bull won't bother going to the cops now, but neither can I.

Nate trudged through the dense undergrowth, mulling over his next move. Pulling the knife from its sheath, he turned around, took several steps, turned back. He paced for several more minutes until he sat down and wondered how much anger it would take to track down the bull, face him, and get the money back. He shoved the knife back into the sheath and took several deep breaths. Grief replaced his anger, as his eyes misted over.

Maybe this was God's way of punishing Nate for taking the cash. Filthy, is what the priest called it. What would his mother call it? How would he protect his family now?

Keep going north. Get a job in Bossier at the cotton gin.

Maybe, by some miracle, Sam Carolla would figure it out and come after the bull. He deserved to get caught, even if he wasn't as evil as Vincent.

But I'm not going to be the one who kills somebody over money. Not this time.

NATE SPENT THE REST of the day and the night in the woods at the edge of a hobo camp. After dark, he sat down and leaned against a tree trunk and tried to sleep. Nearby, two men had wedged a board between a pair of low-slung branches, draped it with a piece of canvas, and sat underneath. They motioned to Nate to join them when the rain started.

In the morning, Nate hopped another boxcar, heading

north once more. To his surprise, two of the men from yesterday's disaster were already aboard.

One of them, a tall man with sandy brown hair, limped over to sit by him. "You okay, son?"

Nate nodded.

"After Batch chucked a dummy, we thought you'd make a getaway with your bag. Too bad you didn't get it back."

"What do you mean?"

"Ol' Batch, he just pretended to faint. 'Chuck a dummy' to us rail riders. Some of us 'bos, we look out for youngsters like you."

"I see. Tell him thanks for me."

"Wish I could. After the bull fired at you, Batch took the next one." The man shook his head. "Been riding the rails since last spring. First sign of serious trouble."

"What happened after I… uh, left in such a hurry?"

"He made us all lie on the ground, face down. We thought he would shoot the rest of us. But I guess he was more interested in getting away with your money."

His money? The old priest hadn't believed it was ever Nate's money. Nate wondered if he had deserved even a small part of it. Perhaps it was best to let it go, for all the bad luck it brought everyone who touched it.

With a forced smile, Nate stuck out his hand and said his name. "Much obliged to all of you."

"Call me Andy." The man shook Nate's hand. "This way of life ain't nobody's choice, outta work and such. But we refuse to let it turn us into animals. All we're doing is going where there might be jobs."

"Me, too. Tell me more about what you do."

"I left home to find work in town after town, state after state. Other places, either the cops or workers already employed chased me to the city limits."

He described the signs that hobos knew to look for, on fences, roads, or any visible flat surface. A circle with an "X" in the center meant the home was a good place for a hand out. Two "Ws" linked together warned to watch out for the barking dog. A squiggly line like a pig's tail indicated a judge lived there.

"I'm steering clear of judges," Nate said.

"The only place we're really welcome is where there's a lack of able workers. The cotton crop was good this year, so the mills are running extra time. The war's over, and people want to settle into their lives again."

Nate grew silent. He wondered when he would ever settle, and where. It couldn't be like his former life. Too much had changed. He had changed.

It all falls on me. Ma can't work all the time, what with a new baby and two little girls.

He refused to dwell on the possibility that Mary and the baby might have already died by now or that someone else had dug their graves.

Enough money was the answer.

While Andy droned on about places in northern Louisiana, Nate pictured a house on the edge of some small town. His mother sat on the front porch in a rocking chair as the little girls played in the yard near a blooming rose bush.

Just as he imagined himself opening the gate leading to the front sidewalk, the train's whistle blew and, empty-handed this time, he scrambled to his feet.

CHAPTER SIXTEEN

After a day and a half of helping Andy scoot from boxcar to boxcar, and taking lost periods to rest, Nate arrived in Bossier City. His new friend's limp had grown worse from a swollen ankle, and when Andy pulled up his pants leg, Nate winced at the blue color of his flesh.

"Swelling needs to go down before I can walk normal again." Andy flashed a sad smile. "Durn this sprain! It'll be hard to get a job when I'm laid up like this."

"You need a doctor," Nate said. "Maybe it's broke instead."

"Oh, he'll just tell me to get some rest."

"That ain't the cure for what you got."

Andy chuckled. "Yeah, but eternal rest might be." He let his pants leg fall and tried to balance. After half a step, he clutched Nate's arm.

Nate steadied him as Andy sat down on a log in the hobo camp. Nearby, someone scraped a spoon against a tin plate, held over an open fire that sizzled and smoked. "How are you even going to get to the cotton gin from here, if you can't walk?"

"I'll be all right in a day or two. You go on and see if'n you can find work. I'll catch up to you later."

By noon Nate had followed the crowd of hobos to McPherson's Cotton Gin on the outskirts of Bossier City. He was hired to move heavy bales into the storage area behind the ginning lines, and then load the trucks every Friday for delivery to the mills in Shreveport and other cities. The leftover seed was sold to Hamilton's Cotton Oil Mill.

In all, fifteen men joined the payroll, while two dozen more were turned down. Nate figured he held an advantage, being the largest and the youngest in the group.

The foreman, a man of about forty-five, stood on the porch of the office. "You'll live in the company quarters out back. Breakfast is at five-thirty sharp. Work starts every morning at six, with a break at noon for twenty minutes. Finish by seven in time for supper. Sunday's work is a half a day, after church."

He tucked his clipboard under his arm. "No drinking on McPherson's property, not even on your time off. You get paid in scrip on Saturday, which you can use for food and supplies in the company store."

Nate glanced at the quarters, built of longleaf pine, he guessed, decades ago for slaves, and frowned. "Is scrip money?"

"It's like money. You spend it on what you need."

"What is the company store?"

"McPherson owns the dining hall and the general store here."

"What if I want to go somewhere else?"

The foreman snorted. "Good luck. There ain't another store around here for miles."

"How do I get money instead?"

"You want to eat and sleep with a roof over your head?"

Nate nodded.

"This job pays in scrip. Take it or leave it. If you have any left by the end of the month—and if you're still working here—you can trade it for cash."

By Friday, Andy hadn't showed up, and Nate asked a few of the new men hired that day if they knew anything.

"His ankle got worse," one man said. "And then he caught the fever. They tried to keep him calm with rum, but he went plum out of his head. Ain't the 'grene awful? I 'spect he'll pass soon."

After plopping down on the bale he and another man had carried to the storeroom, Nate studied a greasy spot on the floor. Other pairs of workers filed past him, lugging their loads.

"I'm sorry," the man said. "Was you and Andy good friends?"

"Hardly knew him." By himself, Nate picked up the end of the bale and dragged it to the stack. He heaved one end after the other to the top and then returned to the workroom, leaving the men in line to stare open-mouthed as he passed them.

ON SATURDAY NIGHT AT DINNER, the older men invited Nate to join them for an evening's fun at the speakeasies along the narrow road leading east from Bossier City. The foreman had provided them with a horse and wagon in exchange for charges against their scrip.

Drinking and gambling, Roy's pastimes, didn't appeal to him, and Nate couldn't understand their jokes. "I don't believe I'd care for any roll in the hay," he said.

The men laughed, and one who sat across the table urged him, "Come on into town with us tonight. Them girls'll go wild for a tall, good-lookin' boy. Probably pay you instead."

Another teased, "What'sa matter, Nate? Promised your mama you wouldn't?"

Picking up his blue tin dinner plate, he nodded and stood up. "I promised her—"

"How 'bout arm wrestlin'?" The first man grinned as he tied his blue bandana around his neck. "I'd bet money on a big 'un who can toss a bale like it's cotton candy."

Nate stared at him. "How much money?"

The man's eyes scanned Nate as if he were buying a racehorse. "All I got."

"How much is that?"

The man checked his pants pocket. "Can you hold out

for—"

"All night, if I have to."

"Okay, my last two dollars says you'll bring in a winner every time. And you better, because Lady Luck been turning me down lately."

Nate sat down and squinted at him. "You can keep backing me all you like, but I want half of what you… what we win."

The man gave a low whistle as the other men leaned in like hungry wolves. "Ten cents!" He shook his head, his red hair gleaming in the candlelight. "Ten cents on the dollar."

"Twenty-five," said Nate.

"Deal!" The man reached his hand across the table. "Name's Clyde Farraday."

Nate shook his hand and held it for a moment. The skin was rough, but the muscles felt tight. "Nate Rut—Wallace. I'm Nate Wallace."

"Looks like I'm your new partner."

"Mr. Farra—"

"Call me Clyde."

"Tell me, Clyde, what's cotton candy?"

"Imagine those cotton boll fibers made of sugar and spun light as air. Wrapped around sticks like thick spider webs. Take a bite and they disappear on your tongue."

Nate grinned at the twinkle in Clyde's eye. "You're pulling my leg."

"Ate some myself. At the circus."

"You been to the circus?"

"Not just been there. I worked there." Clyde stood up, tin plate in his hand. "Son, I was born to separate people from their money."

"Now that we're partners, I'll keep that in mind."

THE FIRST PLACE THE GROUP ENTERED was a bar called Winkie's Tavern. Once inside, the men scattered to order drinks, and while some joined gamblers at poker tables, others headed upstairs with women wearing pale floral dresses that showed their legs.

Nodding at friendly waitresses who passed close enough for him to smell their perfume, Nate waited near the door as Clyde scouted the room. The smoke-filled air and dim lighting reminded him of the Seven Roses Saloon back in Clark's Common. He tried to convince himself no one could die, or even get injured, from arm wrestling.

Clyde gestured him toward a table in the center of the room. "Here's your first taker."

The thickset man across from Nate grinned from under a brown floppy-brimmed hat he wore sideways. One front tooth was cracked halfway off, and his crooked nose flushed to deep red. He set a dime on the edge of the nearby table.

Clyde laid out another dime and shouted, "We got us a new boy here. Who's in?"

Several others plunked down nickels and dimes, and one man left a quarter. Nate calculated Clyde would have to cover eighty-five cents, almost half his stash.

After he rolled up his sleeve, Nate's opponent propped his elbow in the middle of the table and left his hand open, waiting.

Clyde spread his arms and tried to back up the crowd that had gathered around the table. "On three!" he called. "One!"

Nate positioned his elbow about two inches from the other man's and grasped his hand.

"Two!"

Looping his ankles around the chair leg, Nate stared into the man's face without blinking. The man tightened his grip, red-rimmed eyes watering.

"Three!"

From the first instant, Nate could sense his power over the drunk man, but he didn't want to embarrass him with an easy victory, so he let the struggle go back and forth for a short while. Each time their hands crossed into the other man's winning territory, the crowd shouted encouragement.

After a while, Nate saw no point in continuing the pretense, so he flexed his arm muscle harder and slammed the back of the man's hand onto the table top.

Scooping up the coins, Clyde let out a whoop, while the crowd's spirit flattened in disappointment. The man shook his head, stood up, and retreated to the bar.

The next contender sat down, and coins appeared as if by magic on the edge of the next table. Clyde counted to three, and the match lasted about the same amount of time. Same for the two others in line behind him. Each of them had breathed out alcohol fumes, some heavier than others.

Nate figured his take was up to a dollar and fifteen cents by now. Good for less than an hour's work.

His next opponent stepped forward. The man who stared down at Nate looked as if he'd been carved from a tree trunk. As he settled into the chair with deliberate moves, its wooden legs under him creaked. His knees bumped the table's edge when he leaned forward. Without smiling, he set a fifty-cent piece on the table.

Nate looked at Clyde. Clyde shrugged and put out two quarters.

The muttering onlookers grew silent, until one man added two dimes. From the time the rest of them joined the betting, Clyde agreed to match close to eight dollars. More than their winnings, even if Clyde threw in the two dollars he came with.

This man hadn't been drinking. His hand in Nate's felt like a piece of firewood. With his free left hand between his knees,

Nate clutched the seat of the chair until his knuckles hurt.

It seemed all the onlookers inhaled and held their breaths in unison. Clyde took his time counting to one, then two. Everything and everyone shifted in slow motion.

"Three!"

Nate's forearm twisted backward until it hovered about an inch above the table. He held it there, quivering, while the crowd hollered. The man pressed harder, closing the gap to half an inch, but Nate refused to give in. He couldn't breathe.

The man sneered, contempt in his steely-blue eyes. The same look Nate remembered from Roy.

With blood pulsing and muscles quickening, Nate flexed his wrist and raised his forearm as if from the grave. The spectators stopped chattering and watched in an eerie hush.

Nate gained two inches, lost one. Roy's insults echoed in his head. Nate pushed until their arms were upright once more, locked at high noon.

Clyde slid another quarter onto the nearby table. No one so much as twitched for what seemed like a whole minute. Another man matched it, slapping down the coin the way he'd kill a fly. After a moment, a few others added theirs, and the jabber resumed, a little more nervous than before.

Nate forced the man's arm backward, but he resisted and pushed Nate's arm the other way. Inch by inch, gaining and losing, then gaining, Nate held on with more than strength and muscle. He pictured himself digging two graves. From a distance, Mary called his name and coughed.

Nate rammed the man's hand flat against the top of the table and held it there.

No one said anything. Even Clyde froze where he stood.

Once he let go, Nate rose from his chair, but Clyde put a hand on his shoulder, pressing him to sit again. Nate shook it off. "That's all for tonight."

As onlookers drifted away grumbling, the line behind the man vanished. He glared at Nate, pushed back his chair, and stormed off.

Clyde untied his blue bandana, spread it across his palm, and swept the coins into it. Whistling, he reknotted it and tucked it inside his shirt.

Nate turned to him. "You owe me three dollars and ten cents."

Wide-eyed, Clyde grinned. "Every cent is right in here. We can tote it up later, partner." He patted Nate's shoulder. "You were too busy to keep count anyway."

Nate didn't answer.

"That was a good trick you pulled on that last one. The others were drunk, but that monster? He was fooled from the get-go."

"What do you mean?"

"Making him think he was winning before you slammed him. That's when I ran up the bets. If you'd done that for all the matches, we could've cleared at least twenty-five."

"How did you know he wasn't going to win? Maybe—"

"Aw, Nate, can't nobody beat you. There was fire in your eyes." Clyde rubbed his stomach and the coins jingled. "Never seen anything like it. Let me buy you a drink to celebrate."

"No, thanks."

"C'mon, I won't take it out of our winnings."

"I don't drink."

"Then you can buy me a drink!" Clyde took a little dance step and kicked his heels in the air.

As they strolled toward the door, Clyde tried to throw his arm over Nate's shoulder, but gave up when he couldn't reach it. "Just wait 'til next Saturday after word gets around. Keep that fire blazing and we'll make a killing."

Nate followed Clyde back to the wagon and wondered how long it would be until the fire inside him spread out of control.

CHAPTER SEVENTEEN

Days faded into weeks, then months, as the cotton crop kept coming in. Undefeated, Nate added to his weekly wages by making the Saturday night rounds with Clyde, who proved an able hawker. And he was correct about Nate's reputation. The word spread and the lines of men itching for victory grew longer at each saloon.

Nate had never spent time chatting with anyone, but he learned more about Clyde's life in the first week of their acquaintance than he ever knew about Roy. He looked forward to the noon break each day.

Almost thirty, Clyde had joined the US Navy during the Great War. "They send me back and forth across the Atlantic to kill the enemy and pay me to fight," he told Nate one hot afternoon. Clyde wiped the sweat from his freckled forehead back into his mop of red hair. "And then when the war is over, they don't want me to fight no more," he snorted. "I got kicked out."

Clyde took a drag on his cigarette. His words rode out of his throat on little crooked puffs of smoke. "By and by, I could see their point."

"How come?"

"Our lieutenant was always talking down to us like he was better'n we were, even though I know we sank more of the Kaiser's Heinie ships than he did. One day he's calling us names, thought we're too stupid to know the diff'rence. He was from a rich family in Boston, went to a private school, then to Harvard."

Nate's ears perked up at the mention of Boston. Could this lieutenant have known his father?

Clyde dusted ashes off his lap. "One buddy in particular took the insults real hard. Poor kid was always shaking. Couldn't fall asleep without waking up screaming."

Clyde dropped his cigarette butt and stepped on it. "So I slow down a little from what I'm doing, 'cause the looey's making me real mad. Then he starts yelling right up close in my one good ear, and I drop my gear, back up, and take a hard swing at him." Clyde shook his head. "Catch him by surprise right on the jaw."

Nate gulped. "Did you... kill him?"

"Nah, but of course, he doesn't get back up after I hit him a few more times. What with him bleeding and all, spends four days in the hospital, he did. Eats nothing but soup for a whole week."

"How much trouble did you get in?"

"Whistles start blowing and some other guys come in and drag me off, and the next thing I know, there's this hearing in front of some officers wearing fancy uniforms and medals. I get stuck for two months in the brig, and then they kick me out of the whole shebang."

"What's the brig?"

"Prison on a warship."

Nate's eyebrows shot up. "I never met anyone who went to prison. What was it like?"

"Dull. Same thing every day. And the work they give you ain't worth shit. Just like the food." He stood up. "But I'd do it all over again."

"Why?"

"That lieutenant, he was real educated, coddled by his rich family, too. But he had no right to treat us that way, especially that young sailor whose mind was all tore up. He couldn't fight or even protect himself no more, and he deserved better."

Clyde's small frame disguised a hardened, wiry body with arms like whipcord and a neck as thick as a bull's. His quick smile gave the appearance of a good nature, but Nate figured the value of the man lay in the strength of his attitude.

Nate stood up and turned to face Clyde. "I'm glad we're friends."

"Sure thing, you can count on me."

"I'll remember your words."

ON SUNDAY AFTER CHURCH, the men returned to the living quarters to find one of their coworkers sitting on the edge of his cot, sobbing while tears gushed down his cheeks. In his left hand he clutched a piece of paper covered in scribbled handwriting. A torn envelope lay on the floor at his feet.

"They've all died," he said. He stared at the wall as if he could see through it, while tears drizzled onto the front of his shirt.

"Who died?" Clyde bent to pickup the envelope.

"My family. From the Spanish influenza. Every last one of them." He looked at Clyde as if he were a ghost. "I got no parents, no brothers or sisters left now."

Nate stepped forward to stand beside Clyde. "Where did this happen?"

The man's eyes shifted to Nate. "Georgia. I'm from Macon, Georgia." He held out the letter. "Here, you can read it. Our preacher wrote me all about it."

Nate took the letter from the man, holding it as if it would break, then handed it to Clyde. "What's it say?"

Clyde scanned the sheet of paper and read aloud to the crowd that had gathered. "Spanish influenza is sweeping the East Coast. Thousands of people are dying from it every day.

The fatal sickness has spread to the United States from England and other parts of Europe." He let his hand drop. "It says, don't come home. God help us."

Nate broke away from the group and pulled his stash of winnings from its hiding place. While the other men murmured and tried to comfort their friend, Clyde followed Nate and stood beside him as he sat on his bed and counted his money.

Clyde touched his shoulder. "You already know how much is there, down to the last nickel."

"It's not enough. It's not nearly enough."

"For what?"

"You set it up," Nate said. "Come next Saturday, I'm going to bet it all."

"Whoa, there, partner!" Clyde sank down on the cot across from Nate. "That's a lotta risk. You always want to save some back."

"I can't, not this time."

"What's the matter?"

"That 'fluenza. They might take sick and die."

"Your family?"

"My ma and my little sisters. Plus if the baby made it."

"But the bad news is up and down the East Coast. I thought you was from Texas."

"Ma said she'd be heading back to Charleston after the baby came. That was three months ago. If they're already in South Carolina, I have to get them out."

"Unless they… got away on their own. Or didn't make it there yet." Clyde shook his head. "So what's your plan? Other than thrashing ever'body on Saturday night."

After glancing over his shoulder, Nate tucked the money back into its hiding place. "Can you help me write a letter?"

Clyde nodded. "Maybe we can get some paper from the company store tomorrow."

"Why not now?"

"They ain't open on Sunday." Clyde stood up. "Besides, we got to get back to work now. You know how strict that God-fearing McPherson is, 'specially when he needs to make more money."

Nate spent the rest of the day heaving and loading cotton bales until his shoulders and back ached. That night as he lay on his cot after supper, he flipped from stomach to side to back, then again the other way, unable to find a comfortable position. He tried to pray, using words his mother had taught him or Bible verses he had memorized, but his mind wouldn't focus on anything except how he would get to Charleston.

Winning on Saturday night was the key. He had to risk everything.

THE NEXT EVENING AFTER supper, Nate sat down with Clyde to compose the letter. Clyde spread out the clean sheet of paper and held his pencil above it, waiting for instructions.

"How do you spell Rutledge?" Clyde said. "My penmanship ain't the best."

"Starts with R." Nate shrugged. "Give it a shot. The post-man can figure it out."

Clyde licked the tip of his pencil and began to write as he spoke the words, "Dear Miss Rutledge—uh, she ain't married?"

"Not sure. Ma didn't keep up with them after she left." Nate leaned forward and hovered. "It was before I was born."

"You mean you don't even know these folks?"

Nate hesitated before telling Clyde his family history, from Charleston to various other places where Roy could find work, and finally how they settled in Clark's Common. He explained Evie's plan to show up at Vivian Rutledge's front door, leaving out the part about how Roy had died. "At least Ma knows her.

I imagine she'll be surprised to hear from… someone like me."

"Shocked is more like it. But she's your aunt. She has to help you out."

"I don't want her help, just information."

"Jeez, you are the gol'darn stubbornest kid I ever did meet." Clyde laughed. "But that's what helps you win. We should rake in a pile on Saturday night."

Nate pointed to the page on the table. "Ask her if my ma has arrived yet. Evelyn Wallace, but she went by Evie." Nate gasped and sat back in his chair, quiet for a moment. "Goes by Evie," he said in a soft voice. "I know she still does. That Miss Rutledge should recollect her from about eighteen years ago."

Squinting and taking his time as he tried to keep the writing straight across, Clyde scrawled several lines. "Then what?"

"I guess I'll go to Charleston and bring 'em back here."

"You think your job'll be waiting for you while you gallivant over to the East Coast?" Clyde snorted. "Besides, why risk coming down with the Spanish flu yourself?"

"What else can I do?"

"If they already traveled there on the train, surely they can travel back here the same way."

Nate nodded. "Tell her to send Ma and my sisters to Bossier City. I'll pay her for the tickets with what I win on Saturday."

Clyde paused. "Where will they live when they get here?"

"That's the thorn in my side. I can't afford a hotel." Nate pounded his palm with his fist. "Maybe I can find Ma a job. McPherson might need another cook, since he's added more men and another shift."

When Clyde finished the letter, he asked Nate if he wanted to sign it.

Nate took the pencil and slid the page in front of him. "I learned from the priest to print my name." Starting with a large plain N on wobbly legs, he wrote out the four letters, but cringed when he finished. "Damn! He didn't teach me how to write Wallace."

"Just add it at the end. Rutledge can be your middle name."

"She'll think I'm trying to get something out of her rich family and all, by claiming to be her kin."

"Well, ain't you kin to her?" Clyde snickered. "This could turn out to be your best bet ever."

"But Rutledge isn't mine." Nate sighed as he scrawled. "Come to think of it, Wallace isn't either, not really."

"Don't worry about it, Nate. Some day you'll find out who you are and you can start over from there." Clyde folded the edges of the paper toward the middle until it made a square, folded it in half, and wrote "Miss Vivian Rutledge, Charleston, South Carolina" on the outside. He handed it to Nate. "Ask the clerk at the store if he has a stamp to mail this. Won't cost much."

Nate took the paper and tapped it against his fingertips, wondering how someone like him could start over.

CHAPTER EIGHTEEN

All during the week, the men asked Nate if he got plenty to eat. How was he sleeping? Some encouraged him to take it easier on the job. Don't overdo it before Saturday, they told him.

But Nate kept his usual pace, hauling and heaving the same amount, if not more, each day. Work was the only distraction from his worries, and he needed the fatigue to fall asleep each night, if only for a few hours.

Clyde took to calling Nate "Champ" in front of the men, goading them to bet. "Somebody is gonna rake in a bundle on Saturday night, and I ain't talking about cotton. Don't miss your chance."

Nate had no illusion that Vivian Rutledge had received his letter yet, but he couldn't help wondering if the society lady had welcomed his mother and the girls, along with the baby. He tried to convince himself to give up hope that the baby survived its birth in Texas, much less the trip to South Carolina. Yet he was curious to learn the baby's name, and if he had a new brother or sister.

By Saturday, Nate was tired of all the attention. He wanted to do no more than go about his work in quiet, except for the humming of the cotton gin machines.

Clyde was smart enough to leave him alone, but he couldn't stop grinning at lunch. "When you're ready for me to bet more, look up at me and blink twice."

Nate figured his mind had gone into countdown mode.

It seemed no time passed before the men loaded up into the wagon after supper for the trip into Bossier City. Along one side, Nate sat in the middle, while Clyde settled across from him. All their previous winnings were tied up in his blue bandana.

At the saloon, the smoke, the noise, and the drunks hadn't changed. Even the waitresses still gave him the once-over as they sashayed past in search of paying customers.

During each match, Nate signaled to Clyde to raise his bet before he faked a narrow victory. After five opponents, his winnings added almost seventeen dollars to his stash. At the thought of just under seventy-five dollars saved, Nate smiled. "Let's more than double it this time."

Clyde pulled four five-dollar bank notes from the blue bandana and set them on the edge of the nearby table as if they were kings in a deck of face cards. A crowd gathered and a few men laid out coins and paper money.

Blond and fair-skinned, the next man who sat across from Nate had a kind face behind a bristly mustache. Of medium build with a hint of a pot-belly, he looked to be about twelve years older than Nate. His arms, large as ham hocks and covered in scars, dangled from his rolled-up sleeves.

After he placed his bet, one dollar to each of Nate's five, the man stretched out his hand across the table. "Amos Cobb. How are you?"

Clyde frowned and chopped the air above the table top with the edge of his hand. "Sorry, no shaking hands before the match." He grinned at Nate, then turned to Cobb. "Besides, I wouldn't want him to hurt your hand without betting on it first."

Other gamblers, who had abandoned a rowdy game of poker across the room, added more money to the pile of bets.

Clyde pointed to the center of the table. "Ready? On three."

The hollering at the poker table grew louder. Clyde raised

his voice. "One!"

The moment Nate put his hand in Cobb's giant one, he knew the outcome. He couldn't bend Cobb's arm backward any better than he could uproot an overgrown cypress tree.

"Two!"

Nate tightened his grip and stared into Cobb's light brown eyes.

"Thr—"

Bam! Bam! Bam!

Nate shook his hand loose from Cobb's and they both stood up. With chairs scraping the floor, the crowd of players at the poker table scrambled backward. One man toppled forward, face down on his pile of chips. The shooter sat across from him and rested the barrel of his gun on the table.

Shouting, several other men dashed toward Nate and Clyde and bumped against their chests, knocking Clyde to the floor. Clyde grabbed Nate by the lower arm and pulled him down. "Get outta sight!"

Nate and Cobb ducked behind the table as men scurried back and forth behind them, yelling at each other. Tables tipped over, and men and waitresses went sprawling as they tumbled over chairs in the noise and confusion. Nate shifted toward the center of the table and looked over his shoulder. Clyde had crawled to the next overturned table.

Only the crack of a bolt-action rifle quieted the crowd. Nate peeked around the edge of the table. The bartender had racked the bolt, then pointed his loaded rifle at the shooter, who raised his arms over his head.

Within minutes the police arrived, disarmed the gambler, and took him outside. Cobb stood up and watched as several officers came back inside and questioned a few of the players involved in the argument. Other men emerged wide-eyed from under tables, like forest animals after a rain storm.

Nate stayed behind the table until the police left. Only when he tried to stand up did he realize his breath had come in short gasps. He dared not shut his eyes, lest Roy's face haunt him. As other officials arrived to carry out the dead body, Nate leaned one hand on the back of a chair and waited.

"Somebody must've been cheating," Cobb said. He turned to Nate and stuck out his hand again. "Guess we should call it a night."

As he shook his hand, Nate studied the scars on his forearms. One looked like a fresh burn mark. "Mr. Cobb, I'm Nate Wallace."

"Call me Amos." Cobb flexed his right arm. "I'm a blacksmith, in case you're wondering."

"That expl—"

"Holy crap!" yelled Clyde. "Someone took our money!" He scampered between the betting tables, now swept clear of all coins, notes, and bills, his blue bandana nowhere in sight. "I've been searching on the floor for it." He spun around, scanning the room and the floor. "Who's got it?"

A few feet away, a dark-haired waitress bent over to reclaim her tray, while two men set their table upright. They glanced toward Clyde and shrugged. Another man paused on the second step, then continued up the stairs.

Nate sank into a chair, reeling in his head and his gut.

How could this happen? How could I have been such a fool?

"I'll call the police back here," Amos said.

"No!" said Clyde and Nate together. They glanced at each other from the corners of their eyes.

Clyde pulled a small folding knife from his boot and clicked it open. "I'll find the sumbitch."

Nate put his hand on Clyde's arm. "What are you going to do?"

"Somebody saw it happen. I'll make 'em tell me who it was."

"How can I help?" said Cobb. "He's got my four dollars, too."

Without releasing Clyde's arm, Nate said to Cobb, "This isn't your fight. You can go have a beer at the bar. Watch and listen. Let us know if you hear anything suspicious."

As Cobb walked away, Nate rested his palm on the blade and stared down into Clyde's face. "Are you willing to kill someone over money?"

They locked eyes for a moment, until Clyde snorted. "Then I guess we're still partners."

Together they worked the room, asking questions and digging for details. No one was much help, but someone pointed out that a few fellows had gone upstairs.

"I'll check up there," Clyde said. "And you see what Cobb has learned, if anything."

Nate joined Cobb at the bar. While Clyde climbed the steps, his boots thudded like a warning on every riser.

"Nothing," Amos said in answer to Nate's question. "But you should keep an eye out for anyone who wastes a lot of money all at once. Sudden wealth changes people. Makes them do foolish things."

Nate grimaced and wondered how he would be different if the bull hadn't stolen Franco's cash. While Nate kept watch in the smudged mirror behind the bar, Cobb said, "I traveled from Mason's Crossing, over in Texas, to Bossier City to see some clients in the oil business. They need certain types of equipment, which I provide. But I also do repairs, sometimes more important. It's a dangerous line of work, drilling for oil."

"Why?"

"Blow outs. All that pipe tripping down the hole, but no one knows if or when it'll strike. When it does, sometimes it releases tons of pressure. I've heard stories about men and machinery flying through the air, blown sky high by the oil."

"If it's dangerous, it must pay well."

"Better than other jobs, but only when they strike. Either way, it's a risk. I don't —"

High-pitched screams splintered the air. They turned around as a door upstairs opened and slammed shut. A man wearing nothing but a long undershirt ran onto the landing. He made it halfway down the stairs before the door opened again and Clyde barged through, roaring, "Grab him. Grab Harold!"

The man jumped over the railing and headed for the front door. He changed direction when Nate came toward him at full speed. Parting the crowd and weaving around tables, Harold reached the back door and darted into the alley.

By the time Nate made it out the door, Clyde had jumped from the second story window and landed on Harold. He lay on his back, his hips and legs twisted, while Clyde straddled him, punching his face bloody.

When Harold no longer struggled, Clyde drew out his knife and clicked it open. He grabbed a patch of Harold's hair, yanked his head upright, and nudged him in the throat with the tip of the knife. "Where's the rest of the money?"

Spitting sideways, Harold choked on blood and broken teeth. The tip of Clyde's knife drew a tiny red line, which dribbled down his neck.

"Where?" Clyde said through clenched teeth.

Nate stepped forward and put his hand on Clyde's shoulder. "Let him answer."

Clyde looked up at Nate as if he didn't recognize him. "I'm gonna slice him open. He can't talk to us that way. We're a good crew, especially…"

A few men from the saloon had gathered on the back porch to watch. Cobb stood on the edge of the group.

"He's not your lieutenant." Nate squeezed Clyde's shoulder and reached down to clasp his elbow with his other hand. "Come on, let him be."

Clyde relaxed his grip, and Nate lifted him off Harold's limp body. He gestured to the other man to help raise up Harold. When Harold shuffled to his feet, he dangled between the men supporting him.

Nate leaned down into his face. "Now, answer the question."

Harold cast his eyes toward the second floor.

"You hid it in her room?"

Harold winced as he dipped his head a fraction.

"Where?"

"M… mat… mattress."

"Does she know it's there?"

Harold shook his head.

Nate nodded at Clyde. "Go get it. Then meet me out front."

"Yessir."

Inside Nate's head, something snapped. No one had ever called him 'sir.' He wasn't even twenty yet, but he recognized a faint stirring.

Stretching to his full height, Nate jerked his head toward the doorway, and the men propping up Harold edged him back inside. As Nate waited, he felt eyes on him. He whirled around and found Amos staring at him from the shadows. Their eyes met and held for a few moments.

"You did the right thing, son," Amos said. He turned and strolled back into the saloon.

Something lying in the dirt caught Nate's attention. He bent over and picked up Clyde's blue bandana. After shaking the dust off, he folded it and slid it into his pocket.

WORK AT THE COTTON GIN continued while Nate waited for a reply from Charleston. As the days passed, he fretted and tried to come up with a plan that would give his family a place to sleep, food in the cupboard, and some way for his mother to earn wages.

"I don't know whether to ask the foreman about a job for her. She's a real good cook." Nate licked his lips with the memory of her fresh scuppernong pies while he stirred the bowl of watery potato and carrot soup in front of him.

"That'd be a nice change from the slop they serve us," laughed Clyde. "But you don't know where she is yet, so maybe when the letter comes—"

"We'll have to make room for the little girls." Nate sighed. "Plus the baby, if he..."

"How many brothers and sisters you got?"

"If the diphtheria hadn't took four, unless by now Mary has up and passed from the fever, there'd be eight of us. I helped bury three of them in Clark's Common, and the other one, a younger brother, somewheres else."

"Wait a minute," said Clyde. "My math's not that good."

"My mother's had eight children, counting the new baby. Only four are still alive." Nate glanced around the warehouse. "Maybe we can empty out the storeroom. They could all crowd in there. It's near enough to the kitchen."

"That must've been a hardship on your mother."

"Having all those kids?"

"Not just that, but losing them, too."

"She told me not very long ago her heart just felt boarded up like an old house. So many of her children dying, she said she was afraid to get too attached." Nate pulled a piece of bread apart and stared at it. "It wasn't that she didn't take good care of the younger ones, but I don't remember seeing them sit in her lap. She never read to them, neither, like she did me."

"After the others came along, she was a tad bit busier."

"You know something about family life?"

"Heck, I wasn't born in the Navy. Had a family of my own once. A sweet dark-haired Italian wife, an odd thing for an Irishman like me. We had a child on the way."

"Where did you live?"

"New York City. I worked on the docks and my wife was a seamstress."

"What happened to her?"

"Died in 1911. The place where she worked, the Triangle Shirtwaist Factory, caught fire. Lots of young women jumped to their deaths. Them bosses, they locked the doors and the stairwells. They wasn't concerned about safety, only making sure the workers didn't sneak a break to smoke outside."

Clyde blinked, his expression bare of emotion. "Elena couldn't get to the elevator. Someone told me later she made it out the window to the fire escape, but it was flimsy and it pulled loose from the building. Too loaded with women."

Nate had never ridden in an elevator or climbed down a fire escape, but he had seen what looked like an outdoor staircase against tall buildings in Houston. "I'm sorry," he said.

"And then I bounced from job to job until I joined the Navy and went to Europe to fight."

Clyde stood up. "Back to work now."

Nate looked up at him. "If I don't get a letter by Friday, I'm leaving anyway. I got enough money to take the train to Charleston. I can look up Miss Rutledge and..." He bit his lip.

"The guys in town will miss you on Saturday night." Clyde chuckled as he carried both soup bowls back to the serving line to add them to the pile of dirty dishes. "Especially that Cobb fella. He's probably looking for a rematch."

"Tell 'em I'll make it up later, when I get back." Nate followed Clyde to the warehouse. "If I get back."

CHAPTER NINETEEN

By the end of the shift on Thursday night, all the men were exhausted. Perhaps it was the humid weather or the lack of even a gust of air. Everyone grumbled and headed to bed early, while the second crew shuffled to the warehouse.

Nate lay on the cot and planned his trip to Charleston. First thing in the morning, he would go see the foreman in the office and ask for the cash balance in his account. It should be twice more than his winnings by now.

Before he left for the train station, he would stop at the company store and buy a new pair of pants and a white shirt. He wished he could pack a couple of Hootie's newspaper-wrapped muffulettas to eat on the way.

As he rolled over, the breeze picked up and he pulled the thin blanket higher to cover his shoulders. That move left his bare feet exposed. He sat up and jerked the blanket toward his ankles, then tucked it under his heels.

Nate settled on his back and stared at the ceiling. Would his mother think he had changed much since last spring? The girls should be a little taller by now. And the baby, well, he'd just have to wait to find out about the baby.

He closed his eyes, took a deep breath, and tried to relax. His breathing came in a fixed rhythm, and soon he settled into the cool damp air.

The next thing Nate knew, men were shouting and running around the quarters. Outside, the sky was lit up like dawn. He bolted up straight as one man came dashing toward him.

"Hurry!" the man yelled. "Get out quick. The whole place is afire."

Nate leaped off the cot, grabbed his clothes, and headed toward the door. Fire would spread through the now-empty sleeping quarters in a hurry.

At the doorway, Nate turned and ran back to his cot, turned it on its end, and climbed up, trying to keep balanced on the edge. He pulled money, his share of the winnings, from the hiding place in the rafters. After spreading a torn piece of bed sheet across the floor, he dumped the money in it and tied it in a knot.

Nate smelled smoke, while the shouting outside grew louder. A burning timber crashed through the window by the door where he had stood moments ago. The nearby cots collapsed under the weight of the fiery trunk.

Nate ran to the other end of the room and picked up a cot. He rammed the iron frame against the wall but no boards popped loose. On the fourth try, one cracked and he shoved the cot into the opening until he made a hole. As Nate skittered through it, heat smacked his face as something in the warehouse exploded and sent a fireball skyward.

He searched the yard between the warehouse and the dining hall. What if Clyde had panicked and run into the flaming building, thinking to rescue Elena? Nate whirled around and scanned the area. The office was also ablaze, and the foreman and the other men had scattered like dropped marbles.

Behind him, the roof to the sleeping quarters caved in. Nate dashed across the yard and called Clyde's name. No one had seen him. Nate turned back toward the quarters.

Just as he paused, checked by the heat, someone grabbed Nate's arm. He whirled around, fist in the air.

Clyde grinned up at him, his face blackened. "What'sa matter?" His teeth glowed like gravestones against his smoke-darkened skin.

As Nate felt his shoulder, Clyde winced. "I'm all right."

Nate stepped back to get a full look at him. "Your face and arm are all bloody. Are you hurt bad?"

"Nah, but..." Clyde mopped his sleeve across his forehead, straightened his back, and wrenched his head from side to side. "I could use a drink." He tossed his knife in the air and caught it by the hilt with his other hand, then wiped it on his pants.

Nate took him by the arm and led him away from the burning chaos. "What happened?"

"I got up to piss and spied someone duckin' around across the way." Clyde chortled. "He walked with such a limp, at first I couldn't tell what he was up to. By the time I figured out it was Harold, he had already lit the warehouse and was headed toward the quarters. He torched the office right as I tackled him."

"Where is Harold now? The foreman will want to know."

Clyde slipped the knife into his boot and jerked his head sideways. "Over yonder, lying in the woods. They won't need to bother about him." He squinted toward the edge of the property. "I always did think he was a bit of a weasel."

"Why would Harold do such a thing?"

"Revenge," said Clyde. "He got caught more than once, and the bossman finally fired him."

Nate sighed and peered at his friend. "Your face is still bleeding. He cut you pretty bad."

"Not as bad as I cut him."

Nate untied the bed sheet and slid the money into his pocket. He wiped Clyde's cheeks and dabbed at the part above his eyebrow that wouldn't quit oozing. "You need stitches."

Clyde shoved his hand away. "I ain't going to no doctor. He'll just ask me a bunch of questions. Then he'll call the police or the sheriff."

"Well, press this against the cut while I get..." Nate rubbed his forehead. "I have to... uh, the train leaves at..." He stared at the office, now a pile of smoldering boards. His mind went blank for a moment, until he felt in his pocket for his coins.

He turned to Clyde. "Did you take your money with you when you went out?"

"And use it for what? Toilet paper?" Clyde took the bandana from Nate. "Hell, we'll just start over."

Nate had done it often enough to know Clyde was right, but starting over would be hell this time. South Carolina, and his family, would have to wait.

NOW THAT EVERYONE WAS out of a job at the cotton gin, Nate and Clyde trudged to the drilling sites along with the others. As they crowded around a man standing on a wooden crate, Nate shifted his weight from foot to foot and tried to ignore the knot in his stomach.

Addressing the group, the foreman promised them the hardest and dirtiest labor they had ever done, starting at the bottom since they were unskilled. Few were hired, but Nate and Clyde managed to sign on as roughnecks, since they each had some experience with machinery.

As they walked away from the foreman's desk, Nate whispered, "I don't even know what that word 'roughneck' means."

"I'm sure I've been called worse," Clyde laughed.

The foreman, or toolpusher as he was known, hadn't lied. Moving pipe and equipment took all their strength, and Nate was assigned to the rig floor where he learned to operate the tongs and the tugger. He seized upon any other job he was asked to do and went to the tent every night covered in dried mud and sweat.

Clyde helped the boilerman and worked on the steam pump. His smattering of knowledge of engines, acquired in the

Great War, came in handy for Nate, who managed to stand near Clyde and pass him tools. Clyde also served as the laundryman, washing the crew's greasy clothes in the blow barrel and hanging them up to dry in the warm air the boilers gave off.

After several weeks of work, on Saturday night they managed a trip to the speakeasies and taverns on the edge of Bossier City. A handful of men greeted them as they entered.

"There's always money to be made in the booze business," said Clyde, "but since the loss of McPherson's, the bars are less crowded. I ain't had much success at rounding up opponents for you."

"Guess prohibition isn't taken seriously up here in Bossier City," said Nate. He refused to fret about money or talk about his family. He waited at the table in stoic silence.

"Bossier City?" Clyde snorted. "City, my ass. What a podunk place this is. We should get ourselves somewhere else, where the lights are brighter."

"Do you miss New York?"

"Never thought I'd admit it, but yes, I do. Looks like I'm stuck here for now."

Clyde didn't give up on finding ways, as he was fond of saying, "to separate people from their money." When he discovered Nate's natural genius for numbers, Clyde convinced him that learning to play poker would be an advantage.

Shutting out memories of Roy, Nate agreed.

"Finesse, that's what you need," Clyde said as he shuffled the cards.

"What does that mean?"

"You can't be too obvious. If you have a winning hand, don't let anybody figure it out by looking at your face. You have to keep your expression blank." Clyde stood over Nate's shoulder, inspecting the cards he had dealt.

"Like this?" Nate turned his face upward.

"That's good, But don't even widen the dark part of your eyes."

After three nights practice, Clyde thought it was time to try a little game with others. They went back to Winkie's Tavern, where they had started. After seven hands of five-card draw, Nate was down by almost five dollars.

Clyde was just about to suggest they quit the table, when Amos Cobb strolled into the tavern and ordered a beer at the bar. Clyde nodded at him, but Nate concentrated on the cards in his hand and answer.

Each player tossed a dime into the pot for the ante and, after receiving their cards, another quarter for the first round of bets. Everyone stayed in the game.

Starting on his left, the dealer laid out a matching number for what each player discarded. Nate put one card face down. He picked up his replacement card and slid it in place, shuffled the order, and placed all five in a stack on the table in front of him.

After everyone received new cards, betting started on the left. A dollar. The second man folded his hand. The third player said, "Raise." He tossed two dollars into the pot.

Without looking at his cards a second time, Nate picked up eight quarters, counted them again in his palm. He rolled his eyes at the ceiling and dropped the coins into the center of the table. "Call."

The other players grinned, as if they were lions smelling fresh meat.

Clyde, last on the dealer's right hand, folded. The dealer stayed in with two one-dollar bills, and the first player added another dollar to the pot. "Call."

The third player fanned out his cards. "Full house, gents. Ladies over deuces."

"Aw, shit," said the dealer. "Not even close."

The first player threw his cards down. "You got it."

The third player leaned forward and reached for the pile of coins.

"Don't you want to see my cards?" Nate said.

He snickered. "Sure, kid. Whatcha got this time? Another pair of sixes?"

"Almost," said Nate. "Except there are more of them, and they aren't sixes this time." He flipped his cards over one by one until all four nines lay face up on the table.

The dealer gave a low whistle, and the would-be winner dropped back in his chair.

"My, ain't they pretty," said Clyde, smirking as he stood up. "I guess I'll have me a beer to celebrate your win." He wandered toward the bar, stopping to chat along the way.

At the bar, Amos Cobb tipped his beer mug toward Nate and smiled. Nate nodded at him as he raked in his winnings.

"Hold on a minute there," said the third man. "I want to look at those cards you were holding."

Nate narrowed his eyes. "What are you hinting at?"

The friendly banter around the table grew quiet. The dealer set down the deck of cards in front of him and waited.

"I think we better check the deck for nines," the man said. "Something tells me we'll find more besides the four in your hand."

Every muscle in Nate's body tensed. "Go ahead and take a look. I got nothing to hide."

The dealer glanced at Nate, who nodded at him. He scooped up the four cards in front of Nate, and Nate handed him the fifth card.

"Count 'em," Nate said, staring hard at his accuser, "so everybody can see."

The other players leaned in closer to watch as the dealer separated the cards into stacks by suit. When the final card was laid, the dealer shrugged.

Without blinking, Nate sensed the eyes of the other players shifting toward the man across from him. "Satisfied?" he said.

"I may have been hasty—"

"I believe you owe the young man an apology," said a gentle, but firm, voice behind him.

Nate looked up and met the steady gaze of Amos Cobb.

The man muttered, "Sorry," as he scrambled to his feet and turned away from the table. Before he could take another step, another man's voice said in a harsher tone, "I don't think he heard you."

The man turned around to face Nate and winced, as if something sharp had poked him in the spine. "I apologize."

"For what?" growled the voice behind him.

The man gasped and bent his head toward one shoulder. "For thinking you had cheated." He winced again.

"You ain't shooting anybody tonight," the steely voice behind him said. "Now lay the little pistol in your other hand on the table and get out."

The man set a small gun on the edge of the table and when he backed away, Nate could see Clyde, jaw clenched, knife in his right fist, Amos' hand on his shoulder. After a moment, Nate exhaled.

He stood up and clasped Clyde's arm, looking from Clyde to Amos and back. "How did you know he had—"

"Lucky guess." Clyde pulled out a chair and sat down, then emptied the gun of its bullets and set them in the center of the table, as if he intended them for an ante. He slid the gun into his coat pocket. "Another round, anyone?"

As Amos took the seat abandoned by the other man, Nate

heaved a sigh of relief. Who would ever have his back stronger or better than Clyde?

Just as the dealer began shuffling the cards, a man burst into the tavern. "Blowout!" he yelled.

Everyone stopped talking and turned toward him. For a strange moment, no one moved.

"At the southwest patch, number four!" He ran out the door.

Others, including two at the poker table, grabbed their jackets and followed him.

Standing at the same time, Clyde and Nate exchanged grim looks. They had heard about the possible dangers and figured their help would be needed.

Amos Cobb came up behind them. "I was just there earlier today." He shook hands with Nate first, then Clyde, "I've got my truck parked outside. Come on."

As they rode together, Clyde mentioned their new jobs and Cobb explained what he'd been working on. "You can trip all the pipe you like down the hole, but when you strike where the pressure is intense, the oil has nowhere else to go but up. It's an unmanageable force, without something to control it."

"Like a valve on the inside of the pipe," said Nate.

"Exactly, some kind of flap to manage the flow." Amos pulled up to the edge of the southwest patch. "You work the tongs and the tugger, don't you? You understand what I mean about the danger."

"How do you know about that stuff?" Clyde said to Nate.

"Last summer I worked some with my pa... er, Roy when he was part of a crew laying out water pipes in Houston. We mostly did a lot of digging, but after work sometimes I'd get a chance to peek at the engineers' drawings and ask the boss questions. He was nice enough to explain how—"

An ambulance, siren blaring, arrived, along with a fire

wagon. In the distance, dark crude spewed at least two hundred feet into the air, backlit by torches mounted away from the mangled rig. Men hurtled in and out of the shadows, as if some giant god-like creature had stomped on a large anthill.

Amos shook his head. "Tsk, tsk, we got to figure this thing out. Every driller, every wildcatter in the country needs a way to prevent this problem. I've given it a lot of thought."

"You got something you can show me, like a sample, maybe?" Nate said.

"Just sketches, but I'm no artist."

"After we help them, I'd like to take a look." Nate opened the door and climbed out of the truck. Clyde followed him.

"We can go back to my hotel," said Amos, "and work on it together."

As they stood back to let first ambulance pass, Nate pictured Judge Carolla seated behind his desk in his pin-striped suit. The image faded, only to be filled by one of Father Antoine.

If it takes all night or all week, I'll solve this problem.

He plodded through the mud behind Clyde and wondered how a new venture would change his life again.

CHAPTER TWENTY

As Clyde lay on his back snoozing across the end of the bed in Cobb's hotel room, Nate and Amos sat at the table and discussed the problem of blowouts.

"I get the general idea of pressure, but I'm just a blacksmith who repairs equipment. I don't know enough about drilling," Amos said. "And the only way to test anything is under live conditions. Maybe it's worth the risk."

"What if we could come up with something, like an alarm bell?" said Nate. "People would get out of the way and not get hurt."

"How would someone know when to ring the bell? By then it'd be too late." Amos shook his head. "The pot would have already boiled over."

For a moment, Nate chewed the inside cheek of his mouth, then sat up straight. "Let the pot blow the whistle."

Amos laughed. "How's that?"

"When my ma bakes pies, she doesn't want the juice to spill over and burn on the bottom of the oven. She puts a little bird that sings, right in the middle of the pie."

"She baked a bird?"

"Not a real bird, but one made of china. When it whistled, she knew it was time to take the pie out of the oven." He licked his bottom lip and swallowed. "She made the best pie you ever tasted. People paid regular every week for one of her..." Nate studied his palms and wondered what his mother had baked lately. Did she pack her pie tins when she left Clark's Common?

"Okay, so first we come up with a feathery gadget that has a siren to let off steam." Amos smiled. "It rings before the well blows and any fire starts, then what?"

"We don't want to stop the oil from shooting up to the surface, do we?"

"Manage the flow, that's all," Amos said as he looked Nate squarely in the face. "I can see the wheels turning in your head."

Nate picked up the pencil and studied the rough sketches Amos had made. "I don't ever want to be carried out on a stretcher by the ambulance driver." From memory he added the machinery on the drilling floor to the drawing. "Here's where it breaks down. Pinch it close to that spot, we can nip it in the bud, without shutting it off all the way."

Amos leaned over his shoulder. "So if we drive something strong, like another pipe, crossways through the upright, we control how fast the oil comes out. Open and shut as much as we want, no more blowouts."

"It has to be lower down, so it stays in place. Then we add some extra lines with the same gadget so the oil flows to the tanks, maybe three or more of them, depending on how much comes out."

"How difficult would it be to punch a block through when the oil starts surging?" Amos ran his fingers through his thinning blond hair. "How would you get it to slide against that force? Some kind of pulley?"

Clyde stood up and lurched toward the window. After a big yawn, he pushed the curtains aside and tried to raise the lower casement. It wouldn't budge. He pulled down on the upper panel without any luck. "Oh, screw it!" He returned to the bed and flopped face down.

"That's it!" said Amos, clapping his hands. "Clyde, you've still got a brain, even when you're asleep."

Clyde exhaled loud enough for Nate to wish they'd both

get more rest before morning, but he couldn't quit working on the puzzle of the blowouts. Lives, maybe his own, depended on an answer.

Amos dragged a chair around the table next to Nate and took the drawings and the pencil from him. "We put a big screw right here. Make it long enough and it goes all the way through."

"Put another one on the other side to meet in the middle. Two guys like me can get it done faster."

"What could you use to tighten the screws? Can't be a giant screwdriver. What about some kind of crank handle?"

"Something that turns easy when my hands are slippery." Nate stood up and paced toward the window. He leaned on the wooden frame and watched the empty street. In a few minutes, a milk truck passed, making an early delivery.

Nate turned toward Amos, still seated at the table. "A steering wheel," he said. "Doesn't have to be that big, but make it like a steering wheel." He returned to the table. "And we don't have to wait until the oil comes to a head. Every drilling rig should have one of these right from the git-go."

While Clyde slept, they spent the next hour working out the details of length and weight for each section. Amos estimated the measurements with Nate's help, and they both agreed it was simple enough.

Amos figured it could be made from parts already in his shop. "I'll work up a model and bring it on my next trip," he said. "It'll take me a while. Lots of repairs this time around."

"Meanwhile, let's hope we don't have any more blowouts," Nate said. God only knew how long his luck would hold.

DURING AMOS' THREE-WEEK absence, the oil fields near Bossier City suffered two more blowouts. Nate sounded out the words in the newspaper headline:

OIL FIELD DISASTER CLAIMS MORE LIVES

Nate supposed it was only a matter of time before he was blown sky-high as well. He asked Clyde to help him write another letter to Miss Rutledge, this time including instructions for passing on his little stash of earnings to his mother.

"People are supposed to do that, aren't they?" Nate said one evening after supper. "Give their stuff away to next of kin when they die?"

"Stop talking like that." Clyde stubbed out his cigarette. "You ain't gonna die."

"Well, if I do—"

"You don't have enough to mess with," Clyde snickered. "If we didn't work every damn day in the oil patch, we'd have enough energy left to arm wrestle up some extra cash on Saturday night."

Nate was silent for a moment. "I want to make money a different way from now on." He looked west toward Texas and the horizon, where the sun had settled below the pine trees, and wished Amos would return with the working model.

ON FRIDAY, THE DERRICKMAN, who ranked second below the driller, tumbled backward off the monkeyboard, but the Geronimo line caught around his ankle about one-third of the way down. Work stopped while the crew got him untangled and lowered to ground level. Dizziness and a wrenched hip and ankle kept him seated, and the boss called for the doctor while someone else climbed up.

"Gadzooks, that looks dangerous," said a crew member standing next to Nate and Clyde, as they craned their necks to watch the new derrickman climb. "How high you figure that is?"

"Taller than a cottonwood." Nate rubbed his chin and wondered how much more the derrickman was paid than the others. Nate had marked how he tossed lines around the pipes, either to store them on the fingerboards or to trip more pipe down the drilling hole.

"You'd think he'd wear a belt or something," said Clyde. "Like trapeze artists do when they practice a new stunt. Nobody gets it right all the time, even the ones who scare the bejeebers outta folks for a living."

"Holy Hannah," said the crew member. "You worked at the circus?"

Trying not to laugh out loud, Clyde nodded before he traipsed off toward the steam boiler.

Nate squinted as he studied Clyde's retreating back. One more thing to work out with Amos: a safety harness for the derrickman.

He no sooner finished the thought than Amos drove into the yard, driving a bigger truck than last time. He parked on the edge and waved at Nate before he bustled into the lean-to office of the foreman.

After a few minutes, both Amos and the foreman came out of the office and hurried over to the back of the truck. When the doors flew open, Nate couldn't see either man, except from the knees down. One set of legs disappeared into the truck.

Nate climbed down to the drilling floor. He picked up the tongs and waited for the driller's shout.

"You! Wallace, come here!" a man's voice called.

Tensing in the gut, Nate turned around. The foreman stood next to Amos, waving another crewman to take Nate's spot on the floor.

Nate climbed up and walked toward them. "Yes, sir?"

With the back of his hand, Amos rubbed the grin off his mouth, but the twinkle in his eye wouldn't fade.

"This here's Mr. Cobb," said the foreman. "He needs help to unload some equipment from the back of his truck." He headed back to the office, tossing his words over his shoulder. "You do what he says and then get back to work."

As they plodded over the dirty ground, Nate fell in stride next to Amos.

"You'll never believe it!" said Amos. "I already took three orders."

"For the—what'd you name them?"

"Blowout preventers." Amos draped his right arm over Nate's left shoulder." I couldn't come up with a title for what we invented, so I asked Sarah."

"Sarah is your wife?"

"She's good at words, much more clever'n me." Amos laughed. "When I told another foreman about them over in Galveston County, he wanted some right away. So did the next guy. I got a pretty penny for them, leastways a deposit."

"That's good!"

"It started out that way, but here's the problem. Word's gonna get around and my blacksmith business will be swamped. My guys are working extra hours as it is." Amos stopped at the rear of the truck with his hand on the door handle. "I can either make the blowout preventers or sell them. I can't do both."

"Don't you have someone to do that for you?" Nate closed his eyes and tried to picture what it would be like to survive by his thinking instead of his doing. He dared not hope this could be his chance.

"I can get several guys working for me, but…" Amos rubbed the back of his neck. "They're smart, all right, but —"

"So what's the hitch?"

"I believe this sales job will take someone else. Someone special." Turning to face him, Amos put his hand on Nate's shoulder. For once, Nate didn't shrug off someone's touch.

Amos didn't say a word until Nate met his gaze. "I was thinking we'd be partners."

Nate held his breath. If he blinked, Amos might disappear and the whole conversation would be as if he had imagined it.

"You get half of everything we earn, less production cost. It was mostly your idea anyway, and you can sell them because you got practical knowledge working on a rig." Cobb's face muscles contorted as he urged Nate's agreement. "You can explain how the doohickeys work."

Nate stood up straight and looked over Amos' shoulder, but Clyde was nowhere to be found.

"You'll love Mason's Crossing." Amos nodded, struggling to keep his eagerness in check. "Bring your wife, too, if you have one. Hell, bring the whole family. Plenty of friendly folks—"

"Except Clyde, there's no one right now. Not yet, but real soon." He looked down at his dirty fingernails and wondered how they would ever come clean. His mother would insist on it.

"Then it'll be that much easier with just the two of you. I can find Clyde a job at the shop." Amos stuck out his hand. "Partners?"

"Yes." Nate shook hands with Amos, and the 'yes' echoed in his mind first, and then in his heart.

EARLY THE NEXT MORNING at breakfast, Nate told Clyde about the offer from Amos. "He's got a job waiting for you at the blacksmith shop, too."

"Where in the hell is Mason's Crossing?" Clyde shoveled a large slice of pancake in his mouth, drizzling butter down his chin.

"He says it's right outside Austin, in the middle of the state."

"Never heard of it," Clyde laughed. " Or Austin either. So much for the big city, huh?" He shook his head. "What'd that guy say yesterday? Gadzooks… I can't wait."

"Don't you want to come?" Nate set his fork down. "I… I guess I thought we'd stick together from now on."

"Aw, kid, now don't go and get all goofy on me," Clyde said with his mouth full. "You've grown up a lot since we met last year. I taught you 'bout everything I know."

Silent for a few moments, Nate sighed and tried to picture where he would have ended up after he left New Orleans, if he hadn't met Clyde. Hootie had said Nate would land on his feet, but he would have missed the chance to learn how men like Clyde try to make it.

"It's been a real education, that's for sure. And when you got back what little money we had from—"

Clyde put a finger to his lips. "Don't say anything about that. If anybody ever comes around asking, keep calm and act like you don't know what happened."

Nate nodded. "Besides, you know about motors and… and engines. Amos can really use a man like you working for him."

"It's too damn hot in a blacksmith shop. Anyway, like you, I want to try my hand at something else."

"Such as?"

"I might wander up north to Wisconsin and take up dairy farming."

"You know anything about cows?"

"Enough to recognize which is the business end."

"You're joshing."

"Only partly." Clyde's smile disappeared as he stirred his coffee. "Look, you have a fine opportunity here with Amos and the blowout thingamajig, and I want you to go on and take it. You can really make something of yourself."

"So can you, can't you?"

"I got to keep on the move. Maybe I'll rejoin the navy. Or go back to New York."

Nate frowned. "But you're the only friend I got. You're like... the older brother I never had." His tone grew soft. "You saved my life."

"Now, listen—"

"No, you listen!" Nate stood up. "I got no family here and maybe not in South Carolina neither. I can't depend on nobody but myself. We've been a good team so far, 'cause you're the only one who hasn't up and left or died on me."

Leaning back in his chair, Clyde stared at Nate, focused on his eyes. "Nate, I'm just a con man with a dicey past. I never planned on being anything else. Best not to get too mixed up with me, long term. Since my wife died, I go where the cold wind blows me and where the cards are hot." He raised his eyebrows. "And I'm always looking over my shoulder."

Nate returned Clyde's stare, hard as ice. Here it came once more, the separation, the one last look, the uncertain future, the wondering if he'd ever see him again. His breath stuck in his lungs. "Promise me something."

"If I can."

"When you reach the end of that road you're on, come to Mason's Crossing and find me. I'll always have a place for you with my family."

"'Til hell freezes over?"

"And longer."

They shook hands and Nate stood fixed to the spot, watching as Clyde headed out to the oil patch. His friend never turned around. After a few moments, Nate exhaled, then trudged to the foreman's office to quit his job and take whatever pay he had coming.

The hard decision was whether to accept the offer from Amos right away, or to try to find a ride to South Carolina. The Spanish flu kept the death count high as it spread across the middle and southern states. Nate had tried to keep informed by reading the newspaper headlines, and sometimes the first part of the articles.

Nate couldn't guess where his family might be, if they had taken sick, or even died from it. Maybe a trip to South Carolina was pointless, and even dangerous, but he wouldn't know until he wrote again, from Mason's Crossing next time, and received a reply from Miss Rutledge.

Unless the flu had taken her, too.

Chapter Twenty-One

Amos Cobb's acquaintance, a man in the lumber business, offered Nate a ride back to Texas, otherwise he would have been stuck in Bossier City. The truck wasn't any more comfortable than a boxcar, but at least no one would surprise him with a wallop from a blackjack. He shared the driving over rough roads, and they made the trip across East Texas in three days.

The pine trees around Mason's Crossing grew taller than the ones Nate had seen near the coast. Their trunks were straight, not bent, and they crowded the land beside the road. More people lived in the town than did in Clark's Common, and many of the buildings were made of brick. He wondered if his life here would be different as well.

Just after sunset, the driver came to a stop one block off the main street. Nate thanked him and climbed out of the truck at the address Amos had given him. He stood before a large wooden, two-story house with a wide front porch and a deep lawn. A row of rose bushes grew in front of the porch on either side of the stoop. Two empty rocking chairs waited in the shadows, but there was no sign anyone would be enjoying the evening breeze in them.

He took a deep breath, climbed the steps, and knocked on the front door. The knob turned and a little girl peered around the edge of the door. With curly golden hair and bold blue eyes, she couldn't have been more than eight years old. About the same age as Lillie, a little older than Mary.

She was the most beautiful child he had ever seen, so angelic, Nate couldn't speak for a moment. "Ah, hello," he said. "Is your father home?"

"What's your name?" She opened the door wider.

"Nate. Nate Rutledge."

"Weesie," a voice called. "Who is it?" The door pulled open all the way, and a women holding a baby on her left hip appeared. She smiled and shifted the toddler to the other side, not an easy move over her swollen belly. "You must be Nate." She rested her other hand on the girl's shoulder. "Louisa, say hello to Papa's good friend." The woman backed up. "Come on in. We've been expecting you."

For a split second, Nate closed his eyes and prayed he wasn't dreaming. He opened them. The house and the little girl hadn't vanished. Nate ducked as he stepped across the threshold.

"You hungry?" the woman said. "We didn't wait supper on you, but I've got some saved back. Pot roast with potatoes and carrots. Lima beans and mustard greens on the side. Some corn on the cob, too. Amos likes a lot of variety at the table."

Nate inhaled and thought he might faint from the rich aroma. "Yes, ma'am. Thank you." He followed her into a large room, stopping to admire a kitchen and dining table at one end. His mother would have loved it.

She turned around and waddled back toward him. "Oh, I forgot. I'm Sarah, Amos' wife."

The toddler on her hips threw out his arms, reaching for Nate. Nate grinned.

"This here's Joshua. We call him Josh." She handed him over, then tucked a strand of her light brown hair behind her ear. "You mind? Just while I dish up your plate."

"He likes you," said a voice behind Nate. The little blonde-haired girl came to stand beside him, looking up into the baby's face. "See? He's smiling."

"Have a seat at the table," Sarah called.

Nate sat down and slid the toddler forward to his knee, holding him around the shoulders with one hand. Josh took Nate's forefinger and chewed on it. "He's teething, isn't he?"

The little girl grabbed the baby's hands and clapped them together, singing a children's rhyme. The ribbon in her hair matched the one on her nightgown, and the deep blue of her eyes.

"Weesie, honey, take Josh and get him ready for a bath, please." Sarah shuffled to the table and set a white china plate, overflowing with meat and vegetables, smothered in gravy, in front of Nate. "Her real name is Louisa, but we call her Weesie. You want milk or beer with your supper?"

"Milk'll be fine." As Nate let Louisa take her brother from him, he stood up and pulled out another chair for Sarah. "Here, you sit down. Just tell me where it is and I'll get it."

"Maybe I'll put my feet up for a few minutes." Sarah giggled as she sat down. "Oh, my, won't I be spoiled by the time Amos gets home?" She scooted another chair in front of her.

Her laughter sounded like little bells chiming. Nate sneaked a carrot from the plate and slid it into his mouth. "Where is Amos?"

"Taking inventory. It's the last day of the month, and he real strict about keeping good records." Sarah pulled a knife and a fork, followed by a white cloth napkin, from her apron pocket. "He'll be another couple of hours. He said don't wait up for him." She pointed to the icebox. "Milk's in the pitcher. Get yourself a glass from the cupboard."

When Nate returned to the table, Sarah was rubbing her swollen belly. "I declare, you're the easiest houseguest I ever had." She looked down at her bulge. "A lot easier than you!"

Nate hadn't taken more than three bites of the pot roast when a little boy ran out of the other room. His hair stood up straight on top of his head and he had not a stitch on. He came to a sudden stop when he spied Nate sitting at the table with his mother.

Crinkling her eyes, Sarah stood up. "Daniel, where have you been hiding?"

The boy put his index finger in his mouth and stared at Nate. His eyes flickered to his mother. "Unner da bed."

"Well, go get in the bathtub with Josh. It's almost bedtime." She sat down again and groaned. "I'll be in there in a minute."

Nate tried not to gobble his food, but the pot roast was the most delicious meal he'd eaten in over a year. He couldn't remember when he'd tasted meat without a thick covering of fat.

Sarah heaved a tired sigh, and then winced. "I think I can get down on my knees to scrub those two wild Indians, but Lord help me if I can't get up again."

Scraping his plate, Nate said, "Would you like me to lend a hand? I can finish their baths for them."

"How come you know so much about children?"

Nate was silent for a moment. "I have little sisters." He frowned. "And I used to help my ma with all my little brothers, too. Especially when she was near... expecting."

Sarah stood up and began to clear the dishes. "That'd be a big relief to me."

While Nate bathed the little boys, he sent Louisa for towels, diapers, safety pins, and night clothes. When she returned with her arms full, she said, "Mama won't let me use the safety pins yet."

"I can do it." He toweled them dry and dressed the children for bed.

Louisa led Nate upstairs into the children's bedroom. Carrying a child in each arm, he first set the baby in the crib and then the boy in the trundle bed.

"You can turn the light off and move that little chair by the door, where Papa always sits," Louisa said as she pulled back the blankets on the other trundle. "That way you can see to read us a story." She handed him a thick book and skipped across the floor before she jumped into bed.

Nate looked down at the book's cover, a drawing of a kindly but witchy-looking woman in a green dress and red cape, riding on a huge white goose. Over her arm she carried a basket holding a smiling baby. His arms waved like he was on the best joy ride of his life.

He couldn't disappoint the children. Nate sat down, shifting his weight as the chair creaked, and opened the book. He glanced toward Louisa, but could only make out her shadow. "What story would you like?"

"You pick. I don't have a favorite."

"Bear," said Daniel.

Nate flipped the pages to the middle of the book. "Story about a bear? Let's see what I can find." He turned about twenty pages, one at a time, then started over from the front. When he found a picture of a bear, he named the colors and described the forest and the other animals. He scanned the words, trying to remember the lessons from Father Antoine. It seemed like years had passed since he memorized the alphabet. He sounded out a few short lines.

Daniel stood up. "Where's Papa?"

"He'll be here in a while," said Nate. "Lie down."

"I not sleepy," said Daniel.

"Lie down anyway."

Josh whimpered.

"Read us the story," said Louisa, as Daniel got out of bed and toddled toward Nate.

Nate rose from the chair and pointed at Daniel. "Wait here." He hurried downstairs to the kitchen where Sarah stood sideways at the sink washing dishes. "I'll dry those for you in a few minutes. Is it all right if I get one of the rocking chairs off the porch?"

"Whatever you like."

When Nate returned to the children's bedroom with the rocking chair, Daniel was sitting in the middle of the floor, sucking his thumb. Whining, Josh wobbled upright up in his crib, and Louisa leaned against the railing, trying to quiet him.

Nate set the rocking chair down near the doorway and sat in it. Daniel crawled toward his feet and Nate hauled him up into his lap. Mewing like a kitten, Josh rattled the railings until Louisa lifted him out of the crib. She brought him to Nate and plunked him down opposite Daniel.

Louisa backed up and stood looking at the three of them. When a tear slid down her cheek, Nate shifted Josh to the middle of his thighs and patted the arm of the rocker. "C'mon, Weesie. We got room right here, girl."

The angelic child bounded into his lap, settling back against his shoulder. Nate set the rocker moving back and forth, as gentle as a puff of air.

After about ten minutes of pretending to read by just turning the pages, Nate slowed the rocking, then stopped all the way. Neither Daniel nor Josh moved. Louisa sat up straight and looked him in the eye.

"Go get your ma," Nate whispered.

Louisa slid backward off the arm of the rocker until her feet touched the floor. She scampered out the door. In a moment, her footsteps thumped down the stairs.

Nate's left arm tingled under Daniel. He tensed the muscle to see if the boy would stir.

Louisa came back into the room and shook her head. "Mama says she can't come now."

"Then you take Josh and hold him while I put Daniel in his bed."

They managed the transfer without waking either child. As Nate tucked Louisa into her bed, she said, "Will you be here tomorrow?"

He nodded.

"Good," she said as she rolled over, turning her back to him.

Nate tiptoed to the door and closed it behind him. When he returned downstairs to the kitchen, Sarah was sitting at the table with her feet up in the chair, just the way he had left her. He smiled at her, but it vanished when he noticed the puddle under her chair.

"Should I go get the doctor?" he said. "Maybe Amos, too?"

"No time," she panted as she tightened her grip on the edge of her seat. "This baby's decided to arrive a tad early. And fast."

Nate sucked in his breath. He could bathe children, change their clothes, and rock them to sleep, but he had never in his life delivered one. His mother would want him to remain calm, but a panicky feeling arose anyway. He tamped it down. "Tell me what to do," he said.

"Get me into my bed," she panted.

"What's happening?" said Louisa's voice behind them.

As he helped Sarah to her feet, Nate glanced over his shoulder. "The baby's coming real soon." He turned to Sarah. "Can you walk?"

She took a step forward and grabbed his arm, squeezing it so hard he caught his breath. After a few moments she released her grip, then tightened it again. "Oh... my... saints..." she clenched her teeth, "...ALIVE!"

As Sarah drooped in pain, Nate swept her into his arms and strode toward the stairs. The sound of Louisa's sniveling made him turn around. "After I help your mother, I'll be right back.

Can you wait here for me?"

Louisa's crying spiraled up to blubbering as she ran forward and tried to take Nate's hand. Nate put his foot on the first riser, but couldn't step up with the child in the way. Sarah moaned as she stiffened in his arms, and he staggered backward. Louisa tripped on the toe of his boot and fell to the floor. Her wailing grew louder as she rolled back and forth.

Nate looked down at Sarah's face. Her eyes were fixed on the ceiling, not moving, as if she were in a trance.

"Weesie!" he called, using his mother's approach. "Stand up and stop that crying. I need... your ma needs your help."

"She won't stop... for a while," gasped Sarah. "Always been like that." She winced. "You just have to let her work it out by herself."

Nate climbed the stairs, followed Sarah's directions down the hall to the bedroom, and laid her on top of her bed. "I'll get you some linens or something."

He gathered the towels from the bathroom, the ones he had used to dry off Daniel and Josh, and returned to the bedroom. Sarah lay curled on her side with a knuckle in her mouth. Nate wondered how hard she had bitten it. "Don't worry about waking the other children."

She didn't open her eyes, but waved him away. He set the towels on the edge of the bed where she could reach them and returned downstairs to find Louisa waiting at the bottom of the stairs. Her eyes were red-rimmed, but she had stopped crying.

He sat down on the last riser and put his hand on her shoulder. "Weesie, can you be a brave girl for your ma and me?"

Her eyes widened and she stared into his face.

"I need to go get your papa from the blacksmith shop. He'll know what to do. Can you stay here with your ma while I try to find him?"

Louisa shook her head.

"Can you show me where the shop is?"

"Papa won't come until later."

"But how—"

"Ask Miss Gussie. She brings all the babies."

"Where does Miss Gussie live?" Nate hoped it was nearby, or even next door.

"Over yonder." Louisa gestured to the front door.

Nate ran his hands through his hair. Another birth? Another death? He took Louisa by the hand and led her to the front porch. "Which way?" His gaze swept up and down the street, with its darkened houses waiting like secrets in the shadows.

Louisa pointed toward the right, away from the corner where Nate and his travel companion had turned earlier. "She brought Danny and Josh, and even me, in her big black bag."

What did his mother call those women, the ones who delivered babies when no doctors could be had? She had relied on them more than once when Roy was absent, and it seemed to him, Mary and Lillie had had a better chance than the babies who were born without them. He looked up into the night sky and wished his mother stood on the porch with him.

Louisa jiggled his hand. "Aren't you going to fetch her?"

"Which house is hers?"

"That big gray one."

"Do you want to come with me?"

She nodded, and they crossed the lawn. Louisa's pace was too slow, so Nate picked her up and hurried down the street.

The gray house was even grander than the Cobb's. On either side of the wide front door, gas lamps shone bright enough to let Nate see though the fancy glass in the middle of the door. He set Louisa down, and she edged behind him. He rapped on the glass.

After a few moments, a man dressed in a dark suit crossed the entry hall and opened the door. He eyed Nate up and down. "Go around back to the kitchen. Cook will see what's left if you're hungry."

"No sir, thank you, that's not why I came." The words spilled out of Nate's mouth, gathering speed as he continued. "It's Mrs. Cobb. Her time is—"

A woman who must have been the man's wife had come up behind him. "What's going on?"

Nate gulped. "Sarah Cobb needs you, Miss Gussie, right this minute."

The woman tilted her nose and sniffed the air as if she smelled something unfamiliar. "I'll send Gussie over directly." She leaned sideways until she spied Louisa's face. "Don't you worry."

"Thank you." Nate turned to leave. "I've got to find Amos now."

The man spoke. "Ah, who are you, boy?"

Nate spun around until he stood face-to-face with the man. He drew himself up to his full height and looked down into the man's eyes, daring him to question further. "I'm Nate Rutledge. Amos Cobb is my new partner."

Nate returned home to find Sarah sweating and moaning, half her clothes tossed on the floor. He got a clean rag from the kitchen, soaked it in cool water, and laid it on her forehead. Sarah's eyes fluttered back into her head as she squirmed.

"Miss Gussie will be here soon," he said, almost to reassure himself.

"She better," Sarah panted, "or you'll have to deliver the baby."

He had never wished for his mother's presence more than he did in that moment.

Sarah tried to sit up, as she leaned toward the doorway. "Weesie, honey, go back downstairs."

Nate stood up and quick-stepped toward the child, who stared wide-eyed at her mother. When Nate tried to block her view, she dodged him and ran toward the bed.

"Somebody's at the door," she said.

Miss Gussie, a young brown-haired woman with a slight foreign accent, arrived at the Cobb house a few minutes before the baby did. Amos made it home within the hour and was pleased to welcome another son.

"We'll call him James Andrew Cobb, Jimmy for short." He handed Nate a cigar. "Both good names from the Bible."

Fine, as long as his nickname isn't Jimbo. And he survives the night.

Chapter Twenty-Two

Over the next several weeks, Nate settled in with the Cobb family, who let him stay in a small apartment over the carriage house in the back of their property. At first he traveled with Cobb on visits to customers and learned the routes, the buying habits, and the unanticipated needs. He picked up information about who was drilling and where.

And, once on his own, he wrote orders for the blowout preventer, using simple notes, measurements, and numbers. He wondered how much longer he could hide his poor reading skills from Amos. So far, his memory had served him well enough, but he knew one day he'd get caught.

During the few hours he wasn't working, he played with the children, ran errands for Sarah, or helped Amos around the shop. He didn't know what to say when Sarah asked his opinion on new lace curtains for the dining room. His mother was lucky if their windows had glass panes.

Sarah had a few rules, about which fork to use, how often to take a bath, when to be home from business trips. He liked the one about waiting to eat until everyone was seated at the table. Not just good manners. she had told him, but because we don't serve ourselves first. Like a family.

It seemed natural that Sarah and Amos expected him to attend church with their family. His mother would insist likewise and be pleased the local choice was Methodist.

One Sunday, he sat at the end of the pew, children in the middle, while Amos and Sarah occupied the other end. Louisa snuggled in next to Nate, and when the organ started, she pulled out the hymnal from the rack attached to the pew in front of her. After she fanned the pages and located the right one, she held it out for him to share.

Nate took his side of the hymnal but didn't look at the page. The choir joined the organ music and Louisa sang along. At the end of the first stanza, she turned to him and whispered, "Why aren't you singing?"

"Don't know this one."

"Everybody knows this one. It's famous."

"I can't... can't read music."

At the other end of the pew, Sarah caught his eye and held a finger to her lips. Nate handed the hymnal back to Louisa with a grim smile.

After the Sunday dinner dishes were cleared away, Louisa brought her schoolbooks into the dining room. "Nate," she called. "Come help me with my homework."

He pulled out a chair next to her. "What kind of arithmetic problems this time?"

Her eyes twinkled. "I have to finish this story and write a book report. I need someone to read with me. Mommy and Daddy are too busy."

Around the edge of his Sunday newspaper, Amos glanced at Nate from across the table and shrugged. Sarah stood at the sink and scraped plates. Nate sat down, resigned to his fate.

"Now follow along with me and be sure I get the words right," Louisa said. She stumbled over some short ones and made Nate say them out loud. Then she asked him to read the whole sentence and repeat the words she'd missed. Soon they moved on to longer words and phrases.

Amos scooted his chair back and dropped his newspaper into his lap. "Weesie, what's the matter with you? Didn't you already learn all that last year?"

Nate looked up from the page and shifted his gaze from Amos to Sarah and back. Sarah whirled around and held her hands out, palms forward. Her gestures to Amos could only mean 'stop," but he ignored her.

"We should have a talk with your teacher."

"Amos," said Sarah in a firm voice. "Come here, please. I need you to reach something for me." She pointed to a high shelf.

Her husband sighed and stood up. He dragged the chair to the large cupboard between the dining room and the kitchen. "Nate could reach this all by himself," he muttered.

"Nate is busy," she hissed, "learning to read."

"Huh?"

"Act like you don't know anything."

"That won't be too hard." He raised one foot to the seat of the chair. "What are you talking about?"

"Shhhh! Nate needs to improve his reading skills and Weesie is pretending to want help. Don't make a fuss about it. I have a plan already worked out."

"But he gets every order absolutely perfect. What do you mean he can't read?" He glanced at Nate, who watched him for a moment until Louisa grabbed Nate's chin and shifted his attention.

"Keep your voice down." Sarah held his arm to steady him as he climbed on the chair. "Maybe his family couldn't settle for long anywhere and he never had a chance to go to school. Maybe he had to work instead."

"You're talking as loud as I am." Amos retrieved the basket Sarah wanted and handed it to her. "I'll admit I don't know much about his past, only that he impressed me as smart, hardworking, and honest."

He hopped off the seat of the chair. "He'll do the right thing, even if no one is looking."

"When it comes to people, you're not always off the mark."

He gave her arm a little squeeze and then pulled her toward him, leaning forward to kiss her. She backed up and pointed to Nate and Louisa, who both had stopped studying to stare at them.

Clearing her throat, Sarah straightened her apron and returned to the sink. Amos leaned on the back of the chair without moving.

Nate smiled to himself. He decided not to tell them he'd overheard every word.

His smile disappeared when Amos plopped into the chair and leaned forward to hold his forehead in both hands. Nate jumped up and hurried toward him. "What's the matter?"

Amos jerked upright and dropped his hands into his lap. "Nothing. Just a little dizzy spell." With a grin, he nodded toward Sarah's back. "When you find a woman who makes you feel that way, marry her."

Nate returned to the table and sat down next to Louisa. "Writing comes next, don't it?"

BY THE END OF THE MONTH, Nate had expanded their territory to north Texas and learned to copy every word from Louisa's book. His reading aloud flowed smoother, and he asked for additional books.

"I never saw anyone so determined," Sarah told him as he helped her set the table for dinner one evening.

"When my penmanship gets better, I want to write a letter to... someone," he said. "My own words, by my own hand."

Amos sauntered into the room carrying one of his ledgers. His glasses slid down the bridge of his nose as he gestured to Nate. "Take a look at these numbers, young man!" He laid the book on the edge of the table and stood back. "We've had a very good start of the quarter, thanks to you."

Nate sat down to study the page and did some quick mental calculations. "It's more sales than I first expected."

"Some people might say I'm a bit of a tightwad, but I like to keep a firm hand on the costs. This time next month, we'll be ready to do a distribution." Amos picked up the book and smiled. "Your share will be—"

"Almost $120." Nate held his breath and mentally double-checked the figures.

"Mr. Smarty-Pants," said a small voice next to Nate.

He twisted in his chair to find Louisa grinning wide-eyed at him. She held Jimmy in both arms until her mother came to take him and feed him in the other room.

Louisa stepped forward until she stood next to Nate. "What are you going to do with all that money?"

"Uh, I have to take a trip," he said. "To Charleston."

She stuck out her lower lip. "But you already take trips. You're gone every week."

"This one is special."

"Is it to visit your grandma? Does she live in Charleston?" Louisa picked up a spoon and tapped it against the table. "Where is Charleston? Is it far away?"

Amos set the book on the shelf. "Weesie, give the man— give all of us—some peace and quiet."

"My grandma lives on the ranch with grandpa." The child set down the spoon and turned to stare at Nate. "When will you be back?"

"I have to write a letter first."

"Then you better practice your cursive."

WHEN NATE RETURNED FROM his next trip, Sarah had a gift waiting for him. "Weesie helped me pick it out," she said before dinner one evening.

"What is it?"

"Open the box," said Louisa.

Inside was a dark brown leather notebook. He lifted the cover to find a stack of crisp white papers with matching envelopes. He looked up at Sarah and wrinkled his brow.

"Stationery," she smiled. "For your letter."

"This is the best gift I ever got," he said. "I don't know how to thank you."

"Write a good letter."

"I've thought about what I want to say, and I think I'm ready."

Sarah studied his face for a moment, then nodded. "Yes, I'd say you are more than ready."

After dinner, Nate helped Sarah clear the dishes, but she shooed him away from the kitchen sink. "Go on now, and get started on your letter."

He sat at the table with the leather portfolio in front of him. Amos had lent him a pen and he twiddled it between two fingers. He pulled one sheet from the notebook and took the cap off the pen.

Dear Miss Rutledge,

Nate straightened his back and glanced toward Sarah, who stood at the sink. He set the pen down and blew on the three words he had written. Then he wiped the page below his lettering with the edge of his hand. He sighed and picked up the pen again.

This time I am writing to you myself,

He ran his left hand through his hair.

as I am more setled now and can recieve your reply.

Nate held up the page to read what he had written.

It has been sevral months since I last wrote

He crossed out *last wrote.*

sent my last letter.

What could he say to encourage her to answer? Would she mind if he came to visit? What if his mother never made it to Charleston?

I would be pleesed to hear any news of my mother Evelyn Wallace and my sisters Mary and Lillie.

Should he mention the baby?

With your kind leave, I will come visit them in Charleston.

What if she says not to come? Doesn't matter, he'll go anyway.

If they have not come, or you no differnt news of them,

He didn't want any other news.

once you tell me, I will not trouble you any mor.

But he would write to her again, just in case his family arrived later.

Where else would they go?

With sinsere thanks, I remain,

He had never stayed for long anywhere. He wasn't even the same person since he left Clark's Common. Seemed like years ago.

Nate

Should he include Rutledge? How much did she really know about the servant Evie and Ransom Beauchamp Rutledge III, her brother?

Wallace

He didn't care much to be a Rutledge, or a Wallace either, for that matter. Then who was he?

Wallace-Cobb Tool and Machinery

Mason's Crossing

For now, he was a businessman. But something important was missing. He looked around the room.

Daniel and Josh played with toy wooden horses and wagons on the floor at Amos' feet as he read the newspaper. Louisa sat in the rocking chair turning the pages of a book while Sarah put the last of the clean dinner dishes in the tall cupboard.

Nate wanted his own family, the one he lost and...

Chapter Twenty-Three

Toward the end of the next month, after three weeks on the road, Nate returned to Mason's Crossing too late for supper with the Cobbs. In the dark, he climbed the steps of the carriage house, opened the door to his room, and flopped face down on the bed. The iron bed frame squeaked under his weight.

He hadn't lain there for more than a few minutes when there was a knock on his door. He rolled over and let out a deep breath before he got to his feet.

"Nate, you in there?" Louisa called.

"I'm coming." He opened the door. She seemed taller than he remembered.

"Mama says come to the house. She has something for you."

"Already ate dinner."

"So did we." Louisa shrugged. "Must be something else." She turned and hopped down each step, one at a time.

Nate followed her, taking his time to stretch his legs as he crossed the lawn to the back door. He felt too tired to be curious.

Sarah and Amos waited for him at the dining room table. "How are you, Nate?" she said. "We missed you."

"Did you have a good trip?" Amos said. But then he held up his hands, palms forward, and waved them. "It'll keep 'til tomorrow." He pulled out a chair, sat down, and stood up again. Turning toward Sarah, he said, "Well?"

"A letter came for you while you were gone. From Charleston."

Nate stiffened.

She pulled a long white envelope from her apron pocket and held it out for him. "I don't know your business, but I pray it's good news."

Nate didn't move for such a long time that Sarah laid the envelope on the edge of the table. She linked her arm through Amos' and pulled him away from the table. "Come on," she said. "Let's leave him here to read it by himself."

When they had gone out on the front porch, Nate picked up the envelope. The handwriting in black ink looked very formal. He had never seen his name written in such fancy script lettering and couldn't tell whether a man or a woman had penned it.

The return address caught his eye, mostly because the name wasn't Rutledge.

Pinckney, Elliott, Charles, and Lee
Attorneys - at - Law
Charleston, South Carolina

He turned the envelope over and slid his finger under the flap. The paper tore at the point in the center, yet he opened it and pulled out the folded letter.

Dear Mr. Wallace,
No one had ever called him Mister.
I am in receipt of your letter to Miss Vivian Rutledge
Why can't she answer her own letters?
and she has asked me to reply.
Nate held his breath.
Miss Rutledge has news of your family, and she desires
At last, he will join up with his family, they're safe, and he can look after them.

your presence in Charleston

Yes, she wanted him to come to South Carolina!

at your earliest convenience.

He could get money from Amos to buy a train ticket and leave tomorrow.

She will expect you at No. Seven Henrietta Street

A real street address.

within the month.

Sooner than that!

With kind regards, I remain,

Duncan Pinckney, Esq.

Nate read the letter twice more before he headed to the front porch. Sarah and Amos sat next to each other, rocking in the chairs and talking in low voices, as they held hands. When Nate cleared his throat, they both looked up at him.

"Have a seat, Nate." Sarah shook Amos' hand loose and gestured to the porch swing.

"I don't think I could sit still right now."

She pointed to the letter. "Is it good news?"

"Must be." He leaned on the porch railing. "It's my family. I have to go to South Carolina."

"We've been expecting this," said Amos. "How soon do you leave?"

"Tomorrow. As soon as I can get packed and head for the train." He told them a few details of his longing to find his mother and sisters.

"I don't guess you'll know how long you'll be gone." Amos chuckled. "We have so much work in the shop right now, it won't matter if you're not back 'til Christmas."

"Oh, hush, Amos." Sarah squeezed her husband's arm as she spoke to Nate. "Won't you need some things for your trip?"

"Like what?"

"Traveling clothes, a decent suit, some new shirts and shoes. This isn't some drilling camp. You want to look presentable to the lawyers… and to your family."

Amos snorted. "I don't know why. If lawyers think he's got money, they'll figure out a way to get their hands on it."

Nate stood up. "I just want to get my ma and my sisters and bring 'em back here. Would it be all right if they stayed in the carriage house, just 'til we find bigger quarters?"

Sarah shook her head. "There's not nearly enough room for four people up there, but while you're gone, we'll figure out something else. Don't worry."

Nate gripped the letter, rotating it by the edge as he talked. "Amos, I'll have to dip into my share before I go, to buy a train ticket."

"Of course." Amos nodded.

Sarah poked her husband. "And he'll need extra money for his return ticket, too, not to mention ones for his family members."

Amos sighed. "We'll go to the bank in the morning and make a big enough draw in your name."

Tucking the letter in his shirt pocket, Nate headed toward the front door. "I'd best get busy."

This trip would be different, starting with packing his clothes. No running along side the train, but instead he'd hand over his ticket to the conductor and step from the platform into the car. He'd ride in the seat looking out the window until the next station. He wouldn't jump off early and land in the woods or roll through the grass. No one would try to hit him or hurt the other passengers. No one would die.

When he arrived in South Carolina, he planned to… he would…

In the dining room, Nate pulled out the letter and read it again. Why didn't the lawyer or Miss Rutledge simply give him the news of his family? They have to be in Charleston, or why did she ask him to come?

If not Charleston, where?

When he arrived in South Carolina, he would get some answers.

CHAPTER TWENTY-FOUR

Two days later, Nate stood with Sarah and Amos on the southern edge of the platform at the train station in Austin and stared out at the Colorado River in the distance without really seeing it. Not until a fishing boat drifted past and disrupted the rippling surface did his mind turn from images of his mother and little sisters. He was curious how much they had changed in the months since he had last seen them.

Almost a year. I look different, too.

He held a brown leather suitcase full of new clothes which Sarah had helped him purchase two days ago from the City Mercantile at 17th and Lavaca Streets. His new leather shoes came from Capitol Saddlery just down the street, and they felt sturdier than his old work boots from McPherson's in Bossier City.

Nate caught a glimpse of himself reflected in the window and stopped to study the man in the dark pin-striped suit who stared back at him from the shadows. Tall, broad-shouldered, serious expression, hair slicked back to reveal thick eyebrows and dark eyes. Grown up. Ready to assume responsibility as the head of his family. He wondered what Dr. Broomfield would think of him now. Or Spike and Marty.

"I'll have plenty to keep me busy at the blacksmith shop while you're away," said Amos. They had spent yesterday at the shop together, going over the new orders and working on plans to expand the shop in Nate's absence. "Wire me, if you need more money."

The approaching train blew its whistle and Nate patted his left breast pocket, where he carried his sleeping-car-class ticket and the letter from Mr. Duncan Pinckney, Esq. Sarah had helped him with the ticket and the schedule, explaining the overnights and transfers in Dallas, Shreveport, and Atlanta.

The trip would take him over two days to reach Charleston. He could sleep on the train by converting his seat into a bunk bed, draw the curtain for privacy, and cover up with the blanket Sarah had packed for him. Better than huddling in the woods around a campfire.

Nate turned to shake Amos' hand and thank him again. "I shouldn't be gone too long. Just enough to thank Miss Rutledge and get Ma and the little ones packed."

"You take your time, son." Amos grinned. "Who knows? Maybe by next week, we'll have the shop expansion finished and invent something else."

"Just don't let Weesie and the others grow up too much while I'm away." He bent down and reached for Weesie, who had ducked behind her father. "You hear that?"

She pouted in silence while Nate waited for her to speak. When he tried to pat her check, she clutched his hand. "Don't go, Nate. Stay here instead. We'll be your family."

"Already told you twice. I have to do this. I'll bring back my sisters for you to play with. That way, you won't be the only girl."

"But I like being the only girl. I don't need any sisters."

"Well, I do." He stood up and smiled. "So, I guess I'm off."

"Safe travels, and send us a telegram once you're on the way home," Amos said with a wave.

Home, thought Nate. Yes, it would be good to be back here with his own family. Then it would be home.

He picked up his suitcase and stepped onto the train and into his future life.

DURING THE RIDE TO DALLAS, the wheels hummed and rattled as the train sped along the tracks. The padded seat felt much softer than the floor in the boxcar, the passengers more relaxed, the danger non-existent. When he got rich, he would buy a railroad and let the hobos ride for free.

He took a deep breath and considered how to reclaim and rebuild his life upon his return. This time last year, or even last week, he hadn't dared to flirt with these thoughts.

First, find a place large enough to hold everyone. Then figure out an allowance so he could provide food and other necessities. He would have to work harder and sell more. With an expanded territory, he would be gone longer on his road trips. Next, get Mary and Lillie in school, probably the same one Weesie attended. They wouldn't grow up like him, unable to read until now. What about a crib for the baby? Sarah would know where to find one, or he could build one.

Was the baby walking yet? Boy or girl? What name did his mother choose?

He smiled, eager to find out, hoping to build a crib and not a coffin.

AT THE STATION IN DALLAS, he waited five hours before boarding the train to Shreveport. The station offered a small café where he ate dinner, a newsstand where he bought an evening edition of *The Dallas Times-Herald*, and a barbershop where he watched through the window as men enjoyed shaves and got their shoes shined.

He stroked the stubble on his chin and cheeks.

I'll get a shave in Charleston.

He looked down at his new shoes.

Maybe a shine, too.

One of the barbers poked his head out of the door. "Next,

sir? We got an empty chair."

At once, he remembered Amos' words in the saloon after the shooting when Harold stole their money. "Sudden wealth changes people. Makes them do foolish things."

Nate shook his head and kept walking. He'd take extra care with his shoes and he could shave his own face.

NATE SLEPT MOST OF the way to Shreveport, not comfortably, as the seat wasn't long enough when converted to a bed. His feet dangled out the end, with the curtain draped over his calves. He woke up every time someone passed in the aisle to use the toilet during the night.

By the third interruption, he tried turning the other way and propping his legs up on the wall, his bare feet against the cool metal. After he put his socks back on, he fell asleep right away and didn't wake up until the porter came though and announced arrival in twenty minutes.

After breakfast in the station café, Nate stretched his legs on the platform and gazed across the Red River toward Bossier City. Once he got his family settled in Mason's Crossing, he would return there and call on all the foremen for every drilling site until each one signed an order for the new equipment. Not one more blowout bringing its own version of Black Death.

Nate settled on a wooden bench in the waiting room to read the newspaper he had bought in Dallas, starting with the headlines. On page six, he stopped and peered closely at a photo of a woman waving a piece of paper while standing on the running board of a Model T. Her expression and manner reminded him of his mother.

He read the caption: "Women's suffrage leader Minnie Fischer Cunningham celebrates at the ballot box, as Texas becomes 9th state to ratify Constitutional Amendment 19."

Nate wished he could ask Father Antoine what women's suffrage meant, but if anything, he was sure his own mother had suffered enough. He decided to try to read the article.

Until now, it had never occurred to Nate he could vote when he turned twenty-one in two years. According to the information in the article, his mother would now be able to vote when they returned to Texas. That suited him just fine; like Sarah Cobb, she was wiser and a better judge of character than most men he'd known.

After turning the pages to the Business Section, he stopped again at another photograph, this one of a young army officer standing next to a large truck loaded with heavy freight. With his fair skin, light brown hair, and wide friendly smile, he didn't look like a Matranga family member.

Nate read the caption: "Recently-promoted Major Eisenhower arrives in San Francisco after transcontinental trek with convoy to test suitability of US roads."

Nate studied the truck in the photograph, almost twice as large as the ones he had driven in New Orleans. Has to be, if it's going coast-to-coast, he thought. He read the rest of the article, and learned Eisenhower covered almost 3,200 miles, averaging about five miles per hour. More than half the roads he traveled were no better than the dirt roads around Clark's Common or Mason's Crossing. Nate scanned the article again and circled the words he would look up later in Weesie's school dictionary.

I'll buy a truck, a really big one like that, or a whole fleet of 'em. Then Amos and I can deliver our blowout preventers ourselves. Or hire drivers. Bound to be cheaper than the freight we've been paying. Maybe I'll buy me some roads, too.

After several more hours passed, Nate finished reading the newspaper, proud that he circled fewer and fewer words as the day wore on. When the porter came through the waiting room at mid-afternoon, announcing the departure of the train to

Atlanta, Nate tucked the paper under his arm and picked up his suitcase.

"This way, Mr. Wallace," the porter said, as he opened the door to the platform.

Nate stood up straight, squared his shoulders, and strode through the doorway, ready for the next leg of his journey. He prayed the trip would be worth it.

ATLANTA WAS BUSIER THAN Dallas, with more people scurrying to and fro and more morning traffic at the station. Everyone seemed to want to leave in a hurry, and car horns added to the ruckus.

From the white cloths stretched over people's mouths, Nate wondered if the flu epidemic had them worried about mingling with strangers. Even the porters and ticket agents didn't take much time to answer questions.

He bought a ticket on the Atlanta, Birmingham, & Atlantic Railway, which would take him through Augusta, Georgia, east to Charleston. As he searched the waiting room for an empty bench, he noticed a sign across the room that read, "Showers." After several days on the road, he thought, probably a good idea.

The uniformed Negro attendant took his money and gave him a dingy white towel and a small bar of used soap. He pointed down a long hallway with doors on either side. "Right through there, sir. Pick any stall you like."

These colored men were nothing like Hootie, who had never called him "sir" or acted like a servant. Hootie had no boss but himself. Nate had learned that much, and more, from his friend. Perhaps Hootie was blessed with a different spirit, and certainly with opportunity. And Hootie gave a lot of credit, first to God, then to his wife.

Given a chance, Nate decided he would never be anything

except his own boss. He hoped God heard him.

Inside one of the stalls, Nate undressed with care and hung his clothes on a hook. Once under the hot spray, he imagined returning to Atlanta in a few days with his mother and sisters. He would help with their luggage, even carry the baby. Maybe Amos would wire more money, enough so Nate could buy up all the seats in a single car. It didn't seem too extravagant to let Mary and Lillie have the run of the whole car to themselves, while he and his mother caught up with each other's lives since last year. He had so much to tell her.

He should have brought some of Weesie's books to keep the girls occupied during the long ride back to Texas. Nate sighed. He could read to them from the newspaper.

Feeling fortified, he dried off and dressed, but there was no mirror to make sure his tie was straight. He had to comb his hair by touch and wasn't sure he got the part even. Last, he bent over and tied his shoes, using the damp towel to spiff up the leather.

Nate returned to the waiting room and found a seat near the window. One hour to departure. He looked around for another newspaper stand, but could only find a used newspaper on a nearby empty seat.

When he picked it up, the woman in the next seat said through her facemask, "Don't touch that."

"Sorry, I thought it was left by someone." He laid it back on the seat.

"You don't know who put their hands on it or coughed all over it. Maybe they had the flu or they're carriers. You could die if you read that newspaper."

Nate picked it up again. "I'll take my chances."

He returned to his seat and opened the paper, but he couldn't focus on headlines, much less articles. What if someone who already read the paper had taken ill? Nate didn't believe the illness could be passed to him simply by touching the same surface, but the flu was a mysterious affliction, and doctors hadn't been able to cure anyone.

What if Miss Vivian had come down with it, and that's why the lawyer had written to him instead? Surely she would have sent his mother and sisters away until she recovered.

He let the newspaper drop into his lap as he wondered what the first symptoms of Spanish flu might be. Before long, the porter called "Train to Augusta and points east, due in fifteen minutes, platform number six."

Nate rose and picked up his luggage, leaving the newspaper—and, he hoped, any germs—scattered on the floor as he exited the waiting room.

Chapter Twenty-Five

The taxi ride from the station in Charleston to #7 Henrietta Street seemed to last over an hour, but Nate figured he was just extra fretful. Not that there was much traffic in the early evening, but the driver took his time winding through the narrow streets.

Trying to ignore the butterflies in his stomach, Nate gawked at the neighborhoods and thought they looked like New Orleans, only less ornate. He liked the simplicity.

The driver stopped, and Nate paid him and got out. After lugging his suitcase to the sidewalk, he turned around to face the house. His mouth dropped open as he stared beyond the palm trees and tall oaks with the drooping branches trimmed high.

The house wasn't a house at all, not like Nate was used to. Three stories, maybe four, judging by the rows of windows and the height of the chimneys. A high porch stretched all across the front and around each side, with carved white columns supporting a balcony, and a fancy white railing bordering the second level. Beyond the railing were tall windows with their dark shutters opened against the pale peach-colored walls, but no lights shone through them.

The house was wide enough to take up a city block. Nate figured there must be at least twenty rooms, plenty of space for his mother and sisters, plus the baby. If Miss Vivian let him stay, he would probably get his own room, maybe with a fireplace.

He took a deep breath and climbed the steps to the front

door and rapped, using the brass knocker. A few moments later, the door creaked open and an elderly Negro servant, stooped from the shoulders, stood in the darkened entry.

"Evenin'. May I help you, sir?" His white hair shone in the dim twilight.

Nate swallowed twice. "Miss Vivian Rutledge, is she home?" He set his suitcase down. "I know it's late… too late for company, but she sent me a letter and…" Nate pulled the letter from his coat pocket.

The servant opened the door wider. "Mr. Wallace? Come in, please." He reached for Nate's suitcase and after he picked it up, he stood back, eyes down, and gestured with a welcoming sweep of his hand. "Miss Vivian's been 'spectin' you."

"Thank you."

Nate stepped into the entry hall, noting the dark wood floors covered with a fancy carpet. He glanced up at the overhead brass fixture hanging from the ceiling on a long chain which reached all the way past the top of the stairs. When the lights came on, he blinked at the crystal drops shimmering like stars.

"Like magic," he said, as he turned around to smile at the old man.

For a few seconds, the old man nodded, but when he lowered his gaze to Nate's face, his expression froze except for his eyes bulging. He dropped Nate's suitcase to the floor with a loud thud.

"Lord have mercy!" He put a hand to his mouth, as if to shove the words back in.

"What's the matter?" Nate fidgeted, wondering if he had somehow done something wrong.

Before the old man could answer, a woman's voice called from across the hall. "Isaac, what is it? Is someone there?"

The old man shook his head with vigor, as if trying to wake

up. "Wait here, please. I'll jus' be a minute."

He disappeared into the other room, shutting the door behind him, and Nate couldn't help peeking at the other furnishings in the entry. Above a carved wooden bureau flanked by two chairs hung a picture of men in red jackets riding horses across a pasture.

Against the other wall stood a tall clock in a plain wooden cabinet. Its face was made of brass, with a sun and a moon decorating either side. He imagined his mother checking the time as she stood where he waited now.

At the sound of the door opening, he turned and faced the room across the hall. Through the doorway came the old man leading a tall, slightly plump woman who could be none other than Miss Vivian. She wore a long blue dress with a white lace collar. From her ears dangled large pearl earrings, like the strand around her neck. Her gray-streaked blonde hair was piled lopsided on top of her head, and her wire-rimmed glasses had slid down her slender nose until they rested almost at the tip. She looked nothing like any friend of his mother's he had ever met.

Miss Vivian smiled. "Welcome." But when she pushed her glasses up to see his face, her smile faded. She cocked her head sideways and frowned at him.

"Beau?" she said, with a small step forward. "Is that really you?"

Another wobbly step. "Beau… have you finally come home?" Her eyes shone misty and seemed far away as she gazed up into Nate's face.

She raised her forearms and placed her palms on the lapels of Nate's suit. Nate didn't know what to do. Should he step back and avoid an uncomfortable embrace? Try to shake her hand and pretend nothing was wrong? He let his arms dangle at his side and waited to see what she would say or do next.

Her lip quivered as tears welled in her eyes. The scent of rose water floated from her hair, but her breath smelled of whiskey. Then she turned her head to the side and laid her cheek against the front of his shirt. "I always knew one day you'd come home."

Bewildered, Nate's eyes searched for the old man's, but before he could signal, Miss Vivian's body slid toward his waist, and it was all he could to do catch her before she collapsed on the floor.

Isaac lurched forward, but Nate had already swept Miss Vivian up into his arms.

"Carry her this way, sir, if'n you please," said Isaac. He gestured toward the same room across the hall.

Nate followed him, pausing next to the divan as Isaac turned on a lamp on a nearby table. Isaac picked up what looked like a fringed shawl and gestured for Nate to lay Miss Vivian down. Nate waited for him to fluff a small pillow, then squatted to let go of her without dropping her.

He stood up and faced Isaac. "Will she be all right?" he whispered.

Isaac nodded. "Jus' a bitty shock, tha's all." Nate followed his gaze to a half-empty crystal bottle on the table. Next to it lay a carved stopper and a small glass, tipped over. "Po' thing'll be fine, after her li'l nap."

The old man covered Miss Vivian with the shawl as if he had done it a thousand times. Then he led Nate back to the entry and collected his suitcase. "Yo' room be upstairs, sir. Would you please come 'long with me?"

"I didn't mean to assume..." Nate said, reaching for the suitcase. "Here, let me carry it."

The old man wouldn't let go. "Nossiree, Mr. Nate. I gots it for you."

Despite the weight of the luggage, Nate's footsteps made the stairs creak louder than the old man's. Nate wondered if his sisters had been allowed to run up and down. How did they keep busy while his mother… worked? What did they do here?

When they reached the top of the stairs, Isaac turned right and led Nate through the first doorway. He turned on the lamp and crossed the room to set Nate's suitcase on a small stand.

Nate looked around the room. A chifforobe against the far wall by the window, a white mantel over the fireplace, a dressing stand with a large basin and pitcher, a long oval mirror propped up on curved legs, and a four-poster bed with a white canopy and bedspread. He had only seen such furnishings when he carried firewood upstairs for old Mrs. Tate in Houston.

"Would you be wantin' me to unpack fo' you?" Isaac said.

"Uh, no, I can do it."

In silence, Isaac opened the doors to the chifforobe before he turned back the covers and fluffed the pillows on the bed. "You be needin' anythin' else?"

Nate scratched his head. "Who is Beau? And why did Miss Rutledge think—"

"Excuse me, sir," Isaac bowed slightly. "Miss Vivian, she was referrin' to her brother."

"Ransom Beauchamp Rutledge, the third." The name was burned into Nate's brain.

Isaac's white eyebrows shot up. "You know 'bout Mr. Beau?"

"Do I really favor him that much? I learned a few things from my mother."

Isaac's face might as well have turned to stone. "Good night, sir." He turned toward the door.

"Wait a minute," Nate said, blocking his path. "I've come here to find out about her and my sisters. Evelyn Wallace. Surely you knew her." Nate clasped Isaac's shoulders. "Where are they? I'm going to take them home."

Isaac stared at the floor. "I cain't tell you anythin', Mr. Nate. You bes' be askin' Miss Vivian in the mornin'."

Nate dropped his hands and sighed. "You said she would

only take a short nap."

"Yessir, but she won't be wide awake 'til tomorrow mornin'." He sidestepped around Nate and closed the door behind him.

Nate paced the room. Why wouldn't Isaac tell him anything? He hadn't come all this distance to coddle a drunken old maid who mistook him for her dead brother, and who possibly had turned his mother away.

He opened the door and peered into the hallway. No sound from downstairs. He peeked over the railing down the stairwell. Isaac must have gone back to his quarters, wherever that was.

Nate tiptoed down the stairs and crept into the parlor where Miss Vivian dozed. He stood over her and listened to the muffled rasping and grunting. She sounded like a quieter version of Roy after a night at the saloon.

He crossed the room and sat down in a large chair with a high back. The fabric on the armrests felt soft under his palm, and the padded seat was comfortable enough. He could stay there all night.

Nate wanted his face to be the first thing Miss Vivian saw when she woke up.

Chapter Twenty-Six

A shaft of light flitted across Nate's face and he opened his eyes. A pair of blue ones, peering from a puffy face, stared at him. He bolted upright from the chair where he'd fallen asleep, and Miss Vivian stepped backward.

"I'm Nate Wal—"

"Oh, yes," she said as she smiled, "I know who you are. Good mornin'."

Her voice was soft, almost girlish, and her tone sounded giddy. She raised her eyebrows and inclined her head toward him, as if anticipating happy news or an invitation.

Nate rubbed his mouth, which felt dry as old leather. The stubble on his face made him wince. He took a deep breath and studied Miss Vivian. She had changed her dress from blue to pink and wore a cameo brooch instead of pearls. Her blonde hair lay smooth and twisted on top of her head, no longer lop-sided.

"Then, ma'am, you know why I've come," he said.

"Puddy made coffee. Would you care for some?" She turned toward the table next to the divan, where a tray held a china coffee pot and two cups. "Cream and sugar?"

Nate frowned. Coffee would help. "Just black, please."

"How nice. Like my daddy took his."

"Who is Puddy?" That wasn't the question he wanted to ask.

"She's our cook." Miss Vivian poured coffee into the two cups. "Been with us since I was a little girl."

"Speaking of little girls—"

"Breakfast will be ready soon. We'll eat in the garden room. It's pleasant there this time of year." She handed him a china cup. "Careful, it's hot."

Nate took the saucer from her and wrapped his fingers around the top of the cup to steady it. Steam rose from the coffee and he inhaled with his eyes closed. Nothing had smelled that good since he left New Orleans and Father Antoine's café au lait. Or rather Sister Ida-Emily's.

He waited for Miss Vivian to sit down. She took her seat on the divan and gave him an expectant look. "Such delightful manners in a young man. Your mother would be proud."

"Miss Vivian," he said as he returned to his chair, "your letter, or rather your lawyer's letter, said you had news of her. And the rest of my family."

Miss Vivian held a lace napkin to her lips and blinked several times. "That's right, I did." She set the cup and saucer down on the end table and folded her hands in her lap.

"Well?" Nate tried not to sound impatient.

"I was overjoyed to receive your mother's note last fall. She was my only real friend when I was a girl. She helped me through the worst time of my life. Of course, I welcomed her here, but I couldn't afford to hire anyone else after the war, especially since my daddy was gone. I have a hard time managin' all his—"

"When did she come?"

"Not right away. She wrote again and said she had some business to tend to in Clerk's ... ummmm?"

"Clark's Common."

She wiggled her lace napkin at him in an attempt to snap her fingers. "That's right." She repeated it, looking pleased with herself, as if she had remembered all along.

"Because of the baby, wasn't it?"

"What baby?" Miss Vivian sounded insulted. "She didn't say anythin' about a baby."

"Oh." Nate kept silent while he figured his mother accepted the baby's death without much emotion, and he tried to copy her reaction. Evie Wallace just wasn't meant to be as fortunate as Sarah Cobb.

"Did she arrive with any children?"

"Oh, yes, two little girls. Sickly, half skin-and-bones, but sweet as pie. I set right to fattenin' them up again. Had Puddy bake a cake every Saturday. Do you like lemon cake? I'll ask Puddy to bake one for you."

Nate sighed in relief. Then his eyes swept the room, trying to see through walls to search the house. "Where are they? Obviously not still here with you."

"Oh, gracious me, no." She cleared her throat. "They stayed here for quite a while, and Evie looked for you almost every day. I'm sorry to say, when the Spanish influenza hit Charleston like a hurricane…"

Nate drew in his breath and held it.

"Well, the papers have been chock full of the news. Almost 25,000 of our local people infected so far. I insisted your mother move herself and the two little chickadees out of the maids' quarters and leave town. I gave her what scant money I had, so she could buy a train ticket."

"You sent them away? But why?"

"Because, darlin' boy, in this house I was the one who came down with the influenza. It like to killed me, 'cordin' to Puddy and Isaac. With such a ragin' fever, I don't recall much. I've spent the last two months mostly laid up in my sick bed. But I was one of the many fo'tunate ones."

Nate flopped back in his chair and gazed at the ceiling, as if he could see heaven. He closed his eyes. "Then they're safe." He opened his eyes and smiled at her.

Miss Vivian dabbed at the corners of her eyes. "I wish I could agree with you."

Nate sat up straight again and almost glared at her. "What do you mean?"

She patted the seat of the divan next to her. When Nate didn't move, she thumped it harder. He got up and trudged across the room to sit by her.

"Isaac told me later Evie never did leave town. She was workin' as a maid in some hotel. But the health authorities ended up closin' the hotel when people kept dyin' by the hundreds. Afterwards, Isaac made inquiries for me, tried to find the owners or the manager, but..."

She took his hand in hers. "All anyone could tell him was they found a little girl, all alone, half-sick, so they sent her to the hospital..."

"To die?"

She squeezed his hand, but he shook her off and jumped to his feet. "Are you telling me they're all dead?"

"We don't know anythin' for certain, but—"

Not true. His mother wouldn't die from anything. She was too strong. She survived all those babies, even the ones who didn't live, and the beatings from Roy, and the scarlet fever that almost took Mary. He remembered her words: she shut her own heart down. It was her way. It was how she survived.

"They can't be," he said. "Can we go to the hospital and ask? Maybe they have some kind of record. Please, Miss Rutledge."

"But it's not safe to go there."

"I don't care. We're talking about my family. They're all I have."

Clucking, Miss Vivian pushed herself up from the arms on the divan until she stood facing him. "Before she left, your mother told me about you. Insisted you'd be comin' here sooner or later, you were that determined. She had faith you'd make it. I see she was right."

She turned toward the mantel as she whispered, "I never

had any idea she and Beau had …" Miss Vivian's face flushed pink to match her dress. "Now I've laid eyes on you in the daylight, there's no denyin' it. You are my brother's son. I don't care what anyone says, we are family now."

Nate sank down in his chair and put his head in his hands. This was all too much to take in. If only… his thoughts flooded with what might have happened if he'd listened to his mother and not gone after Roy. They could have stayed in Texas and… But sooner or later, Nate reminded himself, they would have come to blows. Life is uncertain, his mother had always said. Sin doesn't go unpunished either, according to Father Antoine.

He stood up. "But I want to go to the hospital. I have to know what happened. Maybe there's a chance—"

"Nate, can you drive a car?"

"Yes, ma'am. I learned in New Orleans."

"My daddy bought a Model T before he passed." She shook her head. "He never thought women should drive. Anyway, it's out back in the shed. What say you and I head over yonder to the hospital after breakfast? I know some people there."

CHAPTER TWENTY-SEVEN

B y "people," Miss Vivian meant the man in charge, as Nate found out when they arrived and were issued cloth masks to cover their mouths, and then were immediately escorted to the administration suite. After they were seated in Dr. Harrison's private office, Miss Vivian took off her mask and introduced Nate. They exchanged a few pleasantries.

"Bertie, we've dared, in the midst of all this plague, to come callin' about the Wallace family," she said. "A mother and two little girls. We need to find out if they were brought here. At least one of the little girls was bound to be admitted."

"When would that have been, Miss Vivian? I hate to bother you, but I'll need their ages and full names, too."

Nate caught the respect in his voice, and, although the doctor could have been older, he addressed her with more deference than she used with him.

She glanced at Nate and, after taking off his mask, he gave the doctor their names and ages, as best he remembered. It felt almost like referring to people he had known from his past life, when he was a different person. He was glad the doctor didn't ask what they looked like.

She added, "Maybe about two or three months ago."

"We transferred lots of patients to other hospitals, once we filled up here. This will take some digging, as our records are not well organized yet."

"We figured as much, but you'll let me know, won't you? I'm countin' on you with all my heart and soul."

"Of course. New cases have begun to slack off some, so maybe there's an end in sight."

Miss Vivian stood up. "Let's all stay hopeful and keep prayin'."

Both Nate and the doctor rose, shook hands, and followed Miss Vivian out the door. She turned to address the doctor once more.

"Bertie, give your lovely daughter Cordelia my regards and tell her I 'spect her to shine at the Cotillion, now we get to hold one this fall. Aren't we glad this awful affliction around here is clearin' up?"

"I'll let her know. She's very grateful you put her name on the presentation list. We all appreciate your kindness."

"Bless her heart." Miss Vivian linked her arm through Nate's. "I haven't been able to attend in quite some time. This year, my nephew Nate will be escorting me."

By this time, Nate knew better than to object or even react. But he would have to let Amos know he wouldn't be returning to Mason's Crossing any time soon. Not until he found his mother and sisters.

As they made their way back to the place he had parked the Model T, Nate swore to find out where his mother had gone. She wouldn't leave Lillie or Mary to fend for herself unless she...

AFTER LUNCH AND A NAP for Miss Vivian, she and Nate sat on the veranda to chat. He thought the chairs looked like thick woven threads and wondered how they could hold his weight.

She sipped sherry, which he declined. She asked him about his childhood, his education, his interests, and his skills, sighing every so often as if something else bothered her.

He thought he made a poor impression. Maybe he reminded

her too much of Beau. Or, more likely, too little.

As he recounted to her what he could remember, it seemed to him he had prospered more in the last year than his parents ever had in their whole lives. If he even still counted Roy as his parent. But he still didn't think he amounted to much.

"Have you obtained a patent on that contraption you invented?" she said.

"A what?"

"A patent. It protects your invention."

"How?"

"The U.S. government grants you a property right which prevents scalawags and scofflaws from copyin' what you made. Nobody else in the whole wide country has the right to produce it or sell it."

"Only me? And my partner." He turned thoughtful for a moment. "What if someone does anyway?"

"You take 'em to court and make 'em stop. Then they have to pay you damages."

He asked her to explain further, which she did, using words such as "public disclosure" and "article of manufacture."

Nate shook his head, wished Father Antoine could shed some light on it for him, and then said, "How do you know all this?" Amos had never mentioned getting a patent, but Nate would explain it to him in his next letter.

"Oh, honey lamb, my daddy was a judge and his daddy 'fore him."

Nate sat up straight as if someone had pricked him with a needle.

"Daddy discussed all sorts of cases at the supper table, after they were settled, of course. Mama and I absolutely hung on his every word, he was such a brilliant man."

Miss Vivian dabbed her eyes with her lace hanky and knocked back a large swallow of sherry. When she signaled, Isaac stepped forward to refill her glass. Nate hadn't even noticed him standing in the corner.

"Beau was destined to follow in their footsteps. That's why Daddy sent him off to Harvard. If he hadn't capsized his canoe in the Charles River, he'd be …" She honked her nose into her handkerchief. "He was captain of the rowin' team, you know. They beat Yale that year."

Nothing she said about her brother meant anything to Nate until he realized she was talking about his father. He decided he should pay more attention.

"Where is Harvard?"

"Up east," she sniffed, "in Boston, smack dab in the middle of where all those Yankees live."

Nate had heard the term "Yankee" more than once, not always meant as a compliment. "But he would've moved back here after he finished school, wouldn't he?"

"He would have settled down and gotten married and had a passel of chil—" Miss Vivian took another gulp of sherry.

Without being summoned, Isaac appeared at her elbow and refilled her glass.

"Mama and Daddy had a right nice girl, too," she said, "all picked out for him. Miss Claudia Wentworth, from a very fine old family, like ours."

Nate had no doubts about the "old" family, but a few about the "fine" part. What man would go off and let a girl carrying his baby get married to someone else? Didn't Beau care anything about his mother? She must have loved him, no matter what.

He decided to change the subject. "How come you never married, Miss Vivian? If you don't mind me asking."

She gave him a sad smile. "When I was younger, I had scores of gentlemen callers, all right, and I was engaged to the best of them. Reid Calhoun Pinckney stole my heart the moment we met."

A gentle breeze carried the thick scent of magnolias across the lawn to the veranda. Miss Vivian drew in a deep breath and let her head fall against the back of the chair.

Nate recognized the last name, Pinckney, from the letter he had received in Mason's Crossing. "What happened?"

"Did you ever hear of Teddy Roosevelt's Rough Riders?"

Nate shook his head. "I don't know much about—"

"Those brave boys charged up San Juan Hill and then chased the Spanish fleet out of Cuba. There weren't many American casualties."

Miss Vivian polished off the sherry in her glass and Isaac poured her another. "Reid was killed durin' the attack. A bullet through the heart."

Nate frowned at him, but the old man paid no attention. Didn't Isaac realize Miss Vivian could catch her death of cold if she spent the night on the veranda? Nate glanced around for a shawl or a lap robe, finding neither.

"Before his funeral, I put my weddin' dress away and never looked at it again."

She took another sip. "Isaac!" she called in a thick, raspy voice. "Get Duncan Pinckney on the telephone for me."

Miss Vivian pushed herself to her feet. "That man came this close"—she held up her thumb and forefinger pinched not quite together—"to becomin' my father-in-law. My daddy relied on him more than anyone." She picked up her glass, drained it, and set it on the table. "All the same, he's a lawyer, and Daddy warned me about them as a breed in general. Wait right here."

Nate watched her teeter into the house, leaning on Isaac. Harvard, Yankees, Rough Riders, Cuba. No telling where Miss Vivian's mind would go next.

A few minutes later, she returned to the veranda. "Duncan Pinckney will see us tomorrow morning at ten a.m. He'll start the process for gettin' a patent on your oil well doohickey."

Nate smiled. Miss Vivian might have taken a lot of detours, but she came full circle at last.

THE COST FOR MR. PINCKNEY'S work on preparing and filing for the patent was more than Nate had brought with him and more than his share of the profits at the bank in Mason's Crossing. He'd have to ask Amos for another advance, or skip the whole thing and take his chances.

"Don't worry," said Miss Vivian with a grin. "I'll take it out of your inheritance."

Nate whirled his head toward her as if he'd been slapped. My what? He glanced at Mr. Pinckney, who continued jotting notes on a stack of papers like he hadn't heard.

"You will be at the Cotillion, won't you, Mr. Pinckney?" she cooed, rising from her chair.

"Wouldn't miss it." He gave her a warm, indulgent smile, but it faded when his gaze switched to Nate. He nodded and offered Nate his hand. "Mr. Wallace, good day to you."

His handshake was firm, and his tone was formal, cool, distant. "I'll contact you when the papers are ready to sign. It will take several weeks to complete the search."

Nate returned his forceful handshake. Another delay in getting back to Mason's Crossing. What would Amos say?

Miss Vivian linked her arm through Nate's, the same gesture he remembered as they left Dr. Harrison's office. "We'll all be admirin' that lovely granddaughter, won't we?"

"Alexandra's looking forward to it. Her grandmother, her mother, all her aunts, and now she will carry on the family tradition this fall. They are positively scatterbrained about the whole thing."

"It's an impo'tant milestone in a girl's life, when she has

her debut." Miss Vivian patted the back of her head, under the wide brim of her silk hat. "By the by, if you recommend it, I'm thinkin' of takin' Nate over to Blakemore & Sons. He'll need fittin' for a new tuxedo."

For a second, Mr. Pinckney's bushy salt-and-pepper eyebrows shot up. "Mr. Blakemore is a… wise choice. The men in my family have always depended on him."

"Although…" she glanced up and down at Nate as if he were a racehorse, "we might could find one of Beau's and have it altered, if it can be tailored in the latest style. Mr. Blakemore made it for him originally, back 'fore he left for college."

"Of course. If you think that's appropriate." Mr. Pinckney held open his office door for them. "May I ask my secretary to call you a cab?"

"No, thank you kindly." She stared him in the face. "Nate's been driving Daddy's old Model T. He's learnin' his way around Charleston just fine. Should know all the impo'tant streets like the back of his hand in no time."

The lawyer bowed slightly from the neck only. "I see."

Miss Vivian seemed to be giving Mr. Pinckney a message behind her words. What did she have in mind?

MISS VIVIAN HADN'T TOLD Nate about their next stop. At her direction, he pulled up and parked in front of Mrs. Chester's School for Etiquette and Deportment on Montagu Street.

"This is where I went to finishing school," Miss Vivian told him.

"Did you get finished?"

She giggled. "Oh, mercy, yes, I did. Top of my class in table manners, curtsyin', dancin', and learnin' how to carry on a conversation. Overall compo'tment, you might say."

Nate figured he might never say that word. "What are we

doing here?"

"Nate, we're goin' to finish your education."

He gripped the steering wheel. "I ain't going in there. It's for girls."

"You don't have to go to school here. We'll get Mrs. Chester to come to the house for private lessons."

"What for? I already know how to carry on a conversation. Been doing it all my life."

"If I'm goin' to introduce you to the impo'tant families in Charleston, you will need to know how to mingle at their level. You have a lot of unrealized potential, and, while sho'tage of experience can be fixed over time, I can't allow lack of social trainin' to hold you back now."

"Father Antoine told me to get a good education. It was one of the last things he said to me before I left New Orleans."

"He was right." Miss Vivian patted his arm. "You seem very bright and responsible for someone so young. I have no doubt, given the right boost, you can become anythin' you want."

"I just want to find my family."

"We have to wait on Dr. Harrison. Meanwhile, let's go visit Mrs. Chester and see if she can teach you to waltz."

Nate rolled his eyes, but got out of the car and followed Miss Vivian up the front steps.

THAT NIGHT AT DINNER, Miss Vivian finished most of a bottle of red wine all by herself. Nate wondered why Isaac kept filling her glass. After Isaac steadied Miss Vivian on her feet, she hobbled toward the parlor.

"You comin', Beau?" said Miss Vivian as she passed Nate, who stood at his seat.

Nate followed them to the hallway but didn't go in. He stopped Isaac as he returned to the entry hall.

"Why do you let her drink so much?"

"For the pain, Mr. Nate. For the pain."

"From what? Is she still sick?"

Isaac shook his head. "Her mama and her daddy, they passed just las' year 'bout six weeks apart. She done lost ever'body. Only she not strong like you. You at the beginnin' of yo' life, but she toward the end. She ain't got no prospects for any day being diff'rent from t'other. Leastways, not 'til you showed up."

"What do you mean?"

"You her nephew, ain't you?"

"I guess so… but…"

"You, Mr. Nate, you is her onliest kin now. You all she gots. Deep down or not, you a Rutledge, ain't you? Tha's the most impo'tant thing to her, you see. Her fam'ly. She 'spects you to carry on the fam'ly name."

The old man trudged down the hallway toward the back of the house. Nate stared after him.

Miss Vivian had lost all her family and maybe all her hope. He had no idea they had so much in common. But was he truly part of her family? Could she be part of his?

"Beau?" Miss Vivian called. "You out there?"

Nate sighed. He went in to the parlor and, when Miss Vivian patted the seat on the divan next to her, he didn't hesitate to sit by her. This time, he reached for her hand and held it until she fell asleep.

CHAPTER TWENTY-EIGHT

A week later, they had heard nothing yet from Dr. Harrison, so Miss Vivian suggested another trip downtown. Nate brought the car from the shed to the side door and got out to help her into the passenger seat.

"How you like drivin' my daddy's automobile?" Miss Vivian said as she pulled her skirt inside the door and tucked it under her. "It's nice to have somebody to drive me around."

"It's real fine, thank you very much." Nate didn't think she needed a driver full time. She never seemed to go anywhere except with him. Shouldn't rich ladies have a life in their own society?

"Are we going to the hospital to see Dr. Harrison again?" Nate shifted the gears and turned from the driveway to the street.

"Not yet. He needs more time. If I've learned anything about him during my illness, it's that he's thorough."

"I expect that's a good quality in a doctor."

She turned to face him. "It's highly desirable in a carpenter or a mechanic, or anybody else, for that matter. If you're smart or lucky, you can survive a calamity, but you'll suffer a lot less when you're thorough, my daddy always said. Let that be a lesson to you, Nate."

"Yes, ma'am." He turned at the corner. "Where to?"

"This mornin', we're goin' to the bank. I have a mind to get some things settled, and Mr. Hodges is just the gentleman to see." Miss Vivian folded her hands in her lap, where they remained until Nate parked the Model T in front of the red brick building with the high arched windows.

He scampered around the back of the car to open the door and help Miss Vivian down to the curb. She held onto his arm as they crossed the sidewalk and he pushed open the glass-paneled front door.

A young man in a dark suit, who looked to be about Nate's age, greeted them and escorted them toward Mr. Hodges' corner office. Nate puzzled over how someone got a job in a bank. What did he have to know to get hired? Lots of schooling, he figured.

As they passed a secretary's desk, she stood up and nodded. "Good morning, Miss Rutledge. May I bring you some tea or coffee?"

Nate wondered if Sam Carolla's secretary would extend the same greeting. More likely, she'd ask if he preferred a gun or a knife.

"Tea would be lovely, thank you." Miss Vivian returned the nod. "Nate?"

"Oh, uh, noth—" He glanced at Miss Vivian. "I'll take some tea also, please." He might as well test his progress on his etiquette lessons with Mrs. Chester.

They entered the office and Mr. Hodges stood up and came around his desk to pull out a chair for Miss Vivian, who introduced them as she sat. He shook hands with Nate, and after the secretary brought the tea and served all three, he settled back in his chair.

"What may I do for you today, Miss Rutledge?" His lips parted without smiling, showing crooked stained teeth. They reminded Nate of the old fence behind their house in Clark's Common.

"You have all my daddy's impo'tant documents," said Miss Vivian.

"Yes, we keep them here in a safe deposit box. The gov'ment doesn't make us do that. It's just a little extra service we provide for our best customers, as well as our board members, like you."

Nate thought his effort to smile was as oily as his slicked-back hair. He knew a little about banks. Roy used to say they kept your money and asked "what for" when you wanted it back.

"Does that include the title to his Model T?"

"Yes, we executed the records for the transaction of sale when he bought it."

"As you know, I am my daddy's sole heir, bein' the only survivin' child of all the chil'ren he and Mama had." Miss Vivian paused as she sipped her tea. "That means the automobile now belongs to me, doesn't it?"

Mr. Hodges sat up straighter. "Why, yes, it does. That's a fact."

Nate peeked at her from the corner of his eye. So Miss Vivian had lost other brothers and sisters, too?

"And I can do with it whatever I wish, can't I?"

"Yes, of course. But… but you aren't going to try to learn to drive it, are you? That would be un—"

Miss Vivian tittered like a schoolgirl. "Gosh sakes, no. I couldn't figure out how to make it go, not in a hun'red years." She shook her head and set her saucer on the edge of his desk. "I want to give it to Nate."

Nate almost dropped his teacup, catching it before it tipped over the edge of the saucer. He turned to stare at her. "You what?"

Mr. Hodges eyes widened. "My, oh my, this is rather… sudden."

"You can draw up… oh, silly me, what did you call them… the transaction papers, can't you, Mr. Hodges?"

Miss Vivian smiled and stood up from her chair to her full height. "And while you're at it, please be sure his name is registered on all my accounts. All the ones my daddy left me."

"But Miss Vivian, you hardly... why, he's not..." Mr. Hodges rose halfway from his chair.

"Let me know when you have everythin' ready for our signatures."

When she eyed him, steady as a hammer on a nail, he sat down again and changed his tone. "What name should I enter for him?" He glanced at Nate.

Miss Vivian whirled to face Nate. "Which will it be?"

Nate stood up and looked her directly in the eyes, searching for something familiar, something of home or family. A glimmer, a whisper, anything would do. Maybe their shared losses would be enough.

"Rutledge," he said. "Nate Rutledge."

She nodded, and after a moment Miss Vivian's eyes twinkled as she turned back to Mr. Hodges. "Say, your daughter Lorelei will be ready for Cotillion next month, won't she?"

"Yes, her brother William will be escorting her. He's home now from the academy just for the summer, but he'll be back in plenty of time."

"We look forward to seeing her, rather, both of them, there."

They shook hands, left his office, and when Miss Vivian and Nate reached the car, he said with a wry grin, "I guess I better learn to waltz after all."

On the way home, Nate wondered what his mother would say. He didn't care what Roy would think, but he couldn't help but suspect his mother had planned for him to become a Rutledge all along.

But had he just traded a name for a car? Was it that simple?

EVERY TUESDAY AND FRIDAY mornings, Mrs. Chester brought phonograph records to play on Miss Vivian's old

Victrola. Nate turned the crank for her and then watched as she placed the needle on the disc record. The music came out scratchy-sounding, like listening through wrinkled paper to the band in the park in New Orleans.

He thought they must look comical dancing together, as she was short and plump. Once he asked Miss Vivian to dance, and she blushed and tsk-tsked, but stood up and took his hand.

Her expression turned dreamy-eyed until the Victrola ran out of steam and Nate had to turn the crank again. She told him he was a natural.

On Monday and Wednesday afternoons, Mrs. Chester made him practice table manners. He thought it was silly to pretend to eat from an empty plate, count spoons and forks from the outside toward the center, and fold his napkin. Even worse was when Isaac held a bare platter next to his left shoulder and Nate faked serving himself.

One evening at dinner, Miss Vivian said, "Nate, I think it's time we give your new table manners a rehearsal."

"We've already been doing a dry run without the food on the plates."

"A dry run?" She served herself from the tray Isaac held, and after he served Nate, he returned to the kitchen.

"You know, like when the fire wagon drivers practice without water, just to get their timing down."

She shook her head. "No, I mean, a dinner party. Now the Spanish flu is almost over, we can start livin' normal lives again."

"Yes, ma'am, if you say so." Nate wasn't sure he knew what his normal life would be like.

"Let's start with the Pinckneys and the Wentworths. Of course, that means the Courtenays as well, since Claudia married into their family instead of ours."

"Won't... er, how do I say this? Won't she get a bit of a shock when she sees me? Seeing as how I look like... well, you know."

"I'll warn her ahead of time."

"Then she might not come."

"Oh, she'll come, all right. She owes me."

"She owes you money?"

Miss Vivian giggled, but turned serious a second later. "No, something else." She cheered up. "All of them should be invited."

"What for? I don't know any of them, except Mr. Pinckney."

"But you will, and they'll become part of your circle, once you get settled here."

"Miss Vivian—"

"Aunt Vivian, from now on."

Nate swallowed. He didn't like going against anything she said, but he couldn't let this slide. "Now… Aunt Vivian, you know I'm headed back to Mason's Crossing the minute I find my mother and my sisters. There was never any talk of me settling here."

"Oh, but Nate, this has become a second home to you, hasn't it? It's what your dear mother wants for you." She dabbed at the corner of her eyes with her lace hanky. "Don't you like it here?"

"Of course, and you've been wonderful and mighty generous about everything, but I came to Charleston to find my family, not…" He sighed.

"Aren't I your fam'ly?" Miss Vivian's voice grew small and quiet, like a shy little girl's.

Nate squirmed. "You're the best aunt I ever had. But I have my work, and there's Amos, and he's counting on me to expand the business, because we're partners and… and… well, anyway, I have to travel to get new customers."

"You could get lots of new customers here. I could introduce you—"

"To who? You know any wildcatters?"

"Any what?"

"Don't you see, Miss, uh, Aunt Vivian, eventually I have to go back? That's my life over there, not this one. This is more like a dream."

Miss Vivian sat up straight and took a sip of her wine. "Sometimes dreams come true."

They finished their dinner in silence, as Nate considered what he should do. After Miss Vivian drained the wine bottle, Isaac came back in the dining room and steadied her on their nightly stroll to the parlor. This time, she didn't refer to Nate as Beau or ask him to come in.

"No, they don't, Miss Vivian," whispered Nate as he lingered in the hall. "Dreams are just dreams."

Chapter Twenty-Nine

The next morning after breakfast Miss Vivian took him to Blakemore & Sons to be fitted for a new suit and tuxedo. She had already searched the closet in Beau's old room, but couldn't find anything acceptable.

"New is better for you than made-over anyway," she said. "Besides, you have shot up into a strappin' young man, even larger and taller than Beau. Maybe you're not even finished growin' yet."

Nate nodded, but thought it best not to stir up conversation about family members long departed. Mr. Blakemore suggested fabrics and styles for Miss Vivian's approval, while Nate stood still for the measurements and nodded when she asked him if he liked everything.

"Yes, ma'am, thank you," he said.

When Mr. Blakemore went to the back of the store and left them alone, Nate sat down next to Miss Vivian. "Why are you buying all these clothes for me? What good will it do?"

She sighed and dabbed her mouth with her lace handkerchief. "I guess it's time to tell you, Nate."

"Tell me what?" He caught his breath and waited.

"Before your mother left my house for the last time, she made me promise to take care of you, in case she ..."

Nate bit his lip and looked down at his shoes.

"In fact, I thought it would be easy to give you a small sum of money and send you on your way." She gave him a feeble smile. "I didn't count on gettin' this attached or findin' so many…"—she shrugged—"things to do together. Like I used to do with Beau before he left for college."

"But Miss, uh… Aunt Vivian, I'm not Beau."

She poked his knee. "Yes, I know that, even after a glass or two of sherry. You see, Beau was quite a few years younger'n I, so it was almost like I helped bring him up. Mama had servants, of course, and a nanny for all the chil'ren, but Beau, he was special. He was like my own little boy, the one I never had. And now you…"

Miss Vivian sniffled. "Don't mind me, Nate. I'm just an old lady indulgin' her memories. And you've made me happier these last few weeks than I've been in decades."

"You're the kindest lady I know," said Nate as he took her hand and draped it over his arm.

What could it hurt to stay a while longer in Charleston? He would write again to Amos and explain his obligations.

If he found his mother and sisters, maybe they could all live with Miss Vivian, just like a regular family. Later he could still travel and sell the blowout preventers wherever anyone drilled for oil. He'd put Arkansas, Ohio, and Pennsylvania on his route. His trips would take longer, so he'd miss out on the hustle and bustle of home life, but—

His thoughts came to a sudden stop. Did he just say *if?* Surely he meant *when.*

When they finished their business at Blakemore & Sons, Miss Vivian and Nate returned home for lunch, followed by a nap for her.

As he had every afternoon since he learned his way around Charleston, Nate drove the car out to the poor neighborhoods and asked every person who would talk to him if they knew anything about a woman named Evelyn Wallace, or her little girls, Mary and Lillie.

The answers were always the same, sometimes in words,

other times just shrugs. But he asked anyway.

ON THE LAST DAY OF the month, Dr. Harrison called Miss Vivian to let her know he could come visit them, if she didn't mind waiting until tomorrow afternoon. She told him Nate was anxious to hear any news, so they would arrive at the hospital within the hour, right after lunch. She would forego her nap.

"How did his voice sound?" Nate said as he drove them toward downtown.

"Saints alive, but you're racin' along. The wind is 'bout to blow this hat clean off my head, with all my hair attached to it." She sat up straight as Nate slowed down. "Goodness, that's better."

"Well?"

"Oh, Dr. Harrison? He might as well've been readin' his wife's grocery list."

After they reached the hospital and settled into chairs in Dr. Harrison's office, Nate kept still and stared across the desk at him. Dr. Harrison took off his wire-rimmed glasses and rubbed his eyes, as if he hadn't slept in days.

"Miss Vivian, we searched through all our records back four months or more. That's why it took so long. We only found one name."

Nate held his breath.

"A Mary Wallace, age approximately seven, was brought here with high fever, on May 23rd," he said as he shuffled a sheet of paper. "She stayed for eighteen days, and when she began to show signs of improvement—"

Nate let out his breath

"—we released her to a convalescent hospital."

Miss Vivian gripped Nate's hand without looking at him.

"Pray tell, where would that have been?"

"Over to Sisters of Mercy in Savannah."

Nate stood up. "Then I'll go to Savannah."

Dr. Harrison put his glasses back on. "That won't be necessary."

Nate sat down. "Why not?"

"The Sisters sent her back to Charleston when she recovered."

Nate grinned and looked up at the ceiling. "Halleluia!" His smile faded. "But where is she now?"

"Well, that's the problem," the doctor said. "Since there was no adult to claim her and we didn't know anything about…"

Miss Vivian shook her head as if she couldn't believe what she heard.

"In fact, we assumed she had no family left, given the circumstances under which she arrived here, we had no choice but to send her to the local orphanage. She couldn't stay here, not with new patients arriving at all hours. We needed every single bed. The epidemic hadn't run its full course yet."

"So now we just go get—"

"I'm dreadfully sorry to have to tell you this," Dr. Harrison said as he smoothed the sheet of paper on his desk, "but the orphanage closed by order of the health department, after the minister and his wife, who ran the place, both died. The children were shipped off anywhere a shelter could be found for them. Two months ago."

"What does your paper say about Mary? Where did she end up?"

Dr. Harrison sat in silence. After a moment, he looked up at Nate. "The record stops there. I can assure you she recovered, but I can't tell you where she is now. Most likely another orphanage, maybe even in another state."

Nate felt like his lungs and guts had twisted from a tornado.

He fought to keep from jumping up and screaming, instead swiveling in his chair to face the wall for a moment so they wouldn't see his face.

"Oh, my dear boy," said Miss Vivian as she sniffled. "We have to keep searchin' for her." She shook her lace hanky at Dr. Harrison. "But what about Evie and our precious tee-ninesie Lillie?"

As he studied the doctor's expression, Nate waited for his answer.

The doctor clenched his jaw until his face muscles twitched. "I'm awfully sorry, Miss Vivian, but I have no history of anyone else named Wallace."

"Lord help us, where are we goin' to look next?" Miss Vivian cast her searching eyes from Dr. Harrison to Nate, and back. "Surely there's someone else we could inquire of, someone who keeps records like that?"

Dr. Harrison lowered his gaze without speaking.

"Oh." Miss Vivian pursed her lips.

If he couldn't find them, if they had died, then Nate had failed to bring their unhappy separation to an end. His family didn't exist, there was no comfort for him. He was nothing. The darkness would swallow him, unless...

Nate stood up and extended his hand. "Thank you for your thorough work, Dr. Harrison. I appreciate your care of my sister."

He took Miss Vivian by the elbow and helped her to her feet. "I know what I have to do."

He could do it. If his mother and Lillie have died, maybe he could find out from the undertaker where they were buried. Then he would do just as his mother taught him by her own example. He would shut down his heart, either bit by bit or all at once, and not let the hurt in.

It's the only way I can survive.

MISS VIVIAN LEFT NATE to himself for several days, while he sat for hours at a time on the veranda or stalked around the porches and out to the edges of the property without seeing the gardens. Sometimes he took off in the car and didn't come back until dark. He was grateful she said nothing, especially when he felt like he might explode.

After dinner one evening, as they sat together in the parlor, he said, "I need to keep busy on something I can see. All this looking around is getting me nowhere."

"Did you find anythin' at all?"

"Only the orphanage that closed. But now the building is partly burned."

"I read where people did that, tryin' to kill the influenza. We're lucky the whole town didn't go up in flames."

"No one can tell me anything. Where could those children be?"

"Maybe they'd come back, if they had a place to come back to."

"What are you saying?" Nate sat up straight and turned to look her full in the face.

"You need a project to keep you occupied, don't you?" Miss Vivian shrugged. "Why don't you rebuild the orphanage?"

He frowned and shook his head. "How would I do that? I don't have any money."

"That shouldn't stop you." She smiled. "I know some people who would help."

Nate was convinced that Miss Vivian could get her "people" to do anything, even if they were bank presidents, lawyers, or hospital administrators. All she had to do was ask.

They spent the rest of the evening drawing up plans for the new orphanage. As she sipped her brandy, she even persuaded

Nate to try a taste. He liked it better than he expected.

MR. BLAKEMORE CALLED TO schedule a fitting for Nate four days before Miss Vivian had arranged for the dinner party. He assured her the new suit and tuxedo would be ready in time.

At five o'clock on the day of the party, Nate came downstairs and searched for Miss Vivian in the parlor, then the veranda. He found her in the dining room, giving instructions to Isaac.

"Oh, there you are, Nate," she gushed. "Turn 'round and let me inspect you."

He obeyed.

"Like a heartthrob in this suit, just imagine what a tuxedo will do for you." Miss Vivian clutched her hands to her chest. "Mighty handsome, yes indeedy."

With a clucking sound, she edged her way around the table, laid with china and crystal and silverware, and tucked a little piece of paper into a gold stand next to each dinner plate. Nate leaned over to read what she had written: Mrs. Pinckney. It wouldn't do if she sat in the wrong chair.

He followed Miss Vivian around the table, reading all the names. He found his own at the head of the table, opposite his aunt at the other end. Mrs. Courtenay would be seated on his right, with her brother, Mr. Wentworth, on his left. Wasn't Miss Vivian taking a terrible chance?

As soon as Isaac left the dining room on an errand, Nate moved to stand next to Miss Vivian. "Can I ask you something?"

"Of course, dear boy."

"What do I say when Mrs. Courtenay asks me about my parents? Especially my mother?"

"Don't you worry your handsome head. She won't say anythin' about that."

"How do you know?"

"I've already spoken to her privately, and she's in complete agreement that it's best to let some sleepin' hound dogs lie."

"Won't Mr. Wentworth mention it?"

"Claudia will have convinced her brother not to broach the subject either."

Nate narrowed his eyes. "What's going on here? Why are these people so willing to overlook my background?"

Miss Vivian gave him a wry smile. "You think the Rutledges are the only fam'ly with an inconvenient secret?" She tottered toward the kitchen, calling Puddy's name.

Nate's eyes swept the table again. How would Mrs. Courtenay and her brother feel if they found themselves sitting next to the Rutledge family's former maid?

CHAPTER THIRTY

At dinner that evening, Nate found Mrs. Courtenay staring at him every time he looked in her direction. She chatted about anything except Nate's parents, and Mr. Wentworth expressed interest in Nate's invention.

"Of course, I wouldn't allow any drilling on my land, even if South Carolina did have oil," he said.

"You'd be missing a profitable opportunity," said Nate. "The oil business will do nothing but grow from now on. It's turned some folks into millionaires overnight."

Mr. Wentworth shook his head and gave Nate an indulgent smile, as if addressing a child. "Our family has depended on cotton and tobacco for many generations, my boy. I'm not about to change now."

"All the same," said Mrs. Courtenay, "how do you know the oil business will grow? It just seems so dirty." She shuddered.

Nate leaned toward her. "Do you own a car, Mrs. Courtenay?"

"My husband does."

"What about your two sons?" He nodded at the young men seated across from each other toward the middle of the table. "They'll each want cars, too, someday soon, won't they?"

He didn't wait for her reply, but turned toward her brother. "Do you enjoy reading history, Mr. Wentworth?"

"Yes, I'm a big fan. Biography and military history, mostly."

"I'd be grateful for some suggestions later." Nate cleared his throat. "Do you know the ratio of horses to men at the outbreak of the Great War? Three to one."

"Interesting. What's your point?"

"Horses consume a lot more food than men. Supplies at the front became a logistical burden."

"But the railroads can move troops, horses, and supplies in huge quantities."

Nate tapped the tablecloth with his forefinger. "When British forces landed in France in 1914, they had very limited means of transportation. By the end of the war, there were over 150,000 cars and trucks, and a few motorcycles, at the front. Including that new armored vehicle. Thanks to the Americans."

"The tank. Yes, I've read about it. It revolutionized tactical warfare from the trenches."

"It's first on the list of what made the German High Command admit defeat. By the way, the tank runs on oil power."

"Pray we don't need to use it ever again," said Mrs. Courtenay. "Let this be the end of all wars."

Mr. Wentworth shrugged. "I think the railroads have revolutionized transportation in this country, much as they did in Europe. Tell me, Nate, do you have much experience riding a train?"

Nate gave him half a smile. "Some, and what I learned is that I can only go where the tracks are laid."

"Then what do you envision as a solution?" He winked at his sister, seated opposite him.

"Recently I read an article about a young Major Eisenhower, who took a convoy of trucks across the whole country."

"What good will that do? He could have accomplished the same thing in less time by taking the train."

"His aim was to evaluate America's roads, which are more flexible than train tracks. More people means more cars, so the country'll need more roads." Nate shifted in his seat. "How did you get your crops to market ten years ago, Mr. Wentworth?"

"Why, in wagons, of course."

"What about now?"

"I ship only to local companies for processing."

"In trucks?" Nate tried to keep from smiling.

Mr. Wentworth nodded, but didn't seem happy about it.

"What if, and I'm talking about the future here," said Nate, "those small local companies shut down because someone else opened a bigger factory in a central location, and took away all the business? Because they process it faster and cheaper, they could beat out the local prices."

"You misjudge the value of loyalty," said Mr. Wentworth in a huffy voice.

"Oh, I'm a big believer in loyalty," said Nate. "I'm just careful not to put it in the wrong place. I want to be faithful to my family, to my business partner, and to those who work hard for us, but I also believe my first job is to make a profit. What good does it do anyone if I don't keep up with the changing marketplace? That includes transportation. Which, in turn, drives the need for oil."

"He's got you there, Horace," said Mrs. Courtenay with a smirk. "Tell me, Nate, what else are you interested in, besides oil wells, trucks, and making a fortune, that is?"

What could he say? She wouldn't want to hear what brought him to South Carolina in the first place, and he didn't think she would find fit conversation in tales of Clyde and him hustling the arm wrestlers and gamblers in saloons.

"Well, I'm looking forward to bringing Aunt Vivian to the Cotillion next month. She's counting on me to escort her."

"Yes, she's shared with me her aspirations for you." Mrs. Courtenay leaned closer to him. "I hope you'll write your name on Georgiana's dance card." She swept her long eyelashes at him and glanced at her daughter, seated next to Mr. Wentworth.

For a moment, Nate studied the girl, about seventeen, pretty, but unremarkable, not as fetching as her mother once must have been. "Does she like to waltz?"

"Simply adores it. Comes naturally to her, of course. She won the top dance prize from Mrs. Chester."

Nate swallowed hard.

The rest of the dinner went smoothly, and during the after-dinner chat in the parlor, Mrs. Wentworth secured a promise from Nate to write his name on her daughter Charlotte's dance card as well. Miss Vivian smiled from her divan, where she had seated herself like a queen on a throne.

Isaac served coffee, with a bottle of brandy on the side for the men. Nate figured Miss Vivian would help herself, maybe even finish the bottle, after everyone left.

Mrs. Pinckney patted the seat next to her for Nate to sit and join her. Her daughter Alexandra sat across from them, listening to Miss Vivian.

By this time, Nate knew what she'd get around to suggesting. After a few minutes of idle conversation, Mrs. Pinckney asked and he agreed.

All three girls were attractive enough, while Alexandra was downright beautiful, and he thought maybe his skill in dancing wouldn't be too embarrassing. Probably he should learn something besides the waltz and the foxtrot.

Mrs. Chester could explain about dance cards and what writing his name on one meant. How much trouble could he get into with three different ones?

THE NEXT MORNING NATE awoke, surprised to find his first thoughts were of Alexandra Pinckney, not his sister Mary or the new orphanage. The granddaughter of Aunt Vivian's lawyer came from a different world than his, but he had started to like it. Was this what his mother had in mind?

Although Alexandra had smiled at him, they had hardly spoken at dinner last night, but maybe the Cotillion would offer more opportunities to get better acquainted. Nate sprang from his bed, determined to get more dancing lessons from Mrs. Chester. He'd figure out what to say to Alexandra later.

Meanwhile, he needed to find out where his mother and Lillie might be, apart from Mary, if they were buried somewhere, if anyone even knew. How would he go about finding Mary?

The empty feeling in his insides returned, like unwanted company that wouldn't leave for good. Keeping busy, ordering lumber and supplies, even working alongside the carpenters would help. He'd have to figure out some way to advertise the orphanage.

After he dressed, he went downstairs to the breakfast room and found Aunt Vivian already seated, drinking her coffee and reading the newspaper. She lowered the paper and grinned. "Good mornin', sunshine."

Nate poured himself a cup of coffee from the silver pot on the buffet, sat down, and waited for Isaac to bring him a plate of eggs and bacon. Aunt Vivian passed him the silver breadbasket and he helped himself to biscuits, along with butter and peach jam.

She set the paper down on the table. "I thought we might go visitin' today."

"Visiting? Who?"

"It'd be nice for you to meet some more people. Like Mrs. Hodges and her daughter Lorelei, and Mrs. Harrison and her daughter Cordelia." Her eyes twinkled more than usual.

"So I can write my name on their dance cards?"

"I never said—"

"No, you didn't, but it's starting to dawn on me that you've got a scheme in mind. Maybe you've been planning all along to put these, uh, temptations in my path."

"What a wild thing to say. I most certainly would never… well, I just thought… you're a young man and you need friends your own age. You can't find my company that fascinatin' all the livelong day." She sipped her coffee. "Besides, it was your mother's brilliant idea, not mine."

Her voice had lost its indignant tone and turned soft, while her eyes grew misty. "She was a lot smarter than I am."

"What did you and she talk about? I mean, when she got here?"

"After we got through reminiscin' about the family, she told me about you. Said you were the brightest child she ever knew. She had consid'rable expectations that you would amount to someone impo'tant, if you could get beyond havin' the same means of employment as your step-daddy."

"I didn't find out he wasn't my father until right before I left." Nate swallowed hard, as a familiar knot gripped his stomach. "Did she tell you about that, too?"

"Only that her plan was to get you out of there and over here to Charleston as soon as possible."

Miss Vivian's hand shook as she sipped her coffee, so much that the cup rattled when she set it in the saucer. "She looked for you every day, never lost hope you would come."

"You said she helped you through the worst time of your life. Was that when Mr. Pinckney died?"

"Oh, yes. All I could do was curl up in a ball and wish I could die, too. Couldn't even get out of bed for two whole weeks."

Isaac brought Nate his breakfast plate, and Nate nodded his thanks. The old man stood at the end of the buffet and waited, eyes down, hands folded in front.

"Your mother stayed by my side all through my grief, even when my own parents gave up. She taught me how to be strong, but I'll never be as good at it as she was."

"That sounds just like her."

"I can't believe she's gone. Jus' like all the others."

"Don't say that!" He softened his tone. "It might not be true."

Isaac cleared his throat and raised his eyes to meet Nate's. He seemed to signal something and Nate resolved to catch him alone and find out what he was hinting at.

NATE HAD TO WAIT UNTIL Miss Vivian finished her morning calls. He drove her first to Mrs. Hodges' home, where he met Lorelei, then to Mrs. Harrison's, but Cordelia was out visiting.

He noted that both homes were of the same size and style of furnishings as the Rutledge's. He believed he could get used to it.

Shoving Isaac's urging to the back of his mind, he tried to be attentive, but couldn't bring himself to do more than agree with their comments about the weather and the upcoming Cotillion. He figured Mrs. Chester would criticize a thing or two about his conversation skills.

Upon leaving each house, Miss Vivian promised the mother a dinner party at her home. "Within a week or so," she said.

When they arrived home in time for lunch, Isaac held out a small silver tray with a handwritten envelope on it.

"It's from Claudia Courtenay," said Miss Vivian, even before she tore it open.

Nate raised his eyebrows.

She pulled out a single folded sheet of paper. "We're invited to dinner next Friday evenin'."

"Why didn't she just call and ask you?"

"That would be too informal. Invitations should be specific and in writin', very personal." She smiled and clasped the paper to her chest. "The social merry-go-round is startin' up again. Oh, how heav'nly it shall be, to have this so-called quarantine lifted."

"If you say so."

"Oh, but Nate. You don't realize what I've been missin' all these months. No, it's more like years since I've had any excuse to socialize. You can't imagine how hard it is, to sit 'round and watch. When Mama and Papa got old and sick, I had to stay home and care for them. Not that I minded, of course, but ever'body else seemed to get what they wanted."

He looked around the dining room, at the silver and crystal and china. "Like what?"

What could his aunt possibly lack?

"Children who grow up and get married and have children. Claudia is already a grandmother, three times over."

"She doesn't look old enough."

"Her son is several years ahead of Georgiana, and he married early, his first year in college, so he could start a family right away." She raised her eyebrows and gave him an intent stare.

"Is that what all these mamas have in mind? Maybe their daughters, too?"

Miss Vivian didn't answer for a few moments. "During the war," she said in a quiet voice, "mothers began to worry there wouldn't be enough young men left to go 'round. Too many of our Carolina boys are buried in France."

Nate wondered if they lay near little Walter's father.

Miss Vivian sighed. "I think my friends are all afraid their daughters will turn out like me."

Before Nate could reply, Isaac came into the dining room to clear away their plates. He caught Nate's eye again, and nodded toward the veranda. Nate helped Miss Vivian from her chair to the hallway and up the stairs to her bedroom door.

When the door closed, he took the stairs down to the hallway three at a time and rushed to the veranda. Isaac stood near the corner, waiting for him.

"What do you want to tell me?' Nate said. He gestured to the wicker chair, but Isaac wouldn't sit down.

Isaac cleared his throat. "Mr. Nate, I sho' hope you don't think I been keepin' nothin' from you. 'Til this very mo'nin', I never figured it was my place to say—"

"Do you know something about my family? Where are they?"

"Miss Vivian, she took so sick, drove clean out of her mind, she don't remember what happened. Yo' family never went to no hotel."

"Did they stay here?"

"Yessir, and yo' mama done tended Miss Vivian, 'til she and ever'body 'cept Puddy and me come down with the 'fluenza. We thought they's all gonna die, right here in they beds." A slow tear trickled down Isaac's wrinkled cheek.

Nate listened without stirring. He wasn't sure he was even breathing.

"Yo' mama had it worse'n the others. Fever like a torment from the devil hisself." His tears flowed until his face was wet. "Mr. Nate, I'm so sorry I hafta tell you. First she passed, then the one little girl, a short spell later."

"Lillie." Nate swallowed hard and stared at Isaac, trying to picture his mother so sick and weak, weak enough to die. He couldn't bring up an image of her at all.

Maybe this was how his mother had pulled through losing all those babies. She had showed him how not to burden anyone else with his sorrows, and he determined to follow her example.

"Tha's right. Seemed like death done planted itself right on the do'step. Puddy and me, we figured the other little girl would do a mite better at the hospital. Miss Mary wasn't so bad off."

"How did you get her there? Dr. Harrison never said where she came from."

"We couldn't carry her over yonder. Puddy was too sore 'fraid to leave the house, on account of the plague, and I can't drive no automobile. We finally got my cousin to bring his wagon 'round, and he took her."

"But didn't he tell them where she lived?"

"Mr. Nate, that hospital's for white folks. Ain't nobody gonna take the word of no colored man 'bout nothin'. Besides, they almos' chased him off after they done took Miss Mary in. I couldn't no way get him to go back and ask after her."

He shook his head. "We didn't s'pose she'd get sent away."

Nate nodded and stared at the floor. "Then Aunt Vivian never knew what really happened."

"She done took it awful hard las' year, when her mama and daddy passed. I figured tellin' her would be same as breakin' her heart again. The grief'd plumb do her in. You think mebbe I was wrong not to tell Miss Vivian the truth?"

"Isaac, you didn't mean any harm. You were just protecting her. In your shoes, I might have done the same."

"You sho' be understandin', Mr. Nate. And I'm powerful sorry you lost yo' family. I knows what tha's like." Isaac bowed his head and turned to enter the house.

"Isaac," Nate called.

The old man stopped and faced Nate. "Yessir."

"Where are they buried?"

"Puddy and me, we done talked 'bout that 'fore we… well, Miss Vivian still wasn't in no shape to make no choices. We couldn't see clear to lay them in the Rutledge fam'ly plot without her say-so. The folks what come for them, they done put them in the public cem'tery, across the river. They ain't no head-stones, but we gots a drawin' what shows the place. They right next t' each other."

Nate had buried enough of his younger brothers and sisters to know how his mother would have liked it. Next to each other was just right.

Isaac went back inside the house, and Nate sat down. For so many months, he had dragged hope around like one of his sister's tattered rag dolls, waiting for good news of his family. He had prayed for some way to find them, bring them all back together, keep them safe from...

Now the lost time, the distance, the fear of sickness had piled on until he felt bone-tired. He tried to imagine what he would do, how he would face each day, knowing his purpose in coming to South Carolina resulted in failure.

He felt strangely relieved. Maybe answers were better than wondering. After he tracked down Mary, he could return to his work in Texas, keep busy and focused, and not be a burden on Aunt Vivian.

Chapter Thirty-One

The next day before breakfast, Nate asked Isaac for the map of the public cemetery. He planned to visit there after lunch, while Aunt Vivian took her nap. When he pulled the Model T out of the shed that afternoon, Miss Vivian stood in the middle of the driveway and waved him over.

"I'm comin' with you," she said as she opened the door before he could climb out of the driver's seat.

"Aunt Vivian, are you sure you'll be—"

"Fiddlesticks!" She pulled in her skirt and slammed the door.

On the other side of the Ashley River, the cemetery lay in a low flat area near the road to Savannah. The graves were crowded together in straight rows by number and letter, according to the drawing.

He parked near the entrance and went around the car to open the door for Miss Vivian. "We'll have to walk quite a ways. Do you mind?"

"I'm fine."

He took her arm and led her to the third pathway from the end. As they picked their way around the mounds, some of them fresh, Nate tried to remember his mother's face. Her voice. Her laugh.

Every step peeled back a little memory here and there. Mostly her fussing with the meals and the children. Sometimes an image of her rocking on the front porch flashed through his mind.

When they reached the place the map indicated, he stood at the foot of her grave in silence, head down, and stared at the runners of grass that had grown from the edge toward the middle. Soon it would be all filled in.

He tried to imagine her lying down with her eyes closed, as she must be in her coffin. He had never seen her resting or sleeping. And keep your burdens to yourself, she always said.

The mound over Lillie's grave was smaller, and the grass was almost knitted together. When he tried to remember her, the only picture he could summon was how she looked asleep upstairs in the loft. Maybe it's best to remember them both that way.

He had come there expecting... he wasn't certain. Surely not comfort. He felt like a cold wind had stiffened his heart and chilled his life. Bracing himself until his feet couldn't move any easier than his feelings, he ached for the warmth of cooking fires and easy visits after a long day spent peddling pies.

The silence weighed on him like a trap around his head, shutting out air and light. Breathing, yes, but he couldn't detect any air in his lungs. Despite the warm day, he shivered.

A sob from Miss Vivian interrupted his conjuring. "Oh, my poor dears," she cried, as she tightened her grip on Nate's arm. "If I'd only known."

"You couldn't save them, sick as you were." He put his hand over hers as she leaned her head against his shoulder.

I could have kept them safe, all of us together, if I'd only had enough money.

ON FRIDAY, MISS VIVIAN ASKED if Nate felt up to attending the dinner party at the Courtenay's home that evening.

"I'm trying not to think about..."

"You are handlin' things better than I ever did." Miss Vivian gave him a sad smile. "Maybe I should order some extra brandy, just in case. I know you must be keepin' your misery on the inside."

"Inside is where it will stay." He softened his voice. "And I don't need any brandy."

Nate was disappointed to learn Alexandra Pinckney and her family had not been invited. Toward the center of the dining table, Georgiana was seated across from him, and she seemed interested in his answers every time one of the older adults asked him questions.

Mr. Wentworth sat opposite at the far end of the table, out of earshot, next to his daughter Charlotte. Nate figured he didn't want to risk exposing his antiquated business practices to anyone else.

Georgiana's elder brother, the married one, settled into the chair next to her, and beyond him sat Cordelia Harrison, the doctor's daughter. She seemed lively and intelligent, but too plain to catch his eye otherwise. Nate figured it would be good manners to promise to add his name to her dance card anyway, before the evening was over.

During coffee in the parlor after dinner, Mrs. Courtenay proposed a picnic at their farm, a not-so-former plantation, during the coming week. "Nate, maybe you'd like to see where we grow cotton and other crops? We can get out the old carriage and take a drive down the path alongside the fenced areas. We won't be in the way of the workers."

"Yes, ma'am." He didn't tell her he'd already seen up close, and picked, more cotton growing in the field than he ever wanted to again.

Miss Vivian nodded her approval and didn't stop smiling until they arrived back at home.

The next morning at breakfast, Miss Vivian sipped her coffee as she studied the fashion news while Nate read the business section. "Oh, my, what a hat!" she said. "It's so tight and low on her head, no wonder she had to cut off all her hair."

She held the newspaper page out to Nate. "Do you think she looks very womanly like that?"

Nate grunted.

"With all that paint around her eyes, she looks like ... well, I dare not say!" Miss Vivian folded the paper and set it aside. "I wonder why we haven't heard from the Pinckneys yet."

Nate looked up from his reading. "What do you expect them to do?"

"Return our invitation, of course. Maybelle Pinckney has to work fast to keep up with Claudia Courtenay. And Mrs. Harrison and Mrs. Wentworth, not to mention Mrs. Hodges, won't be far behind. The race is on."

"What race?"

"The social season in Charleston is always a contest to see whose daughter will get a proposal after Cotillion. This year it could turn into a pressure cooker, since eligible bachelors are scarcer than blue unicorns in a patch of four-leaf clovers." She gave him a wry smile.

"I'm not a unicorn, am I?"

"It cert'nly wouldn't hurt you to make yourself extra agreeable, if one of these lovely young ladies gives you any indication she'd entertain thoughts of—"

"Hold on there." He sat up straight. "I thought we talked about me going back to Mason's Crossing, as soon as the new construction on the orphanage is finished and... I find Mary."

"Yes, we did, but—"

"But nothing. I can't just stay here and go to parties." Nate stood up and rested his hands on the back of his chair. "If I can't find Mary soon, and, it pains me to say it, Amos expects me to get back to work."

Nate paced behind his chair. "But someone has to keep

looking for her, if I can't stay. You promised to keep an eye out for her. Maybe I can hire a detective."

"Well, I guess if you say so… but I have another proposition."

Nate rolled his eyes. "What is it now? More lessons? Should I learn to talk French and play the piano?"

Miss Vivian smacked her lips. "That's a grand idea!"

"Not on your life."

Miss Vivian jiggled her lace hanky at him. "My life is exactly what I want to speak to you about." Her voice sounded solemn.

Nate leaned toward her and peered into her face. "You're not feeling poorly, are you?"

"Oh, no, nothin' like that." She waved him back to his chair and waited for him to sit down. "It's just, well… my daddy left me so much business to attend to—land, investments, prope'ties here in town, stocks, bonds—I have such a hard time overseein' all the accounts. And poor Mr. Hodges tries to explain it all to me, but I'm no good at arithmetic. Nobody taught me how to manage money, only how to spend it."

"Isn't Mr. Pinckney any help?"

"Yes, he's what you call a trustee, which my daddy set up in his last will and testament. But that's only if I fail to act or become incapacitated, in his precise language. There's also a provision to replace Mr. Pinckney, should there be a good reason to."

"What are you getting at, Aunt Vivian?" He squinted at her.

"Now that you're here," she said, looking wistful, "in fact, you've been with me every day for almost three months, and I've come to think of you quite highly. Plus you know your numbers, addin' and subtractin'."

"You've been very kind and generous to me, especially since you hardly knew I was alive before—"

"Oh, I knew about you, all right. I just didn't know if you

were a boy or a girl. And after my darlin' Beau passed, I sorta gave up hope of ever..." She sniffled.

"It's not like you were looking, were you?" Miss Vivian didn't have his same desperation gnawing at her insides.

"Heavens! My daddy would've had a solid gold conniption fit... but that was way back then, and he's not here now to voice any objections. I can be quite independent, if I've a mind to." She pushed her chair back from the table. "So that's what I've decided."

"What have you decided?"

"Nate, you are my only kinfolk. There's nobody else. That makes you my sole heir, and I want us to go talk to Mr. Pinckney about makin' you the trustee instead."

She waved her hand around the room, "After all, someday everythin' I own could be yours, given certain conditions and developm—"

"Huh?" Nate jumped up and stood behind his chair. "You can't be serious."

She folded her arms across her chest. "I'm perfectly serious."

"You're just saying this because I look like your brother."

"You mean, like your *father.* Yes, you are the spittin' image of Beau, only you're more grown-up and sensible. Because you didn't come from the lap of luxury, you'll do a better job of takin' care of the Rutledge fam'ly fo'tune. Beau—bless his heart, he didn't have a lick of sense—would have spent ever' last dime by now. If it was left up to him, we'd be destitute."

"My mama said the same thing, about me favoring him, that is." Nate shrugged. "You have plenty to see you through a long time. I doubt you'll ever be desti—" He jerked his head toward his aunt. "Wait a minute. You said conditions?"

Miss Vivian smiled and gestured to the chair for Nate to sit down again. "Haven't you been sayin' you need somethin' worthwhile to do? What could be more meanin'ful than makin' your fam'ly's assets grow?"

He gripped the back of the chair, but didn't sit down. "What's the catch?"

"The what?"

"Roy always said, if something's too good to be true, there's gotta be a catch."

"Like somethin' hidden?"

Nate nodded and waited. Miss Vivian bit her lip, while her twitching face gave Nate the impression she was searching for the right turn of phrase.

"Let's s'pose you meet someone and fall in love, say, like Alexandra Pinckney. She's the prettiest, while Cordelia Harrison is far and away the most intelligent. But we can't go breakin' anybody's heart or disappointin' their mothers, so give some thought to Charlotte and Georgiana and Lorelei, too. Keep in mind, it's not likely any of them would want to move to Texas and leave her kinfolks. And since your only fam'ly, that's me"— she giggled—"lives here, too, you might as well…"

Nate stared at her and said nothing. How could she forget about Mary?

"Besides, and I don't like to mention it," she said as her eyes turned weepy, "but the rest of your fam'ly—and mine— are buried here. Your grandparents, and our aunts and uncles. You can visit the cem'tery whenever you want. We'll see about havin' Evie and Lillie moved to the Rutledge fam'ly plot. And when Mary comes back home, because she knew you'd arrive in Charleston some day, she can help with the babies."

"What babies?"

"Why, the beautiful ones you'll have with Alexandra, or the smart ones you'll have with Cordelia."

"So what you're saying is, if I stay here, settle down and marry one of these debutants you've been waving in my face, and have children to carry on the family name, you'll make me trustee of the Rutledge fortune, which will one day be mine?"

She raised her eyebrows, tilting her head toward him.

Nate sat down and took her hands in his. "I'll say one thing for you, Aunt Vivian. You sure know how to bait a hook."

"Don't be silly," she sputtered. "I've never been fishin' in my entire life."

CHAPTER THIRTY-TWO

By the time the Cotillion rolled around a month later, Nate still had received no word of Mary or her whereabouts, despite his daily searches.

He had written three letters to Amos, attended five dinner parties and two picnics, met with Mr. Hodges at the bank and Mr. Pinckney at the law office numerous times, and celebrated the completion of the repaired orphanage building. Through his aunt's insistence and generosity, he had acquired another suit, dark blue this time, and a winter coat made of wool and camel's hair.

"It gets cold in Charleston before Halloween," she said.

Miss Vivian had arranged for a young preacher and his wife, both new to Charleston, to head up the efforts to get children settled in the orphanage, but she made them promise to hold one spot open at all times. Nate described Mary to them and committed to staying in contact with them, wherever he might travel.

Or live.

On the day of the Cotillion, Miss Vivian announced she would take an extra long nap after lunch so she could stay up later, but by three o'clock, she had summoned Puddy to arrange her hair and help her get dressed.

"Nate," she cried out, a second time from the hallway, "you need help with your studs? Get Isaac to put them in for you."

"It's too early to put on that tuxedo," he called from the entry hall. "We're not even leaving here 'til seven."

"Nate, where are you?"

"Down here in the library, going over this month's statements from Mr. Hodges."

"Oh, good, I need you to help me open the safe." She came downstairs. "This was my daddy's office. Besides the one at the courthouse."

Nate looked her up and down, as she grinned at him. Dressed in a pale blue evening gown, she whirled around. When he noticed her feet, he frowned. "Aunt Vivian, where are your shoes? You can't go barefooted."

"I know that, silly boy. I save them for last because they pinch my little piggies."

"Why don't you buy a bigger size?"

"I've worn a six-and-a-half shoe all my life, and I'm not about to switch now." She moved some heavy books from a tall shelf in the bookcase behind the desk, revealing a small metal door in the wall. The knob reminded Nate of a clock without hands.

She waved him over. "Here, you turn the dial. I can't see the numbers anymore."

"How does it work?"

"First turn it all the way 'round clockwise, a full circle, then keep goin' past zero and stop on twelve."

"Then what?"

"Turn it ever so slowly back around, and stop on twenty-five. Then go clockwise again 'til you reach eighty-four."

"Twelve, twenty-five, eighty-four. Christmas Day, 1884?"

"Aren't you clever! That's Beau's birthday, too." She stepped forward. "Do you want to try the handle? I haven't opened it in a long time."

He nodded.

"Just turn it like the one on the car door, and it should open."

The metal hinges creaked as the door, heavier than it looked, swung open. Nate peered inside at stacks of folded papers, narrow black boxes, and a few other things he couldn't identify.

"Fetch that red velvet bag outta there for me, will you please?" Miss Vivian cleared a space on the desk.

Nate passed her the bag and she separated the drawstrings to open it. She reached in the bag and pulled out a handful of sparkling jewelry, which seemed to drip from her overflowing palm. She selected a gold necklace and its matching bracelet, both shaped in curlicues dotted with bright white nuggets.

"Are those diamonds?" Nate said, leaning closer, dodging to avoid the frilly blue feathers stuck in a swirl of hair at the back of her head.

"Yes, indeedy, fifteen of them on this one."

She held up the necklace and dangled it toward Nate. "This set was my grandmother's, a gift from Grampaw on her wedding day. Take a more scrupulous look."

Holding the necklace toward the light, he said, "It's really... something." He handed it back to her. "I guess girls like this sort of gimcrack?"

"Oh, it's not paste. The diamonds are rose-cut, from India." She slid a ring on the third finger of her right hand and wiggled her fingers. "This was Mama's engagement ring."

He glanced at the large, pale blue stone surrounded by little pearls. Oblong in shape, it covered most of her knuckle. "Is that a diamond, too?"

"Aquamarine. Colored stones were the custom back then." She dumped the rest of the jewelry back in the bag, returned it to the safe, and shut the door. After it clicked, she spun the dial, turned to face Nate, and held out her hand, as if she wanted him to kiss it. "You may present it to the lucky one, if you like."

"Here you go, baiting that hook again."

"This time, it's a twenty-four karat gold one."

AT A QUARTER 'TIL SEVEN, Nate found Miss Vivian on the veranda, sipping a glass of sherry. When he didn't notice a bottle on the table, he searched for Isaac in the corners, but the old man wasn't there.

"Are you feeling all right?" he said as he sat across from his aunt.

"I'm fine," she said, "just a little... nervous. Aren't you?"

"Why should I be? It's not like these people expect me to do anything unique. Just make polite conversation and waltz with their daughters."

He stood up and crooked his arm toward her. "May I have the honor, Miss Rutledge?"

With a smile, she rose and took his arm, and he escorted her to the front circle drive where he had parked the car earlier.

"Your carriage is waiting, ma'am," he said, as he swept the door open.

"It's your carriage now."

The ride to the Belle Monde Hotel was too short for Miss Vivian to give Nate many reminders, but she cautioned him about gloved waiters and eager bartenders. "Everythin' they serve will be extra tasty, and we'll be tempted to overeat."

And drink, Nate thought. "How can this place serve wine and liquor when the rest of the country's gone dry? Except New Orleans, of course," he said as he pulled the car toward the liveried attendant who stood in front of the hotel.

"Half the people invited are connected in some way to the legislature or the county gover'ment. Nobody's gonna raid a private party tonight. Besides we only serve French wine and aged whiskey."

"I guess federal agents wouldn't want to pour that out, would they?"

After leaving the car with the parking attendant, Nate and

Miss Vivian went inside. Chandeliers cast a warm glow across the dark wood floors of the lobby and lit the grand staircase leading to the ballroom on the second floor. All three bellmen raised their caps and gave a little bow as they passed.

"Good evenin'," said Miss Vivian and called each one's name, as if she had known them all their lives.

To Nate, she said, "Let's take the stairs at a snail's pace so I don't squander my breath 'fore we arrive. Talkin' is 'bout the only fun I get these days."

With each step, Nate's anticipation grew, until he felt like a water bucket about to slosh over. At the top of the stairs, he caught the sound of notes from a group of instruments inside the ballroom, but nothing like he'd heard in New Orleans. The music was softer, one note almost the same character as all the others. He counted the rhythm of steady beats. Three meant waltz.

Through a pair of heavy, carved double doors, they entered the ballroom and Nate couldn't keep his eyes from darting with excitement around the whole room. Tables with tall vases of white roses, set with shiny crystal goblets and gleaming silver candlesticks, groups of people in evening finery, women dressed more elaborately than for the other dinner parties.

On either side, mirrors lined the walls between the windows, and in front of them stood rows of uniformed waiters holding aloft silver trays. At the far end was a platform draped with a gray velvet curtain, pulled shut, but an occasional ripple told Nate something must be planned for later.

For a moment, Nate couldn't move, but only stand and stare. Miss Vivian tugged at his arm and said, "What's the matter, sugar? You rooted to the floor or somethin'?"

Miss Vivian turned and asked the doorman for their table number, and he pointed to the front table just to the right of the center aisle, next to the dance floor.

She told him she was delighted, but Nate could see she wasn't surprised, as if she expected to sit nowhere but there. He glanced up over his shoulder to see where the music came from. A group of musicians sat in a semi-circle on a balcony that overlooked the entire ballroom.

"Good evening, Miss Rutledge," said a voice behind them. "So good to have you back with us, now that we can hold a Cotillion this year. It's been far too long since we've had the pleasure of your company in such a lovely setting."

Nate whirled to see a tuxedoed Dr. Harrison extend his hand to reach Miss Vivian's gloved, outstretched one. He bent forward to as if to kiss it, but stopped short. Nate had never seen him wearing anything except a white coat over his suit. They shook hands.

"You are very kind, Bertie," Miss Vivian said. "It's goin' to be a scrumptious evenin', isn't it? The presentation should be startin' soon."

"My Cordelia's quite exhilarated. She and her mother have spoken of nothing else for weeks."

"I remember my own debut," said Miss Vivian. "Hard to say who was more excited, Mama or I. Daddy, of course, was the calm one."

The doctor nodded and moved on, as other guests, with their sons and daughters, came up to greet Miss Vivian. She introduced them to Nate, referring to him as her nephew. No one asked him any embarrassing questions. In his most polite voice, he inquired if he might put his name on a few more dance cards.

She could say I'm her pet critter from the swamp, for all they care. They treat her like she's the Queen of Sheba, or like her money is. How does she know if they really care about her?

Nate accepted a glass of champagne from a white-gloved

waiter carrying a silver tray loaded with goblets. He passed it to Miss Vivian and took another for himself. Sipping it, he smiled as the bubbles tickled his nose.

The music changed and Miss Vivian looked up at the orchestra. "Time to take our seats."

At once, Duncan Pinckney appeared at her elbow, as if by magic. Before Nate could step forward, he selected the chair with the best view of the stage and the aisle and pulled it out for her. Miss Vivian sat down, dawdling as she settled herself. When Nate caught Mr. Pinckney's eye above her head, his expression was not friendly.

Almost like he's challenging me to a contest, but it's not arm wrestling.

After Mr. Pinckney stood behind the chair on her right, Nate moved to her left and waited for the others to join them. Mrs. Pinckney sat next to her husband, and the other couples from Mr. Pinckney's law firm, the Eliotts, the Charleses, and the Lees, took their seats as well. The rest of the Pinckneys, including Alexandra's parents, were seated at the next table.

Nate sat down just as the lights dimmed and the curtain on the stage parted to reveal five debutantes, dressed in white ball gowns, hands on the outstretched arms of their brothers or male cousins. All with Nate's name on their dance cards.

Each young woman carried a bouquet of white roses, and they took turns coming forward to the center of the stage. One by one, they handed their flowers to their escorts, then dipped down to the floor, with their backs erect and arms spread out like wings. Once they had squatted, which made the skirts of the dresses fluff up like feather pillows, they bent forward until their faces almost touched the floor.

The atmosphere in the room turned tense when Alexandra Pinckney had a little trouble coming back up. Her face froze as she struggled to adjust her balance, and a big smile broke out when she stood completely upright again.

Nate felt like clapping for her, but he checked himself when he noticed Miss Vivian hadn't moved. He sat back and waited to see what they would do next.

Until the debutants descended from the stage, Nate hadn't noticed the steps at the side. Still holding her escort's arm, each girl promenaded around the edge of the dance floor. When the first one returned to the corner of the stage, a line of older men awaited her.

"It's the father-daughter dance, always the first one," Miss Vivian murmured. "My favorite memory."

Nate nodded as he watched the men whirl their daughters around the floor. He tapped his foot to the music and hoped he would look that graceful. All of a sudden, he couldn't remember which girl signed him up for the first dance. Or the second, or any of the others. His eyes darted from pair to pair, as he gasped for a clue.

What a red-ribbon way to offend everybody, straight off. And embarrass my aunt.

He tapped Miss Vivian on the shoulder and leaned forward to whisper in her ear. "I can't recall which girl I'm supposed to dance with first."

She twisted in her chair to frown at him. "How could you forget? First, it's Georgiana Courtenay, then Charlotte Wentworth, followed by Alexandra Pinckney. Then Lorelei Hodges and Cordelia Harrison. After that, you're on your own." Her scowl dissolved into a smile. "Don't worry. If you lose track, they'll come find you."

The supper was served, one course after the other, and Nate watched Miss Vivian select a fork or spoon before he made his choice. So far, everything lined up on the table the way he expected.

"We'll have the first four courses, then break for a little dancing," she whispered to him. "After dessert and coffee, you can enjoy the second set."

The conversation around the table kept to business or national news for the men, and gardening and the latest fashions for the ladies. Miss Vivian commented again on the newspaper article about new hairstyles. Nate decided not to offer his opinion on the oil or transportation industry.

During the first round, Nate enjoyed dancing and chatting with Georgiana and Charlotte so much, he asked them for more slots on their dance cards. Both accepted for the second set.

When it was time for the third dance, Nate searched the ballroom to find Alexandra. The orchestra struck up some unfamiliar music, which caused a buzz of conversation among the older people, who were still seated.

Nate backed up to lean against the wall near the entrance to the ballroom. The music's jazzy beat sounded close to what he had heard in New Orleans. He had not waited more than twenty seconds when Alexandra bounded through the doorway arm-in-arm with another girl, both giggling until they almost stumbled.

"Alexandra?"

She stopped and whirled around. "Oh, Nate, there you are. C'mon, let's do the Cake Walk."

She thrust out her arm and grabbed his hand. At a half-trot, he followed her to the dance floor, mentally chiding Mrs. Chester for not teaching him this one. No getting out of it now, even if he wanted to.

The dance started like a couples' promenade, but soon turned into high stepping and strutting, with shaking the hands at the wrists, like flinging water after washing them. He did his best to follow Alexandra's movements, but felt ridiculous the whole time.

When the dance was over, a group of young people surrounded them, breathing hard and laughing as they rested their arms on each other's shoulders. Nate stood next to her without speaking.

One of her friends said, "You really took the cake."

"What cake?" Nate said when they strolled to the side of the dance floor.

"Oh, that's just what people say, because the dance got started as a contest on the plantations around here, and the winning couple received a cake. Don't you just love the music?"

"It's like what I used to hear in New Orleans."

"New Orleans? I positively adore New Orleans. We always stay at the Place D'Armes Hotel on Jackson Square. Do you know it?"

Nate pictured the historic red brick building and all the ferns in baskets hanging from its black wrought-iron balconies, but he'd never been inside the lobby, only the rear entrance to make deliveries with Franco.

"Yes, I used to pass by it quite often on my way to… uh, visit a friend."

Her deep green eyes grew large. "I hear it's haunted."

She gazed up at him with a smile so charming, he was certain his heart hiccoughed. "Maybe we could explore the attic or the basement together, just to see what we could find?"

"Miss Alexandra?"

"Call me Lexie, won't you?" She arched her eyebrows at him and blinked just slowly enough for him to notice her long eyelashes. "Just Lexie."

"Uh, Lexie, may I please have another dance with you in the second set?" Nate's words tumbled out as fast as he could make them, before her next partner approached.

She winked at him. "I already saved two for you, including the last one."

Nate returned her grin and, once she left with the other young man, he couldn't remember the last time he had felt this happy. The only thing that would make him happier would be dancing with Lexie again. Maybe next round, their hands would touch the whole time. After a moment, he jerked like he suddenly woke up, and scanned the room for Lorelei Hodges.

The dance with Lorelei, followed by one with Cordelia Harrison, was as pleasant as the others, and he asked both of them for dances in the second set. None excited him as much as those with Alexandra.

Once he was seated again for dessert, Miss Vivian asked for details, smiled, and nodded her approval of his good manners. "Did you find out what went wrong durin' her bow?"

"Her escort had his foot on her dress."

"That half-witted second cousin, once removed, on her mother's side."

Nate stared at her.

"He's from Tennessee. What'd you expect?"

When she heard that Alexandra had saved the final dance for him, all she said was, "Oooooh," giving the word three syllables.

He felt his face go warm and kept his eyes down. Lexie, he thought. What a sweet nickname.

Nate looked up to find Duncan Pinckney frowning at him.

CHAPTER THIRTY-THREE

On the drive home, Miss Vivian said, "Except that it's after midnight and you're still wearin' both your glass slippers, I'd stake my diamond bracelet you feel like Cinderella at the ball."

"Who? Was there another girl I should have danced with?" He wheeled around the corner and glanced toward her feet. "Oh, yeah, I bet you can't wait to get home and slip outta your dinky little shoes."

Miss Vivian chuckled. "I mean, you and Alexandra Pinckney. Like Cinderella and her Prince Charmin', only in reverse."

He grinned. "Wasn't she the most beautiful girl at the whole shindig?"

"Well, what do you think?"

"About what?"

"How can you be so pea-brained?" Miss Vivian shuffled the edges of her gown and folded her hands in her lap. "Have you chosen Alexandra or one of the others? After ours, her fam'ly is one of the oldest, but—"

"Hold on a second, Aunt Vivian." He pulled into the driveway and stopped the car. "I haven't even decided whether to stay here yet, much less get married."

"What are you waitin' for?"

"Truthfully, a reply to my letter. I wrote to Sarah Cobb and asked her for some advice. She is a very wise lady."

"Harrumph!"

"You'd like each other. She's kind and thoughtful, like

you. And she's from an old family, too. The Masons of Mason's Crossing. You can't get much more important than having a whole town named after you."

"Isn't it on the frontier?" She pronounced 'frontier' as if the word tasted like pork belly gone sour.

"Texas isn't the Wild West, not any longer." He decided it would be better if she didn't know about saloon fights and drunken gamblers. Or his own past.

"Be that as it may," she said, "are you at least leanin' toward favorin' Alexandra? I could detect an exceptional glow in her pretty eyes when she gazed up into yours."

"She's awful nice, too, and seems… Wait, how do you—"

Miss Vivian opened the car door and slid out, turning as she leaned back in. "Women know these things. Especially mothers."

Nate climbed out of the car and came around the back to take Miss Vivian's arm and help her up the front stoop. "Did Mrs. Pinckney say—"

"You have their permission to come callin'."

"What about Mrs. Wentworth? She seemed to take a particular interest in me from the very beginning, not that I was all that comfortable with it."

"Claudia is disappointed, of course, but Georgiana will have to settle for that Tate boy. His family is not very well off, but they're just as respectable."

"You mean, they only have one family secret?"

"Yes, but I'm not about to spill the beans."

Nate laughed. "Is there anyone you don't know everything about?

She let go of his arm and turned toward him, studying his face and frowning for a moment. "I don't know everythin' about you." Her frown faded and she patted his lapel.

Nate caught his breath. Would she try to find out what he

had done? Why he really left Texas? He could trust that his mother would have kept the circumstances of Roy's death from her, but, without a doubt, his aunt suspected something. Why now?

Miss Vivian waited for him to open the front door. As she glided through, she said, "Whatever else it is you're keepin' inside, Nate, honey, you don't hafta tell me."

Nate exhaled as he followed her into the house. In the entry, Isaac waited for them to pass by before he closed the front door.

As he climbed the stairs behind his aunt, Nate wished Sarah's letter would arrive soon. He wanted to make a decision and get on with his life. He needed to settle somewhere, maybe in his own house, with his own family. One he acquired for himself.

Would Alexandra, or now Lexie, be a good choice for his wife? How much resistance would her grandfather, Duncan Pinckney, throw in his way? Was Aunt Vivian, even with all her fortune, any match for her father's favorite lawyer?

If Clyde were here, he would suggest at least one method of handling the elder Mr. Pinckney. Maybe Nate could follow his aunt's example and bait a hook for Lexie and her mother. He laughed to himself.

There's more'n one way to skin this cat.

THE SUNDAY MORNING FOLLOWING Cotillion, Nate found Miss Vivian risen earlier than he expected, considering the amount of champagne she drank last night. Her head was propped on her knuckles, as she sat at the dining room table, picking through her breakfast of scrambled eggs, biscuits, and bacon.

"Oh, Nate," she said, "hurry up and eat so we can go to church."

"Thought you wanted to skip today. Late night, and all."

"Last night I did, but this morning I've changed my mind." Her voice was firm enough that he knew she wouldn't change her decision again. "Can I go like this?"

She shook her head.

"If I put on a coat and tie?"

"That will be acceptable."

"Why are we even bothering?"

"I want you to meet the preacher."

"I've already met him, remember?"

"The Baptist preacher, not our Presbyterian one."

"No one else will be there. Even the Baptists are hung over." Nate sipped his coffee and nodded at Isaac as he set a plate in front of him. "Do the Pinckneys happen to be Baptist, by chance?"

"What makes you say that?"

"Uh-huh," Nate grunted.

"It's a lovely church, well, maybe a trifle plain—nothin' that some flowers and candles wouldn't fix—but he gives a fine sermon."

"I guess everyone wants to go to confession after drinking all that wine and whiskey last night."

"Honey, folks just want to be sure their neighbors don't gossip about them behind their backs."

AT THE FIRST BAPTIST CHURCH, Nate didn't know the hymns, found the hellfire sermon overly harsh and the pew uncomfortable, and thought his aunt put too much money in the collection basket. His only consolation was they were seated in the fourth row, across the aisle from the entire Pinckney family, including the grandparents and the doltish second cousin. Lexie was seated on the opposite end, away from the center aisle.

During the longest prayer he'd ever heard, with his head bowed, Nate sneaked a sideways glance at the same moment Lexie did. He turned his face toward her and waited. She followed his slight movement and seemed to sigh as she smiled.

By a hair's breadth, he shifted forward to get a better view of her, but instead found himself gazing into the glaring eyes of old Mr. Pinckney. In a flash, he blinked as he faced forward again, bowed his head deeper, and didn't look her way until the service was over.

Following the last "amen," Miss Vivian stood up along with everyone else and stepped into the aisle. Without hesitation, she linked her arm through Duncan Pinckney's and asked him to walk her out. Behind her back, she wiggled her lace handkerchief at Nate, which he could only interpret as a signal to take his time.

Nate pretended to stack the hymnals and dust specks off the seat of the wooden pew, waiting for Alexandra's parents to move toward the exit. Her little brothers and sisters came next, but he could see her over their heads.

Her auburn hair was pulled up and tucked under a green hat. Green to match her eyes. Her skin shone as smooth as the pearls dangling from her ears. One strand of hair had escaped and lay like a copper ribbon against her silky white neck. From under the brim of her hat, she peeked at him, blushed, and flickered her eyelashes.

He was certain his heart skipped a beat again. Maybe he wouldn't wait for a letter from Sarah Cobb.

CHAPTER THIRTY-FOUR

Although he hadn't proposed to her yet, as Columbus Day approached, the upper social circles in Charleston, according to Aunt Vivian, considered Nate and Lexie's marriage a foregone conclusion. Sarah's letter to him had encouraged him to "follow his heart" but "take his time to get to know her and her family better."

Every morning at breakfast, Miss Vivian claimed she would swoon over all the details for the engagement party, just as soon as Nate and Lexie got serious and set a date. "It will be like Cotillion all over again, 'cept without the other girls."

"Should you really spend that much money on a party?"

"Oh, it'll be a drop in the bucket compared to what the Pinckneys'll pay for weddin'."

"I hardly know her. We've been together a lot, but never alone. Her parents or Virgil is always—"

"Nobody knows anybody very well until after they get married. The rules are rather firm on that subject."

"What if she says no?"

Miss Vivian all but sputtered out her coffee. "You silly goose. You think, after all this, she'd turn down the handsomest man in the whole state? Not to mention, one of the richest, some day?"

"Don't say that. It's bad luck." He grimaced as he shook his head at her. "Truly, I'd rather give the money to the orphanage."

"I'll need it to pay for the honeymoon. That's the responsibility of the groom's family. How does Italy sound? Or France?"

He jerked his head toward her. "Not France." Not where poor little Walter's father was buried.

"Well, then San Francisco, perhaps. They've had plenty of time to recover from the earthquake."

"New York," said Nate. "I think I'd like to see New York City. Maybe look up an old friend."

"Would he make a suitable best man? You'll need one."

Nate tried to picture Clyde in a tuxedo and almost laughed out loud.

Isaac entered the dining room carrying a small silver tray with three envelopes on it. Miss Vivian took them and tore them open, one by one.

"Claudia wants to throw a party for you and Lexie, as soon as you get engaged. After our own announcement party, of course. Even her disappointment at not snarin' you for her daughter hasn't kept her from bein' a classy friend, has it?"

The second one contained an invitation to a garden party for Lorelei Hodges and the third was from the Pinckneys.

"Maybelle has invited us to sit with them durin' the parade. All the other men will be marchin' in it, so you'll have your hands full."

Nate grinned. "It'll be a struggle, but I'll manage."

He'd find a way, too, to spirit Lexie away from the crowd and get her consent to marry him. Sooner or later, he'd have to return to Mason's Crossing, whether he found Mary or not.

What would Amos and Sarah say when he stepped off the train with Lexie on his arm? How would Weesie like this new older girl in the family?

ON THE MORNING OF the parade, Nate drove his aunt downtown and parked near the bank building in the spot Mr. Hodges had reserved for them. He took her arm and escorted her two blocks to the high viewing platform, festooned with flags of the State of South Carolina and the Confederacy, where Mrs. Pinckney had saved seats.

Miss Vivian sat in the front row with her friend Maybelle, and Nate shared the bench behind them with Lexie, while the younger children squashed each other in the third level.

Nate slipped his hand around Lexie's and squeezed. Her smile seemed to make the sunny day even brighter.

Citizens of Charleston lined the streets, waving American flags, along with the other banners, clapping in time to the music of the brass bands that passed.

"Daddy's group is last. He and PawPaw ride every year."

Nate smiled to hear the stern Duncan Pinckney referred to as 'PawPaw.' He couldn't imagine himself calling him anything but Mr. Pinckney, not even Duncan.

Three wagons passed, pulled by Negro men. The wagons were decorated to resemble sailing ships. Nate read their signs and asked, "What are Nina, Pinta, and Santa Maria?"

"It's Neen-ya," said one of Lexie's younger brothers. "Didn't you learn the names of Columbus' ships in school?"

Lexie whirled around. "Hush up, you little monkey!"

Nate swallowed. "I guess I missed school that day."

Would he ever get enough education and not worry a kid would know more than he did? By now, Weesie had probably learned more than he ever would. He decided to change the subject. "Why are those men pulling the wagons instead of using horses?"

"The horses always come last." Lexie answered quickly and sat up straighter, studying the next marching group, the Women's Hospital Auxiliary.

"Why is that?" Nate said.

She didn't reply or look at him. He repeated the question.

The same younger brother swatted Nate on the upper arm.

"'Cuz, stupid, horses leave their crap in the street!"

"Virgil!" Lexie stood up, turned around, and grabbed the boy by his ear, pinching it until he hollered. "You quit usin' that foul language, you hear me?"

"Well, who wants to step in horse shit?" he squealed.

She pinched harder and drew back her other arm as if to slap him. Nate caught it before she could strike. The other children next to Virgil shrunk back, fear on their tiny faces.

"Children, behave!" was all Mrs. Pinckney said, without so much as glancing over her shoulder.

The brother slapped at Lexie's arm and tried to wriggle free. After a minute of struggle back and forth, she released him and sat down again. He stuck his tongue out at the back of her head.

Nate had stood up at the same time as Lexie, and he made sure he towered over her brother. He crooked his finger at him. "Virgil, come here."

"I don't hafta do anything you say."

Nate leaned forward, grabbed Virgil by the front of his shirt, and lifted him into the air. He took one step, thrust out his arm, and dangled him over the back of the platform. Eyes wide, Virgil tried to look down to see how far his feet swayed above the street.

"You will apologize to the ladies," Nate said over the loud music, as he glared in Virgil's face.

Virgil squinted at him and said nothing.

Nate caught Virgil's foot in his other hand. "Shall I hold you by your ankles," he said through clenched teeth, "and leave you out there to learn some manners?"

Virgil bit his lip. "Sorry," he muttered.

Nate swept him back inside the seating area, but yanked him close to his face, eye to eye. "They didn't hear you." He set the boy down.

Virgil apologized to his sister, and, after Nate prodded him forward, also to his mother and Miss Vivian. Sulking in silence, he returned to the third row and made another younger sibling trade seats with him, as far away from his sister and Nate as he could get.

Lexie linked her arm through Nate's and beamed up at him. "You're so good with children."

Nate hoped she didn't see him wince.

Drums sounded in the distance. The crowd grew noisier.

"Oh, look, here they come!" Lexie jumped up and pointed down the avenue. "Watch for 'em. Daddy is the standard bearer, while PawPaw is the Grand Marshall."

The final group came round the corner, marching in four straight lines. At the front leading the four lines strutted Duncan Pinckney. He wore a white uniform with a red shoulder sash covered in badges, topped by a red-lined cape and a military-style hat.

Behind him strode men wearing the same uniform, without the sash or the cape. On their heads, they wore white coned-shaped hats with flaps down the sides and back. Bringing up the rear were the men on horseback, at least fifty of them, in the same white uniform and tall hats.

"There he is!" said Lexie, jumping up. "Hey, Daddy! Hey, there!" She yelled and waved, then whined to Nate, "He can't hear me over the crowd."

As standard-bearer, Lexie's father straddled the lead horse, gripping a flagpole attached to his saddle. At the top of the pole, the breeze blew a white flag with a short red cross that looked more like a sideways 'x.' The man riding the horse next to him was the Baptist preacher from their church.

"What group is this?" Nate said.

"A Democratic fraternal organization called the Klan," said Lexie. "They promote Christian values and education and respect for women. As a service project for them, Mama and

Daddy distribute Bibles to the schools, Protestant Bibles, of course."

Nate had heard ugly rumors about the Klan in Texas and Louisiana. Father Antoine and the men who rode the rails had talked about the Ku Klux Klan's violence, even murder, against Negroes, Jews, Catholics, immigrants, and northern Republicans. The big-city newspapers he'd read scorned their members, calling them 'ignorant farmers.'

As Duncan Pinckney and his son passed the platform and saluted their family, Nate thought that description didn't fit them one bit. Maybe Virgil was right after all about what horses bring to the street.

AFTER THE PARADE, Nate and Miss Vivian joined the Pinckneys for a picnic on the lawn at Washington Square Park. A light breeze lifted the midday heat as the Pinckney's Negro servants spread three patchwork quilts over the grass and unloaded the food and drinks.

Maybelle Pinckney sat on the center quilt and fussed over the plates and napkins, but made certain Miss Vivian and Nate were served first, then Lexie. She sent a servant over to the quilt for the children with an extra basket to help themselves, and gave her instructions to set it on the far side to keep their noise down.

"The men will be here any second," she said, waving at Nate to go ahead and eat.

"Maybelle is famous for her fried chicken. She's won blue ribbons at the last three county fairs," said Miss Vivian. "No one serves it up tastier than her Chessie."

Nate took a bite and had to agree, but wondered why Chessie wasn't given the credit. The one who did the cooking ought to be the famous one. Considering the group who brought up the rear of the parade, he figured no servant of theirs would ever complain.

When Nate and Lexie had almost finished their meal, the men arrived, hungry and talkative. On his feet in an instant, Nate listened with half an ear, something about recruitment. Lexie stood up and went over to both her father and her grandfather to kiss their cheeks and tell them how much she and Nate enjoyed the parade.

Lexie's father approached Nate and extended his hand. "Glad you could join us, young man."

"Thank you, sir. It's been a fine morning. Your family is most kind."

"We fellas get a real kick out of it, and ever'one seems to 'preciate our efforts."

Not everyone, Nate thought.

"Well, I don't like to bring up business with the ladies present," said Mr. Pinckney, "but maybe we'll have a chance to visit in private later. There's somethin' I'd like to acquaint you with, maybe bring you in on, which is very important here locally."

"Of course, sir, I look forward to it." Nate wondered how he could avoid becoming a new member of the Klan and, at the same time, ask Mr. Pinckney for his daughter's hand in marriage.

When Lexie's father stepped aside, the next person who came into Nate's view was Duncan Pinckney. He held a plate in one hand and a glass of lemonade in the other. Eyes hard as flint, he nodded at Nate. When Lexie stepped between them, his mouth twisted into a brief smile.

"You looked like an emperor leading his troops into battle, PawPaw," she gushed. "Didn't you think so, Nate?" She turned and raised her eyebrows at him.

"Most impressive," said Nate in even tones. "A striking... figure, for all to admire."

As one of the servants accepted his empty plate and goblet, Nate stepped back and jerked his head at Lexie. "Let's go for a stroll."

She bounded toward him like an eager puppy and twined her arm through his. He led her across the lawn toward the gazebo. Families had occupied all the open spaces, while their children chased each other around the park.

"Is the courthouse open today?" he said.

"Every day, far as I know."

"Let's go inside. I've never seen... my grandpa's office."

They crossed the street and walked a few blocks to the corner of Broad and Meeting Streets. A large three-story building of white plaster took up the whole block. In front of arched windows, a few palms grew in evenly spaced open squares along the sidewalks.

Lexie stood back and looked at the upper windows. "General Washington visited here in 1791 and liked it so much, he hired the same architect to build the White House. Of course, it wasn't called that yet, just the Presidential Mansion."

He held the door open for her and followed her into the lobby. "I wish I knew as much history as you. Good thing I love to read."

Nate scanned the lobby for other visitors. Finding none, he reached for her hand and spun her toward him. As they stood facing each other, he gazed down into her deep green eyes. Without speaking, he laid his right palm against her cheek and felt the familiar hiccough in his chest.

Lexie raised her face to him, lowered her eyes to his lips, and swept her eyelashes back up at him. She sighed and closed her eyes, tilting her head nearer.

A blaze spread across him, warming his body. He leaned down and kissed her mouth, fuller and softer than he expected. In an instant, she wrapped her arms around his chest and bent her head back.

Nate pressed her lips harder and folded one long arm around her shoulders, the other behind her neck. Her curves pressed against him as he cradled her head in the crook of his arm. Gasping, she opened her mouth and whispered his name.

He drew his head back and stared down at her. "Are you mine?"

"All yours." She nibbled the tip of his chin. "No one could ever compare to you."

His blood seemed to stampede, and he plunged forward with an urgency he didn't know he had. Her lips parted a tiny bit, and he licked the wet sweetness. She seemed to like it. Should he shift his hand to the side of her neck toward her collarbone?

"Ah!" she cried, as she turned her head.

He kissed the edge of her hairline, while his hand slid down her arm. She didn't resist. He let his thumb wander toward the top of her breast, sensing her quickened breath under the thin fabric of her dress.

He had just moved his hand onto the front of her shoulder, when she yelped, "Wait! Please!"

Nate let both arms drop to his side and took half a step back. Their eyes met for a moment, then he looked away until his breathing returned to normal.

"You haven't told me you love me," Lexie said in a soft voice.

"Of course, I love you." Nate figured it must be true, since he had never felt this excitement about anyone else.

"And?" Her voice sounded firmer.

"And... I want to marry you."

"Well?"

This was the part for which Aunt Vivian had coached him. He backed up, dropped to his knees, and took both her hands in his. "Miss Alexandra Pinckney, will you please do me the honor of becoming my wife?"

Before she could answer, the front door banged open and Virgil raced into the lobby. He came to an abrupt stop at the sight of Nate on his knees in front of his sister.

Once again Nate felt his face turn warm. He jumped to his feet and turned toward the little boy with what he hoped was a fierce frown.

Virgil gulped and stared, first at Nate, then at his sister.

Lexie put both hands on her hips. "What do you want, you little imp?"

"Mama says come..." He didn't wait to finish his sentence, but spun around and sprinted out of the building.

Dipping her head, Lexie smiled at Nate. "I guess we better head back."

"Do I have your answer?"

"Oh, yes!" she said, breathless. "It's yes!"

He clasped her hand in his. "I'll speak to your father as soon as possible."

They exited the building, not even daring to hold hands as they approached the park. Nate could feel Maybelle Pinckney and Miss Vivian watching both of them as if they were waiting for a signal. Finally Mrs. Pinckney nudged Miss Vivian and they turned their heads to whisper in each other's ears.

When Nate caught his aunt's eye, he nodded. A huge smile spread over her face, and she reached for her purse, where she had slipped the aquamarine ring, just in case.

Nate shook his head. He would wait until after he approached Lexie's father and received his blessing.

At last Nate could picture his future: husband to a sweet

and beautiful wife, a home to call their own, recognized businessman, and soon after, doting father. His dream of a family would finally come true.

A figure passed in front of him, creating a silhouette against the afternoon sun. "Mr. Wallace," said Duncan Pinckney in a low voice. "Please come by my office tomorrow morning at nine-thirty. There are some papers for you to look at."

"It's Rutledge." Nate squared his shoulders and looked the old man in the eye. "Sir."

Duncan Pinckney turned around and walked away as if he hadn't heard.

THE REST OF THE DAY and into the evening, there was no opportunity for Nate to catch Lexie's father for a confidential interview. After supper, Duncan Pinckney had excused both of them, saying they must attend a private gathering of the Klan. Mrs. Pinckney sighed and waved them away.

When the sun went down, fireworks lit the sky over the harbor. Nate found himself seated on the quilt between his aunt and Maybelle Pinckney. They chattered to each other under his nose and, from time to time, asked his opinion on some matter to which he had not paid any attention.

By the time the last rocket was fired, the smaller children had fallen asleep on their quilt. The servants packed up the leftovers from the supper into the trunk and then hoisted the children into their arms to carry them to the car, all but Virgil.

Nate kneeled to pick him up and lifted him to his chest. As he stood, Virgil woke up and, confused for a moment, searched Nate's face. All of a sudden, his eyes grew wide and he bellowed, "No, no! Let me go!"

Nate took a step backward, trying to untangle his feet from

the quilt. All the while, Virgil hollered, "You're gonna drop me! Mama, help! HELP!"

He wiggled and tried to get loose from Nate's tightening grip. The other children woke up, crying and wailing. Nothing the servants did would calm them down. Every time they set one of them inside the car, the wee ones escaped out the other side and ran screaming toward their mother.

Nate stumbled and let Virgil's feet drop to the ground. The boy wriggled free and dashed toward his mother, shoving the other children out of his way and burying his head in her skirts when he caught her.

Lexie came up from behind Nate and tugged on his sleeve. "I thought you were good with children."

They both laughed, then grew serious as their eyes met.

"I will be with ours," Nate said. "I promise."

CHAPTER THIRTY-FIVE

At 9:20 the next morning, Nate waited in the reception area of the law offices belonging to Pinckney, Elliott, Charles, and Lee. Sam Carolla should get a look at this and find out what old money can buy, he thought.

At 9:29, Duncan Pinckney's secretary came to get him and escorted him into the large corner office. "Would you care for something to drink?" she said.

"No, thank you." Nate figured he didn't need any more practice with a teacup. He took a seat in the tall leather chair.

Through his law firm and social standing, Nate was certain the old man had connections beyond Charleston, and even outside South Carolina. Maybe he could recommend a detective to hunt for Mary. Someone who was good at digging around for missing people, who wouldn't quit until he found her.

Duncan Pinckney sat across the large carved oak desk, a stack of papers in front of him. Without expression, he looked at Nate for a moment, then took a sheet from the top of the pile. "This is the result of the patent search. It appears you have a unique invention, and therefore, here is an application for registering the patent. Your signature is required on this line."

He pointed to the bottom of the page and handed Nate a pen. "Congratulations."

Nate read the document and stopped when he saw his name as 'Nate Wallace.' He frowned and looked at the old man. "What do you mean by this? My aunt wants me to use her last name."

Duncan Pinckney laced his fingers together and rested his chin on the pointed tips of the index fingers where they met. "Do you happen to know a Sheriff Kelley of Clark's Common, Texas?"

Nate sucked in his breath, as if he'd been punched in the gut.

"He's looking for the person involved in the death of a man named Roy Wallace. Your step-father, I believe?"

Dazed, Nate nodded. His neck felt stiff.

Duncan Pinckney shuffled the papers and drew another one from the middle of the stack. "How about a Franco de Angelis or a Vincent Rinaldi, both of New Orleans, both murdered?"

Nate sat still as a stone.

"And then there's Father Antoine of the St. Louis Catholic Church." He spit out the word 'Catholic' as if it tasted bitter.

Nate jerked his head up. "What about him?"

The old man read from the page in front of him. "Evidently he's involved in some kind of police investigation related to money stolen from the well-known Matranga criminal organization with ties to the Corolla family, also members of the Mafia."

Nate could feel the panic rising from his insides. "Where'd you get all this?"

Duncan Pinckney set the paper down and stared at Nate with eyes cold as death. "Did you think I wouldn't have you investigated?" He didn't raise his voice or even use any inflection. "After you appeared on Miss Rutledge's doorstep with nothing to recommend you except a resemblance to her wayward brother, who's been deceased for twenty years?"

"Aunt Vivian knew my mother when she worked for their family. They were friends."

"Your mother was a servant, who left their employ in disgrace after she seduced their son and got herself pregnant. She only returned here to swindle Miss Rutledge and take advantage by making her believe in you."

"She does believe in me. Beau was my father."

"There's no way to prove that. Your father could have been any one of a number of men who—"

Nate jumped to his feet and glared down at him. "You shut your dirty mouth!"

"Sit down," said Duncan Pinckney, "and you'll find out what's going to happen next." He held the papers upright and tapped the edges against the desktop until they all fell into place once more.

Nate returned to his seat and scowled at him.

"You have a choice," the old man said. "You will give up any claim to an inheritance from Miss Rutledge, leave Charleston immediately, and never return or contact her or anyone in my family, most especially my granddaughter, ever again."

Nate tamped down the urge to vomit. "Or what?"

"Or I'll be forced to send notice to Sheriff Kelley that his search for Roy Wallace's killer is over. The local authorities will hold you in the county jail until he arrives to take you back to Texas in handcuffs, where you'll stand trial and likely be convicted. Manslaughter, at the least, should bring you no less than twenty years in prison."

"It... it wasn't like that..." Nate turned his face, feeling the edges of his eyes turn hot with moisture.

"It matters not."

"I could go back to Clark's Common, talk to him, clear this up."

"He'll simply arrest you there." Duncan Pinckney shrugged. "Unless the Matrangas or the Corollas locate you first. They do want their money back."

"You're threatening me?"

"I don't have to. You've put yourself in this position."

"But... but I—"

"What's it going to be?"

Nate felt like his insides were boiling. How easy would be it to grab the old man by the throat and choke the evil right out of him? But no, then he would become the killer Duncan Pinckney already thought he was.

Nate picked up the pen and signed the application. "How much do I owe you for this transaction?"

"Nothing. Your immediate departure is the only payment I require." Duncan Pinckney took the paper, folded it in thirds, and slid it into an envelope. "My secretary will send this out with today's mail." He tossed it aside. "Our business is concluded."

Nate stood up. "You don't know how much this will hurt Aunt Vivian."

"She'll recover, enough to thank me later."

"No." Nate shook his head. "You don't know her like I do. It'll be the end of her."

"Either way, you'll never get your hands on the Rutledge fortune."

"So that's your angle? Lexie and I would have—"

"Alexandra is none of your concern."

Nate turned, walked toward the door, and opened it. "You think, if I leave town, you've won?"

"Haven't I?"

"We all reap what we sow. You will, too, someday."

"Are you now threatening me?"

Nate walked out the door without closing it or looking back.

WHEN NATE RETURNED TO the house on Henrietta Street, he couldn't remember how he had gotten there. He parked the Model T in the shed—for the last time, he thought—and trudged up the steps to the side door.

Isaac met him in the hall. "Miss Vivian, she be waitin' fo' you in the parlor." He took Nate's hat and coat. "You all right, Mr. Nate?"

Nate plodded past him and turned toward the stairs without even glancing at the parlor door. He climbed the steps to his room and pulled his brown leather suitcase down from the top of the chiffarobe. The only clothes he packed were the ones he had arrived with, nothing more. Not custom ordered, but decent enough, since Sarah Cobb had helped him select them.

When he snapped the lid shut, he carried the suitcase to the entry hall. Isaac stood nearby, a quizzical look on his face.

"You be goin' somewheres, Mr. Nate?"

"Nate, it that you?" Miss Vivian called from the parlor. "Come in. I have somethin' for you."

Nate looked at Isaac as if he didn't recognize him, not even when Isaac squinted at him. He pointed at the door to the parlor. Isaac stepped forward to open it wider.

Miss Vivian leaned back in her usual spot on the divan, a pile of correspondence on the space next to her, feet tucked up under her legs. She scooped up the mail and set it on the side table, then patted the space and smiled at Nate, expectation on her face.

"Well, what did the younger Mr. Pinckney have to say? I 'spect he's pleased as punch."

As Nate sank to the chair across from her, she rang a little hand bell. "It's early yet, but I think we should celebrate."

Isaac entered the room and gave a short, stiff bow. "Yes'm?"

"Bring us some... ummmm, what would you like, Nate?" She shifted upright and let her feet slide to the floor. "Maybe we have some chilled cham—"

"Nothing." Nate stared at her, not seeing her face.

Miss Vivian shooed Isaac out of the room. "What is it? Did

somethin' go wrong?" She shook her lace hanky at him. "Just wait 'til Maybelle gets ahold of her husband. He'll wish he'd never been born!"

"It isn't that." Nate swallowed hard. What could he tell her? It didn't matter whether she believed him or not, Duncan Pinckney would feed him to the wolves. Then she and everyone else would learn all of his questionable past. He didn't deserve someone like Lexie, never would.

He'd been an idiot to let Miss Vivian convince him he was a Rutledge, when he would always be nothing more than an illegitimate Wallace. She had fooled herself, too, with her blind yearning, no more than an old lady's fancy.

How could he protect her from the pain of this sickening discovery? If he left town, as Duncan Pinckney demanded, he would have to give her a good reason, and she would make him promise to return as soon as he was free. What harm could that do? A small white lie to cover up a black one the size of an ocean.

"I have to go back to Texas," he blurted out. Finding Mary would have to wait.

"How soon? After the weddin', of course."

"There can't be any wedding... not just yet." Nate spread out his palm and pressed the skin in the middle of his hand. "I don't know how long I'll be."

"Surely it can wait 'til—"

"Amos needs me right away."

"That reminds me." She shuffled through the stack of mail. "Here's another letter for you from Sarah Cobb, and one from someone else. Looks like a girl's handwriting." Her voice turned sing-song. "Could it be Alexandra?"

She held out the envelopes and Nate took them, but he only tapped the edges against his fingertips.

"Aren't you goin' to open them?" She handed him a letter opener, silver with a slender ivory handle.

He let one drop into his lap, slit the top of Sarah's, and pulled out a single sheet, folded once. His eyes scanned the printed words, again, a third time before they made sense. He sucked in his breath and held it.

Miss Vivian swung her feet to the floor. "What will you say to Lexie about this slight delay?"

"Who?"

"Nate, you must be in a daze. Lexie? Alexandra? The girl you're goin' to marry?"

"Oh, yeah, Lexie." He exhaled. "I'm catching a train this afternoon."

"That soon?"

Duncan Pinckney warned him never to contact her again. If her grandfather had told her about him, she would fall out of love with him that very moment. Lexie could find someone else, someone more suited to her. She'd be happier that way.

"You know how women think. You can explain it to her better."

"Explain what? I can't just make up some story about your business in Texas. What do I say to her?"

He held out the letter for her to read. "Sarah writes that Amos has some kind of 'health problem.' He's going to see a specialist in Dallas. I have to go back right away and run the business without him."

"Is it that serious?"

Nate stood up. "It's all serious." He stepped forward to sit by her and took her hands in his. "You've been so good to me. It pains me to leave you. I'll miss you more than anyone else."

She smiled and winked at him. "But you'll be back soon. We have an engagement party to plan. It will be the crownin' event of the social season, not countin' the weddin' itself, of course."

"Don't... don't make any plans... just yet," he said. "I can't say for sure how long I'll be gone. And if Lexie doesn't want to wait, I'll understand."

"What are you sayin'? Naturally, she'll wait for you. Open her love note."

Nate slid his finger under the flap and pulled out a single card. He sat down again to read it.

Nate Wallace, I have learned the truth from PawPaw, so there is no way on God's green earth I would ever marry someone like you. How dare you lie to me so bad? I will die of embarrassment, now that my wedding I've counted on is canceled.

Her signature was scrawled to such a degree he could barely make out the letters, but one thing was clear. She loved the idea of a wedding, like another debutante ball, but for only one girl.

All during their courtship, he had wondered why she never once said she loved him. Did she accept him only for his handsome looks and eventual fortune? To keep the other girls from landing him, as Aunt Vivian had hinted. That made her no better than... His fear of getting arrested and his concern for Amos soon outweighed any disappointment.

I can't follow leads about my sister if I'm in jail.

Trying not to flinch, Nate stood up and faced his aunt. "Just tell her I won't blame her if she changes her mind."

"Silly boy." Miss Vivian's face turned serious. "You will be comin' back, won't you?"

Nate leaned over and kissed her cheek.

She giggled and dabbed her eyes with her lace handkerchief. "You silly boy."

Chapter Thirty-Six

Two days after he left Charleston, Nate returned to Austin, without his sister and without the Model T Miss Vivian encouraged him to take.

"I'll be back for it," he had promised her. Another lie.

Since he hadn't known how to give Sarah and Amos notice he would arrive so soon, no one met him at the station. The first three cab drivers refused to take him out of the city, not wishing to return after dark, but the fourth one said, "Get in," after Nate guaranteed him an extra tip from the cash Miss Vivian had tucked into his pocket at the last minute.

The ride to Mason's Crossing was smoother than he remembered and gave him a chance to gaze at the tall oaks and pecan trees and the low, rolling fields, still dry as the Indian summer faded. Nothing like where I've been lately, he thought.

Just at sunset, he climbed the front stoop of the Cobb home, not sure what to expect. He rapped on the front door. No answer. He opened it and entered a darkened house.

"Hello?" he called. "Anyone home?" He set his suitcase by the front door.

Walking from room to room, Nate found no sign that anyone had been there recently. All the dishes and toys were put away, no food in the icebox, a few pieces of mail and newspapers stacked on the dining room table.

Echoes of the Cobb children's laughter haunted his thoughts. The rooms seemed larger than he remembered, and colder. He shivered as he paused by the staircase with his hand on the railing. No reason to go upstairs. He would have heard movement by now.

Is it too late to go to the shop? He sank into Amos' favorite chair. What will I do now?

Nate would have to figure out who would be a good shop supervisor to leave in charge of production while he went out on the road. Someone would need to keep up with inventory and order supplies, while another would have to be responsible for payments, collections, and payroll. Maybe those two jobs could be combined...

Lost in thought, Nate jumped when someone opened the front door. "Who's there?" he called. "Sarah? Amos?"

"'Tis I, Gussie," she said as she came around the corner into the living room. "Oh, welcome back, Mr. Nate." She crossed the room to set the evening paper on the stack with the others. "When did you get here?"

"Just now. Where is everyone?"

"The children have gone out to the farm to stay with their Grandma and Grandpa Mason, and Mr. and Mrs. Cobb should be home from Dallas tomorrow or the next day." She studied his face. "You've been away for some time now, haven't you? You look tired."

"Long journey," he said with a sigh. "I should get something to eat, then go to the shop."

"Mrs. Cobb had me take all the leftover food out of the icebox and send it along with the children. But I can bring you some soup and bread. I made it earlier, so it won't be quite so hot now."

"That's very thoughtful of you."

A half hour later, Gussie returned with a basket containing some warm vegetable soup in a crockery jar and a partial loaf of bread wrapped in a striped dishtowel. "You can bring these back tomorrow morning."

"Thank you." Nate smiled at her and couldn't help thinking how much easier it would be to eat the dinner that Isaac might have set in front of him, if only he had stayed in Charleston. Nothing more than memories now.

After he ate, he made the twenty-minute walk to the shop. Finished for the day, the crew was about to leave. Nate and the foreman exchanged greetings, and Nate heard a quick update on the current production. They agreed to spend more time going over details in the morning.

"I'm glad you're back," said the foreman. "We needed you these last few months."

"What do you mean?"

"Well, Mr. Cobb, he ain't quite the same as he used to be. Sometimes a little forgetful, more so lately. But the worst of it is his temper."

"I didn't know he had one."

"We didn't either, but he's gotten hotter'n our forge over there. Next minute, like nothing happened. Almost as if he's a different person."

"That doesn't sound like Amos. Maybe the doctors in Dallas will figure out what's wrong."

They said good night, and Nate headed back to the house. As he strolled under the darkening sky, he let his heart be relieved for the familiar neighborhoods and street corners, but wished for the Model T.

When he arrived at the house, he discovered someone had left a light on in the living room. Probably Gussie had returned after he left for the shop. The basket was gone, the bread crumbs swept up, and his spoon washed and put away. She'd be a valuable employee, he thought.

He collected his suitcase from the entry and went out the back door. Climbing the stairs to his apartment in the carriage house, he wondered how Miss Vivian or Isaac would react to

Nate's lodging. Nothing fancy here, but it's home. For now.

THE NEXT MORNING, GUSSIE brought Nate some hard-boiled eggs and buttered toast in the same basket. "I'll stop by the grocery and pick up a few things for you. Anything special?"

He handed her a five-dollar bill. "Coffee, please. And bacon."

As he ate, he glanced at the newspaper on the top of the stack. The top article included a photo of someone standing alongside an automobile on Congress Avenue in downtown Austin.

Nate made a mental note to go over the books and set up an appointment at the bank. If he estimated correctly, there should be enough to buy a car. Or, better yet, a bigger truck. Then he could make the deliveries himself and take more direct routes to call on his customers. He'd show Amos how much they could save over the course of a year.

He walked to the shop again and spent the morning going over schedules, orders, supplies, and the backlog. "Why didn't Amos hire more workers?" Nate said to the foreman during the lunch break.

"You know, I tried to get him to see it, but—"

"We could be running two shifts here and still not keep up. We'll be adding to our product line, too."

"I got some guys I could mention it to."

"How many?"

"At least seven, maybe more, once word gets around you're hiring. I'm glad you're taking charge."

"Let me talk to Amos first, and then we'll decide what we're going to do."

The foreman nodded and strolled back to his work. Nate

stood up and walked around the edge of the shop, nodding to the workers, calling each by name. He wished he'd asked Gussie to pack him a sandwich.

Nate was three-fourths of the way around when he came to a sudden stop. He looked quickly in both directions.

"Lose something?" one of the workers called.

"Wasn't there supposed to be more space here? I thought Amos was going to have this wall pushed out about fifteen feet."

"Changed his mind, I guess."

Nate was puzzled. He and Amos had gone over the costs of the expansion before he left for South Carolina, and Amos seemed enthusiastic about the projected return on investment. What could have made him drop the idea?

He finished his turn about the work area and headed back to the office in the other corner. Whenever Amos sat behind the desk, Nate's custom was to take the chair across from him, but today he sat in Amos' place.

Papers were piled up on top of the desk in no particular order. Nate shuffled a few of them. Invoices, requests for bids, several repeat notices from various companies.

With a tightening feeling in his gut, Nate opened the center drawer and found it stuffed with uncashed checks, wads of dollar bills in every denomination, and unopened bank statements. This could be thousands of dollars, just sitting here. Amos had always been so meticulous when it came to handling funds.

What had happened to him?

Nate spent the afternoon organizing the checks, matching them to invoices, and preparing deposit forms. He counted the cash, but had no idea whom it came from or where to apply it. Maybe Amos could tell him.

When he noticed the time, he left for the bank at a brisk pace and got in line at the teller's cage to make a deposit before it closed. The young woman who accepted his paperwork was plain, with slightly bucked teeth and bad skin. She wore a wedding ring, but didn't look much older than he was.

She handed his receipt to him. "Thank you, Mr. Wallace."

"Can you type?" he said.

"Yes, sir."

"I need a secretary, someone who can also handle money and keep accounts."

"A secretary who's also a bookkeeper?" She raised her eyebrows and peered at him. "I can ask around, maybe another teller—"

"If you come work for me, I'll give you a fifteen percent raise."

Her eyes grew wide and her teeth protruded as she grinned. "How soon?" she whispered.

"My company is expanding. I need someone right away."

"I can give my notice this afternoon, after closing." She stretched her hand forward over the counter. "Thank you, Mr. Wallace."

"Please report to my office by 8:00 a.m." He shook her hand and turned to leave, then whirled to face her again. "What's your name?"

"Lizzie. Lizzie Kingston."

Nate returned to the shop, wondering why he offered and the young Mrs. Kingston accepted, both without getting more information. Surely she'd want to know what her working conditions would be. He felt in his gut he was right about her.

He measured the area outside the office he shared with Amos. He'd include some extra funds in the budget for the building expansion, so Lizzie could have a desk in her own space, to make her an official personal secretary and bookkeeper. Just like the ones who worked for Mr. Hodges and Mr. Pinckney. And Sam Carolla.

He hadn't thought of Duncan Pinckney all day, much less Lexie. Staying busy really helped him keep his mind off his old troubles.

Maybe he could get Lizzie to write a letter to Aunt Vivian for him. That wouldn't be going against Duncan Pinckney's threat. Except he should refer to her as Miss Vivian instead, from now on.

He returned to his examination of supplies and inventory, using the unfilled orders to make estimates. Nate called the foreman into his office and together they produced a schedule, including when Nate's next business trip should be.

He glanced at the United States map on the wall behind Amos' desk. Small red flags on pins indicated drilling sites where Nate had taken orders and delivered equipment, covering half of East Texas and parts of central Louisiana. And several in Bossier City.

Nate ran his fingertips over the blue lines of the Sabine and Red Rivers. "Farther north should provide some likely targets, according to what I've been reading." He stuck a pin in the city of Texarkana and another one in El Dorado, just south of Little Rock. His attention wandered to Tulsa, Oklahoma, and West Texas, too, but no pins. Not yet.

"Well, I 'spect I best be getting home to the missus. She's been holding dinner for me," the foreman said, standing up. "See you in the morning."

After the man left, Nate locked the office and walked toward the exit. As he turned out the light, he envisioned a second shift and a night manager to keep the business humming past midnight. That way, he could stay later, too, and delay going home to an empty house.

THE HOUSE WASN'T EMPTY WHEN he arrived. Amos sat at the dining room table while Sarah stood at the stove, stirring something in a pot. The aroma from the kitchen reminded Nate of Sarah's beef stew, something he missed smelling in Charleston.

They both grinned and started toward him. Amos said, "Hey!" as he pumped his hand, while Sarah waited for her chance to hug him. Nate smiled and patted her on the arm, but didn't squeeze her the same way she did him.

"When did you get back?" said Amos at the same time Sarah said, "My goodness, we've missed you."

"Last night," Nate said, as he studied Amos' face. "How've you been?"

Sarah gave Nate a hard stare and shook her head, ever so slightly. Nate took that to mean she would talk to him later.

"We are busy as ever," said Amos. "Having a hard time keeping up."

"It's good to have you back, Nate." Sarah waved him toward a chair. "We didn't know you were coming home now. How was everything in Charleston?"

Nate sighed. "It'll take a while for me to share what all happened, but for now you should know... I came back here by myself. It's just me. There is no one else."

Amos frowned, a puzzled expression on his brow. "But what about your family?"

Nate inhaled, prepared to speak, but no sound came out. He focused on a dark spot on the dining table and bit his lip. Would there be enough money to hire a detective?

Sarah placed a crockery bowl filled with chunky beef stew in front of each man. She stood between them as she removed soup spoons from her apron pocket. "Milk or... milk? No beer tonight. Doctor's orders."

Nate pushed his chair back, but Sarah put her hand on his

shoulder before he could rise. "We are your family now." After a moment, she went back to the kitchen, poured two large glasses of milk, and brought them to the table. Her hands shook as Nate took the glasses from her.

"Aren't you eating?" Nate said.

"Not hungry yet." Sarah's voice was soft, hesitant.

Her protruding belly caught Nate's eye and he jumped up. He held his chair out for Sarah. "Sit here."

When he looked into her face, her eyes were wet. She gave him a crooked half-smile and sat down. Nate didn't know whether to laugh or cry with Sarah. His replacement family, the Cobb family, was growing, and yet...

He gazed at his friend as Amos ate his supper, slurping the juice from the stew and smacking his lips. He seemed to be the same gentle, even-tempered guy Nate remembered.

What could possibly be wrong?

After supper, Sarah suggested Amos must be tired from the trip and ready for bed. He didn't disagree, and, once she signaled to Nate to stay put, she followed Amos upstairs.

Nate shuffled the newspapers while he waited and read articles on local cattle markets, enrollment at the University in Austin, and repairs to homes and businesses after a hurricane had moved north from San Antonio in September.

Sarah came downstairs and sank into the sofa across from Nate. She now seemed exhausted, as if she couldn't move. Nate was about to suggest she go to bed, too, when she spoke.

"I guess your trip to Charleston didn't turn out like you expected. I'm sorry about that."

Nate shrugged. "I learned a lot."

"Hard lessons, aren't they?" She laced her fingers together and placed her hands over her belly.

"Is Amos going to be all right?"

"We don't know yet. One doctor says it's his blood pressure…" Sarah tugged at her apron pocket. "He's going to consult another specialist from a medical school in Baltimore."

"Johns Hopkins, known for its research," said Nate. "I've read about it in *The Wall Street Journal*."

"Oh, is that what it is?" Sarah's voice sounded far away.

"When is the baby due?"

"After Christmas. February, I think."

"What will Weesie say if it's a girl?"

"It would be a shock to her. Just like this… with Amos. She's very close to her daddy."

Like Miss Vivian. All daughters must form a special attachment with their fathers.

"Does she know you're back from Dallas?"

"Not yet. They can stay with my parents for a while longer. We might have to leave again soon. I miss all my babies."

The house would be too quiet without them, but maybe less noise and commotion was what Amos needed.

"Sarah, don't worry about the business. I'll take care of everything. You'll always have plenty of money."

"It's not the money… but thank you, Nate." She gave him a sad smile. "I knew I could depend on you."

"Once I get things settled at the shop, then I'll have to travel some."

"Of course. You do what you have to do."

Maybe that was the hardest lesson of all, Nate thought. Life, or fate, knocked you for a loop, and you fought back as best you could, just by putting one foot in front of the other. At times that wasn't enough, and you had to build something or make something. He'd been grateful the activity of reconstructing the orphanage had saved him from going stir-crazy.

Now was the time to build again. It was how he'd survive.

CHAPTER THIRTY-SEVEN

At the end of Nate's first week back in Mason's Crossing, he had gotten Lizzie started in her new job, with her first assignment to order a desk for herself. His gut instinct had already been proved right, when she produced a report on Friday afternoon showing every last cent in the company account. And where the money had come and gone.

He hired the construction crew to enlarge the shop, and told the foreman to contact the men who might be interested in working the night shift. He placed orders for extra equipment to increase output of the blowout preventers. In the storeroom, he counted and measured old broken drill bits, tagged according to customer, and added new replacements to the production schedule, hoping they hadn't waited too long.

Even with all the activity, he wondered how soon he could travel and sign up new customers. He lounged on the edge of Amos' desk and studied the calendar hanging on the wall behind it. Maybe he could get in a few trips before Thanksgiving.

"What do you think you're doing?" said an angry voice behind him.

Nate whirled around. "Hey, Amos, aren't you supposed to be at the house resting?"

"I can't stay home. There's too much work to do here."

Amos shuffled behind the desk, and Nate moved over so he could open the center drawer. He sat down and pulled out a stack of papers and rearranged it.

Nate resisted reaching for it. "Amos, would you like to—"

"I just want to manage my own business," he snapped. "You've been gone and you don't know what's going on here at the smithy."

"Maybe we could walk through the shop together. You can show me everything, bring me up to date."

"Those men out there..." Amos pointed to the crew as he yelled. "They need their jobs. I can't disappoint them." He shoved the papers off the desk and into the wastebasket and stood up.

Nate waited for Amos to come out from behind the desk, but he didn't move. Amos stood there, blinking as he stared across the room, his expression blank.

"Amos, how did you get here?"

As Amos turned his head to squint at Nate, his lip quivered. "I don't know." He rubbed his forehead and sat down again. "I don't know."

"Maybe you have the keys to the truck in your pocket?"

Amos leaned back and stuck his right hand into his pants pocket, then pulled out a set of keys. "Is this what you're looking for?" He handed them to Nate.

Nate slipped his hand under Amos' elbow. "C'mon, I'll drive you home."

Behind Amos' back, he dipped down and retrieved the papers from the wastebasket, tossing them on the desk as they headed out of the office.

TWO DAYS LATER, SARAH AND AMOS left for Dallas again, planning a longer stay at her sister's house, while the doctors put Amos through more tests. Nate arranged with Gussie to provide his meals, and he moved from the apartment into the big house, choosing a small bedroom in the corner.

When Lizzie suggested installing a telephone in the office, Nate agreed, then asked her to have another hooked up at the Cobb home. He would write to Sarah to give her the exchange number. Her rich sister probably already owned a telephone.

Over the next several weeks, Nate settled into a work routine as he waited for news from Sarah. The building expansion proceeded as planned, the new equipment was delivered on time, and once it was installed, the second crew was hired.

A streak of good luck at last.

Nate planned out a schedule with the night foreman, and then began to consider when he could leave on his next business trip. Each day, he stayed at the shop as long as possible. The house was too big and too quiet without the children, and too lonely without Sarah and Amos. He couldn't bring himself to enjoy the calm.

He checked the map on the wall behind the desk. Traveling to Dallas would take him west of Texarkana. Maybe he could spend the night at the sister's house, which Sarah had described as a mansion, "because we Mason girls always marry well," she said.

Must be like Aunt Vivian's.

At the end of the month, Lizzie handed him the business reports, including a balance sheet and a profit-and-loss statement. Nate studied each line, and when he came to the end, he gave a low whistle.

With all the expenses related to the expansion and additional payroll, their profit percentage had taken a sizable, but temporary, dip. The key would be new customers, and repeat orders from existing ones, to drive their net income back up.

He would pack tonight and leave Mason's Crossing tomorrow morning.

THE WEALTHY SISTER'S DALLAS MANSION was more like St. Louis Cathedral than Aunt Vivian's house, down to the black and white checkerboard tiles in the entryway. Sarah's sister was gone with her older children for several months on a widow's tour of Europe, and she had given Sarah and Amos the full run of her place.

A butler, a white man with a clipped foreign accent, opened the front door and escorted Nate to a parlor. Sarah sat staring out the French doors into the fall garden. Nate followed her gaze. Two matching statues of angels faced each other as they stood watch over the roses.

Sarah glanced up when he entered, but he gestured to her to keep her seat. He couldn't help thinking that Father Antoine would be joining them in a while.

"How are you? Nate said as he sat down opposite her. Her belly had grown since he last saw her. "And the baby?"

"We're… fine."

Nate searched the room. One glass for Sarah to drink water, but no sign that anyone else had been with her. "Where's Amos?"

Sarah sobbed for a moment before she could speak. "He's at the hospital. The doctors don't know what's wrong with him, but he keeps getting worse."

Nate sat up straight and resisted the sudden urge to go sit by her and hold her hand. He hadn't done it when Miss Vivian cried at his departure either, because it wouldn't change anything. He could only do what he had to do. Sarah would probably agree, but for certain his mother would.

She dabbed her eyes. "They say it's probably neurological."

"What does that mean?"

"Something inside his body is slowly attacking his nerve endings. Bit by bit, he's losing his ability to remember, to do things. His personality changes in a flash, while his energy plays out way too early."

Nate squirmed. "Can anything be done for him?"

"Whatever it is, there's no cure. Doctors don't even know what to call it."

"Maybe you could take him to Baltimore, to see the doctor from Johns Hopkins."

"I thought about that. The doctor here consulted with his old professor, who is now head of neurosurgery there." Sarah stood up. "Nate, I've made a decision."

While she paced in front of the fireplace, he watched her and waited in silence as his stomach tightened. He already knew what she would say, as he anticipated running their business by himself from now on, while Amos stayed home and rested.

"My sister has offered to let us live here while Amos is in the hospital. We... the kids and I, we have to move to Dallas."

Nate tilted his head back, as if someone had hit him on the chin, and stared at the decorated ceiling. For a few seconds, his mind went blank, as he studied fat painted cherubs playing among clouds surrounded by gold curlicues.

Running the business alone wasn't the same as living by yourself. With Sarah and Amos in Dallas, who would listen to him or care about him?

"The kids can stay with my parents until I get a few things settled," Sarah said. "Then I have to get Weesie registered in school. There's a boy's academy, the Terrill School, but they aren't old enough yet. Weesie'll attend Hockaday, at the lower school for now. My sister recommends it. Her girls went there. It's a fine boarding school."

Without paying much attention, Nate listened to Sarah's chattering, as she jumped from topic to topic. He knew she had to keep her mind busy. Just as he had done. Busy, or lose it.

"How will you pay all the medical bills? We have money in the business account."

"My parents said they'd help take care of everything. The

expenses are already adding up."

Nate had met Mr. and Mrs. Mason a few times. Plain folks, they didn't seem the type to manage a fortune. Even if theirs couldn't rival Miss Vivian's, all the Masons had worked to make themselves prosperous. Maybe that's how they endured their tragedies.

"What can I do to help?" Nate said.

"Just keep the business running as Amos would. Take care of the employees and the shop."

Nate nodded. No point in telling Sarah he planned to take the business far beyond what Amos ever imagined.

"You will never have to worry about money, I promise," he said.

Before he left Dallas, Nate stopped at the hospital to visit Amos. His friend slept the whole time, so Nate didn't stay long. He whispered the same promise to Amos.

OVER THE NEXT SEVERAL MONTHS, Nate traveled in a five-state area and expanded the business, first by doubling the number of customers, then by increasing the shop area yet again and hiring a third shift.

"We could start calling it a factory now," said the foreman.

"That's the idea."

In the back of his mind lurked the threat of Sheriff Kelley, and after the first of the year, Nate decided to find out what he needed to do. He hired a lawyer with a top Austin firm to investigate what charges had been filed from Clark's Common.

"Roy Wallace's death was ruled an accident," the lawyer told him two weeks later. "The county court records indicate that every witness claimed he attacked you first, and you were merely defending yourself."

The lawyer cleared his throat. "Also your mother's statement seemed to carry a lot of weight."

Nate could picture her talking in a calm voice, reminding everyone of how Roy's mean streak turned violent when he'd been drinking, and whom could she depend on except Nate?

"I guess I'm off the hook, then."

"There never was any hook. The case was closed and no warrant was ever sworn out."

The son of a bitch lied to me, thought Nate. He vowed to himself no one would ever get away with bullying him as Duncan Pinckney had done.

That left the Corollas. And he needed to do anything it took to protect Father Antoine.

"I want you to go to New York for me," Nate said to the lawyer. "Find a man named Clyde Farraday. Tell him I have a job in New Orleans for him."

ONCE NATE WAS CERTAIN Duncan Pinckney no longer held a knife to his throat, he wrote to Miss Vivian, telling her he would be delayed in Texas for quite a long time, but he would come see her again before summer. Just a visit, because his work determined he had to live in Mason's Crossing. He felt certain Alexandra would not want to move away from her family, so he would release her from her obligation.

I will never forget your kindness to me. Please let Isaac and Puddy take good care of you.
Your loving nephew,
Nate

After a moment of deep reflection, he added 'Rutledge' to

his name, writing it, he knew, for the last time.

FOUR MONTHS LATER, Nate received a letter from Miss Vivian's law firm, but Duncan Pinckney hadn't signed it. The partner wrote he was sorry to tell Nate his aunt had "died peacefully in her sleep" and left her entire fortune to him. The lawyer awaited directions for probate.

Nate crushed the law firm's envelope in his fist, as if he could squeeze the life out of it. He picked up the telephone and dialed the number at the top of the letterhead.

"I thought Mr. Pinckney had her change the will," Nate said, after he had gotten the details on arrangements for the funeral.

"He tried, but she was a sweet, stubborn old soul. I 'spect you know that as well as anybody."

Nate gave him instructions to hire a property manager for the real estate, to keep Isaac and Puddy employed at her home, and to give ten percent of the revenues to the orphanage every quarter. But he still wasn't satisfied.

"Why did you write to me instead of Mr. Pinckney doing it?" he said.

"Uh, well... Mr. Pinckney had an accident," the lawyer said. "He's laid up for quite a spell."

"What happened?"

The man's voice dropped to a whisper. "He and the other boys in the Klan were engaged in some... ummm, shall we say, community improvement activities on the other side of town. Mr. Pinckney musta got some kerosene spilt on himself, and he caught fire, too, 'fore that niggra church was even half burned down."

"I just spoke to my aunt last week, but she didn't mention

it. Was he hurt bad?" Nate tried not to sound hopeful, but only because his mother wouldn't approve.

"The doctors think he's not gonna make it. He's still in a coma, covered in bandages from head to foot. If I was in that shape, I'm sure I'd rather die, too."

"I bet." Nate shook his head at the befitting judgment inflicted on the man who chose to be his enemy, then he remembered his manners. "Please give my sympathy to the family, especially Mrs. Pinckney. She was always nice to me."

Nate assured the lawyer he would come to Charleston sooner or later to sign any required documents and pay the legal fees. After he hung up, he stared at the telephone as if he expected it to ring again.

When he couldn't shut out the sound of Miss Vivian's giggle from his mind, he got up and went out onto the factory floor, slamming the office door behind him.

CHAPTER THIRTY-EIGHT

Not long after, Nate received a large brown envelope in the mail. The word "Personal" was written above his name, so Lizzie had set it on his desk without opening it. He squeezed the envelope to gauge its thickness before he slit the flap and shook out its contents.

A folded newspaper tumbled to the desk. He spread it open and studied the front page, first the name of the paper, then the headline.

THE NEW ORLEANS TIMES-PICAYUNE
Judge Carolla Stabbed to Death, Gang War Erupts

The first few lines of the article gave him all he needed to know. During a gun battle between rival gangs and the police, the foreman at the warehouse was one of several Carolla employees killed. Probably shot in the back by his new partner, Nate thought.

At the bottom of the page was a smaller article with a headline more important to Nate.

Popular Priest Resumes Relief Work After Long Recovery

Smiling, Nate made a note to have the lawyer in Charleston send an anonymous $500 contribution to Father Antoine's charitable works, designated for the prison. He tucked the newspaper under his arm and wondered how Clyde had managed to start a gang war without getting hurt. Maybe he caught Judge Carolla in an alley outside a speakeasy. All he had to yell was "Death to the Matrangas!" to get everyone steamed and out for blood.

But what if Clyde hadn't escaped? What if the corrupt police…?

Nate snatched the brown envelope from his desk and turned it over. Postmarked in Wyoming.

He sat down behind his desk, tossed his head back, and laughed. Loud and long enough that Lizzie knocked on his door to see if he needed anything.

"Call that lawyer in Charleston and find out if Duncan Pinckney has died yet. If not, be sure he lets you know right away when it happens, as I will probably be on the road. When you get his call, please arrange to have a large vase of flowers delivered to the First Baptist Church for the funeral. Make it as grand as the florist can manage."

"How do you want the card made out?"

"Have them write 'Rest in Eternity.' Sign it 'Nate Rutledge' in nice big letters."

When she left his office, Nate took the newspaper and the envelope to the fire at the forge and dropped them into the flames. Pretending for a moment they were Duncan Pinckney, he waited until they turned to black ashes, then he walked back to his office.

FOLLOWING HIS NEXT TRIP, which had kept him away for seven weeks, Nate came back to Mason's Crossing to an empty house. The furniture was right where Sarah had left it, but the house felt bare all the same. He found an envelope on the dining room table, with his name written in her familiar script. He sat down in Amos' favorite chair and opened it.

Dear Nate,

We will get settled in Dallas very soon, as my sister has given us the run of the house and left us all but two of her servants. Amos is about the same, and we will move him here instead of the hospital. The doctor will stop by in a few days.

Come see us as often as you can. The children are growing up too fast.

Meanwhile, why don't you move into the big house? Take care of yourself. Get Gussie to cook for you.

With sincere affection,
Sarah Mason Cobb

Nate didn't know whether to feel relieved or distressed. He would miss the family warmth around the dinner table and at church on Sunday mornings, but there was nothing he could do to make the situation better for anyone. He could bury himself in his work and not think about losing his friend.

Traveling, building a business, and managing employees would have to substitute for the bonds of family, friendship, and partnership. Maybe making a profit would be a better choice in the long run. After all, money didn't get sick and die.

His only pleasure seemed to be in working and watching the business grow. He never stayed in one place long enough to get comfortable or enjoy regular companions. After three years of back and forth, he considered purchasing an apartment building in Chicago, but soon decided staying at a hotel would be less trouble.

Nate stuck to his plan for the next decade, only visiting in Dallas two or three times a year on his way back to Mason's Crossing. He always turned down Sarah's invitation to come for Thanksgiving and Christmas. After the fourth year, he quit dropping by the room where Amos was confined to the bed.

When he could manage the time and the travel schedule, he stopped by the cemetery in Charleston, but rarely stayed overnight at Miss Vivian's house or called on her acquaintances. Isaac and Puddy never seemed to get any older, and they seldom had news beyond repairs to the house. Nate kept thinking someday he would run into Mary at the gravesides.

While in Mason's Crossing, he examined the monthly statements Lizzie had prepared and cut large checks to deposit in the Cobb's bank account. Nate invested part of his share of the profits, plus some of the income from Aunt Vivian's estate, in a catalogue company that realized how the automobile would change the way people bought consumer goods.

What impressed Nate the most was their pioneering offer of free parking in a lot next to the new stores they were building. He predicted the company would expand faster than any other, and therefore pay high dividends. When the company, Sears & Roebuck, acquired two suppliers that had merged to produce electric washing machines, Nate purchased more stock.

He would have bought one of their machines for his mother, if only he could. He ordered one anyway, plus a new refrigerator, and moved the old icebox out to the storeroom.

Nate also used some of his inheritance to buy real estate, always paying cash. When stock in the General Electric Company became available, he acquired as much as he could afford.

He believed the future of his fortune, as well as the future of the country, lay in manufacturing. A trip to Pittsburgh convinced him U.S. Steel would be a sound investment.

One day, Lizzie came into his office, grinning like she just heard something hilarious. "Mr. Nate, are you thirty yet?"

"Not as far as I know."

"Well, congratulations!" She waved a stack of reports at him.

"My birthday isn't today." He wasn't sure of the actual date.

"Doesn't matter. You still would make the list."

"List of...?" He cocked his head at her. She didn't often play guessing games with him.

Lizzie laid the papers in front of him. "According to these numbers, you are officially now a millionaire! And you haven't even turned thirty yet."

The idea had never occurred to Nate to celebrate such a milestone. Had he really achieved anything worthwhile?

Thirty. Millionaire. The words bounced off each other in his head.

Accumulating wealth consumed most of his time and all his attention. And he was still alone.

CHAPTER THIRTY-NINE

During one Christmas season, Nate could not avoid going to Dallas to be with the Cobbs, but it was a trip he dreaded. He arrived on the twentieth, the day before Amos' funeral.

"It's as if he died a long time ago, and I've already given him back to God and mourned my loss," Sarah told him that evening after dinner, when they were alone in the dining room of her sister's mansion.

Nate nodded. He didn't know what else to say. He'd had enough of mourning and loss. Why couldn't God be satisfied by now?

That afternoon, Louisa had returned home from her senior year at boarding school, but she barely acknowledged Nate. He glimpsed her as she darted out of the house or escaped to her room. She had no time and few words for him at all. He didn't see her again until the next morning at the cemetery.

Dressed in black wool crepe for the funeral, she had stood at the graveyard slightly apart from her mother and the circle of smaller children gathered around her. Nate waited behind them and to one side, where he could observe both of them, but it was Louisa—grown, changed, and beautiful—who held his gaze.

She had not even glanced at him. The profile of her face glowed through the black veil that fell just below her chin. She blinked often, but no tears trickled down her skin. A wisp of her golden hair had escaped from the comb holding it, tucked below the brim of the black felt hat she wore.

Why did his heart hurt so? Was it only for the loss of his friend and partner? Whenever he looked at Louisa, his breath caught in his throat, and the heartache spread through him.

This is ridiculous. I am almost thirty-one, and she is still a child, not even seventeen.

Yet she was not a child, as the curves of her body and the fullness of her mouth told him. Try as he might, he could not pay attention to the pastor as he read scriptures. Toward the end of the service, at the last second Nate remembered to bow his head for the prayer.

Following the service, Nate lingered in the fellowship hall of Highland Park Methodist Church while he watched Sarah greet friends and other family. If she felt like sobbing, it didn't show. She gave each person a sad smile and a hug, as if they were more important.

After half an hour, he thought she looked tired, so he brought her a plate of cookies and small sandwiches which the ladies of the church had provided. She asked him for a glass of water as well.

He peered into her eyes and wondered how she could seem so peaceful. *She's calm for the sake of their children,* he decided. That was how his mother had acted, too.

"I'M SORRY FOR Weesie's behavior," Sarah said to him over breakfast two mornings later. "She's been altogether too difficult for a while, missing her daddy for so long, and now with the funeral, she's had to be absent from school and being with her friends at the holiday parties."

Sarah picked at the scrambled eggs on her plate. "She's furious with me because I won't buy her that green silk dress from Neiman-Marcus. I took her there to try it on before Amos died, but I haven't had time to even think about anything else, and she still wants to go to a party this weekend. I didn't even decorate much for Christmas because it didn't seem right... so soon, but life has to go on, especially for the younger children... and... and..."

Sarah stopped talking as if she realized she wasn't addressing Nate anymore.

"It's all right," Nate said. "Do you mind if I stay a little longer? I have other business to attend to." He stared out the window.

"It's Christmas Eve. You can bunk here with us as long as you like. It's not like old times, of course, with Amos gone, but it's wonderful to have you here. You were like a younger brother to him, you know."

Later that day Neiman-Marcus delivered a large rectangular box, several feet long and six inches deep, to Miss Louisa Mason Cobb.

Just off the entry hall, Nate sat in the library reading *The Wall Street Journal*. He stood up and tiptoed toward the doorway, hanging back enough to see without being seen.

After the courier left, Louisa sat at the foot of the stairs and tore open the lid. He smiled when she squealed and shouted for her mother to come look. If the windows had been open, he thought, the neighbors would have heard the noise from three doors down.

"I certainly didn't order it," Sarah told her daughter as Louisa held the dress up to herself in front of the entry hall mirror. "It must have been someone else."

"Who else knew this was the very dress I'd been longing for all this time? Who would have bought it for me and had it delivered in time for Christmas?"

"Several people, maybe. I mentioned it to my sister before the funeral, and I told Nate, well, not about the dress, but about your wanting to go to a party, to see what he thought." Sarah rubbed her forehead. "Maybe I did tell Nate about the dress."

Nate returned to his chair and held the newspaper in front of his face, but couldn't focus on the article he had been reading. Near the doorway, footsteps shuffled and a throat cleared. He dropped the paper into his lap.

Louisa stood leaning against the doorway, the dress draped over one arm. She looked at the floor and bit her lip.

"Yes, what is it?" he said.

No answer. He waited and watched as she fidgeted, tapping the side of her foot against the door.

"Thank you for the dress," she whispered, then turned to race up the stairs.

Tilting his head back, Nate sighed and gazed up at the ceiling. "Merry Christmas, my darling Weesie."

THE NEXT AFTERNOON, after a quiet Christmas morning, Louisa came into the library, pulled a book from the shelf, and sat down in the chair across from Nate.

She smiled at him. "I don't miss Daddy so much when I'm with you." She spread the book on her lap and read until the dinner bell rang.

That night, she joined him on his walk after dinner. He found himself talking with her about his travels, sharing his plans

"Nate, you've made a fortune. For yourself and for Daddy. Don't you want something else out of life? Something more personal?"

"Like what?"

"Someone to be with? Someone to love? Why aren't you married?"

An image of Alexandra Pinckney flashed through his mind. "She'd have to want me for myself, not for my money or any other reason."

Louisa giggled. "That's not hard."

Her expression turned serious. "Anything else."

How could he answer without ripping open old wounds? Confronting a lifetime of loss and grief. Never getting what his heart cried out for.

"I guess I want someone to love me, just me, more than anything or anyone else. Someone who will keep on loving me, no matter what. Someone who will never leave me."

Louisa turned toward him and smiled up at him. "And…?"

"Children. I want a family of my own. Babies who will grow up and call me 'Daddy'."

How did Louisa do it? Get him to open up his heart, say words he had never spoken to anyone. For a moment, he couldn't tell if his spirits felt lighter or heavier.

Nate pulled his overcoat tighter and resumed his stroll, slowing down after half a block to give Louisa time to catch up with him. She shivered and slipped her hand in his pocket.

Lighter. Definitely lighter.

They settled into this daily routine, and Nate began to look forward to her company. He spent the time before she arrived in the library thinking of things to tell her, worried she would be bored. She asked a lot of questions on any subject he mentioned, and his uneasiness faded.

During their evening walks, the quiet moments between them were a mystery to Nate. How could a teenaged girl not be eager to chatter or in a hurry to get somewhere? She seemed as comfortable strolling in silence as talking or listening.

On a particularly cold evening, she folded her hand around his arm and pulled him closer. "Brrrrr!"

"Your nose and cheeks are red," he said. "Here, let me wrap your wool scarf better."

"I guess I didn't notice." Her eyes twinkled up at him as he twined her knitted blue scarf around her neck. "That's much better."

Better for me, too, Nate thought. "I've always liked taking care of you. From the time you were a little girl."

They had reached the front porch, and Louisa climbed up one step and turned to face Nate. "I'm glad you've been here. We couldn't... I couldn't have gotten through everything without you."

She stretched up on tiptoes to kiss his cheek. "I want you to stay this time."

"Wish I could."

Louisa frowned and whirled around to race inside the house.

This visit won't be any different than the last time I left her in Dallas. How could it ever be?

ON THE SATURDAY NIGHT of the party, Nate watched from the foyer as Louisa descended the front staircase.

No ornament, no jewel could enrich her beauty. A long thick strand of golden hair curled around her neck and shoulders like an embrace. He could not look away.

She smiled at him and, after drawing on her mother's black velvet evening cloak, hurried out the front door to meet her friends.

"Someone's father is bringing Weesie home by ten, after the supper, but before the dancing starts," Sarah said. "She'll just have to miss that. There will be other parties."

"No doubt," said Nate, as he put on his own wool topcoat.

"Oh, are you going out?"

"Yes, it's not too cold tonight. I think I'll stretch my legs before I finish my paperwork."

Nate ambled through the crisp night air for a long time,

and when he returned to the house hours later, he sat on one of the benches at the far end of the wide porch, smoking his cigar.

Each puff convinced him he should leave Dallas as soon as he could. He missed the wide brilliant sky over Central Texas. Hovering at the edge of any family, even the Cobbs, made him feel his loneliness and his losses more. He needed the solitude to escape.

When the burning tip was within an inch of his knuckles, a car stopped in front of the house. "Good night, and thank you!" Louisa called to the driver as she waved good-bye and walked through the front gate and up the sidewalk.

Her golden hair gleamed in the moonlight, and when she pushed the hood of the black velvet cloak onto her shoulders, she looked like a queen ready for coronation.

As she reached the bottom step, he suddenly flung the remains of his cigar out into the yard, where it hissed and sizzled in the late night dew.

If only I could toss my feelings away as easily.

Already halfway up the front steps, Louisa stopped and turned toward the sound with a little gasp. "Who is there?" she said, breathless, he imagined, as much from being startled as from rushing up the steps.

"Oh, Nate, it's you." She sounded relieved as she stopped at the edge of the porch.

He supposed she would say good night and go into the house, but she strolled toward him. In the chilly shadows of the porch, her breath came out in little clouds.

"Did you have fun?" he said.

"Oooh, it was a lovely party. The tables were loaded with fancy food and candelabras were everywhere, and all the others girls' dresses were bright, but not as beautiful as mine, even after Mother removed the silver sash and the lace. And there was lots of holiday sparkle. It was just grand."

"I'm glad you enjoyed it."

The unfamiliar electric current began again in the center of his body, sending waves to his fingertips.

"I didn't get to dance though."

"I'm sorry. Maybe at the next party—"

"But I want to dance tonight," she pouted. "Dance with me now?"

"There's no music."

"Give me your hand, that one," she said as she stood before him and pulled him to his feet. She placed his right hand at her waist. "Now hold your left arm like this." She moved closer to him and placed her left hand on his shoulder.

As she made him whirl her around the porch, the moonlight shimmered and twinkled in tiny beams across her smooth oval face, her full lips slightly parted. He pulled her to him, quick and hard, before either of them could take a breath, one arm slipped under the black velvet cloak around her small waist, the other arm wrapping her upward to the nape of her neck, pressing her to him.

Nate spread his fingers and plowed them into her thick hair, cupping her head in his hand. He searched her face, but her eyes were closed.

She reached up and locked her wrists behind his neck, and arching her back, she urged his face to hers, his mouth to hers, bending his body to hers. Their breath, their longing, their need for each other came together and urged them into a hungry, devouring kiss. When he tasted the sweetness of her mouth, he tightened his arms around her.

With one hand, she reached toward her collarbone and fumbled with the silken cord until the cloak fell to the floor. Nate kissed her lips, her face, and her neck, and when her white shoulders were exposed, he lifted her off the floor and pressed the curve of her flesh to his open mouth.

She clung to him and, as his lips traveled down to the swelling edge of her neckline, she kissed the top of his head and wrapped her forearms around as if to protect him.

"Nate, Nate," she whispered. "I'm yours. I love you so much. Take me now."

At once he stopped kissing her and let her feet drop to the floor with a jolt. Frowning, he jerked her away from him, but did not release her shoulders. "What do you mean by that?"

"What?" she said, looking a little dazed, as if awakened that very moment.

"Why did you say that?" He shook her slightly as he bent over to peer down into her face, searching, almost angry.

"Because," she said softly, "I love you. I have always loved you. We are meant to be together forever. I want to be your wife. Don't you want to take me for your wife?"

"Is that what you meant?" He let go of her and stood up straight.

"What did you think I meant?" she said, her voice indignant.

He stammered, "I don't know. I wasn't sure you… I thought maybe…"

"No!" she said in a fierce tone. "You are the only one I have ever loved or will ever love." Then she turned to go into the house.

Before she could take a second step, he called in a soft voice, "Weesie?"

She stopped and faced forward but did not look back at him. "Yes, Nate."

"Marry me."

Without turning toward him, she said, "When you didn't

come to Dallas for such a long time after we left, I waited for you. I always knew you would come for me. It was hard to be patient because I longed for you so much, even when I didn't know what it was like to be kissed by you or held like this by you."

She turned and looked at him. "All that time, I waited for you, and only you, and all that I am, all of me, is yours."

He stepped toward her as she fell into his arms again, and he held her so close he could feel her heart pounding against his heavy topcoat.

Chapter Forty

When Nate asked Sarah for permission to marry Louisa, she didn't hesitate to give her approval.

"I think you're the only one who can make her happy, especially after all we've been through. You'll be a calming influence on her, too. She'll be better off in Mason's Crossing anyway. Her Grandmother Mason is nearby, and we'll be moving back eventually, as soon as school is out for the boys next summer."

Nate thought she seemed relieved. "How much time do you need to plan the wedding?" Aunt Vivian and Mrs. Pinckney would have needed many months.

"We'll keep it small and simple. I'll call the church and book the chapel and the minister."

"I'm sorry for the extra burden now."

"Actually, you're doing me a favor."

Nate raised his eyebrows. "How so?"

"Oh, I mean, it will give me something to do since Amos isn't… well… maybe a week or so."

Grinning, Nate said, "That soon? I hope I can be ready."

"Are you sure you want to do this?" Sarah's expression turned quizzical.

Nate thought of the abandoned house in Mason's Crossing, the meals he ate by himself, the empty bed. "I've never been more certain of anything in my life."

CONDUCTED BY THE SAME minister who just weeks ago

had buried Amos, their wedding ceremony was brief, attended only by family. When Louisa and Nate departed for the train station, Sarah and the younger children cried and begged her to write to them.

Louisa blew them kisses from the taxi window as she and Nate settled into the back seat. She had changed from her simple wedding dress of ivory satin into a gray wool gabardine suit.

Nate had already sent three large trunks to the station with the porter. He carried her train case into their private sleeping compartment, along with his small leather valise.

"When you wake up tomorrow morning, we'll be in Chicago," he told her as he turned toward the door.

"Where are you going?" she said.

"To the smoking car." He patted the cigars in the breast pocket of his jacket. "You can unpack and get settled. I'll come back in a little while and we'll go have dinner. Are you hungry?"

"Yes, a little, I guess. It's been such a day, I..." Louisa looked at the floor and the window, anywhere but at Nate.

"Take your time." He closed the door.

About forty minutes later, Nate knocked and entered just as she was coming out of the bathroom. "Oh!" he said. "I thought you were ready to go to dinner."

"I am." She smiled at him, with eyes ever widening.

The dining car was crowded, but Nate had tipped the maître d' extra to seat them in the corner near the window so Louisa could see the rolling plains of Oklahoma. As dusk fell like a purple velvet curtain, he sensed her growing apprehension, and after dinner poured a little brandy into her coffee from a small silver flask he carried inside his front coat pocket.

"This will help you relax," he told her, and he tipped some into his own cup as well. "It's hard to feel comfortable... on a train."

"I guess so." She took a deep breath and exhaled all at once as she spoke, like air escaping from a balloon. "I've never been… on a train… overnight."

They left the dining car and walked down the long dimly lit corridor to their compartment. Nate thought it would take forever, but once they arrived and he put his hand on the door handle, it seemed hardly any time had passed.

"Would you like to change in there?" he said, pointing toward the bathroom door. "I've yet to unpack anything." He lifted his small leather suitcase onto the narrow bed, which the porter had folded down for them. As he snapped the brass locks open, she darted into the bathroom and closed the door.

When Louisa emerged, Nate shut the closet door and turned toward her. He wore no shirt, no shoes or socks, and his suspenders dangled to his knees.

She stared at his dark chest hair and the hard, rounded curves of his shoulders and arms. She smiled, leaned her head to one side, and said, "Now I remember how you looked working in the blacksmith shop with Daddy when I was a little girl. Once I got older, I thought you were the strongest, handsomest young man in all of Mason's Crossing."

He laughed.

Louisa took another step toward him. "It's true, it's true! I still think—"

"You're so beautiful," he told her, and aching for her, he put both hands on her arms and leaned down to kiss her. She tilted her face up to his, but he stopped and looked down at her arm. "How did your sleeve get so wet?"

Louisa clutched the center of her nightgown in her fist and confessed as a small child would. "It's not my fault. There was no towel. My face was wet, my eyes were closed, I couldn't see… What are you doing?"

"It doesn't matter, my darling girl," he said, as he reached up to her hair, still twisted and pinned on top of her head.

She stood motionless, arms at her side, as one by one, he pulled the hairpins out until her long golden curls fell past her shoulders, down to her elbows. He spread his fingers like a comb and placed each hand on the side of her head, lifting her hair layer by layer until it was all gathered in a thick tumble down her back.

He gazed down at the full length of her and realized he could see the soft outline of her flesh through her pale night-gown, which now clung to her. He put his hands on the sides of her neck and the warmth of them made her shiver. His hands slid forward, his fingers fumbling to undo the small rose-col-ored satin ribbon at her neck, then the tiny pearl buttons down the front.

He paused before touching her, first with his fingertips, then caressed her breast in his palm. Under the thin fabric, he ran his hands along her body, from her small waist to the back of her smooth hips.

"Nate," she sighed as he guided her nightgown off her shoulders and let it fall to the floor. "Take me now."

He knew she meant it differently this time.

Nate did take her, take all she had to give him, gave her all he had been saving up, tried to lose himself, find himself in her, gave her all the loneliness of the years behind him. All those years, he had worked to give, but there was no one to receive until Louisa came to him.

As the train hurtled northward and the track straightened and flattened on the dusty plains, passing Kansas City in the predawn gray light, Nate settled himself against the pillows and watched her sleep, exhausted and exhilarated.

He dozed for a little while, and when the sky turned a milky pink, he arose to dress and slipped out in search of coffee and any business news of Chicago. He hoped they would have time to make love again before arriving.

Nate returned to the corridor to find a small crowd gathered several doors down from their compartment. Passengers still in their nightclothes huddled together, murmuring.

Someone turned to look at Nate. "Here he is now, lady. Isn't this your husband?"

The crowd separated to reveal Louisa, tear-stained face, wrapped in only a sheet, shivering in the corner against the wall.

Nate heard whispers of "came out of her room screaming" … "crying and wailing like a banshee" … "no one could go near her" … as he strode toward her and dropped to his knees. "Weesie, what are you doing out here in the hallway? Darling, come back to the room with me. It's cold."

He tried to pull her into his arms. "What's the matter—"

Louisa clutched his forearm in a fierce grip. "How could you leave me?" she shrieked. "Where did you go?"

She dissolved into tears and sobbed, "I thought you'd left me. Don't ever leave me. Promise you won't ever leave me!"

Nate gathered her up, tucking the sheet over her naked body as he arose, and carried her back to their compartment. He felt like a hammer had struck his heart.

CHAPTER FORTY-ONE

As Nate's investments and customer list grew, and thereby his fortune, his business took him away from Louisa for extended periods. In the five years since their marriage, he had hired maids, attendants, companions, drivers, anyone who could help ease the burden of his absences.

He encouraged Louisa to engage in projects while he was gone, having no concern when she ordered the dining room ceiling ripped out or the swimming pool bulldozed and another one installed across the lawn.

Sometimes he considered extending his trips, but knew his absence would only make Louisa's reaction worse when he returned home at last. Half the time, he would find her laid up in bed, scarcely able to move or talk. Not feverish, but weak and listless. Other times, she'd run out the front door down the driveway, shrieking and laughing, hugging him before he could get out of the car.

On occasion, fear—fear that she would end up like Amos— threatened to overwhelm him. He didn't know if she needed medicine or rest or something else. Whatever it might be, the solution eluded him and the doctors he engaged.

Maybe some girls never get over their father's death.

The Italian Renaissance-style mansion he built for her was never finished, from her perspective at least. Louisa always had something in mind that had to be improved or adjusted. After she ordered remodeling or reconstruction, she took to her bed and Gussie, whom Louisa called Mrs. Gussmann, was compelled to oversee the project's completion.

"I'm sorry my wife screams at you, Gussie," Nate said, when he returned from a trip to Paris. "I don't know what to do about it."

"It's not that she's never happy, Mr. Nate," she said. "You miss a lot of the good times with her."

Nate sighed. Would it always be like this?

He wondered if a change of scenery might do her some good, so Nate bought tickets on a luxury liner to Europe for her and her mother. When it came time to pack and prepare for the trip, Louisa would not leave the house or allow Sarah to come visit.

"I don't feel well enough to entertain her," she muttered, "and I don't want her coming all this way just to take care of me."

"Your mother wouldn't mind," Nate said. "She told me she wouldn't. Sarah's able to stand the travel, and—"

"You talked to her behind my back!" Louisa shouted. "She can survive anything! Yes, she's strong, and you think I'm not!" She slammed the door to her dressing room.

Nate could hear her sobbing through the shut door, picturing her collapsed on the silk upholstered divan. He waited a moment, shook his bowed head, and then turned to go downstairs into his library.

A doctor's appointment, he thought, as he descended the stairs to the main hall. I'll have to make another one for her before I go to Pennsylvania. She doesn't seem to be gaining any weight even with the tonics the doctor prescribed for her last visit. Or was it the time before?

Nate entered his study and welcomed the darkened atmosphere for a moment. Without light, the room had no boundaries, and he could imagine himself unhampered by problems that lingered. When he finally turned on the lamp at his desk, all feelings of disengagement vanished.

Just as he opened his briefcase, the telephone rang.

"Middleton, here," a man's voice came over the line.

"Did you find her this time?" Nate said.

"I believe so. "

"Is she there in Atlanta?"

"Yes, but I can try to bring her to Mason's Crossing, if you want," the man said. "Just so you can be absolutely sure."

"No, I'll come there," Nate said, still standing and hovering over the contents of his briefcase, skimming a few documents. "Just keep an eye on her, but don't let her know you're following her. I don't want to frighten her."

"I'll keep my distance," the man said. "When will you be here?"

"I can arrive in four days from now, on Thursday afternoon. A car will be waiting for me at the airport. I'll meet you at the hotel about two-thirty."

Nate hung up the receiver and stared blindly into the center of the room for a moment. His thoughts raced as he considered his next move. How would he tell Louisa he was leaving the next day, but couldn't say when he would return? Atlanta was just one of the stops he would have to make.

He glanced again at the photograph he had received in the mail from the man in Atlanta. He was afraid to examine it too closely. The woman in the photograph had turned sideways and the wind had blown her hair across most of her face. He had no idea whom she really was.

After several hours of reading the papers and reports stacked on his desk, Nate rubbed his eyes. He stood up, stretched, and glanced around the paneled room. A recent painting of Louisa, looking delicate but glowing, hung over the mantel. Painted from a photograph from their first, and only, trip to Europe together, three months after they were married. They had returned home to discover her pregnant, but she soon miscarried. The doctor couldn't give them any reason.

The artist would not have believed she was the same woman now.

Nate remembered to call the doctor and agreed with him tomorrow morning would be best for all.

Maybe he would tell Weesie then.

Could the doctor bring a nurse to stay with Louisa after he broke the news of his imminent departure? Yes, that could be arranged.

Less worried, Nate was still not entirely relieved. Yet the news he had received from the earlier telephone call gave him reason to believe things would get better after the out-of-town matter was settled.

Tucking a newspaper under his left arm, he wandered into the dining room, where the cook took his order for a simple dinner, while another servant laid a place for him at one end of the long empty table.

"No, don't bother to light the fire," he told the young man. "I won't be in here long enough. Besides, it's still summer, isn't it?"

"Uh, no, sir. It's fall now, officially since last week."

Nate ate his dinner in silence, with only an occasional grunt over what he read in the business section. One article on aviation held his attention.

If I purchase a larger aircraft, then... His mind spun through delivery schedules, meetings on both coasts, quicker factory inspections, and a number of other reasons to get across the country faster. He would still keep the smaller one, the two-seater biplane he had purchased from military surplus four years ago.

After he finished his dinner, he carried his own dishes to the kitchen, over the protests of the cook, and returned to his office.

He poured himself a small snifter of brandy, lit a long cigar, and sprawled on the burgundy leather sofa, continuing to read about the benefits of owning one's own cargo plane.

He turned to the front page for articles of international news. Japan had invaded China, and Germany had overrun Poland.

At three in the morning, he awoke suddenly when the clock on the mantel chimed. The brandy snifter stood empty, where he had placed it on the side table. The remains of the cigar looked as if it had also gone to sleep where it came to rest, propped in the crystal ashtray.

Once upstairs, he peeked into Louisa's bedroom. She lay asleep on her back, so still she might be dead. He wondered why she never moved in her sleep. The pale blue silk covers were smooth and almost untouched, as if she might disappear under them. The pillow next to her head, waiting for him, looked newly fluffed, no creases or indentations.

Nate could not hear her breathing, even when he came closer and stood next to the bed. Her thick blonde hair, into which he loved to bury his face and hands, lay spread out like an angel's wing around her head and neck, resting on her shoulders.

He lifted a strand of it, not fearing to disturb her, and examined it as if determining its value.

Louisa sighed ever so softly in her sleep, still not moving. He let go of her hair, turned, and left the room, closing the door quietly behind him.

"I'M GOING TO RUN a few tests," Dr. Grant told Nate privately the next morning, after spending half an hour with Louisa. "Frankly, I suspect she might be with child."

Nate stared at the doctor without flinching. "I didn't think she could… when will you know for sure?" He had quit anticipating news of a growing family, and he was afraid to smile.

"In a week or so," the doctor said. "Will you be back by then?"

"I don't know. I have urgent business in Atlanta on Thursday, then on to Pittsburgh." Nate cleared his throat. "Is she strong enough to carry a child?'

"Oh, her body's healthy all right, if you can get her to eat more. Maybe she will on account of the baby, if that's the result of the tests." Dr. Grant studied Nate's face for a moment. "This will be good news, won't it?"

"Yes, of course. I hope so," Nate words came out fast as he looked aside. "Maybe I should get her mother to come stay with us after all…'

"Whatever you think," he said, picking up his black bag and straightening his jacket. "I know you travel a great deal, so it would be easier on her if you get someone here permanently and soon. Do you have anyone else in mind to help you with this… problem?"

Nate hoped Atlanta would give him a solution.

BY THE TIME Nate's flight landed in Atlanta on Thursday afternoon, he had had few thoughts of Louisa for several hours. The flight across the South had been interrupted by stops in Shreveport, where a few years ago Nate had invested in cotton production, and in New Orleans, where he met with the board of directors of a shipping line in which he was part owner.

In the air since ten o'clock, Nate gave up trying to read anything and just sat. He took the photograph from his coat pocket again, perhaps for the twentieth time, and studied the figure in the picture, as if waiting for her to turn toward him and brush her hair back from her face. He looked at nothing else until the plane landed.

After the chauffeured ride to the Grand Hotel in Atlanta, Nate went directly to the dining room without checking in at the front desk.

"Nice to see you again, Mr. Wallace. Mr. Middleton is expecting you, sir," the maitre d' said, as he led Nate to a table across the room next to the windows overlooking the front sidewalk.

Nate shook hands with a middle-aged man, dressed in a plain brown suit, not shabby, but not new either. Mr. Middleton had tried to hide his boyish face behind a blond mustache, and his light brown hair kept falling across his forehead.

"Do you have any other photographs?" Nate said.

"Of course." Middleton reached in the inside breast pocket of his coat and pulled out a large envelope which he had folded in half. "Here you are, Mr. Wallace."

Nate made no move to take it, so Middleton reached all the way across the table, setting it carefully on the plate in front of him.

With great caution, Nate removed three photographs from the envelope. He stared at them one by one. Why couldn't he get a better view of her face?

"Sorry that one's a little blurry," Middleton said. "It was about to rain that day, and she seemed to be in a big rush."

"Yes. It's hard to tell, but the possibility is there."

The waiter approached, and Nate said, "Just coffee, please," without taking his eyes from the photograph.

"Same for me," said Middleton.

"Do you know where she is now?"

"Not far from here. She's about to leave the public library. She works there until three every day. Then she goes home to change clothes, so she can get to the restaurant by four."

"What restaurant?"

"She's a waitress in the evenings. A family-run place, like a boarding house or private hotel."

"In a decent neighborhood?"

"Nice enough. Not fancy downtown, but not the slums either."

Nate glanced at his pocket watch. "It's almost two forty-five. How far is the library from here?"

"About three blocks. We can walk, if you like."

Nate left cash on the table, too much for just coffee and gratuity, but he didn't care. He wanted to be on the steps in front of the library when this woman emerged. He had to be sure to get a good look at her. So far, it had not crossed his mind what he would say to her by way of introduction.

At eight minutes 'til three, Nate and Middleton loitered at the bottom of the steps of the Atlanta Public Library. Middleton lit a cigarette and paced to the curb and back. Nate stood in one place with his arms folded across his chest and stared straight ahead.

The temperature felt warmer and the air more humid in Atlanta than in Mason's Crossing. Nate unbuttoned his cashmere jacket and waited for a breeze. None came.

When a nearby tower clock chimed three times, Nate looked up. He watched the doors, but the only people who came out were a young woman with a preschool age child. Her hair was dark, and she was taller than average. He glanced at Middleton, who shook his head.

The door opened again. Nate stared into the shadows. Several moments passed until an elderly gentleman stepped forward into the sunlight. He turned to hold the door open behind him for the next person.

Nate sighed and looked at Middleton again. Middleton

stood up straight and jerked his head ever so slightly toward the door. Nate let his eyes be drawn back to the shadow of the doorway.

The elderly gentleman moved to the side to let a woman pass with an armload of books. Nate could not see her face well enough to distinguish any features. Her hair was light brown, and she was of medium build and plainly dressed. Nate might even have said poorly dressed.

She smiled at the old man as she passed him, and he tipped his hat. "Good afternoon, Mr. Carter," she said, "and thank you."

Nate strained to hear his response. Surely the old man would say her name.

"See you tomorrow, I hope," he flirted.

They began their descent together. Nate stood still at the bottom of the stairs. They did not glance at him as they chatted.

"Of course," she said. "You take care on the way home, you hear. Mrs. Carter'll be worried if you miss your bus."

"She'll want to hear all the news today."

"Possible war in Europe again, I suppose?"

"She's worried about her family."

"They'll be just fine. You tell her for me not to fret. There's not gonna be any war."

Nate couldn't restrain himself any longer. "Mary?" he said.

The roar of a bus approaching the bench in front of the library drowned out his voice. Middleton had moved farther away, but lingered within earshot.

"Now look," the woman spoke to the old man as if he were a child. "Here's your bus already. You got your fare handy?"

"Right at my fingertips." The old man patted his pocket.

The doors flapped open, and she stood there until the old man climbed on and sat down. She gave him half a wave, trying not to drop her books.

Nate could see her face from the side, but he did not recognize any features. She seemed too young to be so tired.

As Nate waited until the bus pulled away from the curb, the young woman started down the block in the other direction, away from him. She walked faster, but Nate's long legs soon caught up to her. She stopped to shift the weight of the books to her other arm.

"Mary?" he said. "Are you Mary Wallace?"

She turned and frowned at him, full in the face. He stared at her as sternly as she studied him. She seemed to take in his appearance quickly.

"Why did you call me that?" she said.

"Is that your name? Are you Mary Wallace?"

"No one has called me that in a long time."

"So you are Mary Wallace?"

"Might I ask, who wishes to know?" The friendliness had left her voice.

"Mary," he said in soft tones. "I'm Nate. Nate Wallace. I'm your brother."

She squinted. "That's impossible. He's dead."

"No, I'm here. I've come to take you home." He took a step toward her, to take the books from her arms.

In a flash, she backed up. "What do you mean? How do I know you're who you say you are?"

"Ma took you and Lillie to Charleston after Roy died, to live with Miss Vivian Rutledge. I didn't go with you because… well, for other reasons. I left Clark's Common and got work in New Orleans, then Shreveport. I live in Texas now."

"You're Nate?" She squinted at him. "How can that be?"

"It took me a while to get to Charleston," he said. "After 1920, I received information which told me you had been relocated to an orphanage. But I had no money… then, to try to find you." He nodded to Middleton, who approached them in slow steps.

"How did you find me?" she said. "After all this time?"

"I engaged this man." Nate gestured toward Middleton. "He's a detective here in Atlanta. I hired people all over, just to try to discover your whereabouts. I'm settled on my own property now, with a wife, and perhaps soon a child. I want you to come home with me, so I can take care of you, the way I should have been doing all along. Will you come back to Texas with me?"

Her arms grew slack, and she would have dropped the books, but Middleton caught them just in time. He took the load and backed away.

"Mary, you were about five years old the last time you saw me. I used to carry you and Lillie on my shoulders."

She stood there, peering at his face, struggling to remember it. Nate also stared, trying to imagine this young woman as the little girl he had known all those years ago.

It had been too long and too much had been ripped from their lives for them to be affectionate with each other now. They stood apart, awkward, with no degree of familiarity. How could they get back what they had lost? Could time really mend their wounds, lessen their aches, and restore them as family again?

Nate resolved to convince Mary that it was possible. He would simply work very hard at it.

CHAPTER FORTY-TWO

By the time Nate returned to Mason's Crossing from Pittsburgh, where he purchased more shares in a steel mill, and from Washington, where he was assured of pending government contracts, Mary was due to arrive within a week.

"It's bigger than the public library in Atlanta," she said as she climbed the front steps to their house. "And much grander than the Gleason's home."

"Who are the Gleasons?" Nate said.

"That's the family I worked for in Atlanta... where I lived after I outgrew the orphanage. They were very rich, but nothing like this, like you."

After he guided her into his office, Nate handed her an envelope which contained an unsparing sum of cash.

"What would I spend all that money on?" Mary said, as she faced him across his wide desk.

"Whatever you need." He turned a page in his financial magazine.

She placed the envelope on his desk, closer to him than to herself. "I don't *need* anything."

"Then buy whatever you *want*." Nate pushed the envelope back in her direction.

"You've already sent me more new clothes than I can wear in a month of Sundays... and they're beautiful." She gave him half a smile. "Even Mrs. Gleason didn't have such fine things."

"Then use the money for something special that you'd like

to do."

"Such as? I'm not used to all this luxury. I gave up thinking about anything except work for so long, I can't —"

"Do you like music? Fine art? You can go to the symphony or to the art museum in Dallas or Houston."

"I don't know much about music, except hymns. And the Reverend Haskell didn't allow musical instruments in his church or at the orphanage."

"Well, it's time you were introduced to the full orchestra." Nate felt as though he were wooing her. "Maybe Weesie will feel like going with you."

"Won't you be coming, too?"

"Not likely. I have board meetings and other business to attend."

"Even at night?"

He nodded.

"How will two women get around unescorted?"

"Our chauf… Lennie drives Weesie, only she doesn't care to go out much. Now that you're here, perhaps you can convince her otherwise. Lennie needs to keep busy at his job."

"Is he a good driver?"

"He drove ambulances in Italy during the war."

"Good enough."

"There's something else." Nate put down his magazine and laced his fingers together. "Weesie is pregnant."

"Oh, how wonderful!" Mary clasped her hands as if ready to pray.

"But I can't be here all the time to make sure she eats right and gets enough rest. She's always kicking up some project around the house, but it wears her out before she's half finished."

"What do you need me to do?"

"Watch over her for me. Be on guard against her changing moods and behavior. She can be unpredictable."

Mary waved her hands in front of her face, the way she'd shoo a fly. "Oh, I'm used to that. Mrs. Gleason was downright unreasonable every time she was with child."

"Just so you know what to expect. Also Weesie is… delicate. She has miscarried twice before. It's a source of great unhappiness for her. For both of us."

"I'm sure we'll do just fine."

"Mrs. Gussman will be a big help. Weesie has known her since she was a little girl. Gussie delivered most of Weesie's brothers, but my wife will go to the hospital when it's time to deliver. We'll hire a nurse full time."

"We'll manage. Don't you worry about a thing."

Nate wished he could match Mary's optimistic and cheerful outlook. When it came to his wife, experience had taught him otherwise.

AS LOUISA'S DUE DATE approached, Nate rearranged his travel schedule to be closer to Mason's Crossing. He called home from each hotel in every city and got a report from Mary as to his wife's mood and demeanor. Half the time, Mary gave a full account of what Louisa ate, how long she slept, where they walked, and what they discussed.

The other calls included tales of Louisa's fits, outbursts, and binges of crying. Nate stopped her from tattling about what Louisa broke or threw across the room.

"I know she can be difficult, but this is a distressing stage of her life right now. Even after all these years, she still misses her father, and the thought of being a parent is frightening to her," Nate said. "I'll be home soon."

"You give her too much leeway," Mary said. "She's spoiled, nothing more."

"How I wish that was true," Nate sighed as he spoke. "That

would be simple to fix."

Two days later, he came home to discover the doctor had confined Louisa to her bed.

"It won't be long now, according to Dr. Grant," said Mary, as she fluffed the pillows on the bed. "You'd best cancel your next trip."

Nate nodded and sat on the edge of the bed. "Weesie," he said as he took her left hand. "How are you feeling, sweetheart?" She seemed so small, except for the circular mound under the covers.

She turned her head and gazed at him with vacant eyes. "Like I'm going to die," she whispered. "And the baby, too."

"Nonsense!" said Mary from the foot of the bed. "You won't die. Every baby born in your family came out healthy, and all the mamas went on to have more children. Look at your own mother, why she—"

Nate silenced her with a stroke of his hand through the air. He scooted closer to Louisa. "Would you like me to call the doctor to come over this evening?"

"He'll be too late." Louisa pulled her right hand from under the covers, and when she held it close to her face, she began to weep.

Nate stared at her blood-soaked hand and said to Mary through clenched teeth, "Get Gussie up here right now, and then call an ambulance."

Within a few minutes, Mrs. Gussmann was able to confirm that Louisa's water had broken and contractions would be increasing in frequency and intensity very soon. "She's beginning to dilate, and her labor has started."

They both jumped as Louisa screamed. Nate scrambled to her side and she grabbed his arm, pulling hard until he bent down.

"What is happening to me? Make it stop." She sucked in her

breath, rattling like a drowning person.

Mrs. Gussmann replaced the drenched towel under Louisa's thighs. "Tell Mary to call the doctor to come here instead. She won't make it to the hospital and…"

The look on her face told Nate he needed to hurry. As he left the room, Louisa screamed again.

When Dr. Grant arrived a half-hour later, Nate met him at the front door and escorted him upstairs. Before he let him enter Louisa's bedroom, he put his hand on the doctor's arm.

"One thing I want to be very clear about," Nate said. "If it comes down to a choice between Weesie and the child, you must save my wife. She's all I have."

Dr. Grant patted his hand. "Now don't worry. You'll be holding your son or daughter before long."

"We… I thought we couldn't have children." Nate tightened his grip. "She's everything to me."

The doctor nodded and Nate opened the bedroom door for him. Louisa's screams greeted them, but they soon subsided to moaning and panting, only to be followed by more screaming. Her words came out choppy, as she repeated them, making no sense.

Mrs. Gussmann stood next to the head of the bed, bent over as she propped up pillows behind Louisa's back. "She's about seven or so, Doctor, based on her speech and the musky birth smell."

Dr. Grant entered the room. "Gussie, you've always had a good nose for mothers-to-be." He turned around and closed the door, leaving Nate to wait in the hallway.

He paced, sat, paced again. One of the kitchen maids brought him hot tea and asked if he would prefer brandy or something to eat. Despite his sudden hunger pangs, he shook his head.

Nate sat on a nearby bench and closed his eyes. His mother's face appeared in his mind's eye. She waddled beside him without speaking, rubbing her huge belly. They came around a corner and met Miss Vivian, who held the hand of a little boy. Nate looked closer. Walter waved a white hanky at him, then he and Aunt Vivian faded until they disappeared.

He turned toward his mother, but recognized Amos Cobb instead, with Clyde Farraday standing behind him. Oil and soot streaked their sweaty faces. When he reached out his hand, Father Antoine took it. "Pray, my son," he said. He put his hand on Nate's shoulder and...

Startled awake, Nate found Dr. Grant shaking him by the arm. "Get up, Mr. Wallace."

Nate sprang to his feet and clasped the doctor's shoulder. "Is she... is—"

"You have a fine healthy daughter."

"What about Weesie?"

"She's exhausted, so I gave her something to sleep. Mrs. Gussmann is with them." Dr. Grant smiled. "You may go in now."

Nate peeked through the open door before going in. Louisa lay still on her back. He squared his shoulders and all but marched to the edge of the bed. He knelt down and took her hand, then bent forward to listen to her breathe. Satisfied, he stroked her hair and then arose.

Mrs. Gussmann stood by the window, cooing and gently bouncing a bundle in her arms. She turned toward him and her eyes twinkled. "Mr. Nate, come meet your daughter."

In a daze, he walked toward where the afternoon sunlight streamed through the panes. Mrs. Gussmann stretched out her arms and handed him the soft bundle, then returned to the bedside.

Nate looked down into a tiny, perfect face. Her eyes fluttered open, shimmered, and seemed to search for something to focus on. He lifted the baby's head to his lips.

When he pulled back, the baby's silken face was wet. He squeezed his eyes closed for a moment and more tears gushed down his cheeks and drizzled on his daughter. When he touched her cheek, she opened her mouth and arched her face toward his fingertip, mewing.

Nate sobbed and laughed at the same time. He caught his breath and waited for her to move again. She sighed and his eyes filled once more. Her lips twitched and Nate's tears overflowed, soaking his face until his chin dripped. He wiped it on the fleece of her blanket and stared at her as if she would vanish when he looked away.

After several minutes of memorizing every delicate lash and eyebrow, the crevice in her upper lip, the dimple in her cheek, he found his words.

"Whatever happens," he whispered in a quavering voice, "I promise you, whatever comes, I will never leave you."

MASON'S
KEEPER

Readers Guide
Discussion Questions

Readers Guide
Discussion Questions

1. Who is your favorite character and why?

2. Which of Nate's hardships would be the most difficult for you to overcome?

3. How does Nate manage to keep going in spite of his losses? Is it his determination or the teachings of his mother? A combination?

4. What could Nate have done differently to keep his family together?

5. Could you forgive Nate for some of his drastic choices?

6. If his mother had survived, what other lessons might Nate have learned from her, that he missed?

7. How do the other women in Nate's life influence him? What does he learn from them?

8. Do any of the men Nate encounters represent a better father figure for him?

9. Why is it hard to Nate to make friends as an adult? How do his life experiences affect his ability and his desire to relate to other people?

10. At the very end (no spoiler alert), why does Nate make that particular promise?

11. Would Nate have turned out very differently if he'd been able to stay in Clark's Common and work the same jobs?

12. What is the best way to recover from our significant losses? What tools can we use to "move on" with our lives?

ABOUT THE AUTHOR

C ynthia Stone believes she and Sting were twins separated at birth, because they share the same birthday and original last name. Since she's a native Austinite, some complications in proving their kinship are sure to arise. All of which provides creative fodder for the family sagas she loves to write. Cynthia wrote her first story at age five and has continued to indulge that Muse ever since.

Her checkered career includes magazine publishing, copy-writing, professional fundraising for the fine arts, antiques importing, and interior decorating. She still lives in Austin with her ever-patient husband, Gerald.

Connect with Cynthia online: www.CynthiaJStone.com

ALSO BY CYNTHIA J STONE
Mason's Daughter

Available in print and digital from Amazon.com